She was still overthinking.

...le scrubbed her forehead with one hand. "I have to ...bout a dozen people, finalize plans with the party ...ator, give the caterer the final count, and nail down ...larned DJ." She dropped her hand and rolled her ..."Not to mention—"

...onovan grabbed her up. His mouth came down hard ...rs. She caught his angled jaw with her hands and ...ted his tongue, her worries dissipating with each ...al slide. By the time she was clawing his back for ..., she had to pause to take a breath. He must have ...d one too. When he pulled away, he had to catch his. ...hat help you forget your problems?" His voice was ...nd rumbly, his firm lips damp.

...er hand had come to rest on his chest and she felt his ... thump against her palm. "Yeah."

ACCLAIM FOR JESSICA LEMMON'S NOVELS

BRINGING HOME THE BAD BOY

"Clever, romantic, and utterly unforgettable."
**—Lauren Layne, *USA Today*
bestselling author**

"Top pick! A sexy gem of a read that will tug at the heart-strings. Evan is charming and vulnerable and his sizzling connection with the sweet, genuine Charlotte will keep readers turning the pages. A heartfelt plot infused with both emotionally tender and raw moments makes this a story that readers will savor."
—*RT Book Reviews*

HARD TO HANDLE

"[Aiden is] a perfect balance of sensitive, heart-on-his-sleeve guy who is as sexy and 'alpha' as they come...A real romance that's not about dominance but equality and mutual need—while not sacrificing [the] hotness factor. A rare treat."
—PolishedBookworm.com

"Lemmon's latest is a pleasant example of living in the present and celebrating second, and sometimes third, chances."
—*RT Book Reviews*

"[Aiden is] a fantastic character. He is a motorcycle-riding, tattooed, rebel kind of guy with a huge heart. What's not to love?...I really enjoyed this book and I think readers will find it entertaining and heartfelt."
—RomanceRewind.blogspot.com

"I smiled through a lot of it, but seeing Aiden and Sadie deal with all of their hurdles was also incredibly moving and had me tearing up more than once as well...I can't wait to see what Lemmon will bring to the table next."
—HerdingCats-BurningSoup.com

"Aiden has all the characteristics of a bad boy but with the heart of that perfect hero...Their gradual spark leads to some well-written steamier scenes."
—RosieReadsRomance.blogspot.com

CAN'T LET GO

"I loved Sadie and Aiden in *Tempting the Billionaire*, and I was waiting for their story to finally be told. I love that this novella [lays] the groundwork for what will come in their book. I look forward to seeing how their story unravels in *Hard to Handle*."
—HarlequinJunkie.com

"This novella was long enough to get me hooked on Aiden and Sadie and short enough to leave me wanting more... The chemistry between the characters is fan worthy and the banter is a great addition. The writing style draws readers in. I can't wait for *Hard to Handle*."
—BSReviewers.blogspot.com

TEMPTING THE BILLIONAIRE

"A smashing debut! Charming, sexy, and brimming with wit—you'll be adding Jessica Lemmon to your bookshelves for years to come!"
    —**Heidi Betts, *USA Today* bestselling author**

"Lemmon's characters are believable and flawed. Her writing is engaging and witty. If I had been reading this book out in public, everyone would have seen the *huge* grin on my face. I had so much fun reading this and adore it immensely."
    —**LiteraryEtc.wordpress.com**

"If you are interested in a loveable romance about two troubled souls who overcome the odds to find their own happily ever after, I would certainly recommend that you give *Tempting the Billionaire* a try. It was definitely a great Valentine's Day read, for sure!"
    —**ChrissyMcBookNerd.blogspot.com**

"The awesome cover opened to even more awesome things inside. It was realistic! Funny! Charming! Sweet!"
    —**AbigailMumford.com**

RESCUING
THE
Bad Boy

RESCUING THE Bad Boy

JESSICA LEMMON

FOREVER

NEW YORK   BOSTON

Copyright © 2015 by Jessica Lemmon
Excerpt from *A Bad Boy for Christmas* copyright © 2015 by Jessica Lemmon

Forever
Hachette Book Group
1290 Avenue of the Americas
New York, NY 10104

www.HachetteBookGroup.com

Printed in the United States of America

First Edition: May 2015

10 9 8 7 6 5 4 3 2 1

OPM

Forever is an imprint of Grand Central Publishing.
The Forever name and logo are trademarks of Hachette Book Group, Inc.

The Hachette Speakers Bureau provides a wide range of authors for speaking events. To find out more, go to www.hachettespeakersbureau.com or call (866) 376-6591.

The publisher is not responsible for websites (or their content) that are not owned by the publisher.

For Shannon Richard. Proof God knows what he's doing when he finds friends for me. Thank you for your undying support and for being my water cooler pal in our virtual office.

ACKNOWLEDGMENTS

Donovan Pate and Sofie Martin have led many, *many* alternate lives. As an author, you start out with an idea and as you learn to improve, things change. Ideas shift, making the old idea, well, not *bad*, but not right. Finally, Donovan and Sofie are *right*.

I believe RESCUING THE BAD BOY, after its first inception in 2010 (its last in 2014), has turned out exactly as it should have. That said, there are thank-yous to dole out. Climb into the way-back machine with me, because some of these are long overdue.

Heidi Betts. Long a fan of your work, I couldn't have been more grateful to have access to a "real" author who offered advice, humor, and more importantly, belief that I would succeed before there was any proof that I would. You gave me my first cover quote. You asked me to do a beta read for you. You validated me. Thank you.

Sarah Mayberry, how do I love thee? You live on the

other side of the big, blue ocean, but I connected via e-mail, gushing about how much I adored your writing. I also admitted I wanted to grow up and be a writer, like you. You didn't laugh. You didn't blow me off. You asked if you could send me the transcript of a speech you'd given about plot and character. I was so grateful to learn, to grow, to be taken seriously. Thank you for believing in me.

Cynthia Reese. You were the first published author to read a chapter I'd written. (Thank you, Julie Musil, for the introduction.) While that book will likely never see the light of day, I will never forget your assessment of my very green prose. You told me I could write. You told me my voice reminded you of Patricia Gaffney. I was so overjoyed to hear I wasn't wasting my time, I could have kissed you.

Everyone who followed my blog, Sm:)e Feel Good. You joined me in my journey to publishing, commenting, rallying, cheering me on—even with nothing to gain for yourselves. Thank you for your support.

Thank you, beta readers (new versions and old), Niki Hughes, Amy Wade, Piper Trace, Amber Dunlevy, Charissa Weaks, Teri Anne Stanley, Jeannie Moon.

Thanks to Maisey Yates, not only for your friendship, but for your advice on so many things—including writing a hero who'd suffered a stint of...um...denying himself. You are a master!

Thank you to my readers, for sticking with me from one series to the next. I hope you know how much I truly appreciate your comments online, your e-mails, and meeting you at signings. I love creating characters you love.

As always, thank you to my editor, Lauren Plude,

publicist, Julie Paulauski, agent, Nicole Resciniti, and everyone hammering away at Grand Central/Forever to make this book real.

Every word in this book has been toiled over, fretted about, and above all else, loved into creation. Donovan and Sofie made the journey worth it for me. I hope you feel the same way.

~Jess ☺

RESCUING

THE

Bad Boy

PROLOGUE

The row of sconces lining the hallway cast a yellowish glow across the mansion foyer, doing little to illuminate the floor, the thick drapes covering the windows, or the staircase leading to the murky beyond.

Not that Donny Pate needed light to see what he was doing. *Who* he was doing.

Who I'm about to do...

One hand cradling Sofie Martin's incredible ass, his mouth explored hers, the length of his body pressing her back to the heavy wooden door. Her, he could see.

Every pliant inch felt as amazing as it looked.

He bit her earlobe and she arched her back, rubbing her little black dress against his sweater and jeans. The blood in his head rushed directly to his crotch. He'd tasted her mouth at the bar, sucked on her tongue for several minutes in his Jeep parked outside the mansion, and now, this up-against-the-door thing was trying every last ounce of his willpower.

He might die if he didn't get inside her soon.

It'd been a shit week, one he'd rather forget, followed by a shit night that was turning out pretty damn good. Tonight's company Christmas party had been boring as hell, but the manager at the Wharf required everyone be in attendance if they wanted to get their bonus checks. Donny needed that bonus. He was leaving this godforsaken town the minute the check cleared.

Cheesy decorations had been strewn across the restaurant's dining room, a tinny version of "Rudolph the Red-nosed Reindeer" piping through an ancient sound system. Donny had relegated himself to chain-smoking and drinking with his jackass coworkers, making tonight not unlike any other Saturday in Evergreen Cove.

Until the tip of Sofie's cute, upturned nose poked around a dividing wall. Then his evening took a decidedly more interesting turn.

She'd been sending him furtive glances from the bar all evening, while pretending to sip the beer she'd opened shortly after walking through the door. Caught, a playful smile curled her lips.

Sofie wasn't one to wear a fuck-me smile with a skin-tight black dress, all while blinking bedroom eyes. Tonight, she'd done all three. That was the smile of a girl determined to make a mistake.

Her lucky night.

To quote his recently deceased, formerly belligerent old man, Donny was most definitely "a mistake."

Often, her gaze slid to him in the kitchen at work— amid the clatter of cooking utensils, tall, steel shelves, and fifteen to twenty other servers and cooks. In the midst of clashing pans and the general chaos of a dinner rush,

Donny had caught her moss green eyes on him more than once. And, more than once, he'd allowed his eyes to travel south.

Unflattering khaki pants and a starched, button-down shirt hadn't been able to hide Sofie's killer body. He'd never considered himself an ass man, but Scampi's backside had a healthy curve, and enough cushion to give his imagination plenty of ammo.

Scampi, he thought bemusedly as he slid his lips along hers.

She'd earned the nickname on a dare.

About a month back, after cooking the dinner special for Sofie's tables at least nine times, he'd turned to find the printer spitting out another order from her.

Shrimp Scampi. *Again.*

Tongs in hand, he swiped the perspiration from his upper lip with the sleeve of his chef's coat. He'd been in the weeds all damn night, sweating over four sauté pans going at once. Pissed, he'd shouted a warning across the kitchen. "One more Scampi from you, Sofie, and I'll brand you for life!"

At the sound of his raised voice, the bustling staff had halted for a split second, servers pausing, black books in hand or trays held high. Sofie had approached the divider, put a hand on the shelf between them, and narrowed her green eyes in challenge. Tension knotted the air. The same tension he'd felt buzzing between them like a downed power line since day one.

Typically, Sofie was fairly quiet, but right then, she hadn't looked intimidated or tongue-tied. "Only one?" she'd asked with a rogue smirk.

He'd be damned if she didn't march into the dining

room and sell not *one* more Shrimp Scampi special, but *three* to her next table.

"Scampi," he said now, tugging her bottom lip with his teeth.

At the party this evening, a similar look crossed her face. He'd recognized her determination instantly. Knew there'd be no stopping her from getting what she wanted. And what she wanted, apparently, was him. Ignoring the blaring sirens in his head telling him to leave her alone, he'd made a decision. Good girl or not, he'd have her tonight.

Consider it a farewell present to himself.

"Donny." He could tell by her breathy response, she liked the bite he'd given her sweet mouth. He squeezed her lush body. A squeak left her lips. She liked that, too.

Against her mouth, he smiled.

Every damn time.

Smiling wasn't really his thing. What did he have to smile about? Nothing, normally. But now, a cute brunette rubbing against his cock, her cheeks warm despite the winter air leaking through the gap beneath the mansion's front door, her lips parting in a reverent sigh...

Hell yeah, he had something to smile about.

He grabbed another handful of her ass, admiring the mess he'd made of her hair.

"Library, sweetheart." The closest room in proximity to the front door held an ugly red velvet couch and a thick white rug. He would happily lay her down on either. He'd even let her choose.

"Okay," came her response.

Tightening his hold on her, he lifted her off the ground. Her legs were long, but not too long, her arms hooked around his neck comfortably, her tits in his face thanks to the fact she'd wrapped those not-too-long legs around his waist. He was six-four and guessed her at five and a half feet, every inch of her fitting every inch of him perfectly.

In the pale light, he saw her smile back at him. It made him want her more; a hell of a feat considering the hard-on pressed painfully against his fly.

At the threshold of the library, he paused, careful not to knock her head on the door frame. "Couch or rug?"

Her fingers stopped twirling the back of his long hair. She gave him an innocent, doe-eyed blink. Stunned speechless, he guessed. Scampi wasn't one of the slutty girls he normally took home. And he further guessed, in spite of her best efforts to be a bad girl for a night, "making out" had been the extent of her post–Christmas party plans.

Well, he had other plans. He'd have to encourage her to embrace her inner bad girl. Which meant laying it on thick to get the yes he wanted to hear.

Softly, he spoke. "Scampi, baby."

In response to his gentle tone, her fingers flinched against his scalp. The light from the sconces touched half her face, and in the glow, he watched her eyes grow warm.

She cared about him, he realized, swallowing thickly. Being pinned by the gaze of someone who cared made him simultaneously panicked and horny.

He ignored the pending panic and cleared his throat. Then he asked the question he had to ask if he hoped to get what he wanted tonight.

"Where do you want to make love?" He nearly gagged on the words.

Make love.

Good God.

But it worked. Sofie's expression melted. He'd broken through the last line of her defenses. She was sober, so no worries there. He'd taken her warm, practically full beer bottle away from her at the bar.

She tightened her hold on his neck, lowered her face, and kissed him so softly, so gently, his insides recoiled.

She's sweet. Too sweet.

As her lips moved on his, he silently argued he hadn't had a lot of "sweet" in his life, and he deserved some. Especially after his week had graduated from bad to worse.

"Your call." The oddest tension strained his voice. He'd never been nervous around a chick. Never.

Sofie's tongue darted into his mouth, stroking his. The aggressive move startled and turned him on so much, he tightened his arms so he didn't drop her.

Then her bad-girl smile made a reappearance, and that sinful mouth formed one word.

"Couch."

Music to his ears.

"That a yes?" He felt his lips curve upward. Another smile. Unbelievable.

"Yes."

Angels began to sing.

"That's what I wanted to hear," he said, carrying her into the library and wasting no time getting her flat on her back.

* * *

Sofie's bare back hit velvet, her eyes adjusting to a room lit only by the moon and the scant bit of light eking in from the hallway. The tall shelves lined with books, the antique desk, and heavy red curtains made her feel as if she were in a game of Clue.

Donny Pate. In the library. With the condom…

At the end of the long drive, the enormous stone mansion rose from the center of an army of pines, maples, and oak trees. No chance anyone could see in. They were alone.

Finally.

Donny, in spite of being the last person she imagined might offer to sleep with her, was about to give her a "first time." Thundering heartbeat and parched throat aside, she was ready.

Not a hard sell when the man about to take her virginity was as beautiful as the man between her legs now.

Long, ink-black hair hung over his forehead and brushed his cheeks, shadowing pale, silver-blue eyes. Crystalline, ghostly, they reminded her of winter skies in the Cove. Against his olive skin and dark hair, those eyes had frozen her in place more than once.

But she admired more about him than the physical. There was something about the way he could look at once sad and angry, lost and lonely. Like he didn't have a friend in the world while also not having a care in the world.

She could see his scowl acted as a KEEP AWAY sign. As she was a person who liked people, it hurt her to see him push everyone away.

Well…almost everyone.

She'd watched one by one as different girls hung on him in the bar at work, or followed him to the parking lot after the restaurant closed. Girls who strode through the barbed wire he'd strung around himself, eyes wide open.

Sofie wasn't like those girls, doubted a single one of them had scratched the surface of Donny Pate. Probably because they didn't care about him. Not really. Sofie cared. She wanted to know what was under his façade—and not out of some morbid curiosity but because she wanted to know him.

At least draw another smile out of him.

She'd never forget the first time he'd smiled at her: the slight crook of his lips, the sly way his eyes flickered away from hers. Even at half-wattage, the smile transformed his entire face. Shot light into his eyes, lifted his angled cheeks, and arched his steely jaw. Nothing had turned her on more.

Until now.

She stroked his unsmiling lips with the tip of her tongue, earning a thrill when he opened to her. A hint of whiskey lingered on his breath, and she savored the powerful slide of his tongue, the abrading roughness of his chin against hers.

One hand navigated beneath her dress. His fingers hooked her panties, and wrestled them from her legs, before returning to her bared breast to give her nipple a squeeze.

On a purely physical reaction, her thighs clenched.

She gasped.

He grinned, a flash of white teeth against tanned skin.

God. He was beautiful.

"Ready, baby?"

Baby. She could get used to that.

"Ready," she breathed, unable to strengthen her voice. He'd already put on the condom. Her hands shook slightly as she reached for his shoulders.

His hand disappeared beneath the skirt of her dress and she felt long fingers stroke her center. Her hips raised to meet his rhythm, a completely involuntary reaction to his touch. She was embarrassingly wet—no way he could have missed that. Scrunching her eyes closed, she prayed he didn't mind.

His harsh whisper was almost reverent when he dropped his forehead to hers and breathed, "*Fuck.* You're sexy."

Definitely, she decided, he did *not* mind.

Wrists on his shoulders, she wound her fingers into the ends of his hair and looked up at him. Pale eyes locked on to hers. The tip of his penis slipped along her folds and she tensed. A split second later, he breeched her entrance as she bit the inside of her cheek and reminded herself to breathe.

He thrust once.

Breathe.

Twice.

Breathe.

Then, he slid in *all the way.*

She welded her back teeth together and focused on keeping her facial expressions neutral, not wanting to ruin the moment. Who knew losing her virginity would be so painful?

That's what you get for keeping it sealed up for twenty-one years...

Twenty-one long years of waiting for the right person. Donny was the right person.

Each and every inch of his lean, tall frame was in proportion. Sinew and muscle dipped and shadowed, giving his body a hard, corded hue. She had every inch of his amazing body against her, and quite a few inches nestled inside her. In the sparse light, she could make out his closed eyes, lashes shadowing his cheeks. A grunt, followed by a muffled curse, ruffled her hair.

"Okay," he said, his voice rough.

Donny remained still, his member throbbing insistently against her inner walls. She moved her palms from his neck to his shoulders, ran them down his hard male chest, appreciating the dips and planes of his incredible body.

Seriously. *Beautiful.*

Canting her hips, she bumped against his pelvis with hers, and whispered, "I'm okay." She felt another sharp pinch and gripped his neck. She could do this.

His face contorted, almost painfully before acceptance flashed in his eyes. As if he'd made a decision to keep going—*and why would he stop?*—he slid out, then into her again—one smooth, delicious slide, filling her completely. Another gasp escaped her. He thrust again and again, his movements becoming less gentle, more hurried.

Better.

The pain began to recede. Her eyes fluttered closed and she savored him. Savored them, together.

He felt a hundred times better than when they'd started and a million times better than she'd imagined. He pushed her long hair away from her face and lowered his lips, propping himself on one forearm, keeping a palm pressed to her cheek.

He drove into her, kissing her as he did. Their tongues sparred and her stomach coiled, tension building...

"That's it, baby." He pushed into her again, deeper than before, and like flint to stone, she sparked.

Throwing her head back, she gripped his naked shoulders with the ends of her short nails and let out a raspy, "Donny."

"Come for me, Scampi." He continued winding her, so tight her hips lifted to meet his incessant thrusts.

Tingling. She was tingling everywhere.

"I..." She started to argue she couldn't "come" on demand. But before she made the admission, he plunged into her again, and her body clutched, clamping down on him. Hands clasping him tightly, mouth falling open in stunned awe, a ragged moan escaped her throat.

Sparks flashed behind her eyelids as her toes curled, and Donny continued pumping into her, causing aftershocks to radiate through her limbs. He lost himself a moment later, his groans drowning out hers, his slick-with-sweat chest brushing against her sensitive nipples. One of his hands gripped her hip; the other held the back of the couch.

Sofie's mind spun, her orgasm ebbing and leaving behind a pleasant sinking feeling.

Amazing.

Making love to Donny Pate was an incomparable high. As the sounds of her thundering heart and his broken breaths filled her ears, she became aware of the sensations in her body. The blood rushing through her veins, the pain-to-pleasure pulse between her legs, the happiness lifting her chest.

No matter what happened after tonight, she'd never, ever forget this moment. She opened her eyes to take in the man who'd yet to give her his weight. He held himself away from her and blew out a long, low breath. Their bodies barely touched, except for where they were joined.

She didn't want him to get up—not yet. She wanted him closer. Wanted to wrap her arms around him and kiss him. Snuggle into him and talk about how good it felt to be with him like this.

Donny didn't look interested in cuddling or kissing. Heavy lids narrowed over diamond-hard eyes.

"Forget to tell me something, Scampi?" His voice was low. Cold.

Her blood froze, chilled by his tone. No way could he know this was her first time...

Could he?

No. There was no way he could know.

"*Scampi*," he repeated sternly.

She couldn't tell him. *Couldn't*. Speechless, she shook her head.

Elbows locked, he hovered over her, face growing angry in the silent seconds passing where she said nothing. She lost his warmth when he drew out of her, her body cooling when she lost contact.

The skirt of her dress was rucked up over her hips, her top taken to her waist, her panties...She had no idea where her panties were.

Oh God, I am one of those girls.

Donny stood, shadows slashing across his chest in the moonlit room, and pulled on a T-shirt, then bent and reached for his jeans.

Under his breath, he muttered, "A fucking *virgin*."

Every nerve ending in her body prickled. "H-how did you know?"

He tugged on his jeans and growled, "You're so tight, I nearly broke it off in there."

The insult hit the mark. She cringed.

"Get dressed. I'm taking you to your car."

Dressed? No, she refused to accept tonight would end this badly.

"Can we...can we try again?" she asked, covering her breasts with the top of her dress. She felt so exposed.

He didn't look at her, instead crossing the room and disposing of the condom in a small wastebasket.

"I don't do virgins," he stated, facing her and zipping his fly.

Okay. She took a deep breath and promised herself she wouldn't cry even as her eyes stung and a lump formed in her throat. Another breath and she was able to rein in her frittering emotions.

He couldn't end things now. She wouldn't let him. First of all, it wasn't nice. And second, this wasn't the way first times were supposed to go. He was supposed to be gentle and accommodating. She was supposed to tell him he made her feel like no other man had before. She would remember tonight always, and he was in the process of ruining those memories. She didn't expect perfect. Awkward was acceptable, but this?

This was *awful.*

Even though she was freezing, she dropped the material of her dress and pushed out her breasts. Donny's eyes flickered over her bared skin, but his expression was as placid as before.

"Come on, baby." She tried to purr, but her voice came out taut, nervous. Seduction wasn't really her thing. The rest came out like a question. "Let's try again?"

He ripped his eyes away, snatched his discarded sweater from a nearby chair, and jammed his arms into the sleeves. Leaning over her on the sofa he'd tenderly laid her on moments ago, there wasn't a tender thing about him when he rumbled, "I'm not anyone's *baby*, Scampi." He straightened, pulled the sweater over his head, and added, "There's not going to be a second time. *Ever.* Get dressed."

Wow. That was a solid *no*. The post-coital hum in her body shut off like a switch.

Dejected, embarrassed, and pissed off in a way she knew would devolve into sobbing the moment she shut her bedroom door at home, she finished dressing.

The humiliation had engulfed her by the time she grabbed her coat and purse from the foyer. Donny snatched his leather coat from a hook on the wall and shrugged into it.

Wordlessly, she followed him outside and climbed into his Jeep.

More silence followed during the drive back to the restaurant. The restaurant she'd entered a few hours ago for a work party, determined to kiss Donny Pate before night's end.

Mission accomplished, she thought miserably, unable to dredge up even a humorless smile.

He pulled into the Wharf's parking lot, empty save for her compact car parked in the back. Snow had started to fall, the light flakes sticking to the windshield.

Donny threw the Jeep into Park, then looked straight ahead, his face utterly expressionless. Walls up, shutters drawn.

Closed down.

But she hadn't imagined the part where he'd been gentle tonight. The part when he'd met her eyes, asked if she wanted him. Asked if she was okay. Even his command of "come for me" had sounded a lot like "ladies first."

Determined to leave this night with something salvageable, she turned to say good-bye. Maybe tomorrow when she showed up at work, things would be different.

"Donny, before I go—"

His sensual mouth formed one word, piercing her already tender heart.

"Out."

She blinked at his shadowed profile. *Awful*.

"Can't we—"

He faced her, his gray eyes cold. His voice rose suddenly, echoing off the interior of the Jeep. "Scampi, get the hell out!"

Reacting without thought, a primal urge lifted her hand. The slap cracked across Donny's angled jaw, forcing his head to the side. Appalled, she felt her eyes widen as a shaking hand lifted to her lips. Never in her life has she delivered a physical blow to anyone. Violence—no matter how vindicated—wasn't in her nature.

Through the strands of black hair covering his face, his silver-blue eyes glowed with anger. Before she could get an apology out, his upper lip curled, and when he spoke, it was through a charred throat filled with gravel.

"Get. The fuck. *Out*."

She obeyed and climbed out, feeling a mixture of rage, guilt, and shame. Squealing tires whirred in the gathering snow before Donny peeled from the lot, leaving her to walk to her car alone.

Some first time.

Sofie was wrong about the sobbing. It didn't start in her bedroom, but right then, the icy wind freezing her tears to her damp cheeks. On the drive home, she vowed to make her first time her last, knowing it was a promise she wouldn't keep.

Then she vowed never to let Donny worm his way into her heart again.

That was a promise she could.

$\mathcal{C}$HAPTER ONE

Seven years later

$\mathcal{D}$onovan Pate balled his hand into a fist and gave the front panel of his 1980 Jeep a hard whack. The temperamental dashboard lights had been flickering since he'd crossed the Ohio border.

"Come on, Trixie!" Never before had he raised a hand to his girl, but frustration had reached its peak. A seemingly never-ending drive to the last place on earth he wanted to return had a way of leeching his patience.

The lights blinked one last time before coming on and staying on. Squirrelly electric only one of the many perks to owning a classic. His Jeep had earned her name shortly after he bought her—he never knew which part of her might act up next.

He drove the main drag through downtown, shaking his head at the familiar sights. The local watering hole

Salty Dog and Reggie's Subs were both open, and each as unwelcome as every other inch of this place. When he left years ago, he'd sworn never to set foot in Evergreen Cove again.

"Yet here we are," he told Trixie.

Donovan's phone beeped, an incoming text from Evan Downey, one of his oldest—*and only*—friends, and the only person other than the lawyer who knew Donovan was in town.

The text message read: *The bad boy returns.*

Despite his friend intentionally being a douche, Donovan felt himself smile.

At a stoplight, he keyed in: *FU.*

Evan didn't respond, but Donovan knew he was laughing. Could practically hear his easygoing chuckle now.

The light turned green and his smile faded. Much as he missed his friend, he did not want to be here.

He'd already driven past the library where his teenage, drunken, quick-to-fight self had accompanied his buddies, Evan and Asher, on their now infamous "Penis Bandit" excursion. The "artwork" may be gone from the red-brown brick building, but Evan had returned. Returned with his son, Lyon, fell in love with his late wife's best friend, and was now engaged. Go figure.

Asher Knight had managed to stay away. Good for him. Right about now, Ash was probably touring with his band, female groupies adhered to his side—and likely a few other body parts. Donovan kept up with him through text message mostly. Usually on the receiving end of photos he wished he'd never gotten. The guy saw a lot of drunken, topless girls in his line of work.

Evan and Asher stopped visiting Evergreen Cove, but

Donovan remained. Back then, he'd mostly hung out with the derelict kitchen staff from the Wharf, and his roommate, Connor McClain.

Connor kept in touch periodically via e-mail. Or at least he had during his last stint in the service. Donovan hadn't heard from him since then. He had no idea if his buddy was still deployed in Afghanistan, or if Evergreen Cove had also lured him back into her clutches.

But Donovan wasn't returning to the Cove permanently. No, he was only here because—irony of ironies— he now owned the mansion he once fled.

The sun was down and March's cool air was downright cold the closer he drove to the lake, making him regret taking Trixie's top off. First time he'd ever regretted taking a girl's top off, he thought with a grunt.

He drove by Cup of Jo's, eyed the CLOSED sign on the door. Just as well. He wasn't ready to face Jo, or any other Evergreener who wasn't expecting his presence back in town. Scott Torsett was enough.

Passing the darkened windows of Fern's Floral Shoppe, he parked along the curb next to Torsett & Torsett Law, his destination. He pulled the key from the ignition and glared at Trixie. If she knew what was good for her, she'd start right up when he came back out, no bitching.

He may be bound and determined to vanquish his demons, to finish the unfinished business he'd left behind, but that didn't mean he cared to be bent over the hood of his Jeep in the middle of Endless Avenue on a Tuesday night.

The Cove wasn't exactly a small town, but everyone who lived here had known of his grandmother; knew Pate Mansion. He couldn't take a round of condolences from some overly friendly passerby. Not now. Not ever.

One of many reasons he'd skipped the funeral.

The law offices of Torsett & Torsett were decorated with burgundy and mahogany guest chairs, pine green carpet, and shiny brass light fixtures. Cliché. Ugly.

An older woman, her fingers on the keyboard as she ticked something away on the screen, glanced up as he came in. "Help you?" she asked, eyes behind her thick lenses showing no signs of recognizing him.

"Donovan Pate to see Scott Torsett."

She depressed a button on the phone on her desk. "Scottie, Donny's here."

He cringed at his old nickname, hoping the woman wouldn't start up a polite and needless conversation, or worse—

"I'm so sorry about your grandmother," she said. "She was an amazing woman."

Amazing. Sure, okay.

He clamped his teeth together and offered a curt nod, then turned his back to her and watched the hallway for the guy who used to sit on his battered couch and smoke enough pot to make the entire neighborhood high. Scott stepped out of an office a second later wearing a stream-lined dark suit, his former scraggly goatee shaved clean, his eyes clear, not glassy.

It was a blast from the past in the weirdest way.

"Holy shit, Donny. You look grown up."

"Donovan," he corrected. He ditched the nickname when he'd ditched Evergreen Cove. After his father had died.

Swear to God, Donny, you are a worthless waste of space. What'd I ever do to deserve a piece of shit like you for a son?

Wasn't any wonder why he'd skipped dear old Dad's funeral, too.

"Donovan, it is. Coffee?" Scott offered as they passed a carafe on a cart.

His stomach had soured at the mention of his "amazing" grandmother, at the memory of his father's words. Words often followed by fists. Donovan shook his head. He was only going to be in Scott's office long enough to iron out the kink in the will, then he was out of here and heading straight to the House of Pain.

He sat across from a big, antique desk wondering how the hell Scott had managed to get it through the narrow doorway, when Scott pulled a sheet of paper out of a folder and said, "Problem."

"Another?" *Fan-fucking-tastic.*

"We didn't know about this contract until Make It an Event put an ad in the paper announcing the dinner. Then we started digging."

Contract? Dinner?

Donovan took the sheet of paper and read it over quickly. "A charity dinner."

"Yep. Your grandmother has been hosting these things at the mansion for the last few years, and this one was contracted with the event planning company before she died. It's a binding contract, signed by your grandmother's hand." He clucked his tongue in an *aw, shucks* manner and added, "Hope you weren't in a hurry to sell."

Right. Because what Donovan really wanted to do was stay in this town for . . . he skimmed the type searching for the date of the dinner. "Three months from now."

Scott folded his hands on his desk. "You're stuck, buddy."

Donovan felt his lip curl. He wasn't Scott's "buddy," and he refused to be "stuck." He'd decided seven years ago, after his old man died, that neither his father nor his grandmother would have control over one single aspect of his life. Not ever again.

He groused at the paper in his hand.

Gertrude seemed to have gotten the last laugh.

Last year when he received the call from Scott about the will, Donovan thanked him, then did nothing. He didn't want the mansion or the trust. He didn't *need* the mansion or the trust. Over the years, and thanks to a man in a very high place, he'd been able to carve out a nice living doing stonework and building custom fireplaces in the Hamptons.

When Alessandre D'Paolo offered up his guesthouse, Donovan had looked at it as temporary digs. Aless lent him the garage where he stored his stones and worked on his designs, and where he was planning to repaint Trixie before he drove her here wearing nothing but primer gray. Donovan ended up living there by default. He liked his life in New York. He was able to keep busy, keep his head down, live honestly.

Unfortunately, Caroline, his grandmother's chef-turned-Alessandre's-chef, and Donovan's one saving grace, also had a very big mouth. She'd mentioned the mansion inheritance, and the fact that Donovan was ignoring it, to her wealthy boss.

The bed-and-breakfast kingpin pressed Donovan about his plans—Was he moving? Was he renovating? Was he going to sell it?

He'd replied honestly, telling Alessandre, "I'm bull-dozing it."

That's when his friend's face had gone ashen.

Apparently, one man's House of Pain was another man's treasure, and Alessandre D'Paolo envisioned the mansion as his latest bed-and-breakfast acquirement.

And it would be. Just as soon as Donovan disentangled himself from this contract.

"This my copy?" he asked Scott, standing abruptly.

"It is."

He turned to leave the room.

"It's only three months," Scott called behind him. "Not an eternity."

"Still too long," he answered, and shut the door behind him.

* * *

Despite the late hour, the interior lights were on at Make It an Event, making it one of the only shops still lit on Endless Avenue.

Endless. Like this trip.

Donovan had driven a few blocks until he found the shop, realizing he'd overlooked it the first time he'd come through town. If the owner was in, he'd insist they talk about the contract now rather than wait. Shouldn't be too much trouble to get the venue moved. In a wealthy town like Evergreen Cove, there were plenty of hoity-toity places to hold a charity dinner. He parked next to a meter he didn't have to feed since it was after six p.m. and got out of Trixie, who had done him a solid and started up without complaint.

He hadn't known what to expect an event planning company to look like, but once he was inside, he concluded this wasn't it. The shop wasn't filled with frilly wedding shit, nor was it corporate and bland.

What it was, was orderly.

Clean white shelves lined with silver metal mesh trays and baskets were stacked with papers. Alongside those stood an army of black binders with neatly typed labels on their spines. The shelves and their implements made up the entire rear wall behind an equally neat desk. Save for the huge desk calendar covered in scribbly handwriting.

He studied the loopy scrawls without reading the words. A woman. Most definitely. He put a hand on one of two patterned lavender guest chairs in front of the desk and read the card on a fresh vase of purple flowers. *Courtesy of Fern's Floral Shoppe.*

He wondered if Fern, one of his grandmother's former Bridge buddies, was still alive. Clearly, her business was.

"Be right out!" a woman called from a back room.

Without answering, he meandered to the other side of the small shop where a metal table stood, not unlike the one where he prepped scallops and deveined shrimp when he worked at the Wharf.

He flipped open a photo album on its surface, recognizing the ballroom immediately, the huge chandelier with its dangling teardrop crystals, the navy walls, the gold sconces lining the walls.

Pate Mansion.

He closed the cover to see if the album was titled. It was. With a tag that read USO FUNDRAISER, PATE MANSION and last year's date. He opened the book again and flipped through a few pages, spotting his grandmother in one photo, looking about a hundred and eighty years old instead of seventy-six.

Gertrude Pate had died spring of last year, and he wouldn't be surprised if this was the last photo taken of her. Her ashen skin and sunken, hollow eyes were a far cry from the eagle-sharp gaze and tightly pursed lips he'd grown up around. She'd reached out to him at the end. *Too late.* How could someone live their life horribly for seventy-some years and think they could make up for it with a phone call? There was nothing she could've said he wanted to hear, so he ignored her olive branch and continued working.

Caroline, who up until Donovan turned sixteen had lived in the cottage at the back of the mansion's property, had gone to Gertrude's funeral. She expressed her concern when he didn't fly back to the Cove with her. But then Caroline was an all-around good person, and Donovan wasn't. So, there was that.

He started to close the album when a cute brunette in one of the photos caught his attention. Her familiar smile beamed, her arm wrapped around Gertrude's frail shoulders. Sofie Martin's sweet expression was an odd match for Gertrude Pate's cold demeanor. Seeing her close to his grandmother was startling, if not irritating, but the smile gracing the brunette's face wasn't startling at all. She'd always smiled.

Right up until the moment he'd drawn out of her warm, mostly nude body and told her to get dressed.

She hadn't smiled then.

"Sorry, I was..."

He turned to face Sofie as her words died in the empty air between them. Every detail of her smacked with familiarity, a thundering slam into the center of his chest like it'd been seven minutes since he'd held her in his arms instead of seven years.

Her wavy chestnut hair, cool green eyes that hadn't lost a bit of their shine, and parted pink lips he could still taste on the tip of his tongue. Unbidden, his mouth watered as he recalled snagging that bottom lip with his teeth a long time ago in a mansion not so far away . . .

They hadn't parted under the best of circumstances. *Understatement of the millennium.* His fault. He knew what he was getting into, and once he'd gotten into her, he should have stopped. He hadn't.

Much as he'd like to believe the years had dulled the sting of what he'd done to her, he could see the condensed pain bowing her eyebrows and in the thin set of her normally full lips. He'd been cold that night, arguably as cold and apathetic as his family ever was, proving the apple hadn't had far to fall.

His coldness had earned him a slap on the face. After taking hits his entire life, he concluded the blow from Sofie had been the most deserved. Swallowing thickly, he forced a greeting through his teeth.

One he never imagined uttering again.

"Hello, Scampi."

* * *

A nightmare. I'm having a nightmare.

But she wasn't. If this were a nightmare, she'd be naked.

Unfortunately, the naked part had been very real. Like this moment was very real. Which meant Donny Pate was standing in her shop. For real.

He'd aged well.

Too well, she thought with a frown.

His ink-black hair no longer covered his eyes, but

it was in the same longish mass that tickled her cheeks when he'd kissed her for the first time years ago. Still long and lean, his shoulders were broader, his chest more filled out. Dark denim hugged thighs with far more muscle than she remembered.

He raised one black brow and her eyes locked on to his silver-blue ones. Those hadn't changed. They were the color of the shallows when the lake began to freeze. They were the color of cold, the color of hollow. The color of her heart the night she'd slapped him in his stupid Jeep.

"Nice place," he said, and she realized she hadn't spoken yet. What was there to say?

Welcome home? How did you find me? What are you doing here?

That was a great question, actually.

"What are you doing here?" Rude, but then, he'd invented rude.

The corner of his lips lifted. Not quite a smile, but she could see she'd amused him. Good thing she'd retired from being his plaything, or his enticing smirk may have her swooning.

She'd done some growing up, too.

"Didn't expect to find you here." His tone gave no hint as to whether he thought this was a good thing or a bad thing.

Also: she did not care.

She was a professional. An in-charge, take-charge, confident woman who refused to let her one-time-roll-in-the-hay alter her personality.

"I'm the owner." Pulling her shoulders, she stood straighter and replaced the look of shock on her face with neutrality. "What can I do for you?"

His mouth shrugged as if impressed she'd made something of herself. Not that she wanted to impress him.

He reached into the back pocket of his battered jeans and pulled out a folded sheet of paper. Her eyes grazed his attire: simple gray T-shirt molded to nicely built arms and a muscular chest. Jeans worn from age, but clean. A far cry from the Wharf's checkered chef's pants he'd worn day after day, and the ratty black bandanna tied around his head.

He unfolded the paper, the star tattoo on the base of his index finger a reminder some things never changed. It took her a few seconds to drag her gaze from his hands—amazing hands.

Large, roughened from labor, and marked with a tattoo she never knew the meaning behind. There was a newer tat next to it, she noticed. A black bird—or a crow, wings spread—on the fleshy part of his thumb. She could almost feel the phantom grip of his hands back then, on her hip, on her bottom...

Anyway.

Nice hands.

"I assume this is you."

She jerked her eyes from his hand to the paper he held. He didn't budge, forcing her to walk across the room. When she did, she became aware of how solid he was. Living, breathing, and right in front of her. He'd always been tall, but now he seemed to tower over her. A whiff of spice rolled off his neck, the scent snapping her back to the moment he'd had her back against the door in the mansion.

She closed her eyes against the memories closing in on her.

The rake of his teeth against her mouth, the pain-

and-pleasure pinch of his fingers at her nipples, the way he cupped her bottom and lifted her like she weighed nothing.

"Couch or rug?"

Blinking twice to clear her head, she snatched up the paper and flipped it around to read it. No need. She recognized the contract Gertrude drew up last year, her weakness evident in the scrawled signature next to Sofie's indiscernible, loopy penmanship.

"Yes." She offered the contract to him. "That's me."

He didn't take it, shaking his head, and saying, "Not gonna work for me."

For a second, she was too stunned to speak. Her eyes went to her outstretched arm, then back to his face. "Well...I—it's not up to you." She folded her arms over her chest, hearing the paper crunch, feeling her anxiety creep up alongside her blood pressure. She couldn't lose her composure in front of him, of all people.

The pressure of owning her business had taken its toll these past few weeks, as did pressure from her family— an ongoing affair. Then there was the pressure of going on way too many dates over the past few years and having zero to show for it. On a good day, she rolled with the punches. Today was not that day. She wasn't *rolling* anywhere.

"I'm sure you can find another venue," he stated.

Another venue? Obviously, he'd never planned an event as huge as the Open Arms charity dinner. This wasn't dinner for eight. This was music, this was advertising, this was formal invitations...and that was only part of it.

She forced her dry throat to swallow, the overwhelming list of to-do items stacking one on top of the other in her mind. Too much...*much too much* to reschedule. Her breathing went shallow, her chest grew tight.

Shoot. Wait. No. She was a professional. This was her shop. The contract in her hand was legal. She double- and triple-checked after Gertrude passed away. Uncrossing her arms, she held out the paper for him again. "Sorry for the inconvenience."

Again, he didn't move.

She concentrated on breathing deeply and not having an anxiety attack.

"The dead woman who signed that agreement"—he dipped his chin at the paper in her hand—"left me the mansion in her will. And the new owner, *me*, will not be hosting a charity dinner."

Had he really just referred to his late grandmother as "the dead woman"? Gertrude may not have been the most personable human being on the planet, but she'd earned more respect than he was giving her. She'd donated a lot of money to local charities in her remaining years, working tirelessly until her final fading breath. Who wouldn't find her actions admirable?

Donny Pate. But of course.

Rather than lecture the man in front of her who'd long ago traded his heart in for a lump of coal, she asked him a question instead. "Do you care to know what charity this dinner is supporting?"

"Doesn't matter."

Wow. Seriously. *No heart.*

She decided to tell him anyway. "Open Arms provides emergency shelter and foster care for abused children of all ages," she said. "They've been in the Cove for twenty years this June, offering resources such as tutoring, nutritional education, and psychiatrists to kids who have nowhere else to turn."

The speech poured from her lips, well rehearsed thanks to reciting it over the phone to businesses no fewer than a dozen times today. She was in the process of getting more sponsors for the charity, business owners willing to pay to put logos on table tents or donate gifts for the silent auction.

Using his words against him, she rattled the paper in her hand. "*The dead woman* who signed this contract was committed to supporting Open Arms. She left a great deal of money to them—I'm guessing the rest to you—and left me in charge of overseeing this event. There will be no venue change. Not when this dinner has the potential to fund their program for years to come."

There. Try to turn down a charity for abused children.

His face went hard, his lips pressing together in a flat, unimpressed line. When he spoke, his words were a pick dug into a wall of ice, each syllable a sliver chipping through his clamped teeth.

"When you put it that way," he bit out, "definitely *no*."

She forced herself to breathe and looked around for something peaceful to focus on. Instead, her gaze settled on the most beautiful thing in the room.

Him.

If going for his heartstrings didn't work, she'd have to use good, old-fashioned reason. "Listen, Donny—"

"Donovan."

She felt her eyebrows pull. "Excuse me?"

"Donovan. Not Donny."

Okay, she was absolutely over his attitude. "If you can call me Scampi, I can call you Donny."

He shook his head slowly, the left and right motion

intentional. "You took the dare. You lost. *Scampi*." He smiled. Actually *smiled*. It was a small crook of his lips, but it made him look a little sinister and a whole lot delicious. Her heart pounded harder, and this time her anxiety had nothing to do with the seven thousand things she had to look after for the charity dinner.

"Scott Torsett," he stated.

The lawyer down the street. She'd planned his company Christmas party last year. Wild bunch, those lawyers. Thrown, she replied, "What about him?"

"You and I are going to his office tomorrow morning to get the contract voided."

Voided?

"You still drink coffee?"

Not following his line of thinking, she shook her head.

"Tea?"

She replayed the conversation bouncing around in her cluttered head. "I drink coffee. I mean . . . I don't want you to bring me coffee."

Hang on. This was not the point. Holding the contract in both hands, she tried again.

"Donny—er, Donovan—"

He stepped a few inches closer, his smile slipping. She looked into his crystalline eyes and promptly lost her train of thought.

Geez. He'd been back in town five minutes and she was completely frazzled.

He took the contract, folded and stuck it into his pocket, then gripped her upper arms firmly, but gently. This close to him, she had to lift her chin to take in his full height. Heat rolled off his body, the rough texture of his palms skimming along the thin sleeves of the shirt she wore.

The last time she'd been this close to him, he was kissing her. Touching her. And, dammit, her entire body reacted as if he was doing that now. A full-body tingle radiated from her chest to her limbs. His lips flinched like he noticed.

But she wasn't the naïve girl she was back then, was she? No longer was she the girl hell-bent on losing her virginity to the baddest boy in town.

In short, she was no longer *stupid*.

"Coffee," he repeated. "See you in the morning."

He started to let her go, but she kept him captive with one word. "No."

Thank God. She was afraid for a moment she wouldn't find her voice until he walked out of the door.

He blinked, a subtle look of surprise on his features. Probably not used to hearing the word no. Especially from women, she thought with an irritated flick of her eyes over his solid chest. Once upon a time she'd been one of his women. She knew what it was like to be under his powerful gaze, to be stroked by his powerful hands. She knew how much better it felt to say yes and be rewarded by his attention than to say no and endure his apathy.

Too bad for him, she no longer wanted his attention. And she didn't care if he ignored her. In fact, she *preferred* he ignored her. They were light years away from who they were seven years ago—at least she was. He didn't seem to have changed much.

His lids narrowed over pale eyes. "Pardon?"

"I'm having the dinner in the mansion." Forcing her chin up, she kept her head angled, looking into his eyes as she spoke, making sure he didn't miss her strength and persistence. "I've been planning this dinner for almost twelve months. It's in the final stages," she lied.

According to the *Event Planning Bible* sitting on one of the shelves on the back wall, she was about three months behind. Moving the venue, or changing the date, would be a huge setback. A setback she didn't have time to deal with. And there was no changing the date. June eighth was the day of the organization's twentieth anniversary. Oh crap, had she written the eighth or the eighteenth on the invites she just ordered?

Donovan's hands tightened around her upper arms, pulling her out of her brewing panic. "You're not hearing me."

Oh, she heard him. She'd heard everything he'd ever said.

I don't do virgins.

She felt her face go red at the memory. "Let go of me."

He did, shocking her so much by obeying she didn't immediately back away from him. The thought of him in her shop again come morning sent a river of worry flooding her system.

With less conviction than she'd wanted, she managed, "This conversation is over."

"None of this is *over*, Scampi."

"Wrong, Donny," she snapped. "This was *over* seven years ago."

A muscle in his cheek ticked. His light eyes flickered down her body and back up, making her tingle everywhere as if his fingers followed their path. Once upon a time she believed he was her one. *The One*. Once upon a time when she'd handed over her precious first time to a man who couldn't care less about her.

I don't do virgins.

Now was her chance to make up for the moment when

she'd had no response. After her tears had dried, after she was home and far away from him, she'd come up with the perfect zinger, only it was too late to deliver the blow.

Well. She'd just say it now in the name of catharsis.

Folding her arms over her breasts, she said, "I don't do assholes."

He didn't miss a beat.

"You used to."

Her mouth froze open, but no words tumbled out. Again, she had no comeback.

Damn this man.

He turned on one booted heel and left her shop—the same black, scuffed-with-age boots he'd worn years ago, she guessed. The wind kicked his long hair as he strolled under a streetlamp and toward the curb. She stepped closer to the window, watching as he climbed into a Jeep. Then she realized it wasn't *a* Jeep. It was *the* Jeep.

No longer black, but putty-gray, it was the same Jeep host to her "Ride of Shame" back to the Wharf.

A girl never forgot her first one-night stand, she supposed. Her only one-night stand. As he pulled away, brake lights reflecting red on the dark road, she clicked the lock on her door to keep out any more unwanted visitors.

"I used to," she agreed belatedly in the silence. "But not anymore."

CHAPTER TWO

$\mathcal{P}$ate Mansion sat on twenty acres of manicured land, every inch worth a hundred times more than when Donovan's family purchased it a century ago. At the rear of the property, shrouded by thick trees and unable to be seen from the main house, sat a cottage with a private drive. It was where Caroline had lived before she left Gertrude to work for Alessandre D'Paolo, but that was not where Donovan was headed.

The drive leading up to the mansion was long, flanked by naked trees on either side of the narrow lane. In the darkness, the claustrophobic tangle of branches threatened to squeeze the courage from his chest. He gripped the steering wheel, understanding the fear was displaced, leftover from when he was a kid. It was there nonetheless, causing his heart to pound a staccato.

He set his jaw and reminded himself he'd outgrown fear years ago. By age twelve, he'd resolved to be strong.

No matter what punishment awaited him behind the mansion walls, he would take it. He had, too. Taken the slaps that graduated to closed-fist punches, taken the shoves down the stairs, taken the burns, taken the cuts.

Back then he refused to cower in the wake of his belligerent father. Refused to give the old man an ounce of satisfaction. And now? There was no way in hell he'd let Robert Pate haunt him from beyond the grave.

He parked off to the side of the cobblestone, not bothering with the six-car garage to his left. The idea of shutting Trixie in there bugged him.

Through her windshield, he peered up at the structure more resembling a castle than a house. Built from massive square blocks, he could admit from a mason's perspective, the stonework was impressive. The behemoth boasted a pair of pointed turrets as well, their gold tips scratching the bleak sky.

Foreboding. Desolate. Oppressive.

Welcome home.

Involuntarily, he shuddered.

He got out of the car as a floodlight on a sensor lit the side of the house. A big white dog with brown patches appeared from around the corner, its breed a mystery. As a guess, he'd say part Saint Bernard. It lacked the thickness in its body, the thing too skinny and filthy to be owned by anyone. Or maybe it had been Gertrude's and she'd left it to fend for itself.

That sounded like her.

Donovan stayed still in case the dog was aggressive—wouldn't that be his luck—but rather than charge him, the beast turned and skulked around back, vanishing into the shadows.

He snapped the roof onto Trixie in case the skies gave into rain, then opened the back hatch, the hinges whining. Two suitcases and a duffel bag were the sum of his luggage for the stay. When he'd packed back in New York, the plan—still the plan as soon as Sofie relocated the dinner—was to stay long enough to clear out the mountains of Gertrude's crap prior to selling the mansion to Alessandre.

Donovan had planned on hiring someone to clear it out for him, but now that he was in town, may as well do it himself. Hiring someone would be the coward's way out. The mansion was his load to bear.

Like Sofie, he thought with a frown.

But he wasn't one to avoid the monsters lurking in the dark. He preferred to deal with things head on. Cheaper than therapy.

Hefting his bags to the covered porch, he dropped the suitcase and dug the house key from his pocket.

A charity for battered children, he thought as he wiggled the key into the lock. His grandmother's hypocrisy knew no bounds. He heard scurrying in the grass at the side of the house, reminding him he wasn't exactly alone.

Look at the bright side, you inherited Cujo.

"And I'm not even inside yet."

When the door wouldn't budge, he turned his body to the side and slammed a shoulder into it. The frame swelled whenever it rained, and given the state of the soggy, overgrown brush in the flowerbeds, the puddles gathered in the missing cobblestones in the driveway, it had rained earlier today.

The foyer opened to more dark, but he knew the layout. Straight ahead a curved staircase with crimson carpet soared into the darkened second floor. To his left, an equally dark dining hall led to the kitchen where Caroline fixed nearly every meal he'd eaten. To the right…

The library.

Memories of Sofie flashed in his mind. The cushy give of her backside in his palms, the lushness of her lips, the sigh sounding from her throat whenever he kissed her… every inch of her so different from what he'd been used to.

Gentle. Caring. Soft.

No wonder he'd freaked out.

He came back to town to face his demons. His father or grandmother must have tipped them off. They'd gotten the memo and formed a line, coming at him one after the other since he crossed the Ohio border.

He dropped his bags at his feet and took in the curved staircase in front of him. Another memory hit. One where he was sliding down the banister backward, hair flying around his head. The feel of the waistband of his pants cutting into his belly as his father lifted him from the banister and threw him to the floor below.

Donovan's hand went to his broken collarbone, his eyes straying to the hallway vanishing into the darkness.

The hallway he'd been tearing through after being explicitly instructed not to run indoors. Robert stuck his foot out; Donovan ended up with a chipped front tooth. His tongue brushed the cap there now. That injury, like the others, concealed.

More rooms were visible from the foyer, causing memory after memory to slam into him. And this was only the first floor. There were thirteen bedrooms, eight bathrooms. Thirty-five rooms total. All haunted with memories he thought he'd escaped.

Absently, he rubbed his thumb along the star tattoo on his index finger.

Sofie's words from earlier surfaced. *Open Arms provides emergency shelter and foster care for abused children...*

Kids here in the Cove enduring the same horrific treatment he'd endured. Some probably had it worse. A chill skated his spine. Faceless, helpless. Frightened.

Other than Caroline, he had no safe haven when he was a boy. He lied to her about the cuts and bruises, saying he'd fallen off his bike or scraped his arms rock climbing. If she had known the truth, she would have confronted Robert and Gertrude—would have lost her job. The idea of being stuck in this miserable place without her kindness had been unbearable.

As an adult, he'd stopped sugarcoating Gertrude's and Robert's actions and named it what it was: abuse. His father harming him, and his grandmother turning a blind eye was... wrong. Simple as that.

It was just as wrong for Donovan to ignore children in need now.

"Shit." The quietly spoken word bounced off the foyer walls, echoing up the stairs and dissipating into the blackness.

What if an outside party had intervened on his behalf? What would life have been like for him then—for him *now*—if someone had come to his rescue? Someone who could have championed him when he'd been young enough to be saved.

His past was written. He couldn't change it. But if he denied Open Arms, and Sofie, the upcoming charity dinner, he was as big a hypocrite as Gertrude.

He pulled a hand over his face in frustrated acceptance.

Robert Pate's demon lurked in every cobwebbed corner of this place. Knowing he was looking on made Donovan want to defy him. Because fuck him.

"Bring it," he growled, his voice echoing through the quiet hall. He kicked the front door closed behind him, lifted his bags, and turned for the library, where there was a very uncomfortable sofa holding its own host of memories.

He'd left Sofie behind, having taken her gentleness, her softness, her sweetness for himself. In true Pate fashion, he hadn't given her a damn thing in return.

He gave the couch a long, hard look. There was only one path out of bad memories. It wasn't to go around. They couldn't be avoided. He had to go straight through.

Tomorrow he'd go back to Sofie's shop. But he wasn't going to drag her to Scott Torsett to void the contract.

Open Arms would have their charity dinner in the mansion. He could still gut the place in the meantime and sell to Alessandre after. With that behind him, maybe he'd finally be out the other side.

Straight through.

It was the only way.

* * *

Sofie didn't normally make New Year's resolutions. But this year, overcome by melancholy, or maybe champagne, she had made one. At the stroke of midnight, she'd stood on the balcony of a huge mansion atop Peak Point belonging to one of her wine vendors—and drank out of a crystal champagne flute she'd worried she might break and have to pay for.

She did get a kiss at midnight, though. Granted, it was from her best friend and on the cheek, but hey, better than nothing. After many, many failed dates the previous year, Sofie was beginning to believe she would forever be single.

"You'll find him, honey," Faith had said after the peck on Sofie's cheek. "God's just very, very picky for you."

After the run-in with Donovan last night, Sofie was beginning to think God had a very bad sense of humor.

But that was neither here nor there. What was here *and* there was her new attitude she'd temporarily forgotten she'd adopted for the year.

Struggle now, strength tomorrow.

She ran the tip of her finger over the letters written in Sharpie across the top of her desk calendar. The problem with her mantra was that *tomorrow* never seemed to come. The struggle part, she had perfected.

Donny Pate's arrival in town was the icing on the crap cake.

Or maybe she was being melodramatic. A possibility since she'd skipped her morning coffee. She'd skipped it because a certain someone was supposed to bring her a cup of morning coffee...But then, had she really expected Donny to do anything he said he would? What did a guy like him consider "morning" anyway? It was just after nine now, which was well into morning in her book. Which was why when Faith called from Cup of Jo's offering to deliver, Sofie hadn't hesitated to shout, *yes!*

The cheery bell above her shop's door clanged and Faith pushed in with one narrow hip. Her hands were full of Cup of Jo's white chocolate mocha lattes, but Sofie knew her sugar-loving friend's coffee was laced with extra, extra syrup.

The promise of caffeine and sugar answered, she

started to smile, but felt it fade when she registered the look of fury gracing Faith's delicate bone structure.

Expectantly, Sofie stood.

Faith tromped to the desk, delivered her coffee, and blurted, "I hate men."

On the heels of *Donovan* barging into her shop last night, Sofie found herself in agreement. She was about to open her mouth to say as much, when her best friend did something Sofie had seen her do only once before: she burst into tears.

"He texted me while I was at the coffee shop."

Faith sniffed, blinking furiously. As fast as the tears came, they quelled.

"He" was Michael, the man who had recently incurred a title change. Three weeks ago, he went from fiancé to *ex*-fiancé when Faith caught him with his hand in the cookie jar. Literally.

The other woman's name was Cookie. She was twenty-three and had a tramp stamp. Faith saw it in detail considering Cookie had been—as she put it—"riding Michael like a bucking bronco" when Faith discovered them on the living room rug of the house she and Michael used to share.

"What did he say?" Sofie asked.

Faith gave her a bland look, wiping her eyes. " 'Hey.' "

Sofie blinked. "That's it? 'Hey'? Did you respond?"

"No."

"Smart."

"Yet I'm crying." Almost violently, Faith plucked one, two, then a third tissue from the box on the corner of the desk. "I'm an idiot," she said, dabbing her eyes.

Knowing her friend was hurting, Sofie moved out from behind the desk to take the empty guest chair next to her.

Thinking of Donny's casually sensual smile and all his broad tallness, Sofie argued, "No, you're not. Men are idiots. They are also a necessary evil."

Faith let out a feeble laugh of agreement.

The fact that Michael cheated on statuesque, runway model–worthy Faith with a girl way too young for him left little hope for the rest of the female population. Sofie didn't have Faith's height, metabolism, or cheekbones. She was instead gifted with wide hips and a burning desire to wear skinny jeans that would never be fulfilled. Yes, even bodily perfection hadn't prevented inevitable heartache for Faith.

There was no hope for either of them, which made Sofie sad. But there was one thing she could do to make it better.

"Know what you need, honey?"

Faith batted her lashes. Her brief pretty-cry hadn't so much as run her mascara. "A lobotomy?" she deadpanned.

"Shoes," Sofie answered with a giggle. If there was one thing she was good at, it was shopping for shoes. And helping her friends shop for shoes.

"Funny you should ask what I need. It's kind of why I'm here with a Grande cup of butter-you-up."

"Well, it's working." The white chocolate mocha was sweet, delicious, completely fattening, and horrible for her metabolism. Cup of Jo's lattes were the work of the devil, like every other thing delicious and completely bad for her.

Like tall, sexy, mansion-inheriting, virginity-stealing exes.

"You know how you are looking for an assistant?" Faith asked, snapping Sofie out of the pity party she'd started planning.

Sofie didn't need to turn her head to know there was a massive to-do list with three pages of bullet-pointed tasks sitting on her desk. Plans for the Open Arms dinner. Had Donovan shown this morning like he'd threatened, she would have again refused to void the contract. No way would she relocate this, her biggest, most meaningful project, because it was inconvenient for *him*.

A twelve-page address list sat next to the to-do list, some with addresses, others requiring a phone call to get addresses. Those calls needed to be made, and when the invitations arrived, they would need to be mailed. Then there was the design and printing of the table tents. She still needed to gather the logos and other artwork for local businesses sponsoring the event. Not to mention her e-mail inbox overflowing with responses from DJs, caterers, and pricing for gifts for each and every attendee...

Her chest grew tight and she lifted a hand to her throat. Yes. She still needed an assistant. Badly.

"Sofe?"

She blinked over at Faith, whose face was a mask of concern. "Sorry. Just thinking."

"I quit Abundance Market this morning. I went in to open and there was Cookie. Michael hired her. Like me working with that slimehole wasn't bad enough." Faith's upper lip curled in disgust. "Now *she's* there." She shook her head. "I've moved from paycheck to unemployment line." Smiling prettily, she tacked on, "Unless you still need an assistant."

Sympathy for her best friend aside, Sofie felt weight instantly lift from her shoulders at the prospect of help.

"You'd better not be kidding," she warned. "I have been doing interviews for a month and haven't liked anyone."

Faith's pretty smile turned into a satisfied grin.

"I'm not sure I can pay what you were making at Abundance." Sofie bit her lip. She wasn't "not sure," she was sure, sure. The salary she'd earmarked for her assistant wasn't in the same league as what Faith had previously earned. "As far as benefits go, the insurance plan I have only covers me personally, and since the position is part-time..."

Faith's hand rested on Sofie's, comforting her when things should be the other way around. "It's perfect. I'll take it."

This was why she loved her best friend. Faith was one of the few people who went to bat for her. Faith had money. Plenty of money. But here she was, taking a job she didn't technically need, bailing Sofie out when they both knew she could have been hired anywhere else and earned twice as much for her efforts.

"As long as you're sure..." Sofie found herself arguing.

"Are you kidding? Who would I rather work with than my best friend? Trust me, this will be a dream after having to show up early, stay late, and do the liquor order for the entire store."

Sofie may be a people pleaser, but she knew better than to argue further. "You're hired. The Open Arms charity dinner isn't going to plan itself."

And for the first time in a long time, she was in way over her head.

Donovan's angry, handsome face flashed in her mind.

In more ways than one.

* * *

An hour and a half later, Faith was set up at the desk while Sofie hunched over her laptop on a guest chair. She'd been answering e-mails for the last hour and had tasked Faith with calling the list of invitees to ensure there were complete addresses for the invitations.

Faith insisted on starting today, claiming she could use the distraction.

"Thank you, Mrs. Robinson." She hung up the phone and said to Sofie, "Mrs. Robinson. Oh, the irony."

Sofie laughed at the joke, knowing Faith was referring to her famous mother's reputation for bedding younger men.

They'd been so preoccupied with the planning, Sofie hadn't had a chance to tell her best friend about the man who'd darkened her doorstep last night. When the string of bells over her door clanged, and Donovan Pate strode into her shop, tall, dark, and broody, she realized her faux pas.

Faith had worked at the Wharf when Sofie did, so it was no surprise she recognized Donny on sight. "Oh my God."

"A little less holy," Sofie muttered. She had been prepared to confront him this morning. Now after lunch, she'd assumed he wasn't coming in. She was no longer prepared.

"What is he doing here?" Faith whispered.

Sofie didn't have a chance to answer. Donovan strode over and slapped a single silver key onto the desktop calendar. More specifically, on top of the letter S in strength. Sofie's eyes tracked from the key, to the fingers resting on it, and up the tattooed arm of the man who had delivered it.

"Donny Pate," Faith drawled.

Folding his arms, he spared her a brief glance.

"Donovan," he corrected. Then to Sofie, "Here's the deal. I could fight you if I wanted to. Scott Torsett is an old friend of mine. Don't think for a moment he wouldn't find a loophole around my delusional grandmother's contract."

Sofie bristled. She didn't love confrontation. But she also wouldn't take it lying down. Being good at conflict resolution meant she was also good at keeping her head during said conflict.

"Open Arms is a valued partner in this community," he continued. "I have a responsibility to the man buying the mansion after this fiasco. Part of that responsibility is not tarnishing his image before he gets to town and builds a B-and-B. It's the best business decision for everyone involved that the mansion be synonymous with helping the people in this town."

"How magnanimous of you," Sofie said dryly.

Faith stirred in her chair, ready to rip into Donny if needed.

"Point being, I will not stand in your way." He pointed to the key on her desk. "Skeleton. Fits the front, back, and side door. Also fits the attic, but I don't keep it locked."

Done with his speech, he turned to leave.

"Will you be there?" Sofie asked as his hand closed around the door handle. "Or do I have free run?"

He didn't face her, but he turned slightly, his profile dark in the sunlight streaming through the windows.

"My work will not stop because you're using a room or two. I won't stand in your way. But I expect you to stay out of mine."

CHAPTER THREE

When he informed Sofie he wasn't willing to stop his renovation of the house, Donovan wasn't bluffing. To get the mansion ready for sale, he had land to clear, repairs to make, and an entire basement full of home-shopping garbage and family heirlooms—God help him—to unearth.

Gertrude Pate's spending habit had gotten out of hand over the years. He angled a glance at the full-size carousel horse leaning against one of the bedroom walls, its mouth open in a whinny.

Way out of hand.

Alessandre liked to preserve some of the original pieces from any structure he acquired, so Donovan knew he wouldn't be throwing everything out. There were a few antique dressers, table and chairs in the dining room, and key pieces throughout the house he would leave to Alessandre's discretion. Also staying, the books in the library downstairs, and possibly the hot tub, assuming it was in working order. Currently it was outside on one of the balconies, empty, the bottom filled with dried, brown leaves.

But a few things had met their demise in the Dumpster he had delivered this morning. Mattresses, for example. Worn recliners from the TV room. Anything unfit for a luxury bed-and-breakfast had to go.

He'd been hauling crap out to the cobblestone driveway for nearly seven days, and wasn't close to halfway done. Too bad the hot tub wasn't up and running so he could soak in it. His back killed.

Not only from hauling things up and down—and back up and back down—countless stairs, but because he'd been alternately sleeping on the pile of springs that was the red velvet couch or the lumpy L-shaped sectional in the great room. He'd thrown out the mattresses first, figuring he'd be gone soon enough.

Never before had he been so wrong.

The idea of sleeping in a hotel or cabin in town was out. Last thing he wanted was to rub elbows with the locals. He was at capacity for blasts from his past.

Tonight, maybe he would sleep in the back of Trixie under the stars.

Leaving the painted horse behind, he closed that door and popped open another, hoping to find this room empty. What he found instead were porcelain dolls. Hundreds of them with creepy faces and old clothing. So many damn dolls. He closed the door and heaved a frustrated breath.

Again, he thought about hiring someone else to deal with the rest. But he'd still need to be here. No one knew Alessandre's taste like Donovan, what to keep, what to toss.

He took the stairs down to the foyer. When he reached

the last step, the front door swung inward. In the threshold stood a muscular guy with sandy-colored hair, a scowl on his face, and biceps like tree trunks.

"Son of a bitch. It *is* you," said Connor McClain.

His shoulders had doubled in size since Donovan last saw him. The military had changed Connor's body. *And his face.* There was darkness in his eyes Donovan didn't remember being there when he'd returned from his last tour in Afghanistan.

When Donovan left Evergreen Cove seven years ago, it was Connor who hunted him down in New York. He tracked down Gertrude, which led him to Caroline, who in turn gave him Donovan's phone number.

One minute, Donovan had been watching television in Aless's guesthouse, the next he'd been getting an earful from a guy he hadn't seen in two years.

"Clean out your guest room," Connor had told him over the phone. "I'm visiting before I deploy."

When he showed up the next week, Donovan learned why the sudden interest in serving the country. Connor's girlfriend had been pregnant, and he'd learned the baby was not his. He enlisted in the army the day after he found out.

There'd been no talking him out of it.

He may be several years younger than Donovan, but Connor had always been ten times more mature.

Now, seeing his old friend in the foyer, a welcome light in a very dark place, Donovan couldn't keep the smile from his face.

"McClain," he greeted, extending a hand as he approached. His buddy clasped his palm and pulled him in to slap him hard on the back.

When Connor backed away, his smile was wide. "Scott said you were back."

Nice to know Scott's habit of repeating absolutely everything hadn't changed. "When'd you see him?"

"Ah, I fixed a plumbing problem last night."

Donovan crossed his arms over his chest and lifted an eyebrow at his friend. "Plumbing."

Connor's father's company, McClain's Handyman Services, was run by his father, Roger, and with an iron fist. Roger was as blue-collar as they came. Connor didn't share the enjoyment of repairing sinks or snaking toilets. He'd worked for McClain's because he had to. And he had to because, at the time, he'd believed he was the father of Maya's baby.

"It's temporary," Connor said, his smile erasing. Whenever he came home, he resumed working for McClain's in the interim. Evidently, he'd yet to retire his tool belt.

Changing the subject, Connor tipped his head toward the windows behind him. "You need a professional landscaper."

Did he ever. The brush was so overgrown, Donovan had no idea where to start. He hadn't yet been to the cottage at the back of the property and wondered if he could even get to it through the tangle of growth that had no doubt overtaken the grounds.

"I do. Know any?"

Landscaping wasn't Connor's pastime, it was his true passion. Last time they'd talked, Connor mentioned getting the business off the ground once he was out of the service.

A cocky smile found his friend's face. "For a price, I can hook you up with the best." He glanced around the mansion. "Guy who owns a place like this has to have a ton of cash."

He didn't know about "a ton," but Gertrude left an inheritance with the mansion and it wasn't a small one. There would be money left even after he cleaned the place out and returned to his life in New York.

Connor raised his chin and studied one of the plaster medallions on the ceiling. "I always heard about this place, but I've never seen it. Incredible structure." Before Donovan could respond, Connor gave him another grin. "I'm gonna charge you a shitload."

Hell, if anyone deserved a healthy chunk of change, it was Connor.

"Deal." Donovan slapped his friend's solid shoulder. "You can start today."

* * *

The steering wheel of her unassuming white Honda was damp with sweat. Sofie took one hand at a time from the wheel to slick her palms down her skirt. Nerves were getting the best of her—something she couldn't afford if she wanted to keep her head around Donovan.

It was just a house. A house she'd been to dozens of times before. She'd met with Gertrude Pate, she'd met caterers and florists, she'd planned events, all under the mansion's roof.

She'd just never been here when Donovan Pate was under said roof.

Oh, yes you have.

Right. *Once.*

"Struggle today, strength tomorrow," she said to herself as she parked in the driveway.

Sofie hadn't seen him since he'd darkened her doorstep at Make It an Event to deliver a key to the mansion. She had no idea what had changed his mind but concluded his reasons didn't matter.

After he'd walked out the door, Faith said, "He looks the same as he did seven years ago."

Hot, her tone implied.

Sofie had reluctantly agreed on the inside. On the outside, she muttered a noncommittal, "I guess."

For the last week, she'd been doing everything she could to put off the inevitable visit to the mansion, figuring she'd wait until Donovan left town. But he hadn't left town. She knew because she'd seen his primer-colored Jeep here, there, and everywhere.

Then a few days ago, Ruby Voss had called and invited her to Open Arms. Ruby introduced her to the children either visiting or living there. Seeing those kids had been heartbreaking in a way Sofie hadn't expected. Another thing she hadn't expected was for the nonprofit maven to have a hidden agenda.

Ruby needed a favor. A big one.

"You know how we like the children to help with the charity dinner. Serve, help cook if the caterer agrees," Ruby had started, straightening the sleeves on a smart red suit.

"Of course." Sofie was a step ahead of her. "The caterer loved the idea. We have extra hands in the kitchen to oversee the kids."

Despite her formal dress, Ruby's smile was warm and genuine. "Wonderful." Then she took a breath, her smile dropping. "Recently, we lost our funding for the night before. The kids who are chosen to help with the charity dinner do a campout. We find this is good for them. To get them out of here." She'd gestured at the facility more resembling a big house. "Pate Mansion would be perfect for that endeavor."

For one terrifying second, Sofie thought Ruby was asking if the kids could stay in the bedrooms at the mansion. That was something she was sure she couldn't negotiate. Not with Donovan "stay out of my way" Pate.

"Did you know the mansion sits on nearly twenty acres?" Ruby's brows winged into her stylishly coiffed brown hair.

"Something like that," Sofie had commented with caution.

Her smile returned, pearly teeth bared. "Plenty of room for the kids to make camp. And, right out back. They would need access to a washroom so they can get cleaned up and dressed for dinner. If you think about it, staying on site is kind of genius. They will be there, ready to work, ready to assist the caterer in the kitchen at an early hour. Ready to help you set up in the ballroom if needed."

It was a good pitch, but nowhere near Sofie's jurisdiction.

"This was not part of the original contract, Ruby." Sofie had bitten her lip, thinking how to turn her down gently. "I'm not sure if you know, but the mansion has changed hands since Gertrude passed away. Her grandson is preparing the house for sale. I'm not sure he would be amenable to the campout."

That was an understatement. *Donovan* and *amenable* didn't belong in the same sentence.

Ruby's smile had cooled. "But you can ask." It hadn't been a question, allowing no room for argument.

"Of course," Sofie agreed.

And so, here she was. At the mansion. To ask a favor from the man who simply wanted her to stay out of the way.

Strength.

She parked, noting the obvious: a very large truck standing in the driveway and three very large men at the back of it. One of them she recognized as Connor McClain, local landscaping guy. He used to work at the Wharf back in the day. Now back home for good and warming up his business, Sofie took advantage of his talents and had hired him for several events.

Connor didn't acknowledge her arrival—must not have noticed her before he turned to walk inside the mansion. The other two men wore gray shirts, stitched tags on the material matching the logo on the truck. Local thrift shop.

Dressed in her work clothes, a smart black pencil skirt, cream-colored blouse, her hair pinned back into a twist, Sofie got out of her car and approached the front door. She'd thought about changing into something more casual since she sure as heck wasn't trying to impress Donovan, but by the same token, she also wasn't going to change her appearance for him, either.

Careful not to wedge her new stilettos into the cobblestone driveway, she picked her way in the direction of the front porch, stopping short when a balding man with a large mustache hefted a box. Thick, black Sharpie spelled out the word SILVER on one side.

Sofie pictured the pieces inside clearly—knives, spoons, forks, tongs, ladles, and various other implements, their handles engraved with fleur de lis. She knew what they looked like because she and Gertrude had carefully wrapped the pieces in fabric and packed them into this very box. Sofie had wedged the can of polish into one corner herself.

Last year, for the USO charity dinner, Sofie suggested they use the antique silver flatware for the biggest sponsors who garnered special seating. They charged extra for the perk, which directly benefited the charity and added nothing to the cost of the event.

Gertrude had dug out her fine china as well.

And now the silverware was being loaded onto a truck heading to a thrift store. Adjusting her purse onto her shoulder, Sofie smiled up at the man loading the box.

"Excuse me."

With a grunt, he dropped the edge of the box onto the truck and gave it a shove. The man inside dragged it to the back.

"Excuse me," she repeated. "That box is being donated?"

"Hey, you are smarter than you look," came the mustached man's response.

"Um, you can't take the box of silver. Or that one," she said, tipping her head at another box marked CANDLES sitting in the truck.

"Sorry, lady. You ain't in charge here, so we will be taking whatever the men in the house tell us to. Jim!" the mustached man called to the man inside the truck, "going to need help with the next one."

"What is it?" Jim asked.

"Plates. Don't throw that one around."

"No, no," Sofie interrupted with a strained smile. "You can't take the china, either." She took a calming breath and tried not to have a heart attack. Could be worse. At least she'd arrived *before* they left with the dinner service she'd promised to her biggest contributors.

The man with a mustache turned and glared down at her from his height. "Listen, lady, you are in the way and we have a job to do. I suggest you scuttle your sweet patoot out of the way before we run you over with the dolly."

Her teeth clacked shut, offended in more ways than she'd thought possible. She opened her mouth to defend herself, and her sweet... what had he called it? A patoot? But she didn't get out a single word before Donovan appeared in the driveway, stalking toward the truck.

And he did not look happy.

"Tell me I didn't just hear that, Mario," he told the man with a mustache, his tone eerily calm.

"Hotter than the blazes out here," Mario commented, mopping his brow with a stained orange rag. "Your visitor, while cute, is a pain in my neck."

Donovan smiled at the man, but it wasn't a happy smile. "You think you have a pain in your neck now, wait 'til I lay you out on this cobblestone."

Sofie snapped her head over to her rescuer. Donovan's nostrils flared, his arm muscles coiled. If he were a snake, he would be rattling.

Mario picked up on none of the cues. "Listen, we're on a tight schedule, here..."

Ignoring the other man, Donovan turned soft eyes on her. "Something you need off this truck?"

"Yes," she said, still a little shocked by the conversation so far. "At least two boxes, but I can't be sure there aren't more. Last year, Gertrude and I set aside several items for future charity dinners."

He gave a curt nod and turned to the men. "Mario, Jim, this is Sofia Martin. Anything she needs off this truck, and anything she doesn't want you to put on it, you will listen to her."

Mario's cheeks went ruddy and his dark eyes flashed. He sent Sofie a succinct frown, but then his eyes went back to Donny.

"No problem," he grumbled. She couldn't help thinking he didn't mean that.

Jim, far less bothered by the change of plans, nodded his agreement, grabbed the dolly, and wheeled toward the house. Mario started to follow but before he could, Donovan stepped in his path.

"I ever hear you refer to a single part of her body as 'sweet' again, or if I hear you insinuate any part of her body is a 'pain,' I will lay you out. I don't care how uneven the fight is, how much older than me you are, or that you might sue me or call the police. I. Will. Lay. You. *Out*."

Donovan had leaned a little closer to Mario's face while he was making his threat. The older man wasn't exactly shaking, but Sofie could see he wasn't interested in calling Donovan on the threat, either.

"Understood?" Donovan straightened, gave the older man an unaffected smile, and crossed his arms over his chest.

Mario's eyes danced along the bent tree tat tracking up Donovan's forearm, the inked waves and swirls poking out of his shirtsleeve. "Sure thing, boss. I get grouchy when it's hot."

"I get grouchy where Sofie's involved."

Head down, Mario said no more and walked inside.

Donovan turned to her, what looked like concern bending his eyebrows. "You okay?"

Seriously? She was fine. What he'd done was sort of... sweet. In a scary way.

Then why don't you feel scared?

Because she was too busy feeling flattered.

"I'm sure he would've responded the same if you simply asked him to be more polite. I don't think all that..."—*sexy chest beating*—"posturing was necessary."

My house, my rules," he replied. "No one talks to you like that. Not ever."

Her heart kicked against her ribs. Chivalry was not dead.

He followed the path Mario walked to the house. Sofie was still standing at the back of the truck, gaze snapping from the boxes to the house, unsure what to do next.

A moment later, Connor stepped in front of her.

"I was told by the guys you're taking over bossing them around." He grinned. "Which means I can get back to what I was doing before you got here."

Her eyes scanned the expanse of dirt across the white T-shirt covering his wide chest. With his sandy-colored hair, bulging biceps, and sweat trickling down his temple, Connor was the definition of the word *rugged*.

"Let me guess," she said. "Planting something?"

"Saplings." He stepped to the side. Once his width wasn't obstructing her view, she saw several trees dotting the lawn, roots protected by burlap. A shovel was stabbed into a sizable pile of dirt like a claim. "Trying to get them in before the sale. Make the place look nice."

He grinned, and it was a little blinding. Connor looked like he belonged in a calendar featuring half-nude military guys. All for fundraising purposes, of course. Which gave her an idea...that she shelved for later.

She had bigger fish to fillet.

"Didn't know you were coming over to help," he said as he turned for the trees.

"Oh." She followed him, stopping short of sinking the heels of her shoes into the soft grass-covered ground. "I'm not. Not really. I'm sort of here on my own...agenda." And Ruby's. "What are you doing here?"

He bent, his jeans cupping a very nice backside. "Clearing out a bunch of brush out back, planting flowers"—he gestured at the hole in the ground—"planting trees."

"Donny hired you?"

He pulled on a pair of gloves and went to work wrestling a sapling into a hole. While he did, Sofie mostly stared at the muscles bunching in his arms.

"I insisted," he said, his voice strained from effort.

Connor was a good guy, and though he'd only moved back last year, was already a staple around the Cove. A real-life hometown hero who had done back-to-back stints serving his country. Now home for good, he was working on making his landscaping business his full-time career. Donovan would be glad he entrusted him with the mansion.

"Guess I'll go inside," she said, shuffling her feet. "With Donovan." Apparently there was no avoiding him.

"Who?" Connor teased, wiggling the tree standing several feet over his head to ensure it was in the ground solidly. "Oh, you mean Donny."

She twisted her lips. "I was told he's *Donovan* now."

"Yeah." He squatted and began pulling dirt over the roots. "Being unapproachable is kind of his specialty."

She snorted.

"But then you probably already figured that out." He spared her a glance.

Which she took to mean he knew more than he let on. She had no idea what he actually *knew* about her and Donovan. Not that there was much to know. They'd wham-bam-thank-you-ma'amed and that had been the end of things.

Connor dragged the next tree in line by its skinny trunk to a waiting hole. "He won't bite, Sofe." He winked.

She licked her dry lips, having absolutely nothing to say to that.

Okay. So she'd just...go in there. Apparently she had a job to do, although preventing two burly men, one of whom did not like her very much, from taking things from the mansion was not why she was here. After that task was finished, *right after*, she would talk to Donovan about Ruby's idea.

Putting one foot in front of the other, she squared her shoulders and walked into the mansion.

$\mathscr{C}$HAPTER FOUR

$\mathscr{D}$onovan moved the heavy boxes of china and silver to the ballroom, though Sofie insisted on helping, carrying the smaller container of candles. Mario and Jim had made things very clear—they were here to load the truck, not move boxes around. To her surprise, Donovan hadn't pushed the issue.

"That's it." He flipped the lights off in the ballroom. "Hadn't planned on spending two hours rearranging stuff I would rather throw out."

Great. So he was prickly. And she had yet to bring up the campout.

"There was something I wanted to talk to you about," she said from the darkened shadows of the room, her voice quiet.

He turned and pegged her with those pale, electric eyes. Being under his scrutiny always made her feel kind of small. And she wasn't a petite girl. He also made her feel a lot turned on. Everything about his height, his attitude, and his smile—when he did smile—made her want him.

Used to make her want him, she reminded herself. So, her body was experiencing some leftover physical reaction to him. Perfectly normal.

"And you owe me a coffee," she said.

Half his face in shadow, the other half softly lit from the sunlight in the corridor, he licked his lips. It was a glorious sight. He didn't quite smile, but he was no longer frowning.

"All right, Scampi. Coffee."

She followed him from the ballroom and through the hallway, passing a series of doors she knew to be the bathroom, the great room, and a few other areas not furnished for any one use in particular. In the foyer, they passed the library, which she fervently ignored.

Don't you mean The Deflowering Room?

If Donovan thought about what they had done in that room seven years ago, he didn't show it. Just kept walking. She followed his lead, passing a curved staircase leading to the upstairs, her heels tapping along the elegant, but worn, parquet floor.

The doorway across the foyer from the library led to a massive dining room. In here, the walls bled deep red, the carpet mud brown. The dreaded space opened to the kitchen, one of the only rooms in this place bathed in natural sunlight.

Stepping through the murky dining hall, she followed him into the wide, welcoming kitchen. Buttercream cabinets, pale granite countertops, and a butcher's block filled in the spaces around large, modern appliances. A solid oak kitchen table stood in one corner, eight high-backed chairs encircling it. The room was bright and open, and looked as if it belonged in a different house.

The man standing in the kitchen looked like he belonged in the rest of it. Dark, intimidating...

She thought of Connor's word. *Unapproachable*. That was a good word.

Donovan went to the coffeemaker. She watched his fingers grasp the silver coffee scoop, digging out grounds from a black foil bag, a brand of coffee she'd heard of but had never tried. Her eyes traveled the length of his long legs, encased in worn blue jeans, and ending in those same steel-toed black boots she'd rarely seen him without.

"Those look like the same boots you wore at the Wharf," she blurted before thinking maybe she shouldn't have said that. Nothing like telling the man you slept with years ago you haven't forgotten a single detail about him.

"They are."

Surprised he answered, she asked, "Why haven't you bought a new pair?"

He pressed a button on the coffeemaker and turned to give her a confused expression. He should, she wasn't really making any sense.

"Scampi, if this is what you wanted to talk to me about, I gotta say, I'm underwhelmed."

She cleared her throat. "It's about the charity dinner. Or, well, the charity in general I guess."

He remained silent.

"Your grandmother hired me over a year ago to plan this dinner and raise money for Open Arms. My job is something I take very seriously," she said, warming up to her point. "I know you don't like this town, and you don't like this house, I'm guessing—since you're selling it—but I'm determined to see through my commitment."

He tilted his head, sending a lock of black hair over his forehead. "You have a key to the house, sweetheart. You can 'see through' whatever you need to."

Sweetheart.

She tried not to let the endearment stir feelings so intent on pressing their way forward.

Taking a deep breath, she thought back to the day she visited Open Arms. Not only did the facility need all the funds they could get, the kids she met needed a win in a big way.

One of the children who'd snagged her heart was a four-year-old girl who bore scars from her stepfather's cigarettes, another a twelve-year-old boy who had been beaten by his drunken mother. The boy flinched whenever Sofie talked with her hands, so she'd quickly learned to keep her gesturing at a minimum.

Sofie hadn't grown up in a problem-free home—who did?—but in comparison to what the children at Open Arms had survived, her childhood was utter paradise. Her parents were still married, happily so. Her sisters were healthy and alive, though they bickered like birds fighting over a French fry. Sometimes Sofie felt like the off piece around her mother and sisters, but she and her father had a special bond.

The children at Open Arms deserved to be championed. If Sofie could improve those kids' lives even a little, let them know someone cared, then her efforts would be worth it.

With them in mind, she told Donovan, "I'm doing this for two reasons."

Her voice wavered. She took a breath and steadied it.

"The children at Open Arms need a win. They need money, need the town's attention, need people to stop ignoring and overlooking them."

His jaw had tightened since she began speaking, an unknown emotion darkening his eyes.

"I take it you didn't know your grandmother well. She was an amazing woman. She cared about the people in this town."

A dry, humorless laugh chafed his throat. "'Amazing.' You people need a new adjective." The smile on his face wasn't so much a smile as a grimace. "If she cared about the people in this town, Scampi, it was only because I was no longer one of them."

She felt a frown pull her mouth.

"I'm not fighting you on the charity part, and you know that. I feel like there's something else you need from me. Wanna tell me what that is, or continue practicing your Nobel Peace Prize speech?"

Done delaying, she let him have it—told him about the campout, about Ruby's commitment to the children. About how they would need hardly anything and would stay out of the way if he agreed to the campout. "They have their own supplies and tents. Connor is already hard at work to make the outside inhabitable. I don't see what it would hurt if you let the kids sleep in the yard."

His arms were still crossed, and while he wasn't exactly scowling, he didn't look pleased. "You're asking me to give a dozen homeless children free rein of the grounds at the historical Pate Mansion."

She lifted her chin. "Yes."

His lips formed one word. "No."

Suddenly, she was looking at his back. No?

"Cream is in the fridge," he announced, pouring himself a mug of coffee. "Not flavored like you prefer, but it's all I have."

A fleeting thought about how surprising it was that he remembered she took flavored creamer in her coffee pushed itself forward, but she shoved it away.

"What's the matter?" she asked. "Allergic to kids?"

He leaned on the counter with one hip, the mug steaming in his hand. "I'm not going to be here for this charity thing, and you want to let kids roam around here after the house has been readied, the grounds have been cleared. And before my buyer has a last walk-through."

"It's not like we're letting loose a bunch of feral cats," she said, suddenly figuring out this was a point she could fight. "Ruby has volunteers, assistants. I'll be here."

"You'll be here."

"Yeah," she said quietly, "I'll be here."

* * *

He recognized that stubborn chin-tilt. She'd worn it the night she stomped from the Wharf's kitchen to the packed-with-guests dining room and earned her nickname. She'd looked equally determined the night of the Christmas party when she'd followed him to his Jeep and let him kiss her until they steamed the windows...

Sofie was the same now as she was then: sweet, caring. *Committed*. And frankly, he no longer saw the need to continue this argument.

"Fine." He started for the dining room, or any room where she wasn't.

"Fine?" she called from behind him. "Just like that?"

He turned and paced back into the kitchen. "Just like that. That was the agreement. You stay out of my way. I'll stay out of yours."

He shouldn't want her. He didn't want to want her. But he did. And the closer she came to him, the harder it was not to give in. *Apparently*, since he'd given her exactly what she wanted with hardly a fight.

In front of him now, she said, "You don't have to...be angry."

Lightly scented perfume lifted off her skin, jetting him back to the first time he kissed the soft flesh behind her ear.

In the process of punishing himself for taking what he'd taken from her, his body and mind had also connected her to the one thing he'd been trying to forget for seven years.

What she felt like beneath him.

No longer was he willing to use her as his own personal sanctuary. He'd come back to the Cove to deal with his shit, not drag her into it. She should hate him for the way he'd treated her way back when and, hell, he wouldn't blame her a bit. He hated himself for it.

He remembered their moments in the library vividly, the way her face pinched, the way she bit down on her lip. How tight she felt, how nervous she was. The slight tremor running through her arms had radiated down his spine, mirroring the tremor that shook him to the core.

His father was dead. And Donovan would've thought, after years of bad blood, after the beatings, after Robert Pate was in the ground, that he would finally be free. But Donovan hadn't felt free that night. He felt like a part of him was missing. He felt like crying. He'd laid the confusing swirl of emotions to rest in Sofie's pliant body. Hid them in the softness of her hair, buried them in the bend of her curves.

Flayed open, there was no way not to feel what Sofie gave to him in that darkened library...it was something he'd barely recognized.

Love.

She'd shown him love. *Him,* a guy who could barely manage the meager scrap of a life he'd built for himself.

Greedily he took what she'd readily given. The way he felt in her arms, all that love radiating from her, felt better than the quiet torment chasing him most days.

She had given, he had taken. No question who profited most from that transaction.

After he'd taken his own release he had been filled with self-loathing rivaling the self-loathing he'd felt for years under the hand of his domineering father—and that was saying something.

Way he saw it, Donovan had ruined Sofie. Taken the sweetest, kindest, most caring woman to ever touch him and blackened the last precious part of her.

I don't do virgins.

The words stung to say then. They stung him now. Unfortunately for Scampi, Donovan hadn't known what to do with the mess of feelings he wasn't coping with that night, so he'd latched on to the emotion that had seen him through many hard times.

Anger.

She was wrong when she'd said he didn't need to be angry. He *needed* to be angry. Then and now, but for the same reason: to keep her away from him. The look in her eyes, the way she was taking him in. The sympathy there...

Looked like someone had forgotten what an asshole he could be.

Still am.

Well. He'd remind her.

Moving closer to her, he stepped forward as she stepped back, until she reached the countertop and bumped against it. She had to lift her chin to take him in. He was so close, her breasts brushed lightly against his shirt. Reaching past her, he gripped the edge of the countertop, his arm brushing hers. Touching her made him want to touch her more. She snatched her arm away.

Good girl. Remember how repulsive I am.

Someone needed to remember, because suddenly, he found himself not wanting to push her away, either.

Dangerous. For both of them.

She was visibly flustered, biting her lip, winding her fingers together, yet her steady gaze met his.

"Second thought..." He lowered his head to her ear and breathed in more of her. "We don't have to fight."

Tempting to leave it at that.

The fragrance of her hair, slightly sweet like her, lifted and swirled in his senses. She smelled the same as he remembered. *Sweet.* Sweet like every inch of her tasted back when he didn't know what she was about to give him. She'd offered every part of herself to him. She hadn't been obligated.

Her hand laid on his chest, now, bringing him back to the present. Her small palm warmed him on contact—a touch he hadn't felt in forever.

"I know what you're trying to do," she said, proving herself less susceptible to his manipulations than before.

He backed away from her ear but maintained his

closeness, letting a careless smile grace his lips. The sentiment was fake. He cared. Too much. That was why he needed her pissed at him. "If your guess is getting you to agree to another bounce on the library sofa, you're right."

Her mouth gaped and she pulled in a quiet breath.

"Wrong," she finally managed, her voice cold and hard. There it was. She remembered.

Pushing her further, he said, "Come on, Scampi. I kiss you, you melt to your knees. We both know it."

She shook her head, her palm pushing him away. "You're not kissing me. Not ever again."

Even though it was what he wanted her to say, it cut to hear. His chest took the blow, her words denting the armor installed over his heart.

You deserve it.

A little more prodding, and she'd be good and pissed off. Then he could get done what he needed to do without her distracting him. He could return to New York, leaving the Cove behind permanently. And Sofie could live out the rest of her days in peace knowing he'd never see her again.

Another blow. Another dent. His jaw tightened.

Come on, Pate. Man up.

Whatever emotions she'd kicked up, he didn't get to feel them. Remorse, anger, a dab of guilt, yes. But not this. Not cared for, or liked, or her innate kindness. He didn't get to have someone like Sofie, not after what he'd taken from her. He didn't deserve her, and more importantly, she didn't deserve him.

Stepping back a few inches, he gave her some physical space, enough to allow her angry gaze to burn into him.

Now to shove angry into infuriated.

"Guessing you picked up a few tricks since we were together."

Her eyes narrowed.

Closer.

He smirked. "Or *a lot* of tricks."

Her jaw tensed. Her eyebrows lowered.

Jackpot.

In his peripheral, he registered her lifting her palm.

He'd never been able to watch an incoming hit. Even after he'd pulled himself out of the cage of fear his father had shoved him into. Even after he'd stood up for himself. Even after he'd started fighting back. Out of years of habit, and in the nanosecond before her hand did what he expected—cracked across his face—he closed his eyes. Braced himself to accept what was coming.

Seconds passed.

Nothing came.

Not angry words. Not the sting of her palm on his cheek. Nothing.

He opened his eyes to find Sofie's anger had ebbed, replaced with a gentle expression reflecting her soft-hearted, trusting nature.

Her bleating heart her greatest fault.

People always let you down. Sooner rather than later. Better to be armored up than bare.

Her arm lifted again. This time he didn't flinch. Her hand finished the journey to his face, where she skimmed her fingers lightly over his cheek and down his jaw.

"I'm sorry," she whispered.

What he should be saying to her for everything that had happened in this very house. But the words had come from her.

Pissed, he clenched his jaw tighter and spoke between teeth welded together. "No, Scampi."

Her fingertips stroked from his jaw to his chin. "You thought I was going to hit you again." She looked at his mouth.

Again. Like she had in his Jeep. The moment he'd told her to get out. He'd turned cold and mean minutes after seducing her in the warmest way possible. He didn't deserve her apology. In no way should she feel anything but satisfied for hitting him. He'd deserved that slap.

He hated her vulnerability. Hated more the idea that men must have—had to have—taken advantage of her in the years since he'd done it first. Donovan had one night with her. There'd been thousands of nights since him. How many of those nights had she spent with men who didn't deserve her? Men who'd taken advantage of her vulnerability, had guilted her into apologizing when she'd done nothing wrong.

Too many, he'd bet.

Like you would have treated her better?

No. That was why he left.

He wouldn't use her guilt against her now, turn it on her like a weapon. Like his father had done to his mother, driving her away when Donovan was a toddler. Robert had learned that method from Gertrude.

Patterns. A pattern Donovan was determined to break.

"I lived." He took her wrist and pulled her hand from his face, but found he couldn't let her go right away. Finally, after a few seconds, he released her. He needed to get the hell away from her gentle touch, those green eyes revealing too much of her tenderness. Had to stop feeling the warmth and sweetness rolling off her like fog on the lake.

He stalked out of the kitchen, away from the suffocating air bearing down on him. Accusations followed, the knowledge that he'd been responsible for her at one moment in time; it snapped at his heels, dogged his every footfall.

He blew his chance to save her. From that truth, there was no running.

CHAPTER FIVE

*S*ofie handed over the checklist to Charlie Harris—soon to be Charlie Downey after she and Evan were married. "I made a list of the kinds of photos we'll need for the event. I should have gotten this to you sooner."

An entrepreneur, Charlie was an amazing photographer. Sofie had admired her work since she met her at Cozy Home Furniture. They'd become fast friends, and when Charlie mentioned her love for the hobby, Sofie found a way to get her involved in the next event she planned.

"No, no it's great." With her long, honey-blond hair and sunny yellow dress, Charlie looked like summer arrived early. She slapped the list on the breakfast bar in the house she shared with Evan, wiggled in her seat, and grinned.

Uh-oh.

"Now, are you going to tell me what it was like to reunite with Donny, your long lost first time?"

Charlie's face. So filled with love and hope and heart-shaped helium balloons.

Sofie gave her friend a patient smile. Why was it everyone who was in love thought everyone else should also be in love? Sofie's sister Lacey was the same way both times she'd been engaged. She was all hearts and roses, too. So darn happy it almost made Sofie's stomach turn.

Almost.

She would never begrudge Charlie and Evan the happiness they'd found. Charlie had battled through orc-laden landscapes of guilt for falling in love with her late best friend's husband. And Evan, who had lost his wife five years ago now, fought for Charlie, understanding they deserved each other. Understanding his son, Lyon, deserved to have another shot at a mother.

No, Sofie would never dream of denying her friends what they'd so rightfully won: each other.

Charlie was still smiling at her. "Pleeeease tell me?"

Sofie allowed herself a smile. "Well, first he came to see me at Make It an Event and threatened not to let me use the mansion. Then"—she held up a finger—"he came back, said it would be best for the community if I did use the mansion for the charity dinner, and gave me a key to the house."

Her friend's smile morphed to a frown. "Moody."

Ticking off another finger, Sofie continued. "*Then*, yesterday, when I stopped by the mansion, one of the thrift store guys insulted me and Donny defended my honor. Of course, after that he told me to stay out of his way and he'd stay out of mine." She screwed her eyes to the left in thought, ready to tick off another item if needed. "Yep, that's about it."

No way was she bringing up the moment in the kitchen where he got in her face, clogging her personal space with the smell of spice, those achingly mysterious eyes boring into hers.

She sure wasn't bringing up the part where he'd insinuated he might like to...how had he put it? Give her another "bounce on the library sofa." And why were her palms sweating? That offer was not a turn-on. Not at all.

"Sofia," Evan greeted as he strode into the kitchen in that signature swagger of his. He placed a kiss on his fiancée's forehead, and Charlie beamed at him. Seriously, beamed. It was beautiful.

Sofie's heart pinged with the slightest bit of envy. Not because she wanted Evan for herself—although his dark mussed bedhead and turquoise gaze would give any girl a heart-flutter—but because she would be lying if she said she didn't want someone in her life who loved her as much as he loved Charlie.

And he seriously loved Charlie.

"Hey, Evan," Sofie greeted.

He was dressed in running shorts and a tank, his tattoos on display. A former tattoo artist, Evan hadn't entirely given up the passion when he turned children's book illustrator with Asher Knight at the writing helm. Evan had designed each bit of ink he wore himself. Charlie told her the stories behind them. The roses on his shoulder were for his mother and aunt who passed away too soon. The lion on his other shoulder represented his son, Lyon, the rambunctious eight-year-old who was very much thriving in Evergreen Cove. The town herself was commemorated on one of Evan's forearms, a host of pines tracking up to his elbow. That one earmarked him and Lyon moving here last year.

He'd branded Charlie with a camera tattoo on her rib cage—her passion, adding in watercolor strokes—his passion.

Two lives. Merged.

Beautiful.

As they so often did as of late, Sofie's thoughts turned to Donovan. She wondered the meaning behind the star on his finger, or the raven, the gnarled tree on his forearm, the arrow on the other...

So many. They had to stand for something.

"So that was it? No recognition? No moment of longing settling between you two?" Charlie asked. "It's romantic." Her gaze settled over Sofie's shoulder, then softened. "Reunited after seven years apart..."

When she rerouted her gaze and saw Sofie's look of dejection, she quickly added, "Sorry. Rose-colored glasses."

Sofie cupped her friend's hand over the bar. "Never apologize to me for your happiness, do you hear me? Never. My being single doesn't mean I can't be happy for you." She took her hand back and waved dismissively. "I'm just...frustrated."

And confused. Donovan Pate was a hard man to read.

"I'm sorry. I should be—"

"Ace." Evan interrupted as he poured a cup of coffee.

Charlie rolled her eyes. Evan had been trying to get her to kick the habit of saying "sorry" for everything since he moved here. It was cute, almost as cute as him calling her "Ace." And he was right—she had nothing to be sorry about.

"Did you know your buddy Donovan was a jerk?" Charlie asked him.

A crooked smile played the corner of his mouth as he lifted the mug to his lips. "Yeah."

His eyes flickered to Sofie. "Bet you knew that already."

Oh Lord. What did *that* mean?

Evan winked at Charlie and retreated to his art studio on the other side of the house.

Did *everyone* know Sofie and Donny had done the deed?

After he'd gone, she turned to her friend, whose hazel eyes went wide.

"I only told him what I know."

"Charlie!"

She winced. "Sorry! I tell him all sorts of things. I didn't know he really listened to me."

Evan knew Sofie had lost her virginity to one of his buddies. *Fabulous.*

"How am I supposed to keep showing up there to work?" Sofie buried her face in her hands. "Maybe I'll make Faith do it."

But that made no sense. Sofie had held charity dinners in the mansion for the past three years. She was familiar with the routine of setting up there, of tearing down. Parking. The way the catering was handled. She knew the boxes being donated to the thrift shop shouldn't have been on that truck—Faith never would have known any different.

"Ugh. What am I supposed to do?"

Charlie tugged at Sofie's wrists until she relinquished and revealed her face. "You're going to continue to show up and do whatever it is you do. Who cares if he doesn't talk to you?"

But that was the whole problem. She did care.

Taking a deep breath, Sofie announced, "I slapped him."

"When?" Charlie's big eyes grew bigger. "Why?"

"Seven years ago. The night of the...*incident*," she whispered needlessly. Evan was far out of earshot and Lyon was in school. "After"—she motioned with one hand rather than spell it out—"*after*, he yelled at me, told me to get out of his car. I was hurt."

Sofie covered one cheek with her hand. She could almost feel the cool air from the Jeep's vent blowing on her face. Hurt was putting it lightly. She'd been devastated.

"I hauled off and smacked him." She shook her head. "Right in the face."

Charlie crossed her arms in front of her on the bar. "Good."

But it wasn't good. Sofie's actions may have been justified, but there was no good that came from striking another person.

"Yesterday, he was...I don't know, trying to make me upset or something."

Donny hadn't been warm and welcoming, but he also hadn't exactly been mean. His goading seemed more defensive than anything.

"He stood really close to me and I raised my hand while I was talking—like I do." Sofie waved her hand briefly to demonstrate.

Charlie leaned in the slightest bit. "And?"

She pictured long, dark lashes scrunching over his eyes.

"He flinched."

Her friend's head jerked back in surprise. "Flinched?"

"All six-foot-four of him."

Charlie's mouth pulled into a frown. "What's that about?"

That memory merged into another—the boy at Open Arms who'd reacted the same way. He'd flinched, too.

Ruby mentioned he'd been hit a lot by his mother and not to take his reaction personally.

Her face infused with heat as the visual of the boy's face swapped places with Donny's. Was that the case with Donovan? Had his mother slapped him when he was younger? Had Gertrude? Was that why he hated his late grandmother so much?

The idea of a younger version of him being struck—

God. Sofie couldn't handle the thought.

She also needed to stop jumping to conclusions before she jumped to the wrong one. "I don't know what it meant. Maybe nothing."

There was a possibility he'd simply reacted...but instinct said there was nothing simple about his reaction.

"Hmm," her friend hummed. Sofie didn't like the look of unhappy contemplation on Charlie's face. She didn't like what it might mean, or that it mirrored her own concern for Donovan's past.

"Thanks in advance for doing the photos." Sofie stood and lifted her purse from the countertop. "I have to get going. I have a zillion things to do before the big family dinner."

Charlie walked her to the front door. "Both sisters, I assume."

"Oh, the whole family will be there." Sofie sighed. "Wish me luck."

"Luck?" Charlie crinkled her cute nose, then smiled. "Just remember, Sofe, not everyone is lucky enough to have a whole family to sit down to dinner with."

That was true. Charlie's scattered, distant family was proof.

"You're right," Sofie said.

"They love you. Sometimes families have a funny way of showing it."

And sometimes, Sofie thought, her thoughts returning to Donovan as she headed for her car, families showed it in the worst way imaginable.

She hoped she was wrong about his reaction.

The idea of him being abused was unbearable.

* * *

Sylvia Martin delivered a basket of bread to the dinner table. "Honestly, Sofia, I have no idea why you refuse to plan Lacey's wedding." Her mother sat down and extended her hands to either side of her.

Lacey's *second* wedding. Forget that Sofie attempted to plan her first one. It was a source of contention between her and her older sister... and a source of cluelessness for her mother. Sylvia often pretended the conflict had never happened. Head, meet sand.

The argument was tiresome, but she found herself growing defensive. "I don't plan weddings anymore, Mom. The Cove has plenty of opportunities for event planners. I can make a perfectly respectable living doing fundraisers and—"

"No bragging, dear. We're praying." Sylvia snapped the fingers on both hands, prompting Sofie's dad, Patrick, and Sofie's oldest sister, Lacey, to grab her hands.

Bragging. Sofie felt her hairline start to broil.

"Hurry. Before my food gets cold."

Sofie extended her hands to both sides, took the hand of her younger sister, Kinsley, and her father's. He smiled and gave her a wink and she shut her eyes for the prayer.

Giving thanks went quickly in the Martin household.

Sylvia didn't like to dawdle with piping hot food on the table. After plates were filled and the breadbasket passed, she started in again on Lacey's wedding plans. Lacey looked annoyed when the attention shifted from her to Sofie.

"I'm just saying"—Sylvia cut into her pot roast—"sweetheart, why aren't you eating?"

"I'm eating," Sofie argued, looking at her plate.

She *hated* pot roast. Honestly, was there anything worse than a piece of meat cooked until the toughness bled out of it? She'd filled her plate with the carrots, potatoes, and celery instead, though they basically tasted like mushy pot roast since the food had steeped in the same cast iron pot. Not a salad to be found, but there was a giant bowl of macaroni and cheese on the table. No way was she touching that calorie-dump.

"She's dieting again," Kinsley pointed out, buttering her roll with an unbelievable amount of margarine.

"I'm not," Sofie argued. "I'm just—"

"Point being," her mother cut her off again to change the subject. "Lacey is paying through the nose for this fancy wedding planner when you could simply gift her your services."

"Mom," Lacey started.

Living in a vacation town, most young girls made their living either in the hospitality business or in the food service business. Sofie happened to try both. After serving her time at the Wharf slinging plates, she migrated to the Evergreen Club to sling plates there. It wasn't long before her manager, Belinda, started asking her to run large catering parties in the reception hall. Soon after, Sofie had begun planning events on her own.

The gig had bolstered her confidence, and soon she

was doing her own event planning on the side. Before she opened Make It an Event, the first job she'd taken on was the last wedding she ever attempted.

Lacey Martin's fiasco.

"I don't do weddings," Sofie bit out, purposely keeping her eyes on her food.

If she had the time to plan her sister's wedding—and she didn't—she wouldn't. The rift between her and Lacey was alive and well. The water may be under the bridge, but it churned enough to create an undertow.

Having been the go-to girl at the Club during the years she worked there, Sofie knew how to plan a wedding, so it wasn't her lack of knowledge that had gotten her fired by her eldest sibling. Nor was it fallout because Lacey was nearly impossible to please. *I know it's peach, Sofie, but I want a peachier peach.* It wasn't the demands, the cost, or the time...

What caused the blowout was the groom.

Jeff Bluff. What an idiot. Belching, brash, foul-mouthed...the man was Lacey's polar opposite in every way. He made the entire family uncomfortable, belittled Kins and Sofie in a vain attempt to get a laugh out of their father—Patrick was not impressed—and, to top off that charming package, Jeff had also been jobless.

Lacey and Jeff had dated three months when they decided to tie the knot. Sofie kept quiet as long as she could, but at the cake tasting when she caught him flirting with the young, cute baker's assistant, Sofie said something to Lacey. She cared too much about her older sister to let her be the butt of that butthead's joke. But when she thought Lacey might appreciate the information, Lacey surprised Sofie by firing her on the spot.

Sofie wished she hadn't lost her sister in the debacle. Especially since it was all for naught. Jeff did cheat on Lacey a week before the wedding and Lacey called the wedding off.

What Lacey didn't realize—or wouldn't admit—was that Sofie had acted out of love. She didn't want to see Lacey hurt. After the split and the wedding was called off, Sofie took zero delight in being right about Jeff. She loved Lacey. She wished her sister could see that.

They'd since managed to make their way to the family dinner table, but the "damage," as Lacey liked to call it, was done.

Across the table, Lacey tucked a perfectly straight piece of dark brown hair behind her ear and took a dainty bite of her food. She wore a snow-white shirt adorned with large silver, gold, and bronze circles sewn into a *V* at the neck, and designer jeans that skimmed her figure. Her earrings matched her bracelets. Her nails were professionally manicured. Perfection, as per her usual.

Not that Sofie was a slouch. She'd worn a lightweight striped shirt and a black skirt with her new black heels. Kinsley wore an enormous pair of fuchsia-glitter "stripper" heels, a scrap of a skirt that was way too short for Sylvia's comfort, and a bright fuchsia T-shirt with a middle finger on it.

Twenty-two-year-old Kins liked to push their mother's buttons. Sylvia, as of yet, had not taken the bait.

"Lacey, dear. You could save so much money if you let Sofie help you. And I can help. I used to make flower arrangements, you know. Artificial would be much more cost effective. We—"

Lacey cut her off. "Did you ever consider I don't want

either of you planning my wedding?" Every pair of eyes around the table went to her. "I mean…you're both guests. I don't want you to work."

Minor correction: Sylvia was the mother of the bride. Sofie was a guest. Kinsley was a bridesmaid, along with Lacey's four closest friends from college, for a total of five bridesmaids.

Five.

"Sofie's not in the wedding, darling?" Sofie had over-heard her mother ask Lacey over one family dinner past.

"You know how she feels about weddings," Lacey had responded. "And anyway, all of Kenneth's friends are dating the bridesmaids. Including Kinsley's boyfriend, Mark. I can't pair Sofe up there with someone else's significant other. It wouldn't be right."

Now, chatter continued around the table while her father ate his dinner, head down, letting the women in the house filter through their own stuff. Sofie loved her father, loved that he worked hard, was dedicated to his wife and girls in every way, loved that he'd taught her how to ride a bike, and sneaked her out of bed one Christmas Eve to help eat the cookies left for Santa. But sometimes, she wished he saw how she was feeling. Wished he would interject on her behalf.

Sofie glanced over at Kins, who was slumped in her chair, texting.

"Darling?" Her mother addressed Sofie and changed the subject yet again. Conversations in the Martin household were like the fast-paced card game, War. Sentences were slapped down, then trumped by the highest rank. "Did you ever get a chance to go out with Scott Torsett? I ran into his mother at the bank yesterday. He's still single, you know."

Oh, here we go. Sofie gave her mother a patient smile. Like she hadn't gotten around to it? Like that was the issue?

She felt Lacey's smirk and Kinsley's gaze on her.

"You know he's a lawyer," Sylvia continued.

With a sigh, Sofie put down her fork.

"Yes, I do know he's a lawyer. His office is a few doors down from mine. We've...talked." About Donovan, mostly.

"Delightful!" Yes, Sylvia Martin actually used the word *delightful.* "What have you been talking about?"

"Work stuff. I planned his Christmas party last year, and this year we have a client in common."

A tall, dark, handsome client with a chip on his shoulder. And, so help her, a client her mother and sisters would never meet. She imagined Lacey would love to learn about Sofie's biggest relationship pratfall.

"Well, I think that's lovely. I don't know why the two of you won't go on a date. He's single, you're single..."

Sofie's mind strayed to Donny. The feel of his lips on hers still made her shudder years later. She wondered if he was single. Doubtful. Back when they worked together, he hadn't been taken, but she'd never seen him single, either...

"Yeah, Sofie," Kinsley teased, egging their mother on. "You and Scott should go out. He's a lawyer, you are a professional. You would have professional, event planner/lawyer babies."

"I know what you're doing, young lady," Sylvia snapped at her youngest daughter.

Not missing a chance to put Kinsley in her place, Lacey spoke up next. "Yeah, Kins. Be supportive of your sister." She sent a snarky smile over to Sofie. "I hear he's a good kisser. He used to date my friend Trish."

Great. If she did go out with Scott, it'd be like dating Lacey's friend's hand-me-down. Perfect.

"He's cute, Sofie," Lacey said.

Cute. True. But was that what she wanted? Is that what Lacey wanted for herself? What Kins wanted for herself? Would they settle for "cute"? Didn't any of them long to feel primal attraction to someone? The undeniable physical pull to the opposite sex like a magnet to metal?

That's what Sofie wanted. Maybe she was being too picky. Would explain why she was still single.

"If he's so hot, why didn't Trish stay with him?" she grumbled, picking at her monochrome food.

"Because Trish is a spaz," Kinsley said.

Fact. Trish was a spaz.

Lacey's mouth dropped open. "Trish is my best friend, Kins. She is not a spaz."

The two started bickering. *And they're off.*

While they argued, Sofie's mind went to Donovan in the kitchen, towering over her, trying to intimidate her. Then she reached up to touch his face, and he fled the room like she was emitting some sort of noxious gas.

He suggested they stay out of each other's way. She'd be doing better at that challenge if she stopped letting him into her brain fifteen times a day. She stabbed a brown-orange carrot, making a decision. The best way to keep thoughts of Donny Pate at bay—the best way to physically remind herself he was not a viable dating option—was to go out with someone else.

Her experience with men since Donovan had been less than noteworthy. Mostly, there'd been bad dates interspersed with shortish relationships leading to only a few horizontal mambos. None of them mind-blowing or remotely close to how intense it'd been with—

Nope. Don't freaking go *there*.

Maybe dating Scott would be different. She pictured breezing into the mansion, taking a phone call from him and laughing loud and appreciatively at some witty thing he said. She imagined Donny's pale eyes narrowing, his lashes closing in as he came to terms with the fact she'd moved on.

And she had moved on...hadn't she?

Hmm. That question was worrisome. Mainly because she didn't know the answer.

She tuned into her sisters, and her mother, who had joined the bickering.

"Scott is a great kisser. She could at least get a decent kiss," Lacey was saying.

"How do you know?" Kins asked. "Did *you* kiss him?"

"I'd never!" Lacey pressed her nails to her neck, aghast. "I'm engaged."

Kinsley shrugged. "Yeah, but for comparison's sake. You know, before you lock in with one sex partner until the end of days."

"Kinsley Abigail!" Sylvia scolded.

Patrick shifted uncomfortably, stood with his plate, and ambled into the kitchen. While he rinsed his dish in the sink, he sent Sofie a quick lift of his eyebrows. Sofie covered her mouth to stifle a small laugh.

"I'm merely looking out for Sofia," Sylvia began her argument.

Enough was e-*freaking*-nough, already.

"I'll go out with him," Sofie blurted.

Her sisters and her mother slowly turned their heads in her direction.

She shrugged. What'd she have to lose?

"I'll call him today. And see if he's available for a drink."

Maybe her insistence on waiting for the right spark was futile. She'd had that spark with Donovan—hell, had experienced an entire forest fire with the man. But while they'd burned hot and steady, the spark was snuffed the moment he drew out of her. Now, there was nothing left but embers.

Embers she'd no longer allow Donovan Pate to stoke.

CHAPTER SIX

Donovan propped his hands on his hips, unable to stop the scowl on his face from appearing. "How long were they there?"

Connor looked up from burying another plant of some sort in the ground. His eyes weren't visible behind a pair of mirrored aviator sunglasses, but his smile and the pair of dimples on each side of his face were. His abject glee made Donovan want to hit him. And he'd stopped fighting for fun a long time ago.

"Jealous?" Connor asked.

"Of what? An ex-pothead in a cheap suit?"

Connor returned his focus on the dirt. "Yeah, you're jealous."

Shit. He kind of was. What the hell was Scampi doing in public with Scott Torsett?

"Look, maybe they were talking business. It was just coffee."

Just coffee could lead to something else.

A truck rumbled up the driveway and Connor stood. He motioned the truck to where he was working and the driver answered with a wave. "My mulch is here. You helping, or you gonna stand there and sulk a while longer?"

"I'll get a shovel," Donovan said, not bothering to argue. He was sulking. Sulking because Scampi was sweet and kind and not only bighearted but all-hearted. She had no business having coffee with a dipshit like Scott Torsett.

With anyone.

Deciding to shake it off, he stalked behind the house and across the backyard to the shed. As he opened the padlock keeping the doors shut, he heard a whine come from the other side. He dropped his hand from the door and peeked around the shed to see the same dog he'd seen skulking around the house the night he'd arrived. He hadn't spotted it since and had assumed the mutt had gone back to wherever it called home. Guess not.

"Go on," he said, raising his voice. "Get out of here."

The dog wasn't as big as he'd first thought, skinnier than he remembered. It whined again. Throwing his arms wide, he brought his hands together in a loud clap.

"Get!"

The dog's back legs trembled, which made him feel like a jerk for yelling, then it turned and started to limp away. Its fur was matted, the white filthy, the brown patches filthier. Pale blue eyes turned back to Donovan before it took what appeared to be another painful step.

Great.

Just what he needed.

Lowering to his haunches, he looked left, right, then

behind him. Connor was chatting with the driver and gesturing hither and yon, paying them no attention.

"Guess you're my problem, then?" he asked the dog.

From this vantage point, he could tell by the lack of equipment she was a she.

"Come on." He snapped his fingers and she turned, one paw hovering in the air, and studied him warily. He was getting the idea females didn't like him much. Seven years without experience in that endeavor, he supposed.

Softening his voice, he tried again.

"Come on, dog. Let me look at your leg."

He lowered his head, coming eye-to-eye with her, then remembered how that was a threatening posture and lowered his face. He watched her feet as she crept over, one limping step at a time. She stopped about a foot away, stretched her nose forward, and cautiously sniffed.

He lifted his hand and let her sniff there, too. She did, the look in her eyes so forlorn, it cut him a little.

"See? Harmless," he said of himself.

He scratched her under the chin, petted the front of her chest. He'd read somewhere dogs didn't like to be patted on the head any more than humans, so he tried to respect her boundaries.

She responded by taking two steps closer. Running a hand down her flank, he felt ribs, a lot of them. A wad of white hair came out in his palm and he wondered if the amount of shedding was due to malnutrition, or because summer was coming. Either way, she needed brushing and was likely undernourished.

No collar, either. "Whose are you?"

She crept closer, nudging his other hand with a wet, black nose. After he stroked her coat a few more times, he risked inspecting the paw she'd been favoring. Sure enough, a jagged cut slashed across one pad. He couldn't tell until he cleaned the wound if there was anything in it, or if it was a clean cut. She wasn't actively bleeding, which meant the gash could be surface. To keep infection away, he'd have to pour some peroxide or alcohol on it.

Which would hurt like a bitch.

He knew all too well. The phantom sting of the burn echoed in his memory. How many times had he patched himself up after his father laid into him? Too many times. Made him somewhat of an expert at cleaning and dressing wounds, though knowledge of scar prevention had come later. A little too late, he thought as he looked at the star tattoo on his index finger. Most of his scars showed through the ink if anyone bothered to look closely. Most people didn't.

"My loss, your gain," he told the dog, giving her another scratch. She would have done better wandering into a veterinarian's backyard, but he guessed he was the second best choice.

"You found the right guy." Go figure.

Now to get her into the house. The back door was a good thirty yards from the shed. If he waited to coax her inside a few inches at a time, it'd take all day. He'd have to carry her. For several minutes, he sat on the ground and stroked her, talking to her gently and earning more palms full of fur for his efforts. She began to trust his touch more and more.

Shockingly, when he stood to his full height she didn't bolt, and even more shockingly, when he bent to lift her, an arm under her rump and one under her chest, she let him.

The bones protruding from her wasting body pressed against his chest. Poor thing. Hungry. Dirty. Bleeding. And at first, he had tried to scare her away.

His heart lurched.

She whined against him as he approached the back patio door.

"I know, girl," he soothed as he carried her into the utility room and closed the door behind him.

Minutes later, he hunched over the shower with a sliding door in the utility room, dunked a cup into a bucket he'd filled with warm water and poured it over the shaking, skinny dog.

She was thin, hungry, and now that her foot was wet, bleeding heavily. A trail of red swirled off her paw and down the drain. He'd be quick about the bath, then bandage her.

Then what, he had no idea.

CHAPTER SEVEN

*M*aybe I should have called him first," Sofie mumbled as she checked her rearview mirror. "Not that I have his phone number."

She could have gotten Donny's number from Scott, she supposed. But she didn't want to call Scott and ask for it since they'd sort of gone on a date.

That would be awkward.

Behind her, Ruby Voss followed in a candy-apple red Audi convertible.

"Hey, Donny is the one who gave you a key to his house," Faith said from the passenger seat. "If he didn't want you to show up, he shouldn't have given it to you."

"I know, but I don't think he expected me to bring the director of Open Arms over to see the house before it was done."

Ruby Voss called this morning asking a million questions about the ballroom, the overall setup, and the grounds, which, thanks to Donovan's muttered *"fine,"* they were now able to use for the kids' campout. When Ruby asked to make a site visit, Sofie, flustered, said, "No problem!"

There was a problem, however—Pate Mansion had a lot of acreage. Connor was one man. She hoped he had enough time to get the backyard ready.

When she'd expressed her concern, Ruby had replied, "Sofie, dear, you're talking to a woman who realizes things are not perfect. Often, things are downright abysmal."

Point taken.

Sofie parked in the driveway, watching Ruby do the same.

"Hey, how was your day date with Scott?" Faith unbuckled her belt. "You never mentioned it."

Sofie twisted her lips. What she wanted to say was "nothing special" but that wasn't exactly fair considering they spent all of twenty minutes over coffee at Cup of Jo's. So, she answered, "Fine."

She could feel her friend's dubious expression without looking.

"Wow, don't overwhelm me with your enthusiasm."

"What am I supposed to say?"

"Did he ask you out again?"

Immediately. They had a halfway decent conversation in the short time they spent together, one he concluded with, "Have dinner with me." She said yes, and told Faith as much.

Faith gave her a playful slap on the arm. "You and your secrets! I can't believe you didn't tell me you have a date tonight! Moving on is good."

She didn't know if Faith was talking about herself and moving on from Michael, or if she was talking about Sofie moving forward with a second date. With a lawyer.

A successful lawyer. It was fairly exciting, she supposed.

"Just be careful," Faith said, her voice going hard. "They don't always seem like the cheating kind at first. That comes later."

Said experience.

She thought of her sister's first fiancé. Sometimes, though, they showed their true colors right away.

"Sorry, sweetheart." Sofie sent her friend a small smile.

Faith shrugged, stoic.

"I guess we should go in." She had a key, permission to do whatever she needed, and Donovan never said she *couldn't* bring guests.

The mansion looked gorgeous today basking in the full sun blazing overhead. She thanked the Big Guy Upstairs for the weather. Connor deserved thanks, too. He had been busy. Fresh mulch lined the flowerbeds, new trees poked out of the dirt, and happy, pink flowers blew in the breeze. With the sun lighting the mansion's glittering quartz stones, the trees swaying, and the turrets and their golden points shining regally beneath a blue sky, Pate Mansion looked like a fairy tale come to life.

What better venue for a charity dinner for children whose lives had been less than fairy-tale perfect?

Sofie felt herself smile as she stepped out of her car into the perfectly pleasant spring air.

Ruby walked up a moment later, tucking a large leather planner under her arm and tipping her head back to take in the structure. "Incredible."

"Welcome to Pate Mansion," Sofie told her.

Ruby's eagle eyes left the building and scoured the landscaping. Her mouth pinched and head stopped swiveling when she reached the far side of the building. Sofie prayed her eyes hadn't landed on a scowling, frowning Donovan Pate come to run them off his property with a shotgun.

She turned her head to find it wasn't Donovan who had captured Ruby's eye or, as she noted from her friend's slacken jaw, Faith's. It was Connor.

He bent, jeans curving over his—very nice, if she said so herself—backside, shoveled some mulch, and tossed it around the base of one of the trees he'd been wriggling into a hole when she'd been here earlier this week. Shirtless, a fine sheen of sweat coated his broad shoulders, big arms, and bumps of muscle in between. Military did a body *good*.

He turned, noticed the three of them standing in the driveway staring shamelessly, and grinned.

"Hey, Sofe," he called out.

Faith raised a thin, blond brow, her expression saying everything, but she spoke anyway.

"You know that golden god?"

"So do you," Sofie said on a chuckle.

Faith's expression begged to differ.

"He worked at the Wharf for, like, a minute," Sofie told her friend, then lifted a hand to wave. "Hey, Connor!"

Faith's face scrunched further as they approached. "Really?"

"Busboy," Sofie said, keeping her voice low. "I thought you knew who Charlie was talking about when she mentioned her handyman."

Blankly, Faith blinked. Her friend's disbelieving gaze

tracked back to the sexy landscaper. "She didn't do him justice."

Swallowing a smile, Sofie addressed the "golden god" now regarding her guests curiously. "Mrs. Voss, this is Connor McClain. Connor, you probably remember Faith."

A pair of reflective sunglasses prevented her from seeing where his eyes went, but Sofie bet dollars to dandelions they were not scoping out Ruby's power suit. Faith, on the other hand, her mile-long legs and graceful gait, the sun glinting off her fair hair and illuminating her white knee-length dress... yeah. She'd bet his eyes were locked on Faith Garrett. And Faith's were unmistakably glued to Connor's... well... everything.

"Is Donovan here?" Sofie asked.

"Inside somewhere," he answered, stabbing a mound of mulch with the shovel. He propped an elbow on it and nodded at Ruby. "Mrs. Voss."

"Ruby, please." She didn't show signs of being flustered in his presence, but then, Sofie doubted much flustered Ruby Voss.

His head swiveled and his mouth split into a smile, dimples punctuating both sides of his face.

Voice dipping, he drawled, "I remember Faith."

Faith bit her lip and smiled, twirling her long hair around with one finger.

"I... can't place you," she murmured, almost demurely.

"S'okay. It was a long time ago," he said, his grin staying put. "I didn't work there long, didn't look like I do now."

He didn't. Sofie didn't remember him well, but she got a flash of a somewhat scrawny kid shuffling around the restaurant.

"You look the same." Connor's chin dipped, as if he was taking in Faith from head to toe.

Beautiful, his low tone implied. He was not wrong. Faith was beautiful.

Sofie glanced at her friend and watched her lashes lower as she studied her shoes. Oh yeah. Chemistry burned between those two.

Not that Sofie could blame her. If Faith was in the market for a man, this man would be a good man to be in the market for. They bid the man adieu and headed inside.

In the foyer, Sofie stepped aside and let Ruby and Faith walk ahead of her. She shut the door, ensconcing them in darkness.

"The kitchen is through there," she said, gesturing to her left. *And is the nicest room in the mansion.* "You can see where the kids will be helping prepare the food."

"Well, the front of the house looks amazing," Ruby said, her smile genuine.

"Gorgeous," Faith chimed in, but Sofie was pretty sure the "gorgeous" part had more to do with Connor than the flowerbeds.

"Connor is very good at his job. It's only going to get better." The foyer was dim, and knowing what awaited them in the next room had Sofie holding her breath.

Red walls, brown carpet, dark furniture, the dining room was as warm and welcoming as Vlad the Impaler's castle.

"We were thinking a coat of paint in here will brighten this room up."

Sofie turned to Ruby, who was regarding the room with a look of uncertainty. From behind her, Faith mouthed the word "Paint?"

Sofie nodded. Yep. Paint. It hadn't been in her original plan, but the gloom in here bothered her enough she was willing to suffer manual labor.

"Cream, or maybe a soft goldenrod. I figured we could take care of it ourselves"—at this, Faith's eyebrow hiked up her forehead—"that way we wouldn't have to pay a painter from the budget."

"*We*."

The voice came from over her shoulder and did not sound happy.

"Donny—er, Donovan." She plastered a smile onto her face and turned around. "I'm so glad you're here."

"Lying," he said. "That's new, Scampi."

She pleaded with her eyes for him to behave. Clearly, the chip on his shoulder had only increased in size.

"Mrs. Voss of Open Arms, the charity for abused children," Sofie introduced, "meet Donovan Pate, Gertrude's grandson."

She licked her lips, suddenly nervous. What she needed was for him to cooperate. Sure, she hadn't *asked* to paint in here, but if the place was becoming a future bed-and-breakfast, she couldn't imagine the new owner arguing a color change. The space was ideal. But dreary.

Ruby took a step past Sofie and clasped both of Donovan's hands in hers.

His eyebrows lowered in confusion. Or maybe discomfort.

"Gertrude was a shining example of the goodness in our town," she gushed.

Sofie prickled on his behalf. If she hadn't been sure of the strain in his and Gertrude's relationship before, his creased face and drawn mouth made it loud and clear.

Hopefully, to Ruby, the lines etching his brow looked like grief.

"When she approached us to give a portion of her wealth, I was overjoyed," Ruby continued. "Open Arms has been helping abused children for years and finding new, excited sponsors is a gift." She continued holding his hand in hers. "Your grandmother mentioned you several times. It's an amazing honor to meet the grandson she was so overwhelmingly proud of."

Through his clenched jaw, Sofie could swear she heard his teeth grind.

Please, please. Say something nice.

"Thank you," he said after an extended silence. "It's a worthy institution you run. I'm honored to be a part of it."

Phew.

Ruby's smile was genuine and heartfelt as she let go of his hand. "I'm glad to hear you say that."

So am I. Sofie flicked her eyes up at him. He didn't so much as glance her way, but she knew he watched her in his periphery.

They toured the kitchen, Donovan taking the lead. He suggested where to set up the kids the night of the dinner. Being a restaurant guy, he understood where the prep area would work best, as well as where the expediters could tray the food before taking it to the ballroom.

"The kids won't carry the heavier dinner trays, I'm guessing." He looked to Sofie for that information.

Rapt by his take-charge confidence, she nearly missed her cue. "Hmm? Oh yes. The catering company is providing servers. They'll do the heavy lifting."

"Maybe you could order some smaller trays so the

children could take dessert out?" Ruby asked. "I want them fully involved."

"I will do that today," Faith said. "Would you like to see the ballroom next?"

"That would be great."

Faith led Ruby out of the room, leaving Sofie and Donovan alone in the kitchen. "Thank you," she told him.

He didn't acknowledge her gratitude, instead offering, "Something to drink?"

She moved her tongue around her dry mouth. "Please."

Being alone with him had a way of making her parched.

He opened and closed the refrigerator. She accepted the bottle of water, noticing a weird, yet oddly familiar, smell coming from the closed door to her left. Faint scratching sounded from behind the panel.

"Is that..."

"A dog." He leaned past her and turned the knob, opening the door a fraction.

Sofie peered through the crack. Striking pale blue eyes peered back. "A wet dog." That's what the smell was. Wet dog plus shampoo. "I didn't know you had a dog."

"I don't."

Okay...

"Is it friendly?"

"Seems to be." He opened the door wider and Sofie squatted. The dog reminded her of the Saint Bernard her aunt used to have, but this one was mixed with something else. Shepherd, maybe?

"Boy or girl?"

"Girl."

"Hi...uh, what's her name?"

"No name," he answered tersely. "Found her out back."

"Hi, girl." The dog wagged her tail, though it was positioned low. She took a step in her direction and Sofie held out a hand. She noticed the pooch favored one foot. It was bandaged. "She's hurt."

"Yeah. Cut herself on something."

"Poor girl," she cooed. She offered a hand but didn't pet her yet. "I can't believe she hasn't chewed the bandage off."

"She chewed through three of them."

Donovan stood, hip leaning on the edge of the countertop, arms crossed. She tried to picture him bathing a dog and changing its bandage three times. Tried to picture him being attentive...caring.

She tilted her head and took him in. He stood there looking solid. Strong. Safe.

An illusion.

Donovan Pate was anything but safe.

The dog's wet nose touched her hand and Sofie smiled and reached to pat the dog's head. The mutt's eyes fluttered shut, her ears flattening as if expecting a blow.

Sofie pulled her hand away.

"She's been abused," Donovan pointed out.

Her heart squeezed. It was like a macabre theme.

"You can tell by the way she flinches," he muttered.

Sofie tried again, extending her hand slowly. The dog backed just out of reach and watched her through pale eyes from a safer distance. Eyes the same color as Donovan's.

She's been abused. You can tell by the way she flinches.

Sofie's hand gestures the other day had made the man in this room react in a similar way. She stood, clasping the water bottle with both hands.

Donovan shut the utility room door with a soft *click*. "Don't take it personally."

She met his gaze, wondering if he and the stray had more in common than unique eye color.

As if he sensed her thoughts, he pressed his lips together and, just like he had the other day, walked away.

CHAPTER EIGHT

$\mathcal{D}$onovan chipped away at the fireplace in front of him, listening to Dog snore on the sofa where she'd made herself at home. He hauled her off there twice before giving up and letting her have her way. She'd only be here temporarily, so he justified the potential bad habit wouldn't hurt anything.

After Sofie had joined Ruby and Faith in the ballroom, Donovan had wandered into the great room to keep his hands and head occupied with something other than the forlorn look Sofie gave him earlier.

He didn't want her sympathy. Didn't want her to feel bad for him—to feel bad, period. So, he'd stayed out of sight, avoiding her, though he did overhear the ladies navigating the halls to the front door on their way out. He didn't meet them to say good-bye, but he'd clearly made out their echoed laughter through the vents. Specifically, Faith's voice mentioning Sofie's "hot date" tonight.

His "hot date" had been frozen pizza shared with Dog. He supposed he should get some food for her if she was going to stay here. He couldn't keep giving her people food. And no way was he taking her to a shelter until her foot healed. He couldn't trust a group of volunteers to give her the care she needed. What if they shoved her in a cage and left her unattended? What if she chewed the bandage off again? What if she got an infection?

Dog snored loudly from the sofa, big front paws—one bandaged, one not—thrown over the edge of the cushion. Her eyes were shut tight. Yeah, she was staying here until she was well. He had turned back to the fireplace, when he heard the door to the room squeak open.

"You have a dog," Connor announced from the threshold.

Dog snorted awake, lifting her head from her paws. She gave a halfhearted bark.

Tossing down his tools, Donovan sat on his butt on the dust-covered plastic in front of the fireplace. "She's not mine."

Connor looked from the dog sprawled over the couch cushions, then back to Donovan. "Sure as hell looks like she's yours." He approached, making kissy noises. Dog wagged her tail cautiously.

"Watch her foot. And she doesn't know you, so be careful," Donovan warned.

Connor lifted his hand, palm down. Dog licked it. "Oh yeah," he said as he scratched her chin, "she's vicious." Dog rolled to her back and exposed her belly, which he then scrubbed with his other hand.

Donovan shook his head.

"Hey, girl," Connor said in a soft voice. Dog's tail wagged, beating the back of the sofa like a furry ball bat.

"You are a beautiful girl. Aren't you? Yes, you are. Oh, yes you are."

"This how you get chicks to come home with you, too?"

Connor's mouth cocked into a half smile. "Your daddy's a jealous guy, isn't he?" he asked Dog.

Daddy. A buzz like an electric shock hit his limbs. He knew Connor was giving him shit, but still...Donovan a parent? *Not good.* Not even for a dog.

Connor rose to his feet and Dog righted herself, careful not to put weight on her injured paw. Her mouth smiled, tongue lolled, and tail continued thumping. Happy as a fucking lark.

"It's late," Connor said. "I'm stopping for the day. Thought I'd grab a shower, then a beer. Interested?"

"Not showering with you, man." Donovan nodded to Dog who was staring a hole through the back of Connor's head. "She's starting to look like your dog."

"I'm never home. Plus my apartment doesn't allow dogs." Connor scrubbed her head, which she allowed, then turned back to Donovan. "So?"

He didn't have the overwhelming urge to run into townsfolk while at the local watering hole, but he could use a few hours away from this place. Being in this house was making him cagey. For that reason, he asked, "Where?"

"Salty Dog."

Dog barked, one chuff.

"Sorry girl, misleading name. No dogs allowed." Connor surveyed the damage wreaked on the fireplace. "Looks like you need a break from...whatever it is you're doing."

What Donovan was *doing* was obsessing, and trying not to think about Sofie with Scott Torsett. Trying not to think about whether he took her to dinner, or if they stayed in...

Or if he'd tried to kiss her good night. If Sofie had let him.

Donovan's lip curled.

If he stayed here and continued working, those thoughts would persist. Turning from the debris littering the plastic beneath the fireplace, he brushed his hands on his jeans, knocking dust from his palms.

"You know what?" he told Connor, "I could use a break."

From thinking of Scampi, mostly.

* * *

The bartender at Salty Dog slid two foaming beers down the bar top. The place was fairly busy, making Donovan wonder if Evergreen Cove had turned into more of a party destination than it used to be. Or maybe it always had been. He never really hung out "in town." Most of his partying happened in his apartment.

And had included the guy sitting at his left elbow.

"Back in the day," Connor called over the din of voices, "this time of night, we'd be neck-deep in a bottle of booze."

Donovan sipped his beer and smiled. "Surprised you remember." Connor had been eighteen, underage, and suffering from a wild streak. His friend's life had been nothing like Donovan's. The opposite, actually.

Connor's parents and siblings were overly involved in his life. He'd started working at the Wharf in defiance of his father wanting him to work for the family business.

Shortly after, he started hanging out with Donovan. Connor was a bright kid, and Donovan didn't have a problem with him crashing at his apartment. Before too long, his friend was there more than he was at his own house.

Kind of like he was now.

Connor banged their beer glasses. "To working together again."

Donovan could hardly believe he was back in town. Drinking with Connor. So close to Scampi. A thorough drink of beer wet his arid throat, dry from the dust he'd inhaled for the past several hours.

"I have an ulterior motive." Connor put his beer on the cardboard coaster in front of him, keeping his eyes on the base of the glass.

"Shoot."

"Behind the utility room at the mansion is a hallway leading to several rooms. The largest appears to be where the former groundskeeper kept his stuff."

Donovan had been avoiding that hallway. One thing at a time, and right now, the basement and the bedrooms upstairs had consumed him. Plus the great room, though the fireplace was less something that needed done and more something he needed to do to keep from going mad.

He'd been away from his work for a few weeks now and already his hands ached to create. Building and working with stone had become a reprieve from his life, maybe even an addiction. Craftsmanship had been an outlet for several frustrations.

"Found a few metal and wooden shelves—basically a bunch of old shit in there you're probably going to dump," Connor continued.

He didn't care what Connor took out of that house.

Save him the trouble of sorting through it. But Donovan could also see his buddy was playing down how much he wanted those forgotten shelves. Connor had a way of making old things new again, of seeing the potential in what others viewed as trash. Now that Donovan thought about it, that attribute was probably one of the reasons they were friends.

"And you want it."

Connor's eyes went to his. "Apartment's too small. Be a good place to start an indoor greenhouse. Put a couple of seedlings in there, fresh herbs. Might use the space to start some of my lavender." He took a drink and eyed his glass. "If you don't care."

Donovan swallowed a smile. He knew his buddy needed his hands in the dirt the way he needed his own wrapped around rocks. Putting seedlings in, watching them grow, cultivating life, that was Connor's thing. And if there was any good that could come out of the mansion and his part-time use of it, he'd make damn sure his friends benefited.

"Take whatever you need."

Connor lifted his chin. His eyes brightened. "Yeah?"

Donovan shrugged, even though he knew what a huge deal this was for his friend. "Help yourself."

"Thanks, man. Thought I would start with..." His voice trailed off and when he didn't finish his sentence, Donovan followed Connor's eyes to the front of the bar where a man and woman, linked arm-in-arm, walked in.

"Holy crap. He got her to go out with him again." Connor's voice was an amused lilt. "Will wonders never cease?"

Donovan was not amused. Mainly because Scott

Torsett had an arm wrapped snugly around Scampi's waist, and, he saw as they walked by, his fingers were dangerously close to her ass.

They stopped at the opposite end of the bar and Donovan was grateful for the row of beer taps hiding him and Connor from view. He could see Scampi through the gaps. She wore a royal blue, billowy shirt and pants leaving little to the imagination. Tight, black, kind of shiny, the material cupped her ass in a way that should be illegal. Imagining what was hiding under those pants was enough to make his mouth dry, and his mind wander.

She looked amazing, and something about her being within view yet out of reach—and being touched by Scott Torsett for God's sake—made Donovan crazy.

He was going to need another beer.

"Hey man." Connor's hand hit Donovan's tense shoulder and squeezed. "No brawling. We're just here to drink."

Donovan had a death grip on his mug, the condensation wet and cold against his skin. *Maintain.* Connor was right. They were here to drink.

Scott's hand moved along Sofie's back, his fingers inching lower. If Donovan didn't have hold of the glass, his hand would've curled into a fist.

The lawyer's palm slid to her backside.

A growl pushed its way past Donovan's throat.

Sofie expertly slid away from his touch, casually turning her body so that Scott's hand was on her hip. The smile she gave him was pained.

Connor took his hand from Donovan's shoulder. "God, what an asshole."

He hadn't planned on kicking anyone's ass tonight, but Connor's comment was as good as getting the blessing to rearrange Torsett's face. The rigidity of Sofie's body showed she was clearly uncomfortable. Donovan stood from his seat.

Through the blood pounding against his eardrums, he heard Connor say, "Got your back."

Scott bent his head closer to Sofie as Donovan closed in, walking calmly, trying not to appear murderous. That same—soon-to-be-broken—hand traveled to Sofie's butt again, this time squeezing.

Yep, her date was going to get his ass kicked.

He stepped over to the not-so-cozy pair and interrupted by putting a hand on Scott's shoulder. Scott spun around, which caused the side effect of his hand leaving her body.

Perfect.

"Donny?" Scott blinked a few times and then he smiled like he was relieved. "Hey, long time no see, buddy."

"Get the hell out of here, Scott."

His smile dropped. Tension replaced relief as his shoulders stiffened. "Excuse me?"

"You're excused." Donovan jerked his head in the direction of the front door. "Out."

"What are you doing?" This from Sofie.

Not accustomed to backing down, the lawyer straightened his back and glared up at him. "You have a problem, Pate?"

"You're about to have five problems. The fingers on that hand."

"Okay, okay." Sofie put a palm on each of their chests and applied pressure, inserting herself between them. "Maybe everyone should calm down for a second."

"I'll give him three." Donovan hadn't been in a fight in a while, but he guessed it was like riding a bike. And right now, his fist was twitching for some action. Bouncing it off Torsett's weak chin would be satisfying. Donovan would probably sleep like a baby tonight.

"You're making her uncomfortable," Scott said, his hand moving to grasp her waist.

Donovan leaned into Sofie's palm. "One."

"*Donovan.*" Her tone was a warning.

He kept his eyes on Scott. "Tell me, Scampi, the way this douche is touching you isn't making you uncomfortable, and I'll leave you two to your drinks."

Scott glared up at him.

"I'm fine," she clipped, giving Donovan another shove before dropping her hands to her sides. But she hadn't told him to go away, and she hadn't denied Scott was making her uncomfortable.

"I was right. Lying is your new thing."

She sputtered a disgusted sound.

"I've had her ass in my hands," he told Torsett. "I've had her mouth on mine. I know when she likes someone touching her, and when she doesn't. And man, she does *not* like you touching her. So again, you got two more seconds before I escort you out by the throat."

Scott licked his lips. He was starting to look nervous. He turned to Scampi. "You guys have a thing I should know about?"

"What? No," she answered, sounding a little offended.

"Using me to get back at an ex-boyfriend, really? I was wondering why you asked me out for coffee."

She asked *him* out? Donovan felt his blood pressure raise.

"And you," Scott said to him. "Threatening me? You're as immature as you used to be."

If Torsett was trying to hurt his feelings, he failed.

"You're as chicken-shit as you used to be," Donovan returned.

"Donny's not my boyfriend. Wasn't ever my boyfriend, actually," she muttered to herself.

Donovan slid his eyes to Sofie. She jutted her chin out. He could do without the tone.

"I have to be in court Monday morning," Scott said, straightening his jacket, "or I'd show Sofie how an ass-kicking is really done."

A low laugh left Donovan's throat. "Lucky me, I guess."

"Good night, Sofia," Scott said.

The farther he got away, the better Donovan felt. Until Sofie promised, "I'll call you."

"She won't," Donovan called after him.

Scott started to respond, but someone he knew interrupted him at the door, slapping his arm and extending a hand. Attention diverted, Scott smiled and shook the older man's hand.

Donovan felt himself smile.

"Thanks a lot!" Sofie hissed.

"You're welcome."

"I don't need saving, you know."

That was probably true. But not the point.

"You telling me you like the way he touched you? Because from where I stood, didn't look that way."

Her lips pressed into a thin line. He was right. She hadn't liked it. He thought of her uncomfortable posture when Torsett touched her and his temper shot to eleven. He turned for the door, where Torsett was still loitering.

"I'll be right back."

She gripped his forearm and tugged. "Okay, okay."

Donovan faced her.

"No, all right? I didn't like him touching me. But this is what it's like for a girl on a date. Guys test their boundaries."

He wondered how many other guys had "tested her boundaries," and felt a surge of inexplicable jealousy. She wasn't his. Like she said, she never was. He hated the idea of her being mistreated by anyone, but he couldn't seem to focus on that. Not with her warm palm on his arm. There was always something about her touch that calmed him.

Though right about now, her touch was revving him up.

"What if he would have hit you?" she asked, concern bleeding into her gaze.

He shrugged. "I would have hit him back."

"He could have hurt you."

God, she was cute when she worried about him. Made him forget he didn't want her to.

Chuckling, he said, "No, Scampi. He couldn't have."

She rolled her eyes. "Fine, tough guy. Scott was my ride. Now you have to drive me home. I'm ordering a drink."

Fine by him.

"And you're paying," she informed him.

His lips twitched, curling into a smile. He held up a hand to signal the bartender.

CHAPTER NINE

The bartender shuffled off to get Sofie a glass of white wine. She kept her eyes on the bottles lining the bar shelves and tried to decide if she was more frustrated or embarrassed by Donovan's running off her date.

Coin toss.

She turned to meet his narrowed gaze, determined to get the upper hand before he pissed in a corner and claimed her as property.

"So this is your plan? Follow me around and thwart my attempts to get laid? I didn't know you had more than a passing interest in who I slept with."

Donovan's face went from casually peeved to severe. Granted, she was needling him on purpose, and, technically, lying like he'd accused her of a few minutes ago. No way had she planned on sleeping with Scott Torsett tonight . . . if ever. Yes, he was nice to hang out with—or at least he was until he'd had one too many vodka tonics at dinner. By the time they arrived at Salty Dog, he'd obviously felt comfortable enough to get handsy. His roaming palms were nothing she couldn't handle—was something she'd handled before with other guys. She wasn't kidding about men testing boundaries—they did it all the time—but she certainly hadn't needed Donny to run interference.

"Didn't follow you here, Scampi."

He tipped his head to the left, and she spotted Connor at the other side of the bar. He held up his beer in a silent *cheers*.

"Came for a drink, saw you being assaulted," Donovan said.

"I would hardly call that assault."

"You were alone; it could've turned into one."

An out-of-place shiver iced her spine. She doubted Scott would have gone further, and she hadn't planned on being alone with him anywhere. Then again, he'd had a few drinks. Who knew how much braver one more would've made him? Dating was risky no matter what, but she thought she knew Scott well enough to feel comfortable with him.

Her eyes went to Donovan. Maybe she was a bad judge of character.

But he never made her skin crawl when he touched her, or made her uncomfortable when he stood close. His nearness now was having the opposite effect, dancing on the line of attraction. All over it, actually.

And he'd been right. She hadn't appreciated Scott's hands on her body.

"Torsett, party of two," the hostess announced from her podium.

"He left," Donovan shouted across the bar.

The hostess opened her mouth to ask another question before opting not to and scratching the name off her clipboard.

Scott, done chatting at the door and on his way out, sent Sofie a look of betrayal before storming outside. Fantastic. She'd bet the chances of planning Torsett & Torsett Law's next Christmas party hovered between *slim* and *none*.

Her wine was delivered and Donovan snatched the glass before she could take it.

"My tab," he instructed the bartender, resting his hand on the small of Sofie's back. She noted not a single alarm rose in her head. In fact, she felt safer with him than she did anyone. Safe. That word again.

Strange.

As he led her to where Connor sat, she tried to ignore the warmth spreading along her waist and up her back, the same charged current she'd sworn she imagined the moment he touched her years ago.

Every tingle, every surge, had returned with a vengeance.

Connor stood and offered his seat.

She waved him off. "You don't have to do that."

He tossed some bills onto the bar. "Only planned on staying for one, Sofe. Sorry about the display of vigilante justice."

"Thanks." She smiled.

Couldn't be helped. Connor was charming.

"Don't stay out past your bedtime." With that thinly veiled instruction, and a flash of his dimples, he headed out the door.

Donovan pulled out the barstool for her.

She slid onto the seat. "You have these weird moments of polite interspersed with Neanderthal, did you know that?"

He didn't answer. Just as well since the question was rhetorical.

Lifting his beer, he swallowed a drink and licked his bottom lip. Her eyes zeroed in on the fullness of that lip, remembering the way it felt to have his mouth on hers. If only there were some way to get that part of her brain lobotomized. Cut out the entire Donny Pate part...

She raised her glass and guzzled down a drink, swallowing past the burn in her throat. Wine wasn't a guzzling kind of drink, but her thoughts needed to be bound and gagged. Plying them with alcohol seemed a good start to getting them to comply.

Depositing her purse on top of the bar next to her elbow, she and Donny sat in silence for a while, watching the patrons and bar staff bustle about.

Salty Dog's highly polished wooden walls, booths covered in vinyl the shade of terra cotta, and shining lacquered tables made for a comfortable, warm atmosphere. Framed paintings by the locals were screwed into the walls, one of them she recognized as Evan's star from his and Asher's children's book, *The Adventures of Mad Cow*.

They'd hung the cartoon cow in here after last year's Starving Artist auction. Which reminded her, she needed to ask Evan if he had anything to donate for the Open Arms dinner. A painting of Mad Cow would get a ton of bids.

She smiled at the painting, the character Charlie called "a badass bovine." Mad Cow's attractive scowl reminded Sofie of Evan.

In a way, reminded her of Donovan, too. Though Donovan's scowl was somehow sadder.

"Ruby was really excited to see the mansion," she said, breaking the silence between them.

Slowly, Donovan turned his head. "Sounded like it."

"I couldn't find you to say good-bye. I wanted to thank you for stepping in for the tour. I know I kind of sprang her on you."

"You wanted to thank me for that but not for helping you end your miserable date?" he asked with a small smile.

Unwilling to reopen that can of worms, she continued deliberately. "*So*, I just wanted to *thank you* for the suggestions about how to set up the kitchen. You were convincing." She spun her wineglass, watching the golden liquid wash onto the inside of the glass. "Sounded like you were all in."

"I am."

"Oh." News to her.

"I thought we could stay away from each other," he said, making her wonder if he was suggesting he couldn't resist her any more than she could resist him.

She allowed her eyes to graze him from head to toe. He looked good leaning, his elbows on the bar, battered black boots hooked on the bottom rung of the stool. He was in black tonight—black jeans, snug black tee outlining impressive biceps. Ink tracked up both arms. Years ago, he had a black leather jacket. She wondered if he still did.

"Not going to be able to stay away from you now, Scampi," he said, his voice low. Her heart kicked up a notch. "You have horrible taste in men." His full lips twitched at the corner as another smile curved his mouth.

Gosh, she loved that smile. Would like to see it more often.

"You're hilarious." She shook her head at him but

smiled back. When she lifted her wineglass, he turned serious.

"It's good what you're doing for those kids."

Her heart levitated. It was good. "You're helping them, too."

"Reluctantly."

"Now who's the liar?" They watched one another for a beat. When she couldn't take the intensity of his unwavering stare, she averted her eyes and changed the subject, filling the air with a topic they had in common.

"Ruby said if the children were there, helping serve the dinner, helping cook the dinner, helping ready the ballroom, they would feel more included. Like they belonged. She said a lot of those kids are locked in their own heads."

His eyes went to his beer. He stayed silent.

"Pate Mansion is the perfect setup. For the dinner. For the campout. And the kitchen...I mean seriously, it is a huge kitchen," she continued blathering. She paused to study his expression but got nothing. "They probably resent the idea of that much structure now that I think about it."

"They appreciate it. Kids who don't have any structure secretly want it." His light eyes locked on hers, and for a moment she saw him—really saw him. No veil. She'd seen him like this once before—in a dark library the moment *before the moment* things had turned so very bad. She'd seen him so clearly then.

As clearly as she saw him now. He wasn't only talking about the kids at Open Arms. He was talking about himself. His younger self.

In a blink, the lightness vanished as fast as it'd appeared.

His eyes went back to his beer. He took another sip and said nothing.

"Anyway, thanks for letting them do the campout."

"It's only one night." His comment brought with it a truckload of innuendo.

"Two. Technically," she said softly, wondering if his mind was on the same subject.

His gaze was like a caress, like a hand physically touching her skin. It'd always been like this between them. Always. Even when she tried to resist him.

Even when she tried to forget him.

* * *

Glasses empty, Donovan motioned for the bartender, who nodded and pushed a couple of buttons on the touch-screen computer. A receipt spit out of the printer.

Sofie reached for her purse.

"Don't even think about it," Donovan warned.

"I'm a modern woman, I can go dutch."

He slid her a look. "You really have been dating assholes, haven't you?"

She rolled her eyes.

Shit. He hated being right about that.

On the way out of the bar, he put his hand on her back and steered her toward the door. Her shoes were tall, and the floors appeared recently waxed. At least that's why he told himself he'd reached for her. Not because he couldn't be close to her and not touch her.

Not because she drew him in like he was tethered to her.

Outside, she climbed into Trixie without his assistance.

"The same Jeep," she mumbled. "Thought it was black."

"It's going to be red." His eyes skimmed the pants hugging her thighs before he shut her door. As he walked around to the driver's side, he thought of Scott's wandering hands and lamented not getting to break any of the bastard's fingers.

The drive to Sofie's apartment was quiet, consisting of him fiddling with the radio and her inspecting her fingernails.

"Here." She pointed at the apartment building to their left. Fairly small, the six-unit building stood next to two other identical freestanding buildings. White with black shutters, the staircase open. No security door standing in the way of anyone who wanted to come in. Not that the Cove was unsafe, but wherever there were vacationers, there were strangers.

"Thanks." She undid her seat belt.

"Don't see him again."

Her head whipped around. "Excuse me?"

Elbow leaning on the steering wheel, Donovan twisted in his seat so he could keep his eyes on hers. "I mean it, Scampi. That guy's testing your boundaries too soon."

"I never asked for you to watch out for me. I'm a grown woman. I can take care of myself."

"I know exactly how much of a woman you are."

Her dark emerald eyes went wide before narrowing at him. "You should. You made me one."

Damn. Had him there.

"I'll see whoever I want to see," she replied with fiery determination.

But her words sounded like a dare. The air snapped with the memory of the one night they'd spent together.

Her soft scent wrapped around him in the cramped confines of Trixie.

That was a dare he'd take.

"Who do you see now?"

Her pink lips parted. The anger was replaced with an emotion just as hot, but not nearly as resistant.

She breathed one word. "You."

"Damn straight."

Reaching across the seat, he threaded his fingers into her soft brown hair and cupped her nape. He gave her a beat to react, but she didn't pull back. Instead, she licked her bottom lip, her gaze glancing off his mouth.

He tilted her head, lowered his. She didn't resist, allowing him to tug her closer until their mouths met. Soft lips fused with his. The electricity zapping between them could've powered the city for a week.

God help him, he hadn't tasted anything this sweet since the last time he tasted her.

Her hand came up but not to push him away, which he considered he might deserve. She wound her fingers into a fist, gripped his T-shirt, and yanked him closer. Her teeth scraped his lips, her tongue slipped into his mouth. He savored her flavor—the same flavor he'd tried to convince himself for years existed only in his imagination.

Nope. *Real.*

As real as the sound she just made in the back of her throat. A soft mewl he hadn't heard in far too long.

The heady rush of Sofie in his arms, devouring his mouth, her control ebbing, took over. For a moment he forgot where he was. Until she pulled her lips away and lowered her chin. Stuttered breaths echoed in the quiet of the car.

Her forehead rested on his and she whispered, "Shit."

His hand was wound in her hair. He stroked the silken strands with the rough pads of his fingers and backed away from her some, his heart thundering, his balls aching.

Nothing. Nothing compared to kissing Sofie Martin before or since. *Shit,* as it turned out, summed it up.

Green eyes landed on his. "Okay. Okay." She nodded to herself. "This isn't the end of the world."

He felt his brow lift. "Scampi—"

"We can... we'll just pretend this never happened." She let go of him and gathered her purse, as shaken as he was.

He still had hold of the back of her neck. Gently, he slid his hand out of her hair, along her jaw, and thumbed her bottom lip.

Her eyes turned up to his.

"Like we forgot the night in the library," he said.

"I've forgotten the details."

He studied her beautiful face, her damp lips shining in the streetlight—wet from his kisses. "*Lie.*"

"That was forever ago," she breathed.

He lowered his head, moved his thumb to tip her chin. Her eyes darkened to deep emerald. "I haven't forgotten anything."

When her eyes sank shut, he lost himself again in the heat of her mouth.

CHAPTER TEN

Sofie had never needed a cup of coffee more than the one Faith handed her now. Cup of Jo's fixed life's problems. Especially six-foot-four, tattooed problems with devastating lips and the ability to make Sofie forget her vow never to give herself to a bad boy again.

What had she been thinking? She'd had nothing to drink at dinner with Scott, then, what, one glass of wine at the bar? One glass and she was making out with Donovan in his Jeep in front of her apartment. She couldn't blame her tolerance—wine was her other BFF. She had a sky-high tolerance. Up until *The Kiss*, she assumed she had a high tolerance for Donny, too.

Apparently not.

When they finally managed to unsuction their faces, he offered to walk her up to her apartment to which she replied "NO!" almost comically loud. He grinned—big, and that's when she scuttled up the stairs and inside to gather what was left of her good sense.

He didn't pull from the curb right away, waiting until she was safely ensconced inside. She had turned off the kitchen light and stood in the dark, listening to the clock tick on the wall while chewing a fingernail and worrying maybe she had lost her mind.

She recanted the entire tale to Faith today when she'd shown up for work. Faith left the building and returned with two very large mocha lattes. Thank goodness. Sofie hadn't slept well last night.

Borderline erotic dreams of Donovan made sleep nearly impossible.

She sipped her perfectly frothed mocha. "So? I'm insane? Is that it?"

Faith laughed. "You are not insane." She opened a file drawer and dropped her purse inside. Then sat on the guest chair opposite the desk and lifted her own Cup of Jo's. "Donovan Pate is a tall, hot, black-haired, blue-eyed man. Who, I might add"—she held up a finger to make her point—"rode in and saved your bacon from an evil, ass-grabbing lawyer. Who could blame you for playing tonsil hockey with him?"

"Do not do that." Sofie pointed with the hand still wrapped around her coffee cup. "Do not make him sound like some kind of white knight." He was more like a dark knight, with a big, scrawny dog. And a primered Jeep.

"In case you haven't noticed, I haven't had a lot of men ride in and save the day for me lately." Faith sipped her coffee. "Mmm. I love Jo's mochas."

They were kind of out of this world.

"Delicious." *Like Donovan's mouth*, her mind filled in for her.

Great. These were the types of thoughts she was going to have to endure while planning the charity dinner.

Just fabulous.

Damn her for letting him dive into her mouth last night. She'd reacted exactly the opposite way than she should have—like flypaper instead of Teflon.

Sticking to him. *Clinging* to him.

"That must've been some kiss." Faith lifted a fair blond brow. This is the third time you've spaced out this morning." She smiled a knowing little smile.

Sofie stood and tucked a binder into the multi-pocketed tote bag on her desk.

"Do you think I'm desperate?" She was heading over to see Mr. Wonderful this morning, and if she reeked of *desperate*, she needed to wash off the scent before she arrived at Pate Mansion.

"No," Faith responded firmly.

"How are you newly single and this…this…" Sofie stuffed a water bottle in a side pocket and a handful of pens in another. "*Good* at it?"

Her friend's lips pinched slightly.

Not the most sensitive question considering what Faith had been through. "I'm sorry. I didn't mean to be harsh."

"You are not wrong. Shouldn't I be more upset than this?" Faith gestured to her perfectly springy floral-print dress. "You kissed Donovan and you're torn apart. Michael slept with some girl with a cheap dye job and a tramp stamp, and other than a brief crying jag, I'm"—she shrugged—"I'm okay. Like, *really* okay."

"Maybe you're grieving. Stages happen out of order sometimes."

"Or maybe I'm relieved because I'm more like my mother than I care to admit." Faith pursed her lips.

Sofie rounded the desk and sat in the other guest chair.

For this intervention, she needed to be eye-to-eye with her best friend.

"You don't believe in that curse. You've said it yourself a hundred times."

Faith's mother, Linda Shelby, maintained that "Shelby women couldn't marry." Supposedly, there was a long line of family members on Faith's mother's side who had planned their weddings but never made it down the aisle.

"It was easy to disbelieve when I was engaged," Faith said. "I thought I'd be the first to break the curse, if it was real at all. Now I'm wondering if I said yes to Michael as a test—to see if we'd make it." She shook her head. "We didn't."

A marriage based on a test. That would have been something.

"But...you loved him," Sofie said, trying not to make it sound like a question.

"Did I?"

They watched one another for a long moment before Faith's eyes dropped to her lap. Just as Sofie reached to comfort her, Faith's head snapped up. "Oh! I almost forgot to tell you! Cup of Jo's has offered to set up a coffee bar at the charity dinner."

She smiled, no sign on her pretty face she'd been questioning her love for Michael, lamenting her lost wedding, or wondering if the family curse was real.

"All proceeds go to Open Arms, of course," Faith added.

"That's...great." Sofie wished she had a similar switch. She'd use it to turn off her feelings about Donovan. Just flip it and go about planning the dinner. Then, she wouldn't think about the feel of his firm lips, or the way his palm on the back of her head held her willingly captive, or the way his thumb stroked her lip...

"I figured we could set the coffee up in the far corner," Faith continued. "Next to the cupcakes."

Swallowing thickly, Sofie rerouted her thoughts, stood, and smoothed her skirt. "Sounds perfect."

Faith grabbed a pen and pad of paper from the corner of the desk. "I wonder how much space we have..."

Sofie went around her desk and pulled another binder from the shelf behind it. "I'll find out for you," she said. "I'm going to the mansion today."

"Today?"

She nodded. "Now, in fact."

Faith wrinkled her nose. "You don't look very excited."

What she was, was nervous. About seeing Donovan. About maneuvering around him today after what had happened last night. About him being in her space, in her face...

But Faith was wrong...Sofie *was* excited.

Bad boy kisses did that to a girl.

* * *

Five hours.

She'd been here five hours. Sofie consulted her watch. And twelve minutes.

Other than running into Donovan once—outside while he loaded yet another thrift store truck with old furniture—she hadn't seen much of him. Just his legs walking beneath a hideous floral sofa Connor helped him carry to the truck.

She'd measured the ballroom. Twice. And she'd pulled

out her laptop and researched paint colors and pricing for the dining room. Since the desk in the library was the most sensible place to work, she stowed her emotions about the space and set up in there. Despite her attempt to be a grown-up, the room—and a particular piece of furniture—niggled at her the entire time she surfed the Internet.

That'd been fun—having a momentary standoff with The Red Sofa where she'd cashed in her V-card with the man of the house. The exchange rate on that sucker was *not* good, by the way.

After making a few more calls to sponsors and other locals who'd expressed interest in the charity dinner, her work was far from done, but she was ready to call it a day. She'd prepared herself, mentally and physically, for seeing Donovan. In an effort not to look too nice, she'd changed—forgoing the heels and skirt in favor of jeans and a cotton shirt. Whatever he said to her—whether he tried to come on to her again, or suggested they stay away from each other, she was ready. Only one problem. He hadn't confronted her. He'd avoided her as much as she avoided him.

The sound of the front door opening perked her ears. She heard the dog's toenails on the tile, then Connor's and Donovan's voices echoing in the foyer. Dog sought her out, showing up in the library a moment later, tail wagging.

Dog. Poor thing. She needed a name.

"Hi, uh..." She thought of her mother's neighbor's basset mix and took a stab at it. "Bailey! Come here, Bailey."

Dog's ears stayed down, her mouth panting. No reaction to the name at all. Padding into the room, the dog came to Sofie, tongue out.

"How about...Spot?"

But she didn't have "spots," more like patches.

"Fluffy?" But that didn't work, either. She may be fluffy someday, but at the moment her fur was thin and lank.

Sofie scratched the dog's ears. Silver-blue eyes met hers, reminding her again of Donovan's.

"Maybe we'll name you after the woman who lived here last. That's appropriate for a girl who lives in a mansion, wouldn't you say?"

Dog licked her hand.

"Gertrude is too stately. How about Gertie?"

"Gertie" licked Sofie's face. They had a winner.

"You have got to be kidding."

She pulled her hand away from Gertie to see Donovan standing in the doorway of the library, taking up space in his own special way. He was good at choking a room—or a bar—with his presence.

"She likes it," Sofie argued, scrubbing the dog's head again. "Don't you, Gert?"

"No." His eyes went to the desk where she'd made herself at home. "This your new office?" She wondered if he knew his eyes flicked to the couch next.

She forcibly didn't look, talking gibberish to Gertie instead who, in Sofie's opinion, really did look like a Gertie.

When she continued ignoring him, he prompted, "Scampi."

"I'm done in here."

He took a brief look around and mumbled, "Stay as long as you like."

Stunned, she said nothing, only continued to pet the dog. When she looked back to the doorway, he was gone.

"You live with a grouch bag, you know that?" she asked the dog.

Gertie licked Sofie's chin.

"That's okay," she told the mutt. "We girls stick together."

But that wasn't true. Where Donovan was concerned, Sofie was on her own.

* * *

The thrift store truck had gone, but it wasn't the last. He was nowhere near the bottom of Gertrude's stuff piled in the basement. They'd be back, and Donovan would have another full load for them. Without a doubt.

Earlier, he left Sofie in the library and returned to the great room to chip away at the wounded fireplace. He'd avoided her today on purpose. Mainly because he didn't trust himself to be within three feet of her and not grab her up and kiss her.

She'd stayed away from him today, too, he noticed, preferring to stay out of that perimeter. She must have meant it when she said she was trying to forget the kiss.

Good luck. Her taste had been all he thought about today.

He returned his attention to the jagged pieces of slate crumbling from the mortar, contented to distract himself. Didn't work.

Seeing her in that library—seeing the couch. The only thing he could think about was the kiss last night and how he'd bet if he kissed her again she'd melt into him the same damn way. Maybe gift him a repeat of seven years ago.

He pounded at the fireplace, forcing his body's attention to the physical act of tearing something apart. Cheap rocks. Cheap mortar. Cheap craftsmanship. Nothing he hated worse than a half-assed job. When he first spotted the rock crumbling to the floor, he told himself he'd slap it back into place and be done. Then he noticed a few other loose pieces.

So he pried those off. He noticed a few more and pried those off as well. With half the fireplace's stones strewn across the plastic, he figured he may as well replace each and every one by hand. May extend his timeline, but getting back to what he did best would get his thoughts off the adorable event planner with the tempting mouth.

God knew hauling Gertrude's shit to the curb wasn't doing it.

Plus, he continued arguing with himself, Aless wouldn't appreciate his new B-and-B falling down around his ears the moment he signed the closing papers. Donovan chipped another stone away and dropped it on the plastic knowing that wouldn't happen. Yes, she needed a few repairs—Connor's to-do list was a mile long—but structurally, the house was sound. Pate Mansion may be old, but she had good bones.

Not that he had an ounce of reverence for this house. Not for the curved staircase where he'd ridden the banister and as a result had been given a taste of the parquet flooring. Not the chair rail where he'd raced his favorite Hot Wheels car. Not this very room, where his father had thrown his lit cigarette followed by a full ashtray at him. Quick reaction time, Donovan shielded himself with an arm to deflect the cigarette, earning a burn for his trouble. He lifted a hand and rubbed the scar along his hairline. The crystal ashtray proved harder to miss.

Well, what the fuck ever.

Dog's shrill bark rang through the air, making him jerk in surprise. The chisel slipped off the stone, slicing his finger. He backed away from the fireplace and, much as he wanted to shout, swore under his breath. Dog was adverse to yelling, picked up on human emotions like a tuning fork. He'd seen it happen. Watched as her ears lowered and tail went down just because Donovan had raised his voice to call to Connor from upstairs. She was sensitive to human energy, likely because she'd been yelled at—and struck—by her former owners.

As a kid, he'd been the same way. *Know thy enemy.*

He'd picked up his father's patterns. Knew what mood the old man was in by the sound of his footfalls. Slow and stumbling meant he was lit. Quick and shuffling meant he was pissed. Donovan knew when to wall up, stay silent, not provoke him. He knew when to slip out the upstairs window and shimmy down the maple tree.

He squeezed his throbbing fingers into a fist and, instead of growling a string of curse words, blew out a breath through his nose. Dog had been through enough trauma in her life—no way was he causing her to slink away, repeating the pattern her dipshit owners had started.

"Gertie! Give me that!" came Sofie's playful voice from the hallway. Another bark, this one muffled, rang into the air.

Donovan held his bleeding hand to his chest and ambled to the doorway. Dog, with a strip of long purple material in her mouth, was backing down the hallway playing tug-of-war. Sofie, hunched at the waist, was following each of Dog's backward steps, holding the item gently.

"Give it back, girl," she said softly. "Come on, Gertie."

"Dog."

Dog lifted her head and looked at him, teeth still clamped around what looked like a pair of stretchy pants.

"Drop it," he told Dog.

She wagged her tail left, then right.

He watched her.

She dropped it.

He smirked at Sofie, who screwed her delicious lips to one side.

"Wow. Color you the dog whisperer."

"You're wowed easily."

"Am not."

His hand began to throb. Ah, hell. Blood ran down his wrist. He held out a palm to catch the next drop before it hit the floor.

"You're bleeding!"

"I'm fine."

Sofie raced over to him and wrapped his hand and wrist with the pants. "Bathroom. Go." She shoved him until he obeyed, lurching toward the adjacent half bath reluctantly.

Just as reluctantly, he allowed in a memory of Caroline. Back when she'd been his grandmother's live-in chef. He didn't remember her ever not being there for him.

The cottage at the rear of the mansion was Caroline's home and had become Donny's haven on many nights. Nights when his father was drinking and his heavy steps paced the halls. Most of the time he ran to Caroline's to avoid a beating, but on this particular night, he'd gone there after one.

He came home late when he was supposed to be grounded for what, he couldn't remember. He guessed his father was wait-ing on him; had known it in some deep, dark place in his gut. Donny strode boldly through the front door anyway. Now that he thought about it, he wondered if he'd done that on purpose. Daring his old man to lay into him and give him a reason—as if he needed another one—to leave for good.

Caroline had put in her notice. She was leaving Pate Mansion, leaving Gertrude's employment, and in a way, leaving him, too. Moving to New York now that her son was out of the military. Once Caroline left, Donny had no reason to stay.

None at all.

He entered her cottage without knocking, head down, hair obscuring his face.

"Hey, kiddo." She looked up from a book she was reading, her bobbed silver hair swinging, and pinned him with a smile. A smile that faded the moment he brought his chin up.

"Oh my heavens!" Dropping the book, she hustled him into the bathroom, drag-ging him by the wrist. He was a foot taller than she and twice as strong, but he let her. "Another fight, Donny? What did I tell you about that?"

She didn't know the truth. He'd never told her.

Pushing him down onto the closed toilet seat, she wet a towel and pressed it to the wide split in his mouth. It'd been numb on the way over here, but now it was hurting like a son of a bitch. He had no idea what possessed him to say what he said next. Maybe he needed someone to know. Maybe he felt like he could finally share with her since she was leaving.

"Dad's class ring," he muttered, wincing as she dabbed his bloody face.

Her hands stilled, one on the side of his face, the other wrapped around the towel. His eyes found her worried ones behind a thick pair of glasses.

"How long?" she whispered, her voice frail.

As long as he could remember. He shrugged one shoulder and looked away, ashamed. "Few times."

"Donny." She cradled his face with both hands. "No." She swallowed and he could see the pity well in her eyes. Which shamed him more. "You can stay here. I'm calling the police." She released him and stood. "You should have told me sooner. I would have protected you. No matter the cost."

Cost. As in personal cost. He knew she would have protected him. Would have stood against his father and grandmother, lost her job, lost her home. Donny wasn't about to be the cause for destroying Caroline's life. She was the best person he knew.

Besides, it wasn't like he was a helpless kid. He was sixteen; he could fend for himself.

Wrapping a hand around her arm, he stopped her from walking away. "Don't." He begged with his eyes, the word "please" unspoken on the tip of his tongue. "I'm leaving. Doesn't matter if you call the cops or not. I won't be here."

"Leaving?" She pressed the hand holding the towel to her chest. "Where are you going to go?"

"I have a job. At a restaurant." It wasn't the most upstanding group of guys, but hey, he wasn't exactly living in the lap of luxury here. "Some of my buddies work there and I'm going to stay with them."

He released her arm and she sat on the edge of the bathtub, facing him. She touched the towel to his lip again. "You'll have a scar."

He had plenty of scars. What was one more?

"I'm fine."

She tucked a strand of hair behind her ear and shook her head, sending her gray hair swinging. "All the bruises. Bone breaks. All from Robert?"

Unable to lie to her, he nodded solemnly.

Tears broke free and rolled down the soft skin of her cheeks, making him hate himself for burdening her.

He leaned forward, elbows on his knees, and took her hands in his. "You didn't do

*anything wrong." He tasted blood from the
cut in his lip but gave her a small smile anyway. "We can't pick our family, right? It's
bad luck I got a dad like him. That's it. If
anything, you—"*

Blinking out of the memory, Donovan said aloud,
"Saved me."

Sofie heard. Behind him, she flattened her hand on his
back. "What did you say?"

He tongued his upper lip where a barely visible silver
scar sat. "Nothing."

* * *

Donovan had said *something*. But that wasn't the most
pressing matter at the moment, so she didn't push.

She unwound the material from his hand, aware he
stood over her watching her every move. After so fervently
attempting to save the pair of pants Gertie snagged a minute ago, she'd gone and ruined them anyway. "Shoot."

"Didn't peg you for a velour fan," he mumbled as she
dropped the elastic-waist pants on the floor.

She turned to the sink. "They're not *mine*. Gertie
brought them to me. I thought they belonged to . . . someone
you know."

Some petite girl who shared his bed since he'd come
back to town. Wouldn't surprise her. Sofie had managed
to wrangle up a date since he'd come back to town. Surely
Donovan could rustle up a girl to sleep with him.

"My grandmother had a fetish for home shopping."

She frowned in thought.

Oh.

They were Gertrude's.

She snagged a towel on the rack behind him, relieved it was navy blue so she wouldn't have to watch red blood seep through it. The idea alone made her woozy. Well, she'd have to suck it up. He was injured and she was the only other person here.

"Sit." She gestured to the toilet seat.

"No."

She wet the towel. "Don't be a baby."

"It's not fatal, Scampi."

"You have a first aid kit, right? I mean, that's how you fixed Gert's paw." She bent and opened the vanity door, but before she sank to her heels, his uninjured hand grabbed her arm and hauled her back up. She shook him off. "What is with you?"

"Why do you do that?" He wasn't touching her any longer, but he was leaning close. She backed up until her butt hit the sink. She hadn't had to go far. In the small half bath, there wasn't much room to groove.

"Do what?" She glared back at him, having no idea what he was so upset about.

She watched a muscle in his jaw work, then he bared his teeth and said, "*Care.*"

The word sounded like a curse. She blinked at him.

"I've been nothing but a pain in your ass since I came to town, and here you are. *Caring.*"

She pushed up to her tiptoes, getting in his face. "Too bad." She pressed the wet towel to his finger. The cut was on the opposite hand as his star tattoo, the one with a branchy tree inching up his forearm. "You have new tattoos." Keeping pressure on his hand, she was surprised he let her help him.

"They're not new." His shoulders had fallen, some of his anger dissipating.

"They are to me," she said softly. Her eyes tracked up his arm, where more ink peeked out from under the sleeve. "You have so many."

"Rocks cause scars."

"Okay," she said, not fully understanding his meaning. Maybe it would be best to change the subject. "I'm painting the dining room tomorrow. If you don't mind. It would be nice if I brought some help. Faith and Charlie offered to come over and..."

His palm on her cheek startled her so much, she closed her mouth. When she tilted her face toward his, she found his mouth pulled at the sides, his expression making him look ten years older. His eyes were on her but didn't seem focused—locked in a memory or a thought.

After they'd stood that way for several seconds, she whispered, "Donny?"

His eyes flickered to hers.

"Are you okay?"

He dropped his hand and backed away from her, snapping out of it.

"I'm always okay," he grumbled, then left the room.

$\mathscr{C}$HAPTER ELEVEN

"$\mathscr{Y}$ou guys are my best friends, ever," Sofie said to the two women now pulling supplies out of the back of her car. "Ever. Ever."

"The bribery part of this day is over." Faith hefted a bag filled with rollers and brushes.

"Yes, it has already been established that Faith and I will work for pizza." Charlie pulled out three long extenders for the rollers. They would need them for the high ceilings. "What room are we painting, again? The ballroom?"

"No, the dining room." Sofie took a bucket of paint and stir sticks from the trunk. "Ruby wants to have the bar in there. The setting is more intimate."

"Easier to talk the bigwigs out of their money in an intimate setting," Faith said with a wink.

"And Faith is in charge of the bigwigs," Sofie added.

"Pssh." Charlie, hands full, shut the trunk with her

elbow. "Faith will talk them out of their money, no problem. Open Arms is as good as funded for the next decade."

"Aww, I knew I liked you." Faith smiled. "What can I say? It's a talent."

"Ace." Evan appeared in the driveway, arms out to his sides, frowning at his fiancée. "No lifting." He took the extender rods from her.

Sofie felt her heart both buoy and sink as her eyes strayed to Charlie's stomach. "Are you...?"

"What? No! I mean, I'm not. But it's not like we don't want...um..." She shook her head fervently.

Oops. Sofie hadn't meant to put her friend on the spot.

Evan kissed Charlie's forehead. "Ace. Relax." He relieved Faith of her armload as well and tipped his head toward Sofie when Donovan came outside. "Your girl."

Sofie froze, watching as Donovan approached their little group. They weren't quite at the "your girl" stage. They weren't ever at the "your girl" stage, come to think of it. Evan sent her a wink, one turquoise eye vanishing and reappearing as a smirk slid onto his face. Yeah, he did that on purpose.

Donovan slipped the paint bucket from her hand, his fingers brushing hers as he did. "Making me look bad, Scampi."

Faith and Charlie hustled inside. Traitors.

"Thought you liked looking like a scoundrel," Sofie called after Donovan as she followed him to the house.

He turned his head slightly and she caught sight of his lips twitching.

At the house, he walked inside. She was about to walk in behind him when he kicked the door closed. Slammed it right in her face! Shocked, she froze for a few seconds before reaching for the knob.

The door opened and Donovan, hands free, shrugged a shoulder. "Scoundrel."

She didn't want to smile. Didn't want to have any moment of levity or understanding with this man. But a small smile found her face anyway. Which was dangerous because where he was concerned, a little went a long way.

Or all the way.

Folding her arms over her breasts, she remained on the porch. "I'm not coming in now."

"Yes. You are."

There was no doubting his tone. He was teasing her. Which was fun.

Dangerous.

That, too.

Holding her ground, she shook her head. "No, I'm not."

"Scampi, get your ass in here." Mock seriousness. His light eyes were sparking with mischief. She could see it. She could *feel* it.

An errant zing of excitement flitted through her veins, making her want to challenge him. She didn't move, save to lean forward, purse her lips, and enunciate one word. "No."

He dropped his hand from the knob, stalked toward her in two long-legged steps, and bent over. A second later she was in the air, then upside down, holding on to his pant loops for dear life. He hauled her inside, his shoulder squeezing a giggle from her diaphragm as he carried her into the foyer. When her feet hit the floor she was laughing and pushing a tangle of brown hair out of her face.

Then she found herself staring at his mouth, needing his mouth...

A protracted moment stretched between them and gradually, she became aware she had an audience. *They* had an audience. A very, very interested Charlie with a huge smile on her face. An aghast, open-mouthed Faith, and Evan, who wasn't smiling or gaping, but one dark eyebrow had lifted in a show of mild interest.

Evan broke the silence.

"Ready to go?"

"Yeah," Donovan answered.

Evan leaned over and kissed Charlie good-bye. "Be back." Then to the rest of them he said, "Be good." His gaze lingered on Sofie a bit longer than the others, she noticed.

"No promises," Faith said.

"I'll"—Sofie cleared her throat, realizing what she was about to say sounded very familiar and domestic—"lock up before I leave."

"We'll be back before then, Scampi. Dog!" He put his teeth to his lip and whistled, high and sharp.

The dog trotted into the foyer from the kitchen where she'd disappeared earlier.

"You're taking Gertie?" she asked.

"Fumes."

So he wasn't only protective over her, but the dog as well. That made her feel better...sort of. The guys left the house. She shut the door behind them and turned to face her friends.

Faith propped her hands on her hips. "Any more attraction between the two of you, and Charlie and I would've had to man the fire hose."

"For real," Charlie said, betraying her right alongside Faith. "*Ten-shunnn.*"

Faith nodded her agreement. "Cut it with a knife."

Sofie held her hands out in front of her, mainly because she was afraid her friends were making a point she really didn't want to have made.

"Donovan and I are enduring one another for however long it takes to get this mansion ready for the charity dinner." She clapped her hands. "Painting! That is what we are about to do right now."

Charlie raised an eyebrow and crooked her lips, the mannerisms resembling her fiancé's. "Nice segue."

"Yeah," Faith said. "Smooth."

Sofie grinned, changing the subject again. "Coffee?"

Her friends let her have the reprieve. Faith laid out the plastic on the floor, and Charlie opened and stirred a bucket of paint. Donovan had already moved the table and chairs and the buffet against the one wall they were leaving red as an accent.

Sofie left them to it, walked to the kitchen, and fired up the coffeemaker. She watched out the window as Evan climbed into the Jeep and Donny opened the driver's door. He caught her looking, and paused for a few lingering seconds, before shutting himself into the Jeep as well.

Enduring one another.

Yeah, right.

* * *

The quarry in Evergreen Cove was no pile of rubble.

A fifty-foot wall stood against a blue sky, jagged edges and craggy handholds where Donovan used to attempt to scale his way to the top. Trees and shrubs and other brush grew at the base around where piles of unclaimed rocks rested.

He inspected a piece of quartz before dropping it into a cardboard box. The new design he had in mind for the fireplace required him finding just the right rocks.

"What's your ETA for finishing up?" Evan asked from his perch on a sizable boulder.

He meant the mansion, Donovan guessed.

"After the charity dinner. And the campout." He spared Evan a glance, ignored his friend's surly expression, and went back to picking and sorting.

"Entire town is excited," Evan said. "My agent flipped out when she heard about it. She's calling our publisher and getting advance copies of Asher's and my latest *Mad Cow* book to give away at the event."

"Nice." Asher. There was a guy he hadn't seen in forever.

"Know what that means?" Evan asked, then answered himself. "Penis Bandit reunion."

Donovan chuckled.

Evan was talking about the summer Donovan stole a bottle of liquor from Robert's liquor cabinet. They drank way, way too much, stumbled through town in the dark, and then Evan and Asher painted phallic symbols all over Mrs. Anderson's library walls.

Bright spot in an otherwise dark past.

Donovan shook his head. "I haven't seen that asshole in I don't even know how long."

"That's sweet. I'll tell him you still care."

He palmed a large rock with a rough edge and tossed it into the box. Good size and shape for a corner piece.

"Bust your hand?" Evan asked.

He'd forgotten. So many scrapes, cuts. They blurred

into one another. "On the fireplace I'm now apparently rebuilding."

"Not Scott Torsett's face?" Evan grinned.

"You heard about that?"

"Charlie. Sofie."

"Chicks." Donovan shook his head. "Scampi wouldn't let me hit him."

"Too bad."

"I don't fight anymore."

But he used to. He was young and angry, using his hands for destruction instead of creation. Then he'd evolved to using those same powerful, roughened hands to build works of art rather than use them to prove his strength. It was a necessary part of growing up.

Out of simply not knowing better, he had begun repeating his father's patterns. He had taken his rage out on other people. Until he was about seventeen, then he acquired friends. One was sitting with him now. The other, a rock star coming to town to hock his children's book. The final link in the chain had come later. Connor had looked up to Donovan at a time when no one should have looked up to him, and lucky for him, Connor stuck around.

His support system. He owed those guys a lot.

Back in the day, the quarry had been his refuge. On more than one night he would come down here and smash rocks into the wall before scaling it without climbing gear. Stupid.

But he'd figured he wasn't hurting anyone when he was here, and at the time, that'd been good enough.

"You're not your dad," Evan said.

Every muscle in Donovan's body tightened.

"I know that comment seems random. But I see you beating yourself up over being back here. Know you're struggling being in that house. And navigating whatever is between you and Sofie."

He glanced over at Evan, who shrugged, as if his observation of Donovan's innermost battles was no big deal.

"Thought I'd point out to you that you are not your old man."

"I'm fine," he replied stiffly, not liking how Evan noticed things.

"You know I know, right?"

He clenched his teeth. He knew Evan had a guess at his past, but he didn't think he really knew. Wasn't something they chatted about casually.

"How many times have you and I been drunk together?" Evan's lips lifted slightly. "Approximately."

"A million?"

Evan laughed, an easy sound that relaxed him some.

"Yeah," he said, then his smile fell. "Well. You mentioned your dad a time or three."

Great.

Donovan pushed to standing and looked at the surrounding rocks and the pines, the only refuge—not counting Caroline's house—he'd had in the years he'd lived in the Cove.

"I don't remember mentioning it," he admitted. "Usually not much for chatter."

"Didn't say anything to Charlie." Evan stood and dusted his hands on his jeans. In other words: Sofie didn't know. "It's your story, man."

Donovan nodded, grateful. He didn't exactly broadcast the fact Robert Pate used to beat the hell out of him for fun. That Evan hadn't told Charlie was why he was still a friend. That right there. It was hard to find people to trust in this world. When he did, he kept them close.

"Sofie," Evan said, contemplative.

Donovan crossed his arms over his chest. Now what?

His friend tilted his head. "She and Ace are close."

"I noticed."

Evan took a step closer to him. "Sofie gets tweaked about something you say or do, she's gonna be upset, and that's gonna make Charlie upset."

Ahh. Evan had assumed the role of big brother to Sofie.

"This the part where you tell me if I hurt Scampi, you beat my ass?"

Evan shook his head as if frustrated, his eyebrows sinking into a pair of angry arches. "I thought you posed a threat, dumbass, I never would've let you near her."

His turn to frown. "You're seven years too late."

"I know you've been through some shit. But I also know you, Donny. You're loyal. You believe you don't deserve any better than you have. Which also means I know you would chew off your own arm before you'd hurt Sofie. You're safe with her. She's safe with you."

Safe with him.

Donovan worked his jaw while he thought.

"What you're doing for those kids—"

"Sofie's doing it." He was quick to correct. He wasn't some sort of benevolent do-gooder. The charity dinner, camping…The only reason Open Arms was infiltrating Pate Mansion was because he'd agreed to get out of the way so Scampi could let them pass. It was the right thing to do, especially in a house that'd been so filled with wrong.

"Trust me, Ev"—he crouched to dig through a nearby pile—"my interests are self-serving."

"Keep telling yourself that," Evan grunted, not buying his bullshit. Another reason Donovan kept him around. "You have to hand-pick every one of these goddamn pieces yourself, or you want me to help?"

"You can try."

"You're lucky we're friends." Evan squatted next to him and began sorting through another pile.

Bitch of it was, he was right.

Donovan was lucky to have him.

* * *

Faith emptied the final wine bottle into the highball glass in Sofie's hand.

"I told you, I don't want any more." Sofie had stopped drinking after the first half a glass Faith poured for her. She was too nervous about what might happen to the wall—worried she'd end up with trim lines as curvy as her hips by the time she finished.

Each time Faith refilled her glass, she'd dumped the wine back into Faith's or Charlie's glasses instead. Meaning she was stone sober, while her giggly friends were not in the same vicinity as sober.

"Come on," Faith urged.

"Yeah," Charlie agreed. "Have some fun."

Sofie looked at the drying paint, head swimming from the fumes even though they'd opened the windows. Well, she was almost done anyway. "Okay, I give."

They'd finished the coat on all three walls. And to be honest, there wasn't *that* much more to do. The one wall where she removed the sconces might need touching up after it dried, the fixtures rehung. But all in all, a successful paint job nearly completed. She lifted her glass and clinked it with her friends' glasses. Faith had found a wineglass somewhere, but Charlie was drinking from a glass coffee cup with a cartoon of Garfield painted on one side.

Faith finished off her wine, licked her lips, and sucked in a breath. Then she exhaled, looking pained.

Sofie lowered her glass. "What is it?"

"Would it be completely awful for me to ask about Connor's . . . status?"

Charlie shook her head. "Heck no, I'd hit that."

Sofie had lifted her wine to take a drink and now sputtered into her glass. She wiped her lips and laughed. Charlie wasn't usually one to trash-talk. "I love when you drink. Evan is wearing off on you."

"He is," she said, her voice taking on a dreamlike quality.

Sofie turned to her other friend. "And my answer is no, it's not awful. I have no idea if he's seeing someone," she said, thinking. "But he's never mentioned a girlfriend and he's here a lot. Connor is a really nice guy."

"It's true." Charlie gestured with her glass. "And I was kidding earlier. He's been my landscaper since he got out of the service. I've never once considered hitting that." She studied the ceiling for a second. "I mean, not for real."

Faith laughed, a loud *ha!* "Yeah, because you have a very fine hunk of man at home waiting for you each and every night."

A silly smile covered Charlie's face.

"And a boy who calls you Mom." Sofie witnessed the first time it happened. She'd watched her friend nearly disintegrate beneath the weight of that title. Lyon's mom, Rae, was Charlie's very best friend before Rae passed away. When Charlie fell in love with Evan, it took her a while to accept she hadn't "stolen" Rae's family.

"It's true. I hit the jackpot." Charlie turned to Faith. "You have nothing to feel badly about. Lust away. Connor's hot."

Faith smiled but it was weak. "I'm not sure how long I should be in the grieving stage over my lost fiancé." She twisted her mouth, her expression going hard. "Lost is the wrong word. He's not *lost*. He's still living in his house on Meyer Avenue. And I'm sure he's still banging Cookie, the tramp-stamp wearing, bull-riding twentysomething, so what the hell do I have to feel badly about?"

"Absolutely nothing." Sofie squeezed her friend's slender forearm, hating the way Faith's future had been crushed so completely.

"There's no predetermined grieving timeline," Charlie said. And she knew of what she spoke. "By the way, how are things going with your mom? Getting better?"

Faith grunted. "As well as you'd imagine. This is why thirty-year-olds shouldn't live with their mothers."

"Amen," Sofie said, thinking of her own mother. When she moved out of her parents' house, she'd never returned. She may be a long-suffering middle child, but her independent streak was thick. She offered Faith the remainder of her wine.

"Linda's new boyfriend is twenty-six," Faith said of her mother, accepting the glass.

Charlie's eyebrows hit her hairline.

"*Twenty-six*," Faith repeated.

"At least he's a good-looking guy. Maybe you should enjoy the view of him hanging around her pool shirtless," Sofie said, but she was teasing. Faith had expressed her distaste for Marco. He was waxed hairless, always covered in tanning oil, and looked in a mirror every time he passed one.

Faith laughed and threw a hand through the air. "I'm done bitching. I have plenty to be grateful for. I live in a beautiful house. I have beautiful friends." She batted her eyelashes. "And my beautiful friends are surrounded by beautiful men, one of which is a sexy, sexy landscaper who I can't quite picture from my days of working at the Wharf." Her smile vanished and she blew out a sigh.

"He's hotter now," Sofie put in.

"Well, whatever." Faith took a swig of wine. "Unless he's interested in a one-night stand, I'm out."

"He might be," Sofie said flatly. Weren't they all?

"No, Faith. Don't give up on love." This from Charlie. "I wasn't looking for it, either. And the last person I was looking for it with was my late best friend's husband."

Sofie remembered how upset Charlie was when Evan started pursuing her. His wife had been gone for four years at the time, and his son, Lyon, loved Charlie like a second mother already. It took a while for Evan to convince her, but when Charlie accepted, it was the best thing for them all.

But hers was a unique situation. That kind of thing didn't happen to everyone.

"Charlie, you got lucky." Sofie smiled when her friend looked at her. "I have to say, I'm about to climb into the one-night-stand boat with Faith. This dating thing is crap.

Most men do not want anything long-term. You start to wonder if you should give up."

"You're further along than you think," Faith interjected. "Donovan kissed you."

"He *kissed* you?" Charlie's big eyes were huge, her smile huger. "O-M-G tell me all about it. Was it good? I bet it was good. Did he bring up the past? Did you? Did his lips feel the same?"

Sofie held up a palm. Instead of answering with *yes, no, sort of,* and *better...definitely better*, she said, "It was an impulsive kiss."

"And?" Faith prompted.

Deflection was not going to work with these two. Turning, she studied the drying paint on the wall and thought of how to best say it. "The chemistry...the attraction"— she shook her head—"hasn't gone anywhere." Which made being near him all the more dangerous.

"What if he changed? What if he wasn't what you needed back then—but he is what you need him to be now?"

Ah, Charlie. So full of hope. More than anything, Sofie wanted to grab hold of that hope with both hands. There was a time she would have. A long time ago.

There was a moment when Donovan's lips were on hers and temporarily, she forgot the past. *Need* was the dominant feeling. Then the moment in the bathroom, when he wouldn't let her bandage him, when he'd been angry with her for caring...*Frustration* had been her dominant emotion.

"He's...I don't know what he is," Sofie answered honestly. "I used to think I could save him." She'd been so naïve. "There isn't a more futile pastime than trying to save someone who doesn't want to be saved." He didn't want her saving him any more than she wanted him saving her. "Trust me. He doesn't want anything from me."

Except the one thing he'd already claimed.

There wasn't any going back to the way things were. They'd just have to move forward from here.

And somehow, Sofie vowed anew, she was going to keep her heart to herself.

CHAPTER TWELVE

"Workaholic," Charlie said as her fiancé slipped an arm around her shoulders.

"Am not." Sofie turned from her paint bucket and pointed at the wall with the loaded brush. "I'm just going to touch up two things."

Faith yawned. "I have an hour-long drive after I leave here."

Oh, that was true. Faith had carpooled from the shop rather than bring her own car to the mansion. Sofie hadn't expected to be here well after dinnertime.

Sofie sent a longing glance at the wall, then to her very patient, darling friend. "Ten more minutes?"

They'd long since sobered from their day of wine drinking, especially after eating fully loaded pizzas that had been delivered. Thank God her friends worked cheap. Earlier, the guys had argued they could have taken care of the painting in half the time, Evan's grumbling a cute

"I paint for a living," but the girls had shooed them away. The two of them needed their male bonding time as much as Sofie had needed girl time.

"We can drive her to her car," Charlie offered.

Faith's shoulders dropped in relief. "Oh, thank you. I need to get home."

Which would mean Sofie was on her own. "Um…" She flashed a glance at Donovan, who came into the dining room, pizza slice in hand, mouth chewing.

Evan politely pointed out the pachyderm in the room. "You sure you and Donny can hang out without killing each other?"

Donovan's brows jumped. He flicked his eyes to Sofie and took another bite.

Concentrating way more than necessary, Sofie ran the brush along the wall. "We'll be fine."

Satisfied, Faith grabbed her purse and bolted for the door. "Perfect. I have to get up early."

Right. Skylar, Faith's sister, was moving out of her boyfriend's house—yet another relationship-gone-bad. The Shelby curse. Maybe there was something to Faith's family's urban legend after all.

Evan, Charlie, and Faith made their way out the front door and Sofie kept painting, acutely aware of Donovan behind her, polishing off his pizza and brushing his hands on his jeans.

"Thanks for dinner," he said.

"Was there enough left for you?" The girls had eaten almost two entire pizzas on their own, and Sofie ate three slices herself. "I ate too much. Should probably put down this brush and run a few laps around the house."

"You worry a lot about what you eat."

She peeked over her shoulder. "All girls do."

"Not all girls."

Well. He probably knew what he was talking about, considering he had a wide sampling of ladies to pool.

I use the word ladies *loosely. And the word* loosely *literally,* she thought with a smile.

"You look good, Scampi. I wouldn't sweat it." He pulled his thumb and index finger over his lips. She watched him draw his mouth open, watched his lips close again. The star tattoo on his finger caught her eye and her stomach fluttered to life. So did parts much lower.

Paint fumes. She turned back to the wall. She'd blame the fluttering on the paint fumes.

"I see you went with a Band-Aid after all," she said.

"Yeah."

"Find what you were looking for at the quarry?" If she kept the conversation flowing while she finished this wall, she might stave off more inappropriate thoughts about his mouth.

"Mostly."

Another one-word answer. He wasn't helping her in the conversation department.

"Want a beer?"

She looked over her shoulder again. His black hair was wavy from the humidity today, his shirt covered in dust from the quarry. The man was sexy, tall, and made her think of sinning ten different ways. She should have gone with Faith and let the painting go.

Shaking her head, she muttered, "No, thanks."

He turned for the kitchen.

Adding alcohol to the equation would not do her any favors. Though it might dull the synapses snapping in her brain. At current, they were lobbing suggestion after suggestion at her, mostly about kissing.

Kissing Donovan was fun in a way that made no sense other than physically. She thought about Faith's proclamation to only have one-night stands, and then Sofie thought about the fact that, technically, she and Donny had already had a one-night stand. Then she wondered if they did it again, if it'd be a two-night stand.

"Oh my gosh, brain, shut up," she whispered.

Crazytown had a population of one, and her name was Sofia Martin.

Done with the area she could reach, she saw there was one more spot over the doorway she wanted to fill in before calling it quits for the evening. Her right wrist ached and pins-and-needles numbness prickled her fingers. She'd had a death grip on the paintbrush for most of the day in an effort to carefully trim around what seemed like *acres* of hand-carved wooden molding. Worth it, though. The molding stood out better against Pale Walnut Mousse than the dark, light-sucking red she and her friends had spent the day covering.

She dragged the six-foot ladder to the wall and climbed the rungs. If she rested her left elbow on the top and reached out with her right hand, she could hold on to the small container of paint with one hand and touch up the spot above the doorway with the other.

A little more stretching, a little maneuvering...

The tips of the bristles were almost on the wall...
Allllmost.

Her plan would've worked if it hadn't been for Gertie's poor timing.

A shrill bark rang out, startling Sofie and causing her

to reel. Thankfully, her reaction time was quick. She slapped a hand onto the ladder, righting herself before she fell.

Sofie swiveled her head to find Gertie smiling and panting up at her, tail wagging. Before she could breathe a sigh of relief she hadn't fallen off the ladder, Sofie noticed paint sinking into the grooves of the ornate, hand-carved, *antique* door frame.

"Oh no." She pulled her shirtsleeve over her hand and wiped frantically at the smudge, all while trying to stay balanced on the ladder and not spill her paint.

"Of course I'd ruin it at the end," she grumbled. Not like she could replace the molding by making a quick trip to Lowe's. This particular feature had come with the house.

She nearly had it, all she needed to do was lean a little farther out on the ladder to scrub a spot just out of reach...

The ladder tipped. And this time, Sofie couldn't prevent the fall.

* * *

Donovan took a slug of his beer and headed for the dining room. He was going to tell Sofie to wrap things up or else he was going to grab a paintbrush and finish for her. He got that she wanted to do this on her own, but there was no way he could stand by while—

At the threshold, he stopped cold. The ladder rocked, Sofie on it, and before he could think, he'd slammed his beer bottle onto the dining room table and rushed to her. He caught her a millisecond later, his hands grasping her hips. The bowl of paint and the brush glanced off him. He barely noticed. His mind was more on her and the adrenaline rushing through his bloodstream than on paint stains.

She grappled onto the top step of the ladder, backing her ass—her incredibly fine, round ass—directly into the center of his chest. He blew out a breath, teeth wedged together, hands still on her hips.

"What the hell are you doing?" Vaguely, he became aware of paint oozing down his arm.

"Let go of me!" She straightened, but he kept his hold tight. In a different scenario, he might enjoy her ass in his face. But her almost falling to her death and/or dismemberment pushed every ounce of lust from his brain.

"Not a chance. Not 'til you're down safely."

"I don't need your help." She glared over her shoulder at him. "I would've had it."

"And by 'it' you mean a concussion?" He let her go but stayed close in case she slipped again. "That's all you *would've had* if I didn't save your ass."

Her eyelids narrowed to slits. "Which you had no problem grasping with both hands, I noticed."

"That doesn't sound like a complaint," he growled. Not a single part of her, from top to toenails, had recoiled from him.

She stepped down a rung, then two, but he kept his hands firmly on the rungs. Denim-covered thighs brushed his forearms. Still, she didn't try to escape him.

"You're in this house, Scampi, you exercise safety," he said, his voice raising despite her proximity. "You do not climb six goddamn feet into the air and risk a brain injury to paint the wall. I'm a foot taller than you are. Ask me."

"Ask you?" she snapped, taking another step down.

He kept her caged with his arms until she put one foot

solidly on the ground. Then and only then did he let go of the ladder.

"*You*, who has been oh-so-approachable."

Fair point. Not that he'd admit it.

"I need a wet cloth and paint thinner." She left the ladder to poke around in her supplies.

"Leave it."

She ignored him and continued rummaging. "Do you have paint thinner?"

"Scampi, leave it."

"You don't understand. There is paint on the molding and if I don't clean it off it will—"

"It's not a big deal." He could feel a headache forming over his right eye.

"I want it to be perfect."

He rubbed the spot with two fingers.

"Are you sure there's not a container in the basement?"

"It's just a fucking house!" he bellowed, gesturing with one hand at the door frame. "I don't give a shit about the molding!"

Dog lowered her head and skulked out of the room. He could feel badly about yelling later. Right now, he needed Sofie to listen to him.

She spun to face him, a look of alarm in her rounded green eyes. If he worried he'd scared her, he didn't need to. She looked pissed. Hands propped on her hips, she cocked her head. "Excuse me?"

"I don't give a shit about the molding," he repeated. Calmly this time. "You know why I don't give a shit about the molding?"

"Because you don't give a shit about anything?"

Now? Now she was giving him hell?

He unclenched his jaw, took a deep breath, and then blew it out through his nose. "When I was nine..."

He swallowed past the bitterness in his throat. Not wanting to finish, but needing her to know the truth. The same way he'd needed Caroline to know the truth that long-ago night in the cottage. Needing to tell this story for the first time out loud. Needing to get it out. *Let* it out. *Straight through.*

Taking another breath, he started again. "When I was nine, I had a rust orange 1972 Impala Hot Wheels. My favorite car."

He looked past Sofie at the chair railing running along three walls in the room, his gut churning with acid and stale fear that had no place in him anymore.

"If I balanced the car just right, I could roll it on two wheels on the rail. Nearly made it the length of the wall once." His smile faded. "Until my father caught me, and I quote, 'ruining' the wall."

He'd never forget the look of rage on Robert's face. The way his lips pulled away from his teeth, the putrid smell of alcohol on his breath. Mostly, Donovan would never forget the brain-jarring slap to his face, the warm sliver of blood trickling from a small cut at the corner of his eye.

Sofie's face went pale, her hand lifted to her throat. "Oh my God."

Like that, she'd figured it out.

"I only had to be told once," he said with a hollow laugh. "Never did it again."

She took a step closer to him. "He...he hit you."

Hearing Sofie say it out loud made the truth uglier. Her eyes were wide and full of sympathy—his least favorite look on her. He didn't want her to feel badly about anything, especially for him.

Still, part of him drank in her sympathy. The fact that she cared—that *anyone* cared—made his chest ache. And reminded him how empty he was.

"More than once," he answered. "But that's not the point. Point is, I don't want you to worry about the molding being ruined." Words came into his mind unbidden, slashing him inside, parting his hollow chest and spilling out dust. His father's words.

You don't appreciate nothing. That's why your mother left! Because you were an ingrate then and you are now. Little bastard. Get the fuck out of this room. No dinner or breakfast! You starve and think of what you did!

His father had stomped the toy to pieces. Donovan had run upstairs and washed the blood away. He'd cried that night. He cried several times after, until he turned twelve and decided to never let Robert see him cry again. That was the year he threw a punch at his old man. Big thing for a twelve-year-old to attempt, but he'd had the element of surprise.

Robert hadn't been able to believe his son had hit him.

Donovan hadn't believed how much he liked feeling the skin of his father's lip split open, or how satisfying it'd been to spill his father's blood for a change. At the time, it made him feel powerful. Now, it tossed his gut.

"I'm sorry." Sofie took another step closer. Her soft touch landed on Donovan's arm, and the anger shuddering inside him shifted into an ache.

"Don't be. He's dead. And I hope wherever he is, he sees that"—he tipped his chin at the paint marking the molding—"and the bastard's bones roll."

The air between them radiated enough heat to set him on fire. But like the fireplaces he built, he could handle it. He could handle the heat from her, not because he was impervious, but because he was strong enough to soak her in and not burn to ash.

She swiped his arm where the paint was drying with one of her shirtsleeves.

"Sorry about the mess."

"Don't...I can..." Her soft touch rendered his brain useless. "There is a shower in the..."

He lost his train of thought when emerald green eyes hit him. He lowered his face, watching those eyes grow dark and wide. Watching her chin lift and her delicate throat work as she swallowed.

Heat.

He wanted more. If only to test his own strength.

He moved his lips gently against hers but resisted holding her to him. She held on to him, though, grasping his forearms with both hands, her fingers wrapped around his elbows. Then she pressed closer, her warmth fusing with his, her tits resting against his ribs.

Hell, sounded like an invitation to him. He thrust his tongue into her mouth, deepening their connection, and reached around grabbing her ass in both palms. When he squeezed, she sucked in a breath.

"Told you," he rumbled against her parted mouth.

"Told me?"

"You weren't complaining, Scampi." He squeezed again. "Perfect."

A choked laugh left her throat. "Big."

Still moving his hands over her backside, he said, "First thing I noticed about you at the Wharf."

He'd been plating up a chicken scaloppini when the manager walked in to show around a few new servers. Two he couldn't remember, and Sofie. Bent over the plate, he'd peeked between the metal shelves framing that perfect ass. He'd stood to get a better look, and she'd pegged him with those moss greens.

"Second thing I noticed was your eyes."

Her lips parted into a small smile.

He kissed that smile. Couldn't help it. She tasted incredible.

"And the third thing?"

"The first time you talked to me."

She rolled her eyes. "And what did I say?"

She didn't think he remembered. She was wrong.

" 'Can I get a side of cock?' "

Laughing, she shook her head.

He grinned, unable to help himself. "Then you cleared your throat and said, 'cocktail sauce.' "

"Worst abbreviation ever."

"Kitchen guys are immature."

She blinked up at him, studying him, like she was trying to piece him together. He didn't want her to. Once she pieced him together and had the whole picture, she wouldn't like what she saw.

He kissed her again, deep and slow, moving his hands gently on her body.

"Are you testing my boundaries?" she asked, her tone teasing.

"Mine," he corrected.

She bit her lip. "I don't date much."

"Me either."

At all, actually.

She hummed, more in thought than in argument. "I don't think I have any boundaries with you."

He was beginning to think he had none with her, either. So far since he'd been back in the Cove, he'd stormed into her office, backed her against his kitchen counter, bullied her date out of a restaurant, and was now holding her ass in both hands and refusing to let go.

Keeping his palms where they were, he tugged her closer until her breasts were smashed against his chest again.

"You know the best way through a bad situation, Scampi?"

She shook her head.

"Straight through. Straight through all the crap."

Slender brows met over her nose. "Is that what you're doing? Going straight through?"

"Yes."

She raised a hand, playing painted fingers along his collar. "Is that what I should do?"

For a second, he didn't get her meaning. Then he did.

She means me.

He was her straight through. He was her bad memory. He was the one who had robbed her of something precious.

Donovan knew that. He'd *known* that. This . . . kissing her, and if he could get lucky enough to have her under him again, would relieve the simmering ache throbbing in his dick now but wasn't going to make anything better for her.

He hadn't earned her the first time, and he sure as hell hadn't earned her this time. But that's what penance was. Paying for the past and not getting what he wanted.

One good thing about practicing penance, he'd gotten good at not getting what he wanted. Practically a pro.

He let go of her and promptly backed away.

Drying paint tangled in the hair on his arm. That, he could focus on. That was a mess he could clean up. A goal with a finite timeline.

"Gonna wash this off," he told her, ducking his head and pointing for the kitchen. "Try not to kill yourself while I'm gone."

CHAPTER THIRTEEN

That was intense.

Sofie stared blankly at her sleeve, covered in Pale Walnut Mousse paint. She wiped her fingers on her jeans, but instead of getting paint off her hand, it came back covered.

Covered in paint because she'd been covered in Donovan a few short moments ago.

How had it happened? One minute she'd been falling, the next being rescued, the next being kissed.

Maybe the better question was, how could it *not* happen? Where they were concerned, neither of them was very successful at avoiding the other.

Then he confessed a past she'd begun to suspect. Abuse. At the hands of his father. Donovan had told her one story. *One.* How many more were there?

He . . . he hit you.

More than once. But that's not the point.

Sadness left a residue on her skin, a film on the roof of

her mouth. A similar film coated the walls. No, not the walls. The molding. Her eyes went to it now, to the paint drying in the grooves.

She pictured a nine-year-old Donovan with his toy car. His father, large and angry, bearing down on him. She shut her eyes and bristled.

When she opened them her vision narrowed at the paint smudge on the door frame.

He was right. Who cared? Who cared about preserving what he was beaten for when he was a child? Right about now she wanted to get a crowbar and pry every damn piece of *antique* molding from the wall.

This house was possibly the worst location to host a charity dinner for abused children. What had Gertrude been thinking? Was this her way of apologizing to a grandson she should have stood up for? By extending an olive branch alongside this dinner, which was nothing less than an example of utter hypocrisy?

Sofie thought back to how angry Donovan used to be when they worked at the Wharf. Or so she'd thought.

Beneath that veil of anger was sadness. So much sadness, in him, in this room, she could feel the emotion clotting in her throat.

But there was also something else. The confusing spark of electricity between them. Inescapable. Palpable. Electricity they were powerless to resist.

Why were they trying? Maybe one more night together would be cleansing. Straight through, right? That's what he said. Maybe lying skin-to-skin with him would help him. Would help *her*. Would give them another chance to be together without any secrets between them.

Thinking back to that night, she realized how prematurely

they'd acted—as if sex required nothing more than two people and a wild amount of attraction. But she hadn't truly known him—at all, as it turned out. And he'd been so angry with her...she thought because she was a virgin. But maybe there was something else? Some hint of self-loathing. Because he believed he'd taken something from her? The only thing she'd been able to see or feel that night were her own haphazard emotions. By the time the Jeep ride ended at the restaurant, she'd built enough steam to—

My God.

She'd hit him. Like his father had before her, she'd slapped Donny right in the face.

She dragged her nails over her palm, paint rolling under her fingernails in the present, but a shadow from the past causing her palm to tingle.

Donovan found a way to blame himself. Because that's what kids who were abused did.

Tears welled in her eyes, but she blinked them back. She refused to cry. She would not go to him and treat him like a kicked puppy. He would never stand for it.

Straight through.

Stomping from the dining room to the kitchen, she followed the direction he'd disappeared. In the utility room, she found him bent, shirtless, half in the shower, scrubbing paint from his arm.

Tanned, rounded biceps flexed as he washed away remnants of paint in the streaming water. Veins stood out from his skin. An arrow tattoo ran the length of the inside of one forearm leading to the hand marked with the black bird, and the star on his finger.

She couldn't look away. He was *glorious*.

He tossed his mass of black hair out of his face and noticed her standing there. More ink covered his shoulder, a pattern of waves and swirls she couldn't make out the details of from here.

When she'd asked before about the new tattoo on his arm, he'd mentioned how rocks caused scars. Had he meant the tattoos covered scars caused from his work? Or other scars...

No.

Her eyes slid over all the tattoos covering his arms and hands. His shoulders. His flank. There were so many. Did they cover scars from an abusive father? A man who was not a man at all.

A monster.

The puzzle pieces slid together, and suddenly she understood why Donovan was the way he was. Disconnected, angry, short-fused.

But... what was he now? What was he to her? Right now he looked nothing short of beautiful. Like a wounded animal backed into a corner, growling whenever someone nice got too close. Because what did he know of close? What did he know of nice?

What had he known of virgins?

The kinds of girls she saw him leave with at the restaurant weren't nice. They sure as hell weren't virginal. Sofie remembered the way it hurt to see him go home with girls who didn't give a crap about him when she cared so very much.

No, she wasn't that kind of girl. But he'd gone home with her.

The blurry edges of the past narrowed and focused.

Unaware, he continued scrubbing his arm under the

running water from the showerhead. He tipped his chin to direct her upstairs.

"I have a T-shirt if you want to clean up and change. There's an attached bath in my . . ."

He trailed off, and the reason he trailed off was because Sofie whipped her shirt over her head. Stripping herself bare the way he had a moment ago when he told a story about a boy who had deserved compassion, not closed fists.

She swiped the paint from her arm and fingers and dropped the soiled shirt to the floor.

Standing in her bra and pants before him, she asked in a small voice, "Do me?"

Her request hung in the air between them for exactly half a second. Donovan slammed his fist into the faucet to shut off the water and reached for her with one dripping wet arm. He pulled her body flush against him, his mouth hitting hers hard.

Her eyes closed in relief—in sweet, sweet bliss. She ran her hands over his naked chest, his muscles, his tattooed skin. This kiss wasn't as desperate as before. It was as if an understanding had passed between them because of what he'd told her. Now that she knew, she saw him in a new light.

Coming into the light.

Just a little. Just enough.

* * *

Stop.

Dammit, stop.

Donovan ignored the warnings in his head. Now that he

was drinking Sofie in, her warm half-naked body pressed against his, there was no stopping. There was nothing he wanted more than to taste her, to feel her against him. To feel the noises she made when he turned her on vibrating along his rib cage.

There'd be no more telling himself how he didn't deserve her, or reminding himself he was paying penance. There was only Sofie and there was only him and there was only the scorching heat burning between them. The same heat that had burned between them the last time he had her.

The last time he'd had anyone.

To say remaining celibate hadn't been easy would be the understatement of the decade. His only method of survival was burying the sexual frustration in his work. Which was why he was a damn good mason. Why he had a waiting list of clients who paid handsomely for him to build custom fireplaces up and down the East Coast. There were no women pulling his hyper-focus from the one thing he did morning, noon, and night.

Like monks who made the best beer in the world, Donovan was a man without the distraction of sex.

Was.

With his tongue in Sofie's mouth, and her hands climbing his body, his extended bout of celibacy was about to become a memory. If having her meant he couldn't wrangle enough brain cells to construct another fireplace ever, so be it.

He wanted her. Only her. The dam had burst, and there was no holding back the flood.

He reached around her back and unclasped her bra. She continued kissing him, running her lips over his, making him forget his name, or what anyone's lips had tasted like before hers.

"Scampi."

"Yes," she said, kissing him again and again. "That's going to be my answer no matter what you ask."

He hadn't planned on asking her anything, but he'd take it. He needed a yes.

God, how he needed a yes.

He ran the straps of her bra down her arms, before tossing it to the floor. He took in every inch of her smooth, bare skin like a man savoring his last sunset before going underground forever. Fingers following the path of his eyes, he ran them over her rib cage, up the sides of those fabulous tits, and down over pink, supple nipples.

Soft. She was so fucking soft.

She tilted her head back and he kissed her neck. Her nipples peaked, hardening beneath his fingertips. He pulled his lips away to watch her, to bask in her glow.

He didn't know how long he had. This moment could burn hot, then fizzle out like a dollar-store sparkler. If this was it, this was *it*. More penance could be paid after. For now, he could only think of committing the crime to do the penance for.

More than anything, he wanted this touch. *Her* touch. Gentle touch hadn't been something he'd had a lot of over the years. Save for Caroline's motherly hugs, or shaking Alessandre's hand. Or the occasional pat on the back from a client. Aside from that, there had been no touching. Not since Sofie.

He worked her breasts with his thumbs and forefingers, pulling high mewls from her throat. His own skin sizzled in response, all of him on the brink of boiling over. Her fingertips glided along his abdomen, up his torso, over his pectorals. Lost in the feel of her touching him, his eyes sank closed. A groan left his throat. She made him feel . . . she made him feel . . .

That was it.

She made him feel.

He hadn't felt in a long time.

"Is this okay?" she breathed as she raked her fingernails over his chest.

"Sweetheart, better than okay."

She had no idea how much *more than okay* this was for him. Flushed pink nipples drew his head down. He tasted one precious bud, while the fingers of one hand worked the button on her cotton pants. The snick of the zipper sounded as his tongue swirled around her nipple, making it pebble.

Her hands grasped his shoulders. He palmed her back, arching her closer, feeling the tips of her dark brown ponytail brush his hands. She tasted like his past, but a good past. Good memories were very few and far in between. He continued pulling her breast into his mouth and drawing the same high, tight sounds from her throat. His cock throbbed in time with his heartbeat.

He had to have her. *Now.*

He gripped her butt in both hands, lifted her, and deposited her on top of the washer. Wrestling with her pants, he managed to free one of her legs, tossing her shoe to the floor as he did. Her hands went to the stud of his jeans. She had them open, her hand inside grasping him one mind-numbing second later.

Through his boxers, she stroked his shaft, and for a moment all he could do was drop his head back and enjoy the sensation of being touched by a hand other than his own.

Her lips caressed the underside of his chin, moved down the length of his throat, wetting his skin, making him crazy. He opened his eyes, grasped the back of her neck, and kissed her. She accepted his tongue in her mouth, joining him in the intimate dance. This was the tension simmering just beneath the surface since he came back to town. Unhinged, unresolved, overwhelming attraction for the woman in his arms.

Sofie had come to him this time. She'd been the one to say yes. And had asked him to "do her," he thought with a smile.

There was one problem. He hadn't planned on having sex while he was here. Even after kissing her in the car, even after he'd thrown her over his shoulder this morning, sharing a brief moment of lightness. He didn't expect to have her practically nude, on top of the washer hours later.

He pulled his lips from hers, and she let out a frustrated grunt, her hands tightening on the back of his neck, ruffling his hair. He had to tell her before this went any further.

"Scampi."

"Don't." She kissed him again, two, three times, quickly on the lips. "Do not try to talk me out of this, Donny."

He almost laughed. Talk her out of it? Not on her life. He managed a smile, a strained one, but still. "Not talking you out of this. But bad news, sweetheart." He did some quick math—figuring out how long it would take him to get to town, park in front of Nelson's drugstore, and run inside to buy condoms. Then drive back, breaking a minimum of nine traffic laws on the way.

Thirteen minutes, he figured. *Fifteen, tops.*

Risky. Fifteen minutes was enough time for the boiling-over heat between them to simmer. Hell, five minutes. *Two.* He took in her nakedness, the simple but sexy pink cotton panties she wore, the pants dangling off one leg, the shoe she still wore.

"No condom," he announced bleakly. "Wasn't planning on getting into your pants."

She blinked up at him, eyes going wide for a second. Then she smiled, a gentle, sweet Scampi smile from way back. "There's one in my purse."

Later, he would worry about *why* she had one in her purse. But for now, he could kiss her. So he did. Quickly.

He raced from the room, pausing in the doorway, pants open, chest heaving, the taste of her lingering on his lips.

"Where the hell is your purse?"

CHAPTER FOURTEEN

Dining room," she answered.

He took one last look at Sofie who was leaning back on her hands atop the washer, the room a sea of white behind her. Her ponytail was lopsided, some of her hair hanging over her face, her bare breasts begging for his tongue. Her panties begging to be tugged off with his teeth. He wanted her so much, he hated to leave her for a second.

Focus. A condom was around the corner.

He found her purse hanging on the back of a dining room chair, snatched it up, and dashed back to the utility room. Thrusting the small bag into her hands, he kissed her neck while she dug through the pockets.

"Here." A small foil packet was pressed to his chest.

She reached for his pants and pushed them down his hips. He let her. She freed him from his boxers next. Her hand wrapped around him again, stroking once, twice, while he tore the foil packet open with his teeth, a shake working down both of his arms. He clasped her wrist with one hand, pulled her hand off his cock, and kissed the inside of her wrist.

"Trying to make this last, Scampi. You're not help-ing." He let go of her to roll on the condom, worrying for an insane second he may have forgotten how to do it. He hadn't.

Thank God for small favors.

Grasping her butt cheeks with both hands, he pulled her closer, her ass squeaking along the washer's lid. Her breathing had increased with the same anticipation firing through his bloodstream at the speed of sound.

He watched her breasts lift and fall, lift and fall. "I've never seen anything as beautiful as you naked." He hadn't meant to say that out loud, but it was the truth. Every inch of her was perfect...at least, the inches he could see. Should have laid her down in a bed where he could strip her completely bare, but beggars couldn't be choosers.

And, yeah, he was the beggar in this situation. Taking whatever she was willing to give.

"Compliments are not necessary," she told him. "I've already said yes."

He wasn't feeding her a line, but now wasn't the time for that conversation.

He lifted her foot and eased her out of her panties, leaving her dressed on one side. As he lined up with her entrance, she fisted the back of his hair, her green eyes trained on him. In the still moment between them, his heart raced.

"Straight through," she whispered.

He tilted his hips and plunged deep inside her.

The surprised, satisfied sound from her was an elixir,

bathing him, healing him. He didn't have to ask, he knew from that reverent sound she liked how he felt. From the sound, her pink cheeks, her open mouth, and the way her short nails bit into the muscles in his shoulders.

Subtly, she stiffened, and he knew he'd lost her mind and attention. Maybe she was remembering another moment similar to this one. The last time they'd done this.

Pulsing, and in too deep to dream of pulling out, he tightened his arm around her waist and waited for it. Waited for an accusation, for her to call him on his crap from years ago.

"Say it," he commanded.

Her unfocused gaze met his. "I forgot how big you were." Her fingers lovingly stroked his jaw and sifted into his hair, pushing it away from his cheek.

When he smiled, so did she, the slightly crooked tilt taking him back to the very first time he touched his mouth to hers. Dipped his tongue into the curve of her top lip.

Not able to keep from it, he kissed her there now. "I'm trying to hold out, Scampi. This. Is not. Helping."

He pulled out and eased into her again. The feeling so consuming, he wondered if he'd be able to hold out at all. Pursing her lips, she let out a little "ooh" sound, also *not helping*.

"Good. So good." She bit her bottom lip.

Concentrating, he tightened every muscle in his body to the point of pain.

"Was it ever this good? Ever?" She sounded like she was asking herself that question, but he knew the answer. *No.* No was the answer. He'd had a lot of girls in his bed in the blurry years before he'd slept with her, and yeah, on a purely physical level, sex had been satisfying. But now, nestled between Sofie's thighs, "satisfying" was a lame descriptor.

What they were doing was mind-melting. Knee-exploding. Tendon-tearing.

Or it would be if he didn't loosen the muscles in his legs.

His cock tingled at the tip and he clenched his ass cheeks. *Hold out. Hold out. Come on, boy.* Through teeth he was grinding into pea gravel, he managed, "I mean it, Scampi. Talk about something else if you want this to last at all."

"I want it to." Her voice was as tender as her touch, her fingers running from his earlobe, down his jaw, and ending at his chin. She kissed his bottom lip. "Please, I want it to."

A shiver having nothing to do with the fact she was wrapping him tight in every way possible worked its way down his spine. That shiver was the reason he'd taken her home the first time. The reason behind it one he'd ignored back then, pretending not to recognize what it meant.

Not many women in his life had given a damn about him. His mother left when he was three, probably to get away from Robert, and really, who could blame her? Gertrude saw what she wanted to see, and ignored the rest. Most of the chicks Donovan had taken to his bed didn't give a damn about him. They wanted what he wanted. To use him up, get a quick fix, and move on.

Then there was Scampi. She didn't want to use them for anything. She cared about him, cared about what he said, how he felt about things, his opinion. The night of the Christmas party when he approached her, she'd given him a shy smile. He couldn't remember another time a girl had given him a shy smile.

When she came with him to the mansion, allowed him to take her inside, kissed him back, and finally allowed him to enter her... she blew his mind.

And by "blew his mind" he meant "freaked him the fuck out." It wasn't hard to figure out she was a virgin. She was tight. She was tense. She'd held her breath and scrunched her eyes.

He was being selfish, but she hadn't seen it that way. She gave the gift freely. For a man who hadn't received many gifts, it was a gift he'd taken with hardly a second thought.

Until after.

"S'mores," she panted now.

The word snapped him back to the present like a rubber band stinging flesh. The last thing in the world he'd expected Sofie to say was...

"S'mores?" he asked.

She kissed the underside of his chin and wrapped her arms around his neck.

"Can you work with that?" She flexed her hips and drew him deeper, and he felt a tingle buzz from tip to shaft again.

His mouth dropped open. She kissed his chin again. *Right.* The distraction he asked her for.

"We'll see. Keep talking, sweetheart."

She licked her lips and nodded. He kept pumping, slowly, watching her face contort while she tried to keep up a conversation.

"I figure... Since we will be camping out... We are going to need a fire pit..."

He tried to concentrate on her words; the picture she was painting rather than the feeling of how tight and wet and warm...

Focus, dammit.

He tried to focus on the cool metal of the washer's lid under his palm instead of the expression of lust on her face.

"That, I like that," she said on a sensual sigh. "Where was I?"

"S'mores," he somehow got out through a jaw of welded steel.

"Dark or milk chocolate?" Her words came out in uneven bursts, punctuated by little, panting breaths.

Now he was thinking about covering her in chocolate. Melted chocolate. Licking it off her body, suckling it off her nipples.

"I like my marshmallows golden brown...Oh *God*... Roast them nice and slow...uhhh, oh yes, *yes*...so that they melt on my tongue."

Yeah, this wasn't working. He stopped moving and her eyes snapped open, meeting his.

"Scampi, baby, how about you shut up and come instead?"

"Yeah." She nodded. "Okay."

She wrapped her legs around his waist, her half-off/half-on pants brushing the back of his calf, her naked inner thigh damp against his. He reached under her ass, angled her body, and drove into her deeper. A sharp, loud cry came from Sofie's mouth. Her nails dug into his shoulders once again.

There. She was about to blow and he was grateful, because it wouldn't be long before he followed. He just had to get her over, and he knew how to do that. Maneuvering his thumb between their bodies, he pressed gently against her clit, swirling the tiny nub until her breaths grew closer and closer together.

"That's it," he encouraged, watching her eyes sink closed.

He dropped his head and pulled her nipple deep into his mouth, running his tongue over and around it, increasing the suction until she pulled his hair and swore into his ear. With that four-letter word reverberating through the room, she came. Her inner walls clamped down over and over again, drawing his own orgasm before he could say the word *s'mores*.

Letting loose her nipple, he dropped his forehead against her collarbone, his entire body shaking, his lungs squeezing, still coming, for God's sake. It was the longest, most draining, orgasm he could remember. The best fucking thing to happen to him in a long time.

He didn't know how long he stayed that way, bent over her, blissed-out. When her hands gently stroked the back of his hair, his shoulders, down his back and across his ribs, he came to like a man who'd lost consciousness.

"Baby," she whispered.

He didn't argue the sentiment. Simply enjoyed being held.

* * *

Her entire body was buzzing. And what was that last move with this thumb? He filled her, his length and thickness a heady mix. She'd either forgotten how big he was, or had blocked it out after the underwhelming lovers who followed.

Sofie hadn't slept with a lot of men since Donny, but dates had turned into temporary boyfriends. Frankly, she saw no reason to stay celibate after she lost the one thing you stay celibate *for*. Once the "big V" was gone, what was left to hold on to?

So yes, there had been a few men. She was far from slutty, but she was also a modern woman, with modern needs. Only now that she'd had Donovan again, she realized those needs hadn't been met until, possibly, right now. In retrospect, he really overshot her expectations for a first time.

Christopher. Christopher would've been a better choice for a maiden voyage. He didn't have much length or girth, and he wasn't overly strong or confident. His body didn't bow powerfully, making each thrust a physical blow in the sweetest, most delicious way imaginable...

Unlike the man still inside her, breathing against her skin while he recovered. Donovan had an amazingly beautiful body, gorgeous eyes, and enough knowledge and experience to do whatever that last extra credit bit was, the move that had made her orgasm so hard she *still* saw stars.

She couldn't stop her next thought from coming, like she hadn't been able to stop herself from coming, she thought wryly. That thought trickled from her lips now.

"What did we do?"

"Dunno." His voice was muffled against her chest, the side of his face resting on her breast. "But if you give me fifteen minutes, we'll do it again."

Again. That'd be...gosh. *Awesome*. Her heart slammed against her rib cage. It wasn't something she should want. They should be cutting their losses. Getting dressed. Discussing what happened.

Painful words from their shared past whispered in her

mind. She ignored them. Numbly, she heard herself ask, "Fifteen minutes?"

He lifted his head, his silver-blue eyes making her feel, making her want, making her forget the past and cling to the present instead. His lips landed on hers, his longish hair tickling her cheeks.

"Ten, Scampi. Ten, tops."

He blew out a breath that tickled her stomach. She fed her fingers into his hair.

"Ten," she agreed.

Gone. She was gone for him already.

That was fast.

* * *

Sofie couldn't read the look on Faith's face at all. One of her eyes was scrunched closed, the open one dark blue and filled with judgment. Or admiration.

Or...jealousy?

Sofie lifted her arms and dropped them to her sides. "Okay I give up. Let me have it. Did I officially screw the pooch, here?" She slapped her hands to her mouth, then held them in front of her. "You know what I mean."

Faith folded slender arms over her breasts, and for a moment didn't give Sofie a single damn clue as to what she was thinking. A second and a half later, she let her have it.

"Fly free, my little bird." Faith rounded the desk, bent over Sofie's chair, and hugged her neck. When she stood, she gave an overexaggerated shrug. "I don't know why you insist on beating yourself up. You should have what you want. Everyone else in the world seems to get what they want. And no one seems to care about the consequences."

Uh-oh. This did not sound good.

Faith walked around the empty shop, her voice escalating in frustration. "Michael. Didn't Michael have what he wanted? He had Cookie. He *still* has Cookie. He's probably taking her on the cruise he bought for my birthday. And what about my mother? Doesn't Linda Shelby always get what she wants? Does she not have a way-too-young male hand model prancing around her house, lounging at her pool, drinking her beer—which makes no sense by the way because he has abs of steel. How can he drink beer?"

Oh yeah, Faith's meltdown was bad. The pressure of living with her mother had finally gotten to her. When Faith left Michael, she'd tried to find an apartment in Evergreen Cove, but the only place not too close to rental properties teeming with kids and noise and vacationers had a hellacious waiting list. Faith put her name in, but until then, she was stuck under her mother's roof.

"And what about Skylar?" Faith said, tossing her hands into the air. "My baby sister gets what she wants. Guess where I moved her when I helped her out of her boyfriend's house?"

Cautiously, Sofie asked, "Where?"

"Into her own house! *Her own house!*"

"Let me guess." Sofie crossed the room. "Your mom furnished the house. As in paid for the house?"

"Furnished as in bought furniture, and furnished as in paid for the damn house." Faith's voice went quiet, losing steam. "Here's the clincher. I can't decide why I'm so upset. If my mom offered to buy and furnish my house, I would never let her."

She wouldn't. Sofie had known Faith for a long time, and the woman was independent. Faith's mother gifted both her girls thousands of dollars each year, but Faith insisted on working. Refusing the money caused a huge rift, so Faith kept it, investing it instead. Up until recently, that nest egg was supposed to fund a wedding for her and Michael.

Faith blew out a breath. "We were talking about you. Not me. I'm sorry."

"Don't be. You've been through a lot."

A resilient smile found her friend's face. "You and Donovan did the hanky-panky. Now you're not sure if you want to do it again..." She motioned with one hand for Sofie to tell the rest.

Well, that was some conversation starter. Sofie walked to the window and watched the quiet street. May as well admit the truth.

"I want to do it again," she announced to Endless Avenue just beyond her reflection on the pane. "I want to do it again and again *and again*. He's crazy sexy, and he..." He knew how to move his body the right way to give her an orgasm propped against a washing machine. But she had some pride, and she wasn't about to tell Faith that part.

Gosh. The washing machine. Sofie had never done it anywhere other than a bed. Or the couch.

And that'd been with Donny, too.

Anyway.

Moving on.

"So what's the problem?" Faith asked when Sofie turned around to face her. "Do him. Do him while he's in town and when he leaves town you can stop doing him."

Sofie crossed her arms over her stomach. Holding on

to . . . she didn't even know what. "But isn't that stupid? If you look at our history, it's not like he was great to me seven years ago. Would I be dumb to get involved with him again?"

Faith grasped Sofie's shoulders. "Your eyes are wide open. They weren't back then. Now, you're in control. You know who Donny is, and who he isn't."

Sofie locked her arms around her stomach tighter. She knew way more about him than she used to. Part of her did feel like she knew him.

"You have the power to walk away. That's all the power you need." Faith's voice went soft, her eyes sad. "You can trust me on that."

$\mathcal{C}$HAPTER FIFTEEN

$\mathcal{R}$uby came into Make It an Event at her scheduled time, and Sofie and Faith ironed out the last of the details for the charity dinner. Ruby was pleased Sofie handled planning for the kids to be involved both at the camp-out the night before the dinner, as well as having them involved in serving and preparing the food.

Sofie contacted the caterer and arranged to have her make a trip out to Open Arms to meet the kids before the charity dinner. All volunteered of course. Thanks to Faith, who was a silver-tongued devil on the telephone. And Sofie had taken on the task of convincing Abundance Market to donate quite a bit of food for the dinner. Faith's wounds were a little fresh for her to be contacting her former workplace.

Faith stayed at the shop to finalize the plans with the decorator and get an updated headcount for the dinner.

Sofie, though it was likely the last place she should be, climbed into her car and drove to Pate Mansion.

Her best friend had made a good point about Sofie embracing her inner harlot and sleeping with Donovan while he was here. Sofie was still making up her mind about whether or not she could be that girl when she pulled into the driveway.

She got out of her car and counted two... wait, no, *three* incredibly attractive men in the backyard.

The temperature was hovering in the mid-eighties and the humidity was a million percent, making for a very hot spring. Which might explain why the three guys in the yard, their arms bare, one of them shirtless, were glistening with sweat.

It was a most beautiful sight. Shame Faith wasn't here to enjoy it with her.

Sofie stood in the driveway, keys in her palm, purse in hand, staring. But she hadn't been caught yet, so she continued to stare.

Connor wore work gloves, low-slung jeans, and instead of a shirt, a sheen of sweat shined off his broad, muscular back. He lifted a bundle of sticks tied with twine, his biceps bunching with the movement.

There was another guy she didn't recognize standing next to Donovan. He was pointing at a tall tree, a chainsaw resting on the ground next to his work boots. He was in loose cargo pants and a tee, his big arms crossed over his chest, a battered straw fedora askance on his head.

Donovan stood in a similar stance, arms crossed, tight tank top hugging the contoured muscles in his back. Battered, threadbare jeans hugged impressive thighs. Her mouth watered as her eyes tracked up to the tattoos on his arms. She was really going to have to get a closer look at those. Yesterday, she couldn't seem to take her eyes off his face...or separate her brain from the amazing sex long enough to study his tats.

As many a fantasy took root, she blinked Donovan into focus to notice he'd looked over his shoulder and caught her staring. The corner of his tempting mouth slid upward. He turned and prowled toward her in a long-legged lope she now recognized as more cautious than careless.

It was like all the things she thought she knew about him seven years ago were slanted, off-center. Her perspective had shifted. Or maybe her focus had intensified.

"Scampi. Didn't expect to see you today. Aren't you tired?"

She had started walking toward him, but stopped dead in her tracks. Did he seriously say that?

The brown-haired guy with the hat cocked a smile in her direction.

"All that painting," Donovan said, squinting in the sunlight. He smirked.

She blushed.

"Ant," Donovan called.

Ant?

The man wearing the hat paced over to them.

"Meet Sofie."

Ant closed the gap between them, arm extended. "Anthony Renaldo. Tree guy."

His huge hand clasped hers and he gave two solid pumps. He was big, wider than Donovan and almost as tall. Attractive as he was, he paled in comparison to the six-foot-four, black-haired, silver-blue-eyed, tanned man standing next to him.

As she cataloged every inch, she realized her hand was still in Ant's but she was staring at Donny. She pulled away after an unnaturally long handshake. "Nice to meet you."

Donny winked, a smile sitting on his lips. Her thighs heated.

She really was a goner.

No, you're not. You're just taking what you want. When have you ever taken what you wanted?

The only time she had was with the man she was admiring now. Things hadn't ended well for her the first time. Not at all.

But you are different now. You're stronger.

She was. But was she strong enough to endure another broken heart?

"Don't listen to him," Donny interrupted her thoughts. "Ant is a carpenter more than a tree guy."

Ant regarded the ground, looking humbled, and for such a big guy, it was kind of adorable.

"I'm just going to..." She pointed toward the house, then lifted a hand to return the wave Connor gave her from the other side of the yard. Seriously, the man candy here was bordering citation. *Penalty: Too many hot men on the field.*

Before she could embarrass herself by drooling down her shirt, she hustled inside.

What she found in the dining room surprised her. The plastic covering the floor was gone, the table and chairs back where they belonged instead of shoved against the back wall. The paint buckets were sealed and stacked in the corner of the room, the paintbrushes cleaned and lying on a towel in a neat line. She tipped her head to study the top section of the wall that needed another coat yesterday.

Wet paint gleamed.

Finished. The dining room was finished. The pictures and sconces hung, the outlet covers screwed back into the wall. She'd come back here to take care of it herself, but now there was no need.

"Thought you might be too tired to come in today."

She turned to find Donovan leaning in the doorway separating the kitchen and dining room. "That's the second time you said that." She walked a few steps closer to him, his magnetic pull too much to resist. "I can't help but think you might be referring to what happened"— she tilted her head toward the direction of the utility room—"yesterday."

A sinister, downright sexy smile curled his lips. "Don't know what you're talking about."

"Don't you?" Oh yeah, her resolve was melting like ice cream under hot, hot fudge.

He pushed off the door frame and came to her in three strides.

Really hot.

When he reached her, he dipped his head, capturing her lips in a brief, sweet kiss. And sweet was just about the only thing she didn't think she could handle from this man. She didn't have a category to file it under in her head.

"You got me," he murmured, and for a second her heart stopped. Because that's what she wanted. *Him.* He hooked a finger under her chin. "I like thinking about what we did yesterday. I liked doing it more."

His fingers left her chin to graze her neck, his body heat radiating and mingling with hers, the smell of his sweat-and-sunshine-soaked skin tickling her nose. The fight—not that there was much of it left to begin with—drained out of her.

Donny was more fun to kiss than he was to fight. She tipped her chin to accept the next kiss he offered.

"Probably don't appreciate me this close to you after working outside. Other than yesterday, been a while since I've been this close to a woman."

She felt one of her eyebrows raise. "What constitutes 'a while' in Donny Pate's world? Seven days? Twelve days? Don't tell me it's been three whole weeks?"

His lips twitched. "When'd you get that smart mouth?"

He winked again, and her knees melted. Or maybe her knees were melting because his fingers had left her neck and were currently toying with the low neckline of her shirt.

"Bit longer than three weeks," he said, fingers trickling over her collarbone. He bent to give her another kiss. Then his hands left her and he walked into the foyer. "Gonna grab a shower. Assume you'll be here a while?"

Well. She wasn't leaving now. Surely, there was something else she could do here. Too bad it wasn't within the vicinity of Donovan's shower. His eyes went from her face to her shirt, and she felt her nipples tighten as if he'd touched her.

"I'll be here," she promised.

"Good," was all he said.

She bit her lip and listened to his heavy footfalls on the stairs.

* * *

He should've invited her to join him. A shower wasn't just a shower with Sofie Martin in his house. Now that he'd stripped her bare and had driven inside of her, being under the hot water was distracting to the nth degree. Not like he'd never taken care of himself in the shower before. Sometimes he had to clean the pipes, if for no other reason than to get blood pumping back to his brain.

His stint of celibacy over, all he could think about was sex. Not just sex, but sex with Scampi.

Right about now, felt like he'd lost fifty IQ points.

He scrubbed quickly, ignoring the twitch of his dick, attempting to keep his hands moving rather than settle on any one area. A swipe here, a wash there, just enough to get himself soaped up and wiped down.

Old habits died hard.

Once there, he wrapped his hand around his shaft. He squeezed, giving himself one slow, sudsy stroke...then another.

Thoughts of Sofie filled his mind. Her parted lips, sensual sighs, the way she'd made s'mores sound sexy in the wrongest way...

He blew out a breath and flattened both palms on the back wall of the shower. When he bent his head into the stream, he took in several deep breaths through his mouth. Hot water streamed down his face, flooded over his eyes, and soaked his hair.

Suck it up, Pate.

But that thought introduced new imagery into his head—a head already filled with images of Sofie. Memories of her bare nipple tightening on his tongue, the way she moved like silk beneath his hands, sinking into her warm, wet puss—

A sharp knock on the bathroom made him jerk.

He pulled his face from the water. "Yeah," he called, wiping his eyes and pushing his hair back. "Hang on."

One last rinse, and he turned off the shower. He stepped out, running the towel over his hair quickly, over his body just as quickly, before wrapping it around his waist. He pulled open the door, the lust he was feeling a second earlier evaporating into the atmosphere.

"Connor," he said flatly.

His buddy gave him a knowing grin. "Sorry to disappoint you."

Donovan pushed past him and stepped into the master bedroom, digging in his dresser for fresh clothes. He'd given up the suitcases earlier this week. Seemed ridiculous to continue digging through bags when he wasn't going anywhere for a while. He pushed the drawer shut. "Get it straightened out?"

"Ant doesn't want paid," Connor said.

Ant had come by to help remove some of the brush and dead tree limbs for the campout the night before the charity dinner. Connor was only one guy, and clearing a big enough space for that many kids required more manpower than just him and Donovan.

"Yeah, well, I'm paying you both." Donovan stuffed his legs into jeans and pulled them up, tossing the towel on the floor after his ass was covered.

He hadn't gotten a bed for this bedroom yet, but he did find a blowup mattress. It was not comfortable, but ten times better than sleeping on the springy red sofa in the library downstairs.

"I appreciate you guys wanting to donate your time but I have money set aside to handle the house. No sense in being noble to a fault."

"You know I would do it for free."

Donovan slapped his friend's shoulder. "I know you would. I'm not asking you to." He reached for the T-shirt next and pulled it on.

"Fine," Connor said. "I'll donate what you give me to Open Arms. Those kids deserve better than their shithole parents."

On that, they agreed. "Planning on making a sizable donation myself."

Connor nodded, his lips pressed into a thin line. "My father called. Cabinet installation in Somerset."

Somerset was a neighboring town, not far from Evergreen Cove. But Donovan knew the short drive wasn't why Connor was upset. He was upset because his father had a way of mixing guilt and obligation like a cocktail and serving it straight up Connor's ass.

"Hate to leave you high and dry." Connor's mouth pulled into a deeper frown.

"Do what you gotta do, man. You know the timeline."

Hell, he knew Connor wouldn't leave him high and dry. He was loyal. That loyalty likely the reason why Connor insisted on helping him. Without him, Donovan would be more behind on getting the house ready. And he'd already been stuck here long enough.

Sofie's face flashed in his mind. If he hadn't been stuck here, he would have missed out on yesterday. On this morning. On seeing her again, period. He pushed the thought away.

He had a job to do, and when it was done, he was gone. He may have agreed to do extra, to see the preparation for the charity dinner through, but after, he was going back to New York.

Distracting brunette or not.

* * *

Donovan had returned to the great room to work on the fireplace after he and Ant finished in the backyard. He'd heard Sofie on her cell phone earlier, her voice filtering into the hallway. Just as well she was working, he could use an excuse for a diversion himself. Thanks to a fresh heap of sexual frustration.

Easier to forget he had primal urges after having denied himself for so long. Now on the surface, they were proving harder and harder to ignore.

No pun intended.

On the bright side, the fireplace was coming along. The rocks he'd excavated at the quarry, and a few Evan had found, fit nicely into the design. So far Donovan had managed to reface the entire right side. Progress.

"Looks good."

Sofie strode into the room and his breath caught in his chest. It had been a long while since anyone hitched his breath. Since anyone had taken him by surprise at all.

Just her. Just yesterday. When she let him kiss her, and then pulled her shirt off over her head in an invitation he hadn't been able to refuse.

Do me?

There went the twitch coming from his pants again. He'd forgotten how much it was like having an untrained stallion running free in there. Horse out of the barn, it wouldn't stay still.

Whoa, fella.

He pushed to standing and faced her, subtly adjusting himself as he did. "Gives me something to do."

Besides picture you naked and under me.

"I'm done"—she pointed over her shoulder to the direction of the ballroom—"making the floor plan in there." She pushed her hair off her face and wound it behind her ear in a nervous gesture. He liked that. A lot. He hadn't been out of the game long enough to forget that when a woman touched her hair around a guy, it meant she liked him. Good news for him.

And Shadowfax, down there.

"I wanted to come in and..." She waved a hand in an uncomfortable gesture. Then she blew out a breath, her shoulders sagging. "Okay, I'm not going to lie about why I came in here." She looked everywhere in the room but at him.

"I'll bite." He let the offer hang.

She didn't miss his attempt at a cheesy joke. Tilting her head to one side, her mouth pulled into an expression more indecision than humor.

"I came in here to talk about what happened...on the washer." She winced, clearly uncomfortable bringing it up.

Should've seen this coming. The big talk about how she didn't want to keep doing what he knew damn well they both wanted to do. He'd let her have this discussion. Frankly, he owed her that. Talking her into sex wasn't on his agenda this time around.

Ever again.

Didn't mean he wouldn't get in as many preemptive strikes as possible. "Did you sleep well?"

That threw her. She blinked a few times as he ambled over to her.

"Did I . . . y-yes. I did sleep well."

In front of her now, he touched her face, knowing it would unevenly stack the deck in his favor. He tipped her chin and rested his other hand on to her hip. "Me too. On a shitty air mattress. In a house I hate. Have you to thank."

Her brows bowed in sympathy. His Scampi. So fucking sweet.

He let go of her, scrubbing his face before pulling both hands through his hair. He pushed it off his face, but it fell over his forehead anyway. "Hell, I can't do this."

He hated himself for saying it, but later he wouldn't. Because giving her an out was the right thing to do.

Maybe.

"Do what?" Her voice was a barely discernible whisper.

He backed up a few steps and collapsed into a big, gold chair, unearthing a few months' worth of dust mites in the process. He rubbed his nose when he spoke. "Scampi, you wanna walk away, and I am not going to argue. I don't want that, but I deserve that. More than that. Hell, I know—"

"No."

He lifted his head, elbows perched on his knees, words he hadn't wanted to say still sitting on his tongue. She stood over him, reversing their roles, forcing him to lift his chin to look up at her. All that flowing mahogany hair, T-shirt hugging her body, the womanly flare of her hips leading down to an ass he wanted to take a bite out of . . . God. *Gorgeous.*

"I don't want to walk away." She stepped closer and

parted his knees, wedging her legs between them, lining up his face with her stomach.

"No?"

"No," she whispered.

Testing her claim, he lifted his hands, watching in wonder when she didn't smack him away. She let him grab her hips and tug her toward him. Willingly, her muscles loose and accommodating. He didn't feel the tiniest bit of resistance. He liked that she wanted him to touch her. It was one thing for him to trust himself, a whole other for her to trust him.

Her fingers fed into his hair, no longer damp from his shower. "How long are you staying?"

"'Til I get done." Not the most forthright answer, but it was the truth. He didn't specify what he'd have to get done doing, leaving himself an escape hatch.

More old habits.

"Okay." She didn't flinch, didn't ask him to clarify, which bothered him.

He didn't like that it bothered him.

Her hands moved from his hair to his hands, still at home on her hips. "I figure while you're here, we could... satisfy our curiosity."

He swallowed around a lump in his throat, her offer humbling him. "You sure about that? I'm pretty curious."

Clutching his hands into fists at the waistband of her pants, he tugged her closer. She had to lean forward and put her palms on his shoulders to keep from falling into him. The tips of her hair tickled his face, turned up at a severe angle since she was leaning over him.

"I'm happy to satisfy your curiosity," she said down to him, a sexy lilt in her voice. "And after the charity dinner, I'll be done. That will be the end of assignments from Gertrude. That will be the end of my needing the mansion."

The end of them.

Her fingers brushed the hair out of his eyes. "Straight through, right?" The honesty in her green eyes flayed him.

But he didn't argue. "That's my motto."

Her lips came down to meet his in a soft, slow, wet, light-his-pants-on-fire kiss. His eyes sank closed. *God.* Her taste. So sweet. It'd been twenty-four long hours since he'd had her tongue in his mouth. After seven years had nearly driven him out of his mind.

He threaded his hand into her hair, the fingers of his other hand cupping her ass and pulling her into his lap.

She straddled him, one knee on each side of his thighs, settling over him. He moved his hand from her hair and put both hands on her butt, holding her tightly against him and grinding against her through his pants and hers.

"Too many clothes," he said around another kiss.

"Is anyone here?" she asked.

"Don't care."

"Connor—"

"Gone." Maybe. Who cared? Another kiss, with tongue.

"Ant?"

"Gone."

He pushed a palm under the hem of her T-shirt. Her skin was baby soft, her ribs expanding with the next breath she drew.

"Do me," he murmured into her mouth, his tongue sliding along the length of hers and causing his hips to buck.

She smiled, and when she did, his lips glanced off her teeth, which was sexy in the weirdest way. Everything about her was sexy. Everything about her made him think of sex, sex with her, and where he wanted to have sex with her.

Her tone was cute, playful when she said, "You're making fun of me."

He kissed her bottom lip and tugged it gently with his teeth, capping it with a soft kiss. "I would never," he lied.

Lifting the material, he exposed her flat stomach, adorable belly button, and bra. White with tiny blue flowers on it.

"I used to be a lace man, Scampi, but you make cotton sexy."

A sultry laugh tumbled from her lips. He felt it under his palms, both of which he'd wrapped around her ribs in an attempt to get her upper half undressed. "Like I told you yesterday, I already said yes. There's no need for flattery."

Thumbs brushed over the bra and she gasped. "How about I flatter you because I want to."

And he did want to. It'd been a long time since he'd allowed himself to say anything suggestive to a woman. Sofie struck him as a woman who didn't hear it often enough. Crying shame, that.

While they were together, he wasn't holding back on the compliments.

He tugged her shirt off and watched as her wavy brown hair fell over her shoulders. The bra went next. "Front clasp. I approve."

He freed her gorgeous breasts, peach with pink tips—reminding him of the fancy desserts served at the snooty parties in the Hamptons. Raspberries on sorbet.

He wasted no time taking a taste. Suckling one while he thumbed the other. She arched against him, riding his hard-on and making him grunt.

Self-control has left the building.

Reluctantly, but before he went too far and couldn't think at all, he pulled his mouth off her delectable body and cursed under his breath.

"What's wrong?" Her eyes were wide, her palms resting on his shoulders, those perfectly delicious breasts in his face. Nothing. Absolutely nothing was wrong with half-naked Scampi straddling his johnson.

Unless they wanted to go further.

"Sweetheart." He shook his head and tore his eyes away from her chest to look into her eyes. "No condoms."

The way her shoulders sank told him she hadn't planned ahead, either. "I didn't decide about us until I saw you outside earlier." Looking slightly guilty, she added, "You're sexy when you're sweaty."

He dropped his forehead between her breasts and let out a dry chuckle. Her fingertips slipped into the back of his hair, her touch making him tingle from scalp to balls. It was the best feeling of his life. Cruel because he couldn't act on it, but awesome all the same.

"Ironically," he said, "I'm relieved you don't have a huge stash of rubbers to pull from."

"Excuse me." She gave his hair a sharp yank and drew his face back so he was looking up at her. "I believe of the two of us, you are the one who has round-the-clock care for your privates."

He felt his lips curve. He liked her feisty. Cupping her ass with both hands, he stood, lifting her as he did. A narrow table stood behind the sofa in front of the fireplace he'd been repairing. He carried her there while she held on to his shoulders, plopping her down on the surface.

"You flatter me with how much you think I get laid," he told her.

If she only knew.

She peeled his T-shirt over his chest, which was as high as her arms went. He helped her, taking his shirt the rest of the way off. When his chest was bared, her lips landed on his ribs, her tongue darting out and wetting his skin.

His hand went to her hair as her mouth moved on his body. He forced a breath between his teeth.

"We can do other condom-less things," she suggested, sucking his skin as her lips moved across his chest. Her fingers dipped into the waistband of his jeans, her tongue mimicking the motion she had in mind. His hips thrust forward involuntarily.

It took a dose of superhuman strength, but he managed to reroute her lips to his.

"Nope, that's not on the docket, babe." He kissed her lips, her throat, and down to her bare chest. Her bra, open, still hung on her shoulders. He tossed it aside.

"Why not?"

Because I'll come like a freight train and pass out instantly.

"Because I said so."

"I need to know..." She sighed as he pulled a nipple into his mouth again. "For safety reasons..." Her breath stuttered from her lips; losing control already. "How many since me?"

He pushed his hand between her legs, parting her pants-covered thighs. She grasped his face, he thought to guide him, until she yanked his head up, robbing him of the breast he was happily working.

"Donny," she said, her face serious.

Too serious.

Resting his hand on her thigh, he watched her gorgeous mouth form two words, and that's when he knew he was screwed.

And not in the fun way.

CHAPTER SIXTEEN

$\mathscr{B}$allpark me."

He felt his eyelids narrow as he took her in. She was asking this... why?

"Important all of a sudden," he grumbled.

Her lips went tight.

He guessed she was asking because there were no condoms, and she wanted to play without one. That thought made him hard in an instant—could split a tree with the erection raging in his pants—but the risk was too great to get her pregnant.

"I'm on the pill."

Correction: *now* he could split a tree with the erection in his pants.

"And I can promise you, uh..." Her gaze skittered around the room before she met his eyes. "I'm clean. Are you?"

In that manner? Squeaky.

"I'd trust you if you said you were," she said. "You wouldn't lie to me about that, right?"

He wouldn't lie.

"I was also curious...wondering who I've been measuring up to since then." She shrugged, her luscious breasts rising and falling with the movement. "That's fair, right?"

"Clean, Scampi." He stroked her ribs with his thumbs, wanting to kiss her again and abandon this conversation entirely. "Could eat off me."

Her cheeks colored and a small smile found her face. But she wasn't done yet.

"I've had four lovers since you, bringing my grand total to five." She held up her hand in front of his face and wiggled her fingers. "Lame, I know. But that's the truth."

Silence ate into the conversation. Her brows lifted as she waited.

He sighed, straightened some. "Zero or one hundred, Scampi, what's it matter?"

"A hundred?" She would latch on to that number. Zero was too unbelievable. Hell, it was true and he didn't believe it.

He laughed, but it wasn't funny. "No, sweetheart. Not a hundred."

* * *

Not a hundred.

Zero was impossible. One hundred was improbable. She hoped.

So, she guessed that was sort of comforting. But why did it matter? Why did she need to know now? Knowing would only make her think of the faceless, nameless women Donovan had bedded. And might make him think of them, too.

Plus, she'd already announced they were biding time until he left. Wasn't like they were permanent. Pain crept into her chest and she willed it away.

What does it matter?

It doesn't, she decided, focusing instead on what he'd said before that.

Could eat off me.

Mmm. She could.

Rough hands moved up and down her torso and this time, Sofie raised her ankles, crossed them over his back, and pulled him closer. His lips twitched with surprise. Probably thinking he was off the hook.

He was.

Getting him to say a number, admit there was even one girl in his bed since her, hurt her in a way that wasn't logical. Because she wasn't going to be with Donovan forever. She was going to be with him now. And hopefully a few more times before he left town. Once he was gone, he could go be with fifty more women—at once if he wanted.

He wouldn't be her concern.

There was a certain freedom in knowing he was leaving. She thought about Faith's speech about power, understanding her point. Caring was powerful. But not caring? That was just as powerful—maybe more. Sofie could use a dab of power to fortify her resolve. A whole truckload.

"There's no one now. No one but you," he said.

"Same," she returned.

He teased her with a kiss. "No more Scott Torsett?"

A chuckle tumbled in her throat. "Not unless I want to see his nose broken next time I see him."

"Naw." Donovan kissed her jaw, then a path down her neck. "I was going to break his fingers."

That shouldn't be sexy. But it so was.

She had Donovan until he went back to New York. He'd leave like he did last time, but at least she knew he was leaving. She knew now, knew going in. That was something.

That was everything.

Tilting her head, she let his lips work down her neck, to her collarbone, until he took her breast in his mouth again. She arched her back, sensations electrocuting her limbs as she squirmed on the narrow table he'd plunked her onto.

"Hope this holds me," she muttered absently.

He let her go, his lips leaving her skin, his expression *not* happy.

"You think you're fat for some reason, and I'm telling you, Scampi, it's starting to piss me off."

"I didn't say I was fat. But I know I'm not built like Faith."

"No. Neither am I."

Grasping her thighs, he spun her so she was lying lengthwise on the table, unbuttoned her pants, and drew down the zipper.

"Donny."

"Let me look at how beautiful you are."

Leaning on her elbows, she allowed him to tug her pants off, stunned absolutely speechless. Beautiful? She'd been told she had pretty hair. She'd been called cute. And her aunt Kay always told her she had a "healthy" build. Sofie knew she wasn't obese, but she also knew in the hip/butt area, she could stand to drop a few inches.

But beautiful? Donny was beautiful. Practically a work of art. But her?

"Do you mean that?" she asked.

He tossed her pants aside and reached for her panties. She watched his eyes wander up and down her body. In response, her skin tightened.

"You don't believe me?"

"I—"

"Zero." His eyes left hers as he worked her panties down her legs. "Do you believe that?"

"Zero?" Surely he couldn't mean...

Climbing halfway up her body, he flattened his palms on the table and got in her face. "You, Sofia Martin. *You* are who I've had in the seven years since I've had you. Yesterday in the laundry room. And here, in about ten seconds."

Her mouth dropped open, went dry. She blinked.

"Lie back."

"Donny—"

His fingers found her folds and stroked, long and slow. She was wet in an instant.

"Scampi. Lie back."

Over her, his hair tickled her face and neck and chest while he kissed her body, his fingers wandering, slipping, sliding.

Sofie decided to let it go. To let the whole thing go. If he was lying about her being beautiful or that she was the last person he'd slept with, things would be almost simpler. She couldn't handle that information right now.

Didn't know what to do with it. Problem was, she didn't
think he was lying.

While he worked her into a lather, she panted her
approval. Moving her hands to his pants, she undid them
and reached inside.

A brief male grunt came from his perfect mouth.

"Explains why you were trying to hold out," she said.

His tongue delved into her belly button and she nearly
shot off the table.

"Building endurance takes practice," came his heated
breath on her skin.

He was getting really close to—oh no. Not that. With
her free hand, she moved his head back up her body.

"Not there." She was not mentally ready for *that*. His
face between her legs was so . . . so . . . personal.

Donny didn't argue, only continued to move his talented fingers between her legs, relocating his tongue to
her breast.

After many panting, pleading moments, she clutched.
He didn't let up until she threw her head back and climaxed,
mind dissolving, her every muscle tensing. Only when he
moved his mouth on hers did she come back to herself and
realize her hand was still in his pants. She gave him a gentle squeeze. His penis throbbed, no doubt painfully.

"You," she said weakly, coming back down from yet
another amazing orgasm. *Wow.* He was spoiling her.

"If you insist." He kissed her.

Oh, she insisted. Turning on her side, she wrapped him
in one hand, stroking him while he hovered over her. A
few minutes later, he found his own release, both hands
flat on the table on either side of her. The sheer force of his
reaction blew her away—the way his entire body coiled.

The way his lips froze over hers, open and letting loose a deep, reverent sigh. The way the muscles in his arms, the tendons in his neck, tightened. The way his long, black eyelashes cast shadows on his cheeks.

Continuing to stroke him long after he'd let go, she basked in the awe of the hold she had on him.

He snagged her arm to stop her movements. His eyes opened. He licked his lips, his voice a broken whisper when he spoke.

"Damn, woman."

She smiled.

Power. She had it.

He dropped his head on her chest, bent over her for several long seconds. She'd buckled his knees. Again. *Amazing.* Unable to keep from it, she stroked his hair, feeling his breath on her stomach like she did yesterday.

"We do it on appliances and furniture," she pointed out.

"No bed."

Her fingers stilled in his hair. "You don't have a bed?"

Standing, he took her hands and helped her off the table. He grabbed up his T-shirt, turning his back while he cleaned himself up, then zipped his pants.

"Not staying."

There it was.

The undeniable truth said out loud. Echoing through the great room while she clasped her bra, turned her underwear right side out and put them on.

"You'll be here a while, though," she mumbled.

Where was her shirt? She pulled on her pants, snapped them, then her shirt appeared in front of her face. A second later, a third voice sliced into the air.

"Good God."

The voice from the doorway startled Sofie so much, she yipped. Actually yipped.

Connor stood in the threshold, palm over his eyes. "You need to start putting a sock on the doorknob, man."

"My house," Donovan answered as Sofie hid behind him and scrambled into her shirt.

She arranged her hair and stepped out from behind Donovan. "Safe."

Connor dropped his hand from his eyes and gave Sofie a perfunctory glance. "Dog needs dinner."

"Gertie," Sofie corrected.

"*Dog's* food is in the utility room." Donovan's eyes slid to hers.

"Yeah. About that. Not that I overheard much yesterday, but the hallway to the indoor greenhouse is attached to the utility room and—"

Yesterday. The utility room. No, no. This was not good. Sofie knew from the heat infusing her cheeks her complexion was a hectic mess of red and pink.

"In your defense," Connor told her with a crooked grin, "I like s'mores."

She hid her face in her palms.

"You're a dick," Donovan told him, but he sounded like he was smiling.

Damn male pride.

"I need dinner, too," Connor said.

"Leftover lasagna in the fridge."

Yep, carry on. Meanwhile, I'll just stand here and die of embarrassment.

"Got it." Connor snapped his fingers and Gertie, who'd poked her nose into the room, followed on his heels. At least from what Sofie could see from between her parted fingers.

Donovan pulled her hands away from her face and tugged her close. "Dinner?"

Like she could sit across from Connor McClain knowing he'd seen her in her bra today, and had *heard* her moaning yesterday.

"No, I uh, I've got to get back."

"Okay."

No argument. But what did she expect? Her tender heart ached. And that, she decided, was something she would not tolerate. The moment her "feelings" entered the equation, she needed to knock them off and move along, little doggie.

"Working here tomorrow?" His voice was calm, face placid, clearly not sharing her plight of too much thought.

"In my office," she said through a thick layer of disappointment. She really didn't want to come back to reality yet. But that was all there was. The reality of a very big project intermixed with the knowledge Donovan Pate hadn't slept with a single person in seven years.

Gosh. Why not?

Frustrated because she was still overthinking, she scrubbed her forehead with one hand. "I have to call about a dozen people, finalize plans with the party decorator, give the caterer the final count, and nail down that darned DJ." She dropped her hand and rolled her eyes. "Not to mention—"

Donovan's mouth came down hard on hers. She caught his angled jaw with her hands and accepted his tongue, her worries dissipating with each sensual slide. By the time she was clawing his back for more, she had to pull back to take a breath.

"That help you forget your problems?" His voice was low and rumbly, his firm lips damp.

Her hand had come to rest on his chest. His heart thumped against her palm. "Yeah."

He kissed her again. "Rain check on doing me," he said against her lips.

How was he this sexy? So consistently? Losing the battle of worry and shame, she smiled. "Thought that's what I just did."

"Appreciate it, Scampi, but I want all of you next time."

Next time. She liked the sound of that.

Too much.

* * *

"Incoming," Faith said at the same time the bell dinged over Make It an Event's front door.

Sofie turned, coffee cup in hand, to see Donovan stride in on those long legs of his. Every inch of him looked good enough to eat, and she would know since she went to bed last night starving for him.

Sad, but true. She had *so* jumped from frying pan to fire.

Standing, she allowed her eyes to graze his charcoal gray T-shirt, cut in a *V* over the smattering of chest hair she'd admired yesterday. His long, black hair brushed his cheekbones and tickled his collar, matching thick lashes dipping over a pair of ghostly eyes that didn't miss a thing.

He was a beautiful, beautiful man.

"Gets better-looking every day," Faith said between her teeth.

No kidding.

"Hey, Scampi. Faith." He came deeper into the room until he got to Sofie's desk. "Busy?"

She looked down at the piles of paperwork, then glanced

at her computer at fifty unread e-mails. A *ding* sounded. Fifty-one. Before she could say a word, Faith stood from her chair.

"She's not busy at all. I was about to take over for her so she can have the rest of the day off."

Her friend, the liar. "*Faith*."

Donovan's eyebrows rose slightly, and his gaze tracked from Sofie to her friend.

Faith grinned to beat all. "Go, go. Don't worry about a thing." She waved her hands frantically, then physically pushed Sofie closer to him.

As if Sofie needed help in that endeavor.

Nervously, Sofie straightened her skirt and her shirt. "I can take a break for a . . . a while, I guess. What did you have in mind?"

His smile nearly floored her. She wanted to kiss that smile so badly, and if she had less self-respect, she might throw her arms around his neck and lay one on him right here, right now.

"You'll see," was all he said. He took her hand and pulled her to the door.

$\mathcal{C}$ HAPTER SEVENTEEN

$\mathcal{W}$ hen Donovan came back to Evergreen Cove, the mansion didn't feel like home at all. But the quarry, with the tall rock face he used to scale, and the piles of quartz, limestone, and other rocks he picked through, was as familiar and comfortable to him as any home could be.

The day was overcast, unlike yesterday when the sun blazed hot and the air was almost too humid to breathe. The wind cut the humidity in half, and the cloudy skies were gray and forlorn, but didn't look like rain.

Dog was loving life, poking around the rocks and sticking her nose into every crevice and crack. Donovan took Sofie home to change before he brought her here, and instructed her to wear sturdy shoes. She'd need them for wandering through all this rock. She looked cute, too, in her double tank tops, cotton shorts, and tennis shoes with short socks. He shook his head. Those legs and that round ass—he couldn't get enough.

"This place is so cool. I can't believe I didn't know this was here." She looked left, then right, her long ponytail brushing her shoulders.

Before he could think about why he was doing it, he reached for her hand, pulled her close, and dropped a kiss on her lips.

They parted and she smiled up at him. "What was that for?"

"Glad you're playing hooky with me." Glad, about anything, was a new feeling, but he was in his element so it sort of made sense.

"What are you searching for?"

"Rocks."

"Ha-ha. I mean what *kind* of rocks. Can I help?"

"Probably not. I'm picky. I have a design in mind for the fireplace in the great room." He slid her a glance. "You remember the great room."

Her smile was pretty, almost modest. He knew better. She wasn't as innocent as she liked to pretend. With him, anyway, which made his chest puff with pride.

"Know the right pieces when I see them," he said, dropping her hand. "It's like a puzzle."

"Like you," she said.

He bent to pick up a piece of limestone, rough, but flat. "No, Scampi. I'm not the kind of puzzle you want to figure out." In an odd way, it flattered him she'd thought to try.

They continued picking, Donovan dropping rocks into a box he'd brought along for that purpose. Sofie hadn't contributed any, proving pickier than him.

"Hey." She knelt about three feet away from him and lifted a stone. "This one kind of looks like a heart."

It did. A jagged, imperfect heart. Like his? Poetic.

"It's not very smooth though." She wrinkled her nose and started to put it back down.

"In the box," he muttered quietly. Maybe it had a place in his design.

Maybe? Denial much?

The rock Sofie had found was a piece—possibly *the* piece—he'd been looking for. He could picture exactly where it fit. Not making a big deal of it, she dropped it into the box, dusted her hands on her shorts, and stood.

He pulled his bottom lip under his teeth and whistled. Dog's head shot up and she tracked over to where he stood. "Don't cut that paw again," he told the mutt. Bending, he scratched her ears when she sidled up to him.

The dog leaned against his leg, content to be petted. She'd put on some weight, and her hair had started coming in thicker. Must be the gourmet, three-dollar-a-pound food he'd purchased at the pet shop.

Well, she deserved it. Any dog put through her paces the way this one had been deserved a little spoiling.

He was smiling down at her panting face when Sofie spoke. "What are you going to do with her when you leave?"

Something he preferred not to think about. He continued scrubbing Dog's head. "I'm sure I can find her a home."

Probably should start asking around. He wasn't keeping her and knew finding the right fit for the stray wouldn't be easy. He was gonna be particular about Dog's new home. Make sure she found a family who would keep her for good.

He patted her flank with a few solid thumps. Her tail beat his leg.

"So what did people do here?" Sofie asked, stepping around the boulder Evan sat on the other day.

"Dig. Most of the rock was mined for construction projects, I'd guess. Roofing, flooring, countertops, that sort of thing." Donovan pointed at a small body of water beyond a large pile of rock. "Deeper you dig, more water you find. When it's active, they pump the water out. When it's abandoned, you get a lake."

"This place is bigger than I thought it'd be."

"Forty acres. Give or take."

When he was a kid, he'd sneak out here and risk getting caught by Colin Rink, the man who owned the quarry and the attached golf course. Donovan suspected Colin knew he was out here, busting up rocks and climbing the rock face he and Sofie stepped up to now. The old guy never stopped him.

"Used to be a lock on the fence to keep out trespassers." He tipped his head and took in the scale of the wall, hardly able to believe he'd attempted to climb to the top. "Gone now. Guess the kids have better things to do than come here and screw around."

He'd climbed the wall a time or two, pushing himself until the fear melted away. Fear was a pussy. Lost its power when challenged.

Like with his dad. After Donovan stood up to him once or twice, he was no longer scared of him. Didn't mean his old man quit hitting him, but Donovan got better at enduring it. And learned not to cry.

"Do people ever climb this wall?" Sofie's hand found his, squeezing his fingers. He lifted her hand and kissed her knuckles.

"Some people." He dropped her hand and walked three feet to the right, finding a familiar hold he thought he'd forgotten. But no, it was still there. He tucked his fingers into the crevice and found another hold above that one with his left hand.

His left leg automatically found a piece of jutting rock. His right followed, finding another.

"What are you doing?" She sounded worried. *Cute*. He wasn't used to anybody worrying about him.

He hoisted himself using his arms, the familiar burn lighting his biceps. Been a while since he'd hauled himself up a wall using only arm strength. He balanced, grabbed another bit of rock. His foot found the next perch like he'd climbed the face yesterday. Not much had changed about this place. From what he could see, no big chunks had chipped off or eroded away. The sheet of rock where he used to come to forget was as intact as when he'd last scaled it.

He did fall once, back in the day. Broke his ankle. Gertrude turned a blind eye, which hadn't surprised him. No matter the injury, cut, or bruise, she preferred to pretend Donovan was fine. Admitting he was hurt meant seeing Robert Pate for the tyrant he was, and Gertrude refused to see her precious son in any light other than a false, shining one.

At that same spot, he looked over his shoulder. Sofie held her hands over her mouth in prayer pose, fingers laced together as if she might start praying then and there.

"I'm very impressed," she called as Dog made her way to stand next to her, tongue lolling. "Now will you please come down here, so I won't have to call an ambulance to splint your leg when you fall?"

He grinned at her before turning back to the rock.

"So damn sweet," he said to himself. He hauled himself up another two or three feet, feeling the exhilaration, the shot of adrenaline course through his veins.

The next hold he reached for crumbled to dust under his hand. He grunted a curse as bits of the now-obliterated rock pinged off the wall he hung from. Losing his stability caused his arm to swing behind him, threatening his already precarious balance. Biceps burning, he held fast with the hand thankfully still anchored to the wall.

"Donny!" Sofie gasped, and repeated her plea for him to come down.

He blew out a breath through pursed lips as he carefully shifted his foot to brace his weight on his left side, the fingers on that hand aching, arm muscles beginning to shake. He prayed the bit of rock he clung to held him until he could get his balance.

It did.

Bending awkwardly, he dug the fingers of his right hand into a hold several feet below, knowing his weight was unevenly distributed. With more solid footing than before, he risked a quick look down at Sofie's fear-filled green eyes, and gave her a smile and a wink.

Her expression hinted her fear had receded some, and that's what he'd been going for.

"Please come down," she said. "I'll do whatever you want."

The promise was almost enough to make him jump. Broken ankle be damned. Adjusting his hold, he stepped down another few feet, peeking over his shoulder as he did. For her benefit, he raised an eyebrow.

"Whatever I want?"

She dropped the prayer pose and crossed her arms over her chest. "Come down here without brain damage, and we'll talk."

So fucking cute.

A minute later, he was on the ground, leaping the two feet and wiping chafed palms on his jeans. No cuts. Nice.

He inclined his head, finding the spot where the rock had given beneath his hand. No wonder she was scared. It was way up there. Stupid to try to climb without gear, given the risk. But Sofie had never seen him climb. And he'd never shied away from risk.

Broken bones healed. Scars could be hidden. Impressing a woman was fleeting. He had to grab the opportunity when he could.

"I believe you said 'whatever' I want," he told her, stepping in front of her.

She shook her head, but her smile was undeniable. He liked how much she wanted him. He wanted her right back.

"Fun as this has been," she said, taking her eyes off his to look around, "I have a very big, very involved charity dinner to plan. Don't you have a mansion to get ready?"

Smartass. He opened his mouth to retaliate, when his text chime dinged from his phone. He checked the screen. Connor.

"Was going to take you to lunch," he told her, still frowning at his phone. He needed to get back after all.

Shit.

"You were?" she asked.

He tried not to be insulted by her surprised tone. "No way to talk you out of work and into coming with me?"

She shook her head, but the only reason her refusal didn't hurt as much as it could've was because she looked like she didn't want to go back to work. "There's so much to do."

"Okay." He whistled for Dog, and she came obediently to his side. No leash needed.

As they paced back to Trixie, Sofie said, "I'm scheduling something at the mansion with the caterer. Probably for Wednesday. Does that work for you?"

He opened her door for her. Wednesday would work. And would give him time to get something else ready. "You got a key, Scampi."

She was free to come and go as she pleased. What he wanted was for her to come way more often.

And yeah, he meant that in every way imaginable.

* * *

"*Holy shit.*"

When Connor texted him at the quarry asking how soon he could get to the mansion, Donovan assumed he had a question about the grounds. Then he'd arrived home and Connor met him in the driveway.

"Follow me," he'd said, eyebrow cocked.

Donovan had followed him through the backyard, around the side of the house, and through an open door leading behind the utility room to the maid's quarters and beyond.

Then he'd followed him into the recently renovated indoor greenhouse. Connor had done a good job cleaning out the massive space. The cluster of shelving formerly filled with home décor and boxes of collectables had been cleared. They were now lined with pots of all sizes.

Or had been.

Donovan gaped at the mess and repeated, "Holy shit."

Several pots were busted and lay in a terra cotta heap, their seedlings lying like dead bodies on the ground. One shelf leaned back against the wall, lucky it hadn't fallen in the other direction and busted out the window.

In the center of the mess stood a doe, probably not full grown, but definitely not a fawn. Her wide, brown eyes were panicked, her nose wet and dripping.

"How the hell did it get in here?" he asked, keeping his voice low. Evidently an earlier panic attack had caused the mess he was looking at now.

"Left the door open while I was carrying in the wood." Keeping his hand gestures subtle, Connor pointed to the half-built flowerbed dominating the room. The raised bed looked about six by eight feet, not yet nailed together, boards held together by clamps. "When I found her in here, she freaked out."

Which meant the deer walked in through the outside door, through the hall, and into the greenhouse.

Eyes on Donovan, her tongue came out and licked her face.

"Okay. So we get her out." Couldn't be too hard.

"Without her destroying my seedlings."

That might be harder. He surveyed the shelves again. If she started bucking, she could shatter the window and cut herself to shreds in the process.

"Apples," Donovan said. "What if we leave a trail of apples and let her find her way out? We can wait outside and watch her leave."

"That's it? Leave a trail of apples?"

"You want to go in after her?" Donovan took a half step into the room and the deer backed into a shelf she hadn't yet overturned. Pots wobbled on its surface.

Connor stayed Donovan with one hand. "Okay, okay. Apples."

An hour later, Connor and Donovan were perched on top of a picnic table just out of sight of the door where a fat and very happy deer should be exiting any moment now.

Annny moment now . . .

"Hope she's not in there eating your lavender," Donovan said, swallowing the end of his beer. He dug a fresh one from the ice in the cooler.

Connor held out a palm and accepted it. "Deer don't like lavender."

"Lucky you." Donovan uncapped a beer and rested on his knees, watching the door. When he was about to give up, a black nose poked out of the doorway, lifted, and smelled the air.

"Jackpot," Connor whispered.

The doe stepped out, sniffed the air again, and left the mansion. When she turned her head and noticed the two men watching her, her ears fanned out to the side. Dark eyes studied them silently for a few seconds before she broke into a run for the trees.

Donovan blew out a breath. "Least we didn't have to shoot it."

Connor chuckled, mirroring Donovan's pose, elbows on his knees, beer bottle resting in his hands. "Like you would've shot it."

"I wouldn't have," he agreed. "Would have been a hell of a mess."

Another chuckle made him bristle. Connor took a swig of his beer. "You act like such a hardass. When really, you have this gentle touch." He held his index finger and thumb together and motioned like he was pricking the air. "So soft."

"Happy to black one of your eyes for you and prove

you wrong." He wouldn't, though. Connor may have been the one friend Donovan hadn't tussled with. By the time they met, his preferred method of self-destruction was whiskey.

Connor's good humor vanished when he looked Donovan dead in the eye. "You know the best way to handle a deer in your house, and an injured stray dog, because you know what it feels like to be afraid. To be cornered. To have no way out."

His childhood wasn't something he talked about much, but Connor knew. And Evan—apparently. Connor was one of his closest friends, and when he'd started staying in Donovan's apartment, they'd had a shitload of personal conversations.

Among them, Donovan's father.

Donovan took a long drink of beer and looked at the house again.

"I didn't know what to do," Connor said. "I just rushed in. My fault the doe made confetti out of half my planters." He shook his head.

"I'll buy you new ones."

"You'll kiss my ass."

Donovan swallowed a smile. "No deal."

Silence gathered in the air between them.

"You need a cornhole game or something," Connor said half a beer later. "Boring as shit out here."

"Cornhole," Donovan grunted.

"What's the matter, Pate? Cornhole too lowbrow for you? Been up on the East Coast living champagne wishes and caviar dreams for so long, you've forgotten your roots?" Connor slid off the table and put his beer bottle down.

"You suggesting I've gone soft?"

"As a marshmallow." Connor put up his fists.

Donovan drained his beer in a few long guzzles and hopped off the table as well. "You think because you have arms like telephone poles you can kick my ass, but you forget how scrappy I am."

"Nothing above the neck. I might try to get a date with your girlfriend's cute friend soon."

He was supposed to react to "girlfriend," but Donovan refused. He lifted his arms. "Faith's too classy for a grunt like you."

"Always was," Connor agreed, nodding. "Not going to stop me from trying, though."

Donovan rushed him, hitting Connor's torso. Solid as the rock he climbed today. When his buddy trapped him around the neck and spun him out, Donny's shoulder throbbed from the hit.

"That was easy," Connor bragged.

But Donovan wasn't done. He swept his friend's leg, dropping him to his ass. Arm over his chest, he held Connor down. "Had enough?"

Connor shook his head and grinned. "Loser has to clean up after the deer."

"Deal."

Donovan was thrown to the ground a second later, but nowhere near giving up.

After wrestling and trading places pinning the other to the ground several times, they rolled to their backs to catch their breath.

"Tie," Donovan said, exhausted.

"You forfeiting?" Connor asked, sounding equally exhausted.

"Hell, no."

"Neither am I."

They smiled over at each other.

God, he'd missed his friends. Connor was right about him being in New York for too long. No one there knew anything about him other than the loner workaholic he'd shown them. But Evan knew him. Connor knew him. Asher, too, wherever that son of a bitch was hiding.

It hadn't occurred to Donovan how important it was to be around people who knew his crap. People who knew him through and through. His relationships in New York seemed shallow in comparison.

Not that he'd admit any of his thoughts out loud. "Arm wrestling?" he suggested.

"Beer chugging?"

"Sounds better than cornhole."

Connor laughed, pushed himself off the ground, and offered a hand. Donovan accepted, but when his friend leaned over him, he used that hand to send Connor tumbling into the grass.

Rookie.

CHAPTER EIGHTEEN

"All set then?" Gloria Shields stood, her red nails pressed onto the edge of Sofie's desk. The woman was a force to be reckoned with—Sofie had noticed when she met the literary agent last year. If anything, Gloria's intensity had only increased.

Glo represented both Evan Downey and Asher Knight for their *Mad Cow* children's books. She'd also arranged to have a special print run and donate hundreds of copies to Open Arms.

They'd discussed the charity dinner, the books, the signing where Evan and Asher would set up, but Sofie had one more favor to ask. She'd been trying to get her courage up to ask before now, but failed. She was running out of time.

Sofie made scribbly lines on her desk calendar, took a breath, and said, "I know you don't really handle Asher's music career, but I'm having trouble nailing down a DJ. Do you think he might—"

"I don't handle it." Gloria's eyes were as hard as the sapphires they resembled. She flicked her silken black hair off one shoulder and sniffed.

Something had gone down between those two in the Cove last year when Asher was in town working on the second book with Evan. Charlie had told Sofie about how Asher and Gloria were lovey-dovey one minute, and at each other's throats the next.

Sofie shuffled some papers. "Of course, I'm sorry to ask."

Gloria peeled a Post-it note from the pad on the desk and fished a pen out of the cup on the corner. "Here's his personal cell. He has a scheduling manager, but she's an insipid twit. He gives you hell for calling him personally, tell them I told you to do it. It's a good charity. And if Asher has a scrap of self-worth, he'll say yes without too much argument."

Sofie accepted the Post-it note with a cautious smile. "Will you be in town long?"

"Leaving late tomorrow." Sharp, blue eyes trained on Sofie. "Why?"

Because Gloria looked like she needed a drink. Maybe two.

"Wine night at Charlie's studio tonight," Sofie said. Charlie, who had moved in with Evan, had kept her house on the beach, using it as her photography office-slash-studio. Her back porch was enormous and perfect for entertaining. Perfect for Girls Night Out.

Faith stepped into the office from the back room and said, "Oh, that would be great. I'll pick out a new bottle of wine. We had so much fun on the boat with you last year. I'm sure Charlie would be excited to have you."

"That's sweet." Gloria looked as if she might offer a polite "no" behind that statement, but surprised Sofie by asking, "What time?"

* * *

Charlie threw the best Girls Nights Out ever.

A cool breeze blew off the lake, framed by the plantation-style back porch. Appetizers covered an outside table, dressed in a flowered tablecloth with matching seat cushions. Hummus and chips, a vegetable platter, and courtesy of Faith, Devil Dogs for everyone. The dessert had become something of a tradition since she introduced them to Charlie last year.

Fat-packed goodness of layered chocolate cake, cream filling, and dark chocolate coating proved to be too good an indulgence for any of them to pass up.

Sofie, Faith, and Charlie had already started on the wine when Gloria rounded the back of the house, making her entrance.

"I know you told me not to bring anything, but I happened to find my best friend in need of a break." Gloria tugged a woman with midlength wavy red hair alongside her. The redhead lifted a hand and gave a bashful wave.

"I hope that's okay." But Glo's smile insisted she knew it was more than okay.

"Kimber!" Charlie exclaimed, rushing off her porch to close the redhead in her arms. "How? What are you doing here?"

"She has a very wealthy husband who put her on a plane immediately when I called and told her about wine night," Glo said.

"Are you staying?" Charlie asked.

"Not for long," Kimber said. "Gloria and I are flying back to Chicago tomorrow."

The three of them scaled the steps to the porch. "Faith, Sofie. Kimber Downey. Landon's wife," Charlie introduced.

Sofie had heard of Evan's oldest brother, Landon. He was a Chicago-based ad executive who married family friend Kimber after an unexpected twist of events. Charlie and Evan had busted out their cell phones to show Sofie pictures last Christmas. The unexpected twist? Their son, the adorable Caleb Downey.

After a round of introductions, hugs, and compliments on Kimber's attire—finds from her Chicago-based clothing stores—the ladies circled the table, filled their glasses, and the gossip began.

"I think a date at the quarry is romantic," Charlie said after Faith spilled the proverbial beans about Donovan coming to pick Sofie up at her shop.

"Not romantic. We were just...hanging out," she said, her eyes on her wineglass. "I need a refill for this discussion."

Faith obliged her.

"Sounds like you're in deep, Sofie." This from Kimber, who probably knew what she was talking about. She'd mentioned how all she'd done was agree to a nanny position with Landon to watch Lyon for a week. After that week, she and Landon agreed to a list of "extracurricular bedroom activities"—her words—that ended with a surprise neither of them had anticipated: love.

"I thought Landon and I were keeping things casual, but I quickly learned sex is anything but casual." Kimber elbowed Gloria. "I knew I was right."

Glo held out her palms. "I admit I'm horrible at giving advice to other people. I'm better at giving advice to myself."

"And the advice you are currently giving yourself?" Charlie fished.

Glo sat up straight in her chair and lifted her glass. "Never bed the bad boy and expect him to change."

Faith raised her glass. "I can drink to that. Michael wasn't exactly a bad boy, but a 'good' boy doesn't cheat on his fiancée, now does he?"

They toasted the inarguable fact.

Charlie held up a finger to make her point. "Evan is a bad boy, but in the right ways."

Kimber smiled. "Mm-hmm. And Landon's emotions were buried until I unearthed them." Those two *cheers*ed next. "Just goes to show, sometimes, a bad boy can bring out the best in you."

While Gloria and Faith scoffed, and Kimber and Charlie playfully argued their point, Sofie sipped her glass, feeling very alone, and a little worried. Looked like this thing with Donovan could go one of two ways for her.

Was Donovan still cut-and-run like Ash, or ready for a fresh future, like Evan?

Was Sofie more like Glo, embittered to the point of giving up, or Charlie, who embraced the second chance and was happier for it?

Time knew. But it'd be a while before it told.

* * *

By week's end, Donovan was making himself at home. *Apparently*, he thought, having just watched the movers set up the king-size bed in the master bedroom.

With all the junk he'd been hauling out of the base-ment, and all the bending he'd been doing over the fire-place in the great room, he needed a better place to sleep than a crappy air mattress or a springy couch.

His and Connor's impromptu wrestling match hadn't helped, either. Connor was younger than him, so the bas-tard bounced back instantly. Meanwhile, Donovan iced his shoulder and wondered when the hell the new aches and pains had started.

Al, the head delivery guy for Cozy Home, sliced the plastic off the mattress with an expertise that only came from moving mattresses for a living. He wasn't a small guy, with a sizable gut and a black brace wrapped around his lower back. Nor was he young. Donovan put him at fifty or fifty-five, and that was being generous.

"All set, Mr. Pate." Al extended a beefy mitt, and Don-ovan shook his hand. "I'll see myself out."

"Thanks." Donovan stood over the newly delivered bed dominating the room. The room could hold it—it was the master suite, after all—but he'd also ordered a big-ass bed. At his height he wasn't risking his feet hanging off the end. And after many restless nights, he was ready for a good night's sleep. He'd like to fall into it now. But he couldn't.

A reporter was coming today from *The Evergreen Gazette*. Sofie called this morning to give him a heads-up. She'd come by on Wednesday as promised, to meet with the caterer, but he'd been out. Got home as she was fol-lowing the woman to her car. Other than a wave over her shoulder, he hadn't seen or talked to her for a week.

Until this morning. His heart had hit his gut when his phone rang with a local number. Connor never called—didn't need to call since he was here all the freaking time—so Donovan figured it was Scampi. He answered, and Sofie told him the paper wanted to do a piece on the mansion for the charity dinner.

He'd be lying if he said he wasn't looking forward to it if only to get to see her again. Sighing, he turned and found Connor in the doorway.

"We won't have everything done today," Connor said. Ant had come out to help with some last-minute yard cleanup. The indoor greenhouse had been cleaned up, too, by Connor since he conceded the wrestling match. To be fair, Donovan had tried to warn Connor he was scrappier than he looked. "But the yard will be photo ready by the time the paper gets here. No worries."

"Not worried." Donovan knew things would come together. Plus, Charlie was taking the photos and he trusted her to shoot the place in its best light.

His friend's eyes cut past him. "Giant mattress."

"Huge."

Connor gave him a shit-eating grin. "You bought her a bed."

"Piss off. I bought *a* bed."

"To sleep with her in."

More than sleep … if I can get her to stay. Laying Sofie on the table in the great room, boosting her up on the washer—both fun. But Donovan was sick of fighting one structural impediment or another. He wanted to lay her down and take the time to do the things he wanted to do to her.

And there were a lot of things.

"Lotta room to groove," Connor put in.

"Don't you have something to mulch?" Donovan grumbled.

"Yeah, yeah." He turned to leave.

Donovan followed, but before he flipped off the lights, he studied that big, spacious bed again. And thought of Sofie on it.

Acres of room to groove.

With a smile of his own, he closed the door.

* * *

Sofie arrived an hour before the reporter was due to show. She wore her best navy blue pencil skirt and a tight, but not too tight, white shirt with beaded navy blue, silver, and white jewelry around her neck, wrists, and dangling from her ears. Her hair was up, her heels were tall, and she was ready to kick some reporter butt.

Theoretically. Robin from the *Gazette* loved the idea of the mansion pairing with Open Arms. He wanted nothing more than for the dinner to be a success. Charlie, who often took pictures for the paper, had the idea to call them, and Ruby had given her wholehearted approval. The last link in the chain had been Donovan, who had agreed with nary an arm twist.

Sofie stepped out of her car and took a deep breath as she scanned the grounds. She was pleased with what she saw. And not only because Anthony Renaldo was back there buzzing through a tree trunk with a chainsaw, sawdust stuck to the sweat on his arms, hands, and dotting his longish hair sticking out from beneath his ever-present Fedora.

The passenger side door opened and closed. "Who the heck is that?" Faith asked, awe prevalent in her voice. "Oh, wait. You told me about him. He has a bug name or something."

"Ant," Sofie said with a laugh.

"Yes, that's right."

"Don't even pretend you're not looking for your landscaper. He's here, don't worry."

Charlie pulled her car into the driveway and parked, waving as she did.

Faith tugged her sunglasses from her face and rested them on her head. "I'm here to support *you*," she told Sofie. "Not look at the eye candy..." Her voice trailed off as her gaze flitted to the backyard where Connor walked into view.

Uh-huh. Sure she was. Sofie clucked her tongue. "He is not a fan of wearing a shirt, is he?"

"No, he is not," Faith murmured.

Charlie, camera in hand, stood next to Faith. "Would it be wrong for me to snap a few candids of these guys? You know, for practice."

"Only if you promise to blow one up poster size for my bedroom," Faith quipped.

Sofie shook her head at her friends, but couldn't blame them. When did the Cove suddenly fill to overflowing with man candy?

Delicious as these two were, her thoughts went to her own sweet piece—*dark, salty, sweet Donovan*.

She headed for the mansion's front door, waving to Faith and Charlie to follow.

CHAPTER NINETEEN

*L*ongest. Interview. *Ever.*

Four hours later, Sofie had just about enough of smiling. She was a cheerful person, but the pressure of representing Open Arms and the stress of making sure she smiled enough for both her and Donovan had taken a lot of face muscles.

Robin Derringer, reporter for the *Gazette*, finally showed signs of slowing. Around her height, he was short for a man, with dusty blond hair gone half-gray. His nose was large but regal, his teeth white but not too white. He was a powder keg of energy. About a half an hour ago, Sofie wondered if the interview might last until dark.

They'd covered most of the thirteen-thousand-square-foot mansion, Charlie alongside them snapping photo after photo. Several rooms weren't camera ready, but there was no shortage of rooms that were. After traipsing through the inside, their group—Donny included—walked the entirety of the grounds.

High heels, she had concluded, were not the best choice in footwear.

Donovan wore the smarter outfit of baggy cargo shorts, boots better suited for the long grass, and a comfy-looking V-neck shirt. Dog looked equally smashing, wearing a red bandanna around her neck, her hair brushed and fluffed courtesy of Faith's talented hand.

Faith left earlier. About an hour into the interview, she tracked Sofie down to let her know Skylar had an emergency of sorts—an ex-boyfriend emergency. Even though Faith had rolled her eyes, Sofie could see she was worried about her sister. Without hesitation, Sofie handed over her car keys.

Connor and Anthony had also vanished while they toured the inside. Just as well. Two dirty, sweaty, and yeah, okay, *sexy* guys traipsing around shirtless would be a fine photo if they were publishing a calendar, but for the newspaper...not so much.

The photos Charlie took now—of Dog, at Robin's request—were going to be the perfect attention-grabber for the article. Sun shined on glossy fur, Dog perched on her back haunches, pink tongue panting, bandanna bright against her white-and-brown hair. She looked happy. An absolute showstopper with the mansion in the background.

Charlie smiled from behind her camera. "She's going to win so many hearts!"

Without a doubt. She'd won Sofie's already.

Donovan stood, arms over his chest, and watched the photography session with mild interest. In what she hoped was a subtle move, Sofie slipped out of her Manolo Blahniks and flexed her toes in the cool, thick grass. *Ahh*, so much better.

"What's the pup's name?" Robin asked, pencil at the ready over the notebook he'd been scribbling in all day. "For the photo caption."

Donovan exchanged looks with Sofie, who stayed quiet. His black eyebrows lifted slightly.

Not knowing whether she should say "Dog" or "Gertie," Sofie hedged. "She's, um, she's a rescue. Donovan found her out back and nursed her back to health."

Robin's pencil moved furiously over the pad. "She was injured?"

"And starving," she added.

"You have veterinary training, Mr. Pate?" the reporter teased.

Donovan's face stayed rigid. "Patched myself more times than I can count. Masonry is dangerous business."

Masonry. Sofie felt her heart pinch. She knew the truth. He'd patched up more than injuries occurring on the job.

"Will the pup be attending the charity dinner?" Robin asked. "Seems friendly." He watched Donovan, waiting for an answer.

"That's Sofie's area of expertise."

It was?

"Oh, um. No, probably not the formal dinner." She smiled brightly. The dog was well behaved but the fancy dinner was no place for her. "She will be attending the campout the night before. Some of the kids relate better to animals than they do people," she said, remembering what one of the counselors told her. Charlie lowered her camera and Sofie stroked Gertie's head. "People have let those kids down. Open Arms often uses animals in the facility to get the quieter kids to open up."

"That's great. Great stuff, Sofie." Robin wrote in his notebook. He looked up when he was finished. "Article will run in the next week or two. I'll shoot you an e-mail when we have the slot finalized."

"Thank you, Robin." She extended a hand and he took it, his smile revealing an attractive fan of crow's feet on either side of his eyes.

Charlie flipped through the photos in the camera, head down as she shuffled through the grass to where they were standing. "I think we have everything. I'll get these organized and e-mailed over to you," she told Robin. "By Monday?"

"Perfect." Robin nodded at her and then turned back to Sofie and Donovan. "Oh, the dog's name?"

There was an unnaturally long pause hovering in the air between them. A pause that shouldn't be there. The question was simple enough. A rescued dog, clearly at home at the mansion, obviously had a name. Technically, the dog *did* have a name. But by Donovan's silence, he must have realized "Dog" wasn't the best name to give to the newspaper. Naming a dog "Dog" made him seem either really disconnected or really dim.

And he obviously didn't want to share the name Sofie had given the pup. Because it would bring up the topic of his grandmother. Just when she was about to make something up, she heard an intake of breath over her shoulder.

"Gertie." His voice was tight, but she doubted anyone noticed.

The reporter's pencil stopped on the paper. "Gertie as in Gertrude? Like your grandmother?" Robin smiled gently, not knowing the truth about her. But then, no one knew the truth, did they? It hadn't been public knowledge the woman who should have cared for Donovan had neglected him.

Sofie would just tell Robin a white lie—that she'd blurted out the name and it stuck. "Actually—"

"Yes," Donovan interrupted. "Open Arms was important to Gertrude. And the dog showed up at the mansion the night I came back to town..."

He trailed off, and again she felt the truth of that statement spear her heart. What he told Robin was true, yet there was so much more truth buried beneath it.

"Like a sign," Robin filled.

"Right," Donovan said, but Sofie heard the flatness in his voice.

"Nice." Robin tucked his notebook away. "It's a lovely tribute."

Sofie smiled, but her heart wasn't behind it.

Robin shook Donovan's hand, then Sofie's again. Charlie said good-bye before she and Robin walked to the driveway, talking the entire way.

Once they'd climbed in their respective cars and driven down the driveway, Sofie turned to Donovan. "I'm sorry about that." Lame. But it needed to be said.

Donovan was stalking—yes, stalking—toward her, his jaw set. His eyes fierce. For a second she thought he might go on a tear about Gertie, or about Sofie's insistence to name the dog Gertie. She held up her palms to speak in her defense, but rather than get a single word out, she ended up with two handfuls of very hard, male chest.

An arm wrapped around her lower back and a hand grasped her backside. He lifted her off the ground, knocking her off balance. Her arms wrapped around his neck, her ankles around his lower back. A fraction of a second later, her mouth was accepting his tongue.

Oh. Oh, his mouth was glorious.

The kiss was slow and deep—so deep, she felt a ping between her legs as he lit her on fire again and again. So hot, she would swear the ends of her hair sizzled.

Well. This confrontation was going much better than she'd expected.

Carrying her, he walked them toward the house, Gertie jogging past them to the side door leading to the kitchen. Probably looking forward to a nap on the stack of blankets in the utility room.

Spotting her shoes still in the grass, Sofie pulled her lips from Donovan's. "My shoes."

"Don't need 'em," he replied lazily, propelling closer to the house, the hand on her back moving into her hair and pushing her lips down over his again. He worked her mouth while she clung to him like a treed cat.

"I need to get them," she panted when he gave her a chance to breathe. "What if it rains?"

His eyes were not amused. Then they were. Then the corner of his mouth—which was so close she could see the stubble pressing to the surface of his skin—lifted in amusement.

"Seriously," she whispered.

"I'll buy you new ones," he countered.

Before she could argue they were clearance, or the last pair of seven-and-a-halves at Cobbler's Cove, *or* tell him the price and cause him to have a seizure, he lit her up again. That same ping and sizzle returned, this time with a vengeance she either didn't want to want or couldn't refuse.

He opened the door and carried her into the kitchen. Propping open the door with his hip, he set her on her bare feet, let Gertie pass, then followed behind her.

Fading sunlight filled the kitchen, shining warm orange and yellow on Donovan's face. His pale eyes held a certain spark, making him look like a heavenly body. He had one of those, too, she thought, eyes tracking down his tattooed arms.

Hadn't she been about to do something? Oh, right. Her shoes. She took a step to the door. "It'll only take a second—"

He reached for her and quelled the flow of words yet again, his mouth plundering hers, and more putting her panties in danger of getting wet than her precious shoes.

"Argue with me again," he dared, his hands sliding around to her butt and cupping it.

"No, thank you."

His lips lifted again and she had to mentally restrain her heart from doing the same. Gloria's words from wine night—though slurred—rang in her ears. Had Sofie bedded the bad boy expecting him to change?

Of course she had. Even now she found herself hoping he'd stay in the Cove instead of leave when this charity dinner was over.

Donovan, his hand linked with hers, walked from the kitchen to the dining room and into the foyer. She floated behind him, the promise of what she guessed was more kisses carrying her on the air.

Which...was a very bad idea.

"I should get out of here," she said in a last feeble attempt to keep her heart intact. "Can you still take me home?"

The plan after she'd relinquished her car keys was for Donovan to drive her home. She thought back to something Faith said when Sofie had excused herself to get her purse in the foyer, leaving Robin, Charlie, and Donovan chatting in the ballroom.

Her friend's hand had closed around the key ring and she offered one parting piece of advice. "Don't let Glo scare you."

"What are you—"

"Donovan isn't Asher. I can see how much you like him. How much he likes you."

Which was so *not* what Sofie had needed to hear.

Had Faith's earlier comment given her hope? Softened Sofie's heart to room-temperature butter? She really should leave, if for no other reason than to preserve her sanity. But she was stuck here unless Donovan agreed to take her home.

Since he hadn't answered her yet, she tried again. "Give me a second to get my things." She started for the library but didn't get far.

Before she knew what had happened, her back was flat against the front door, braced there by Donovan's body.

He didn't kiss her, only trained his eyes on hers. "What happened?"

"Pardon?"

"I made you come on the washer," he blurted without preamble.

She blinked at him. *Oh-kay.*

"I made you come on the table."

"Donovan..."

"You avoided me for a week."

All true.

"I was busy. Not avoiding you," she responded quietly.

"Thinking I should've lied and told you there were a hundred."

He meant girls since her.

"No." She shook her head. "You shouldn't have."

"Would've been easier than zero." His voice was low and edgy, his glare burning through her. "Getting laid a hundred times over would've been easier than coming in my hand with your name on my lips for the past seven years."

Was she supposed to be...flattered by that admission? She wasn't. Her mouth dropped open, her blood pressure skyrocketing.

"I never asked you to...to...do that. You're the one who left town."

"You're the one who took me out of the game," he bit out.

This time the fire burning within was from anger. Well, he wasn't the only one who had a grievance. "Oh, you were so gone for me, you instructed me to, and I quote, 'get the fuck' out of your car?"

His cool eyes flamed. "Scampi."

"Care to have a repeat of that night? You can drop me at my apartment instead of a parking lot this time. After that, feel free to get back to those *hundreds* of women you'd like to bang."

"*Scampi.*"

"I never asked you to make me the last of your conquests, Donny. Were you waiting for me to forgive you? Fine. I forgive you." She waved a hand. "Go forth! Get back in the saddle, cowboy."

She pushed against his chest. Which was as successful as moving a stone wall.

He continued hovering and glaring. Giving up on getting past him and back through the house, she clutched the doorknob behind her, intending to slip outside. She didn't make it. He caught her arm and tossed her over his shoulder while she held the waistband of his shorts. Blood rushed to her head, her hair swinging as he carried her up the stairs.

"This is ridiculous!" she shouted, voice jarring with every step he took.

"Tell me about it," came his calm response.

At the top of the stairs, he turned, opened a door, and plopped her on her feet. Her head spun as the blood drained from her face and settled elsewhere. Donovan flipped on the light. They were in a bedroom. A very big bedroom with a very big bed, covered with a gray and black comforter, and four pillows. The massive black headboard took up most of the wall behind it.

Donny stood sentry in front of the bed, anger rolling off him in waves, yet he still managed to be the sexiest thing she'd ever seen. No one wore dark and dangerous quite the way he did.

He jerked his chin toward the bed. "Get in. And take off your clothes."

"No."

One of his eyes twitched. "You don't get in that bed, Scampi, I swear..."

What. *Ever.*

Huffing, she crossed her arms. "You listen to me, Donovan Pate—"

"Bed." He pointed. "Now."

Her hands went to her hips, brushing over her skirt. The prim and proper blouse she'd chosen slinked over her body, turning her on. Or maybe it was the demanding man ordering her around who was turning her on.

Swallowing thickly, she tried to sound angry but her voice held a tremor of excitement she hoped he didn't hear. "And if I don't obey... What are you going to do, spank me?"

"Never," he growled.

It took her a second to get why that one word was lined with disgust... then she did get it. Of course he'd never.

His eyes went to her necklace. "Leave the jewelry on."

Her argument wasn't an argument at all, instead two weakly spoken words. "Excuse me?"

His lips twitched, the anger fizzling out of his expression. "Maybe I should get your shoes."

"Donny!"

He fingered the small plastic tab of the zipper on the side of her skirt.

"You said you would drive me home." But she didn't want to go home anymore. *Weak. So weak.*

A thin *zip!* sounded as he undid her skirt in one swipe. "I will."

"I... I can't stay," she reiterated, in case he tried to talk her out of leaving. She was overwhelmed. Her heart... her head. So overwhelmed.

"You want to."

She did. If she were being honest with herself, she wanted to stay. Her hands came up, trickled down his shirt, across his firm chest, and over the bumps of his abs. "I can't."

"You're staying."

"Shouldn't we—"

Donovan's lips slammed over hers.

"You can't take it back," he said when he tore his mouth away.

Her fingers had tightened into fists, clasping his shirt, holding him to her. The man could *kiss*.

"Take what back?" she breathed, feeling the flush of her cheeks.

"Your body. *Mine*."

He pushed her skirt past her hips, his hands curving over her bare thighs, then traveling beneath her silky blouse and brushing the skin at her waist.

"I can take it back." Her argument was as thin as her last breath.

"Yeah. You can." He flattened his palms against her bare back and pulled her against his hard-on. "But don't."

He was asking. Asking her not to leave him. Asking her to stay with him. How could she refuse? This close to him, his hands on her, she couldn't refuse him. And she didn't want to.

His hands left her skin to undo one of the buttons of her blouse, then he palmed her jaw and said, "Continue."

She licked her lips and slipped the next button out of the hole, her own hands shaking with excitement.

He kissed her cheek and whispered against her temple, his voice low. "Another."

She continued to strip, earning a kiss after each one. When she ran out of buttons, he instructed, "Take it off."

The silk brushed her upper arms, coating her body in a layer of goose bumps. Shirt off, she stood in the center of the bedroom in a snow-white bra and matching high-cut panties.

His gaze danced over her skin, taking in every inch of her while she nervously chewed her lip. He met her eyes. Something reverent crossed his face.

"Scampi."

Exposed. She was so exposed. She balled her fists at her sides.

He grinned, a wide, genuine, gorgeous grin.

"Stay the night with me."

Her heart thudded. Blood rushed through her veins. She wanted to stay. So, so much. Rather than argue or try to be rational, she gave into the promise of his wicked grin.

"Okay."

CHAPTER TWENTY

Hallelujah. Donovan had never considered himself a religious man, but hearing Sofie agree to stay made him believe in the Almighty.

Scampi looked like an angel, reddish-brown waves whirling around soft shoulders, powder-white panties and bra making her appear pure and beautiful. Her simple answer of "okay" had granted his wish: time to explore every last inch of her. The way he'd wanted since he first saw her in her shop on Endless Avenue.

They stood in front of the bed, but before he threw her onto it, his hands went to her round, plush bottom. "I love your ass."

"So I've gathered," she said, her dry tone suggesting she didn't love his attention on this part of her anatomy.

Too bad.

He pulled her close. "I'd like to bend you over, see

these cheeks in the air in front of me. You'd better get used to the idea of me looking at it."

He wanted her that way. Wanted those contours and curves bouncing off his hips while he drove deep. His dick gave an insistent pulse.

Her smile was shy. "I don't think so, buddy."

He'd see about that.

When she reached for the blankets he grasped her wrist. Her brows came down in confusion.

"Naked," he told her.

"Let me cover up, then I'll get naked."

From what he could see, from what he *had* seen of Sofie, every inch of her was as gorgeous as the next. Body issues were her own neurosis.

"You could see what I see," he told her, "you wouldn't take that away from me, either."

She opened her mouth to argue.

He cut her off. "Seven years, Scampi. Give a guy a break."

Her lips flattened. "Now you're trying to coerce me."

"Is it working?" He smiled.

She smiled back. Yeah, it was working.

"We'll go slow," he promised. "Bra."

Biting her lip, she gave him a wary look before reaching around her back. A moment later, the cups of her bra loosened.

"*Slow*," he reminded her. "First one strap, then the other."

She slid one strap from her shoulder before crossing her arm over her body to slide the other strap off, too. His throat went dry. He wondered if it was possible to die of anticipation. But this wasn't about him. This was about Sofie. She needed to reveal herself, to stop hiding, to trust him with her body. Every part of it, especially the parts she viewed as imperfect.

He suffered no such delusions. Perfection was often found in imperfection. Like the jagged pieces of rock in the fireplaces he built, fitting together as one beautiful whole.

Her hands cupped her bra to her breasts. But there'd be no hiding. Not anymore.

He nodded his encouragement. She let the material fall away. Nipples yet to chill in the mansion's cool air stood soft, begging for his tongue. He resisted.

"Now the rest," he said, his voice tight with lust, his hard-on straining against his fly.

"What about you?" Her voice the only sound in the room other than his pounding pulse.

"I'm next."

"Why do I have to go first?"

He caught her hands before she could cover herself. "Scampi."

She gave up the fight. "*Fine.*"

"Yes, you are."

She rolled her eyes.

"Panties." He released her hands and crossed his arms, watching her openly. "*Slowly.*"

She slipped her fingers into the waistband, which had the side effect of pushing her breasts out. *Nice.* Wiggling, she pushed down one side, then the other. His heart rate ratcheted as he watched her supple body shift and move. His eyes latched on to where her thighs met. He balled his hands into fists, aching to touch her.

Not yet.

"I feel silly," she said.

"You look sexy." He stepped forward and replaced her hands with his, sliding them into the back of her panties, around and over her bottom, gripping those cheeks in his hands. "Beautiful."

Her fingers went to the hem of his T-shirt and raised the edge a second before her warm touch abraded his skin. "You have a rain check to cash in."

Like he needed reminding?

"Trying to."

She hauled his shirt halfway up his chest, then ran her fingers along the words etched over his rib cage. His abs tightened as she read, "We live with the scars we choose."

Before she could ask what it meant, he leaned down and kissed her. She pressed her almost-naked body against his bared chest and moved her hands from his torso to his neck.

He took his hands from her bottom and pushed her onto the bed and followed her in. One hand on the small of her back, he inched her up, crawling with her until her head hit the pillows.

"There. That's better." His knee went between her legs, his mouth fusing with hers, before leaving her breathless and taking a nipple to his tongue.

"I'm not naked yet," she panted.

He groaned, not speaking since his mouth was full.

Her hands went to his hair, kneading the top of his head. Moving down, he slid his tongue over her ribs, over her belly button. When he attempted to sink lower, she clamped her legs shut.

He looked up to find her giving him a shaky smile. For some reason, she didn't want his face between her legs.

He guessed this was another of her body hang-ups. She'd stopped him when he tried this in the great room, too.

"You don't want me to kiss you here?" he asked.

Her throat moved as she swallowed. She shook her head no. But he didn't believe her.

As a test, he lowered his head again. She squirmed but her thighs relaxed the slightest bit. He lowered his lips and pressed a kiss over the top of her panties. Her hips bucked.

Proof she didn't know what she wanted. But her body did.

He pressed a second kiss right over her sweet spot, opened his mouth and breathed hot, knowing she felt that breath beneath the material. Knowing, because he dragged a plea from her throat.

A tight, high, "*Donny.*"

Sounded like a yes to him.

He moved her panties to one side, took a short, but appreciative, gander at what lay before him, then dove in. Tongue first.

* * *

Sofie's back arched. She had no idea how long he'd been down there—long enough to lick every protestation from her brain. At first, she'd been uncomfortable, having never been able to relax enough to enjoy…um…*that*.

Now, she was clawing the sheets, eyes scrunched closed, helpless sounds eking from her throat along with each truncated, strangled breath. Donovan, as it turned out, was incredibly skilled at what he was doing. And what he was doing was drawing her to the very edge of a cliff she never would have voluntarily stood on.

Then he pushed her over.

"Oh, oh God!" she shouted, actually *shouted*. Her entire body tightened like a drawn bowstring, then released, every nerve ending pulsating, light bursting behind her eyelids. He moved up her body, pressing kisses to her thighs, her stomach, her ribs, breasts, and finally to her still-open mouth.

"Need to know if you're good with no condom, Scampi."

Lazily, she opened her eyes. He hovered over her, so close, his long hair tickled the sides of her face. His silver-blue eyes unerringly met hers and when his tongue came out to wet his lips her back arched again. Because his mouth: *wow*.

"Yes." She wasn't about to turn him down.

"You trust me."

She did. "I trust you."

"Open your legs and let me in," he whispered against her mouth before capturing her lips with his.

She parted her knees and he worked the snap on his shorts, sliding down the zipper and freeing his length. Without undressing, he slid inside her and Sofie's eyes rolled back into her head.

Oh-so-sensitive down there, each delicious slide echoed through her body, making her pant and plead as he stroked in and out slowly.

"Another," he said, sounding pleased. "That's what I like to hear."

She opened her eyes but rather than find him grinning cockily, when he drove into her again, his mouth dropped open as his eyes squeezed closed.

"Tight. *Jesus*, Scampi."

Every one of her limbs went rigid, froze solid. Her hands on his shoulders clutched, her fingers flinching. Pinching her eyes shut, she tried to push away the memory of a time he'd said something similar. And failed.

You're so tight, I nearly broke it off in there.

She'd never forgotten how disgusted he'd sounded. How embarrassed she felt.

"Don't," she whispered, her voice as thin as the shield she raised to protect herself now.

His palm was on her face in the space of a heartbeat. "Scampi." He stilled. "You need me to stop?"

She shook her head, eyes still shut.

"No. Don't stop. It's...it's not a big deal," she said, reassuring both of them. She opened her eyes. Forced a smile. "It's nothing."

"Lie." His upper lip curled.

He flexed his hips and drove in to the hilt, then came down on his elbows and sifted his fingers into her hair. There was no escaping him. No escaping his piercing eyes. He brushed her hair from her forehead.

"Straight through, sweetheart."

Dammit. Inhaling a breath she hoped was laced with courage, she spoke quickly. The truth this time.

"In the library. That night. You...said the same thing to me. I was humiliated," she finished on a whisper, humiliated still.

His brows bent, pale eyes flooded with regret. "Fuck."

"Yeah."

His gaze was unwavering, his body embedded in hers. "Want the truth?" he asked after a lengthy silence.

She bristled, but said, "Yeah."

"You're still tight."

A new wave of shame covered her, but he wouldn't let her look away this time.

The fingers he'd sifted into her hair anchored her in place.

"I had a lot of anger back then. So much, sometimes I shook with it." His fingertips pressed into her scalp. "At times, I felt like I was falling apart." His mouth closed over hers in a soft kiss. "Being inside you, Sofie, is like being held together."

Lost in the moment, she drank in the honesty in his face. Took in the fact there was absolutely nothing between them—no barrier between Donovan's body and her own.

"Difference was," he continued, "back then, I didn't know what to do with that feeling." The pressure lessened on her head and he massaged gently. "Your sweetness wasn't something I knew how to deal with."

"I hate being sweet. It's a nice way to say I'm weak."

"No, Scampi." He eased out of her body oh-so-slowly, taking her breath with him. "Not true." He stroked into her again, hard and thick, and grinned. "That was the sweetest sound I've ever heard. And there isn't a damn thing weak about you."

Except for where he was concerned. There, she was weak. Like wet-paper-plate weak.

Tilting his hips, he drove into her again.

"You have a decision to make, Scampi." He drew out, muddling her mind. "Slow and smooth or hard and fast?"

Given that the slow and smooth was making her feel all sorts of things she knew she shouldn't, she said, "Hard and fast."

His grin suggested he didn't mind her request.

"You got it."

He made good on both counts. And the second time he mentioned the word "tight," it sounded a lot like a compliment to her.

* * *

Sofie woke with her hand over the words tattooed on Donovan's ribs, her entire body sealed against his. Her left leg was thrown over his thigh, the bottom of her foot against the side of his foot, and her right cheek against his left shoulder.

The sun streaming through the balcony door woke her at least twenty minutes ago. She'd had several thoughts since her eyes opened. Like how she should get up, get dressed, get ready to make her day into whatever it was going to be. But she hadn't. She just lay here. Enjoying the feel of his rising and falling chest. And remembering each and every moment of what they did the night before.

Her fingers traced the ink decorating his torso. Then she moved to the ink tracking up the arm she wasn't wrapped in. Carefully so she wouldn't wake him, she shifted so she could see his face. Black hair a disaster, long lashes covering eyes she'd never forget, Donovan looked like a dark angel. There really wasn't any debate over why she'd given him her virginity.

Or why she'd fallen in bed with him last night.

Seven years ago, she had been ready to have some unscheduled fun, to do something wild with her straight-and-narrow self. He had been the answer to both desires. When the night they spent together went south, it haunted her for years, following her into her next relationships. The memories were etched deep into her skin, into her bones. And now... Well, now she didn't know how to summarize what he meant to her. She wasn't a virginal, naïve girl any longer, but neither was he the same hot-headed, angry guy.

Sighing, she flattened a hand on the center of his chest and rested her chin there, her eyes tracing the tattoos decorating his shoulder. A series of waves, indiscernible patterns, mostly shapes she couldn't make out looped up his arm.

"Morning, Scampi."

Her eyes flicked up, finding his closed. "I didn't mean to wake you."

"You did." His arm wrapped her tightly, his palm closing over one butt cheek. Lashes fluttered, and then those silver-blues were on her.

"Your eyes are beautiful." She didn't exactly mean to say that, it just sort of fell out of her mouth.

The side of his mouth frowned. "Delicate things are beautiful. Paintings, flowers." His hand squeezed her backside, cradled in his palm. "*You*."

Flattered, her cheeks warmed. She never thought of herself as beautiful—or delicate, for that matter—but somehow, he made her believe it.

"Beautiful is also how you describe things that are powerful. The ocean, a herd of wild horses..."—she tapped his chest—"*You*."

He stayed silent, searching her face for a moment, his expression indiscernible. She traced a finger over the waves on his shoulder. "You have so many."

Tilting his chin, he looked to where she pointed.

"Do they mean anything?"

"I'd like to say yes. But truth is, most of them were selected by shape and size."

She thought back to what he'd said about the tattoo on his arm, to the words emblazoned over his ribs. "Because they cover scars?"

"Yeah."

She traced a finger along his collarbone, felt the unnatural way the bone raised. That's where a serpentine line started, blending into the waves on his shoulder.

"He threw me down the stairs." Donovan smiled, but it wasn't a happy smile. "Parquet floor is harder than it looks."

She flattened her palm over the broken bone. Not trusting her voice to come out steady, she traced her fingers over to his shoulder and raised her eyebrows in question.

"Bat."

A baseball bat. Her stomach flipped. Pain flared in her chest, forcing her eyes closed. She felt his fingers in her hair a moment later and opened her eyes. He pushed the length of it over her shoulder and brushed her cheek with the back of his palm.

He'd had to be so strong as a child. Too strong.

"Don't look at me like that, Scampi."

She didn't need a mirror to know the look on her face. Hurt. Hearing details of the abuse caused by his father—the one man who should have protected him—hurt her.

Taking his hand from her face, she rubbed her finger over his star tattoo. This one was the most familiar to her—he'd had it since she met him. In her mind, the star was his defining mark.

"Past is past," he said quietly.

"Tell me." She shouldn't want to know, but the truth was his truth. Straight through was the only way out; he'd said so himself. And she wanted him out. Free.

"Sweetheart—"

"I want to know." She didn't. But she did. This was who he was.

Who he is.

He blew a long breath from his nose, then said, "My father had this pocketknife. Antique. White bone and brass handle. I borrowed it, after strict instructions never to touch his things."

Worse. This story was going to be worse than the bat or the fall to the parquet floor. She clenched her jaw, suddenly angry. His eyes met hers.

"I broke it."

"You were a kid," she said, her defense of him too little, too late. Way too late.

"He found out and decided to teach me a lesson so I'd never, ever borrow his pocketknife again."

She wanted him to say he'd accidentally cut himself but knew from his toneless voice that wasn't where this story was headed.

"It worked. I didn't."

She examined the tattoo closely. Then she saw it. Beneath the filled-in black-blue ink was a scar. White, jagged, and running the width of his index finger. She rubbed her fingertip over it. Flat, save for a raised edge between his first and middle finger.

"The bastard cut you." She felt sick. Infuriated. With no one to spew her anger at, she growled, "I hate him."

"No, sweetheart, don't give him that. He doesn't deserve any feelings from you."

Donovan's calm voice dampened the spark of her anger. He was right. Wasting energy on a man—a beast— who would harm his own child was a waste. It was better spent on the man in front of her. The man who was gentle in spite of having a million reasons not to be.

She lifted his finger, pressed a kiss to the star. "I wish I could make it better."

Hand on her lower back, arm around her, he pulled her closer and pressed his lips against hers.

"Trust me. You are." He lifted his arm and tucked it under the pillow behind his head, propping himself up, looking at her. "Bones heal. Scars fade."

"But you've immortalized yours."

He was quiet for a long time, so quiet she didn't think he was going to comment.

"My body is my life's roadmap, Scampi. Erasing those scars completely"—he shook his head—"wouldn't be right."

Plopping her chin back down onto her hand, she lay there, allowing her finger to trace the lines and ink decorating his imperfect skin. She was beginning to see what he meant about the rocks he chose for his fireplace.

There was much more beauty in imperfection than perfection.

"My shoes are still in the yard," she mumbled after a long bout of silence.

His chest shook with gentle laughter. She felt her smile as she took in the lines on either side of his mouth. His tongue darted out to wet his bottom lip as his eyes slid to hers. Bedroom eyes brimming with hot intention. Remembering how he'd loved her with his mouth last night, she squirmed, going damp between her thighs at the thought.

"Why are you laughing?" she asked, hoping to hide her reaction to him. "Is it because you have new clothes to change into, and I'm going to be stuck with the wrinkled and rumpled ensemble strewn across your bedroom floor?"

His hand was at home on her butt, his smile intact.

She flicked her eyes to the balcony. The sun was shining bright, the clock unstoppable.

"I should get out of bed." Sad, but true. "There are so many things I need to do today," she announced glumly. "So many calls..."

"Slow down." His arm tightened around her body, sliding up to her ribs. Goose bumps popped up on her naked skin. "In my world," he said, his voice a seductive murmur, "this is not how mornings go."

Her nipples pebbled at the notion she might get to find out what was under his gravelly tone.

"How do they go normally?"

"Don't want them to go the way they normally go." He gave her a sleepy smile. "Want to know how they go with you."

The breath halted in her lungs. She held it there like she could hold on to this moment. As if time would stop if she willed it to obey.

"*Normally,*" he said, "I get up, feed Dog." Gertie, hearing her other name, padded to the edge of the bed and rested her chin on the blanket. Large, pale blue eyes that matched her temporary owner's stared them down. Donovan reached out and gave her a pat. "Morning, Dog." To Sofie, he said, "I let her out, feed her. Shower, shave. Get to work on the house."

The house. So many things to do and a looming deadline for the dinner—the campout—lay before them both. She lifted her hand to rub the headache forming over one eyebrow. "I have a zillion things to do."

"You say that a lot."

"Because it's true."

"You have time, Scampi."

"I really don't."

Grabbing her up, he pulled her until she was lying on top of him, skin to skin, absolutely nothing in between them. Well, that wasn't exactly true. *Something* was between them. Something large, nestled between his legs, nudged her suggestively.

He smiled, tilted his hips. "Make time."

Dog whined low in her throat, begging for some of that time neither of them had to give. Donovan slid out from under Sofie, leaving her in bed, and threw the covers back over her body. He strutted bare-assed naked across the bedroom and shrugged into a pair of jeans while she snuggled into a pillow and enjoyed the show. Watching a worn pair of denim cover his perfect butt was almost as fun as watching him take them off.

Almost.

Shirtless, he pulled open the bedroom door and commanded, "Do not get out of that bed."

Which, of course, she ignored.

CHAPTER TWENTY-ONE

It might have been the most stunning shower she'd ever seen in her life.

Stone walls, various sprayers at varying heights, and a huge round shower head hanging right over the middle of the enclosure. There was no door, just sort of a hallway leading into the shower.

Yes, she'd gotten out of bed. She wasn't trying to be obstinate; she had to pee. On the way through the bathroom, she'd spotted the shower and was drawn to it by no fault of her own. The tub in her apartment was small, narrow, and the plug designed to stop the drain, broken.

But this massive, luxury veritable wall of water? Yeah, there was no way she was passing up the chance to get in there.

Sofie tilted her head back to rinse the shampoo out of her hair when she heard a familiar, deep voice echo off the stone.

"Thought I told you to stay put."

She pushed the water off her face and blinked, sweeping a mass of wet hair back. Donovan leaned on the edge of the shower, out of the spray's range, jeans on, shirt off. He ran a gaze—a hot, hungry gaze—down her body and up.

"Second thought, this might be better." He grinned, reaching for the waistband of his jeans. Shamelessly, she watched him undress. He did so proudly.

Guys. So secure with their bodies. They would never know what it was like to be a woman. To obsess over cellulite, bathing suit season, breast size, butt size, *shoe size* for Pete's sake. Of course, the naked man stalking toward her in the shower had nothing to be insecure about. His long, lean, marked body was perfection in the flesh. More amazing than years ago when he'd been more lanky than broad.

Donovan wasn't lanky now. His body was still lean, yes, but strong. Dips and curves and protruding muscles, laced in warm hues of red and orange and blue on the artwork on his shoulder, black and white ink decorating his arms, his hand. His ribs. His wide chest tapered down to a waist leading to those "V" thingies curving over his hips. And his *legs*. Covered with a smattering of hair, his thick thighs proved he was a runner, or at least used his legs to lift. Because seriously, those suckers were *fit*.

He stepped in the shower with her . . . well, not so much with her, as against her. He walked right into her personal space, under the cascading water, cupped her bottom in both hands, and pulled her to his chest.

She went willingly, palming his pectorals, watching water spill over the ink decorating his skin. She didn't care how he defined it. Donovan Pate was *beautiful*.

"You owe me an apology." He backed them out of the overhead spray, but water shot out of every wall, covering her in warmth and infusing the air with steam.

She tipped her head back to study his face. He raked a hand through his hair, now damp.

"For?"

"For that." He backed away, revealing the soldier saluting her from between his legs.

She smiled, knew he was teasing. Liked him when he was teasing. Liked him with a matching easy smile on his face, rather than a formative scowl. Just *liked* him, period.

"That's not my fault." She made no effort to look away. Matter of fact, she was kind of staring.

A brief, deep chuckle rumbled from his chest, making her heart rise like a helium balloon. *Definitely*, she liked him more when he was teasing her.

"Scampi, sweetheart. Your fault."

Steam billowed, but that was only half the reason why she was hot. Warm and loose, with no immediate place to be, a drop-dead gorgeous man standing naked before her, she did believe she'd just discovered her brazen side.

"I can take care of that for you, you know," she said, her voice husky.

She'd thought his gaze was hot and hungry earlier, but that was nothing compared to now.

His eyes flared, fire in their depths. "I know." He was focused on her intently, arms surrounding her.

The ends of his wet, dark hair clung to the sides of his neck and she touched his throat, running her fingers over his chest, over his inked skin. "Did Evan do any of these?"

Blinking, probably out of the thought she'd inserted

into his head, he glided her fingers to the words on his rib cage.

"This one. And...another," he added, his voice rough.

She ran the pads of her fingers over the words, thinking about the meaning behind them. *We live with the scars we choose.* Poetic.

"Where is the other one?" She cocked her head, appreciating the way his body looked with water droplets clinging to his muscles.

He tensed beneath her touch. Just a little, but she noticed.

"Donny?"

He licked his bottom lip before he moved her hand to a spot high on his left rib cage, under his arm. Wordlessly, he palmed just behind her left breast and rubbed her tattoo with his thumb. They stood, their hands on one another, arms extended.

Her tattoo.

He couldn't mean...She moved her hand aside and revealed the tattoo on his flank. An infinity symbol.

Like hers.

The one and only bit of ink she'd had done.

A memory from years ago hit her front and center.

A light summer drizzle fell on the parking lot when Sofie left the Wharf at midnight after her shift. Donny was there, leaning back against his Jeep, cigarette between two fingers, smoke trailing through his nose.

"Scampi! Where you going, girl?"

Butterflies swarmed her stomach at the sound of his voice. Sexy, sexy Donny. Would she ever get over what his voice did to her insides? She'd worked with him just two months and already had the biggest crush on him imaginable. He scratched his nose and she spotted the star tattoo on his index finger.

Her car was parked next to his, so it made sense for her to walk in his direction.

"I got it done yesterday." She tipped her chin at his tattoo, blinking away the tiny raindrops. They'd been talking about tattoos in the kitchen last week. What she wanted and why.

"Bullshit." He grinned. "Show me."

"No way. I told you where I was getting it. You're just trying to get a free peek."

"Scampi"—serious now, he gestured to himself as smoke curled from the end of his cigarette—"who do you think you're talking to? I am a professional. I have tattoos."

He'd mentioned another on his shoulder, but she hadn't seen it. She fantasized about a quick game of I-show-you-mine-you-show-me-yours.

"I can give you my expert opinion." Even in the moonlight, she could see the silver in his eyes. Those pale, pale blue eyes she saw in her dreams the moment she closed her own each and every night.

"I don't know . . ." She flirted back, shrugging a shoulder, and what the hell—just went for it. "Maybe if you show me—"

"Fucking finally!" came a shrill female voice from behind her. Sofie turned to find Heather Conrad, her face pinched. She aimed a scathing glance at Sofie, pushed past her, and walked up to Donny. "Hey sexy, you got the stuff?" she asked him, clasping his leather jacket in one taloned fist.

"You know it, sweetcheeks." He threw an arm around Heather's neck and pulled her close.

Sofie's stomach flopped, filled with gut-wrenching envy. Sick. She was going to be sick.

He dragged Heather to his Jeep and called over his shoulder, "Later, Scampi."

Sofie snapped back to the present, brought back by the feel of Donny's rough palm on her jaw. She blinked up at him, the man in her memory feathering at the edges and evaporating into the air. Years, knowledge, and seasons separated him from the man he used to be. He wasn't the same. Neither was she.

She traced the tattoo on his left side. An infinity symbol the same as hers, but it was a universal symbol. Could be a coincidence. Probably was a coincidence.

"I got it a few years back," he told her. "Ev came out to visit, did the quote on my ribs. I had this one added at the same time."

She hadn't taken her eyes off the symbol yet. Didn't want to see his face, or embarrass herself by blurting out she'd thought for a moment his tattoo matched hers.

"Endless possibility," he said.

"*What?*" Her head snapped up, her eyes finding his.

"That's why you chose an infinity symbol. You said it represented 'endless possibility.' "

She had said that. She'd been twenty-one and so full of hope. Before she knew bad things happened to nice girls... that bad *boys* happened to nice girls.

"I never showed it to you," she muttered, almost to herself.

"Not intentionally." His fingertip rubbed the tiny tattoo on the side of her left breast. "I saw it the night in the library..." he trailed off but he didn't have to say more.

He'd had her naked that night. Mostly.

"And you...got your own?" She refused to ask the question she'd been wondering since she laid eyes on it: *Why?*

"Remember when I said my tats cover scars?"

"Oh my gosh." He couldn't mean...

There, under the spraying water, pressed against him, his fingers left her body and dug into her wet hair. He lowered his lips to hers and in a soft voice confirmed her fear.

"You are one of my scars, Sofie."

* * *

It was the truth. But not in the way she was thinking.

"The tree." He took his hand out of her hair to show her the gnarled branches crawling up his forearm. "That one was bad."

Her fingers slid through the water running down the scar hidden in the trunk of the tree. Delicately. *Sweetly.* Trying to make him hurt less, he knew.

"Few years back, I was building this outdoor fireplace

at this massive, massive mansion on the beach in the Hamptons. Twelve feet up on a ladder, I'm hauling this big-ass rock, my arm shaking, my shoulders burning."

Stupid. It was completely stupid. He should've had a spotter, much like Sofie should've had a spotter at the bottom of the ladder in the dining room the day she was painting.

"There was nothing but concrete to catch my fall," he continued. "The stone was the perfect shape for the center of the fireplace. I searched everywhere and finally found *the* rock—right size, color, the right everything. It started to slip, and I did what I could to keep from dropping it and busting it to pieces."

Sofie's eyebrows bent into a look of concern. This girl. She felt so damn much. Her thumb stroked back and forth over his skin. He wondered if she knew she was doing it; if she knew how much he liked her hands on him.

"You could've broken your neck," she said.

"Didn't." He'd held on to the finished section of the fireplace for dear life, until his muscles shook from exertion. Until he was able to both right himself on the ladder and salvage the stone.

"Got the fucker on there," he said with pride.

She smiled up at him, in an expression that looked proud as well. She shook her head. "And cut yourself, I'm guessing?"

"Tons of stitches."

Her eyes went to his arm again.

"Poured my heart into that piece." After a silent moment, he asked, "Get it, Scampi?"

The dent between her eyebrows answered his question. She did not get it. He was going to have to spell it out.

And for a guy who wasn't used to admitting his feelings, or that he had them, he wondered for a second what he'd gotten himself into.

Sofie. Sofie was what you've gotten yourself into.

Like she was embedded under his skin, infecting him and making him feel the things he'd spent years teaching himself not to feel.

He touched his hand to her infinity tattoo again. "Not all scars are bad memories."

She locked her arms around his neck and tugged his face down to meet hers. Then her lips were on his, slanting over his mouth and kissing him deeply while he sought purchase on her hips. Her tongue plundered, tangled with his as rivulets of water ran into his ears, down his throat, and dripped from his lips to hers. She tasted minty from toothpaste, and like Sofie—like hope, and care, and every part of her was turning him on.

He didn't think, only reacted. Reacted to the way she pressed her body against his, the way all her soft, warm flesh felt under his kneading palms. She freed one hand and reached for his cock, stroking him slowly. His mouth dropped open and for a moment he forgot how to work his tongue.

"Want you." She stroked him again.

His arms were steel around her as he pushed her back against the smooth, tiled wall of the shower. Both hands cupping her ass, he pried his lips off hers to turn his head. There was a sprayer in here that should be just the right height for what he wanted...

Finding it, he slid her down the wall a few inches until—

"Oh!" Her eyes flew open, her butt cheeks clinching beneath his palms.

"Stay there. Lean back," he instructed.

Watching him with wide green eyes, she did as she was told, which was amazing, because she never did anything he told her to do. But the sensations the water pressure was causing on a certain part of her body must have been worth it, because her eyes slid to half-mast. With the water doing its work, he thumbed her nipples and kissed her deeply. She moaned and the vibration slid down his throat and radiated off his spine. He explored the length of her neck with his tongue, nudging her head back with his nose. Impatiently, her hips wiggled.

Yeah, she liked this a lot.

Continuing to roll one nipple between his fingers, he slid his other hand between her folds until he found her clit. This might be his favorite part of her. That tiny spot of perfection packed the biggest punch. The most bang for his buck. He knew, after being between her legs last night, that she reacted to the slightest—

"Oh God!" She jerked her head back again, her face pulled into a beautiful mask of pleasure-and-pain. He continued torturing her, slipping along her silken skin until her cries turned to muffled whimpers and her teeth dug into her plush bottom lip. His hand left the nipple he'd been rolling between thumb and forefinger to catch her when her knees gave out. And they did. A few strokes later, Sofie gave him her weight. He supported her, while her arms around his neck held on tight.

He kissed her ear and whispered, "You are gorgeous when you come."

Hands on her ass, he lifted her so that her back rested against the wall and her thighs wrapped around his hips. He positioned himself at her entrance.

"Now let's see you do it again," he said, sliding home.

A sharp cry rang from her throat as he encased himself in her liquid heat.

"Can't," she argued, clinging to his shoulders.

"Yeah, sweetheart, you can." He slid in and out smoothly, given how she was wet and ready for him. The high, tight sounds in her throat had started already. "Told you."

He grinned, loving the feel of her wrapped around him absolutely everywhere. Loved the way her nipples abraded his chest, the way her hands pulled at the ends of his hair. Loved the way her ankles ground into his back, hard enough to cause bruises, urging him to continue.

Their shared breaths echoed off the shower walls, blending in with the sound of water spraying in every direction. He pumped into her, encouraging her with his words.

"Come."

It wasn't fancy; he just told her what he wanted.

"Come for me, Scampi." He drove into her again. "Come, baby."

He didn't know how long he repeated his request—until his legs had grown tired and the water had gone cool. Still, he did not give up. When she went over, she did it with a full body shudder, locking her arms around him. Her lips on his ear, she moaned and pleaded. And the feel of her warm breath, the sound of those pleas and cries, and knowing he took her there, that she'd obeyed his commands, were what he needed to reach his own climax.

His release shot down his arms and legs, across his back, making the water feel electrified as it pierced his skin.

Holding himself and her, he turned his back to the

shower wall, then slid down, keeping hold of her hips. When his butt hit the floor, he rested his head against the wall, his legs and arms spent. He caught his breath and opened his eyes, his lashes fluttering to keep out the cool water spraying around them. Didn't help. Water blurred the scene in front of him, blurred Sofie's face.

Even blurry, he could make out her smile, her honest emerald eyes. He was inside her, wrapped in her from head to toe.

And right now, she was everything he needed.

CHAPTER TWENTY-TWO

*E*xhaustion never felt so grand.

Currently, Sofie was battling her well-earned tiredness with her third cup of rainforest-certified coffee. She could get used to being oversexed, sleep-deprived, and caffeinated. Yes. Yes, she could.

Donovan made a huge avocado bacon omelet for breakfast. They shared it, hovering over the countertop, feeding each other bites. She was wearing one of Donovan's T-shirts, a strange match for the prim pencil skirt, and was scuttling around in a pair of his socks. The weather may be warming up, but the floors of the mansion had not received the memo.

Shuffling into the ballroom, Sofie sipped from her coffee mug and decided to check in with Faith. She asked if there were any messages. There weren't. "Well, I'm here if you need me to measure anything else."

Faith snorted. "Hmm, there is something I'd like to know the size of..."

"I'm talking about the ballroom."

"Well, I would hope there's room in his pants for those, too." Laughter trickled through the phone.

"Are you through?" Sofie sighed, but she smiled.

"Do not play innocent with me, missy. I know you've been sexed up, down, and probably sideways from the sound of your voice."

She was not wrong.

Faith sniffed after her bout of laughter and got down to business. "*Anyway.* Pretty slow morning. The normal glut of e-mails to answer, but I've got it under control."

Sofie could kiss her. "Did I give you a raise yet?"

"Not yet." She seemed to sober. "I happened to talk to Gretchen today." A friend of Faith's who worked at Abundance Market. "I guess Michael and Cookie are no more. He found her banging the stockroom guy. Told you she was a tramp."

"With the stamp to prove it," Sofie added helpfully.

"Damn straight." There was a pregnant pause, then Faith said, "He called me last night."

Uh-oh.

"I didn't answer," she was quick to add. "Which is why I called Gretchen this morning. To get the scoop. He's single. And she said he's not doing too well. He's miserable, apparently. I think we're both trying to figure out where to go from here. How to move on from a future that didn't go as planned."

Sofie clucked her tongue. "Honey . . ."

"I know what you're going to say." Her friend heaved a sigh. "But you don't know what it was like with Michael and me, when we were alone. Everyone makes mistakes. God knows I've made mistakes."

"Yes, but you didn't make a mistake with another person."

"Sofie," Faith said, her tone both resolute and gentle, "I'm not going to lecture you about climbing back into bed with the guy who stole your virginity and broke your heart."

Silence clung to the seconds stretching between them.

"It's a bad idea. If he cheats once, he will cheat again," Faith said. "That's what you want to tell me."

"No." Sofie put her coffee mug down on the bar and sat on a backless stool. "That's not what I want to tell you," she said, her voice echoing in the cavernous ballroom. I *want* to tell you he made a mistake he will never make again. I *want* to tell you he still loves you. I *want* to tell you that you and Michael will walk down a long, white runner in a big garish church where you both say your I dos. I *want* to tell you you'll buy a house with a picket fence and have two children. Honey, that's what I want to tell you. That's what I want for you. But I don't have a crystal ball. I'm not sure what's going to happen between the two of you."

"I want that, too," Faith said quietly. "I want all of that. Watching the years I had with Michael wash down the drain... What if I let him go and I wasn't supposed to? What if this is my destiny? What if we are meant to have those two children you just mentioned?" Her voice was full of hope, and it broke Sofie's heart to hear.

Hope.

She could relate. A very similar emotion was swirling in her chest now. She was filled with hope. And wasn't Donovan proof that people could change? He was different from what he used to be. Wasn't it possible for Michael to change, too?

"I'm going to call him, Sofe. I can't see the harm in a phone call. And I can't push him away, pretend he doesn't exist. We had a home together at one point."

"I know."

"He never did anything like this when we were together. And it is no secret that I have been putting off planning our wedding for a very long time. Maybe we both got cold feet…it was just that his led him to someone else."

She had to give it to her friend. If Faith was willing to overlook Michael cheating on her, she had a more forgiving heart than Sofie. She just hoped Faith wasn't making the biggest mistake of her life by making that phone call.

* * *

Sofie found Donovan outside, bent over a round hole in the ground where he was stacking bricks. The sun blazed hot overhead and he wore a pair of sunglasses, a black folded bandanna over his head. He looked so much like the Donny in her memory her heart gave a little leap.

Donny. The man who'd made her see stars this morning after making her see fireworks last night. The man who had a tattoo matching hers because he considered her one of his scars. Was this really happening to her?

Rather than say what she was thinking, instead she went with, "Hi."

"Scampi," he greeted, continuing to place bricks in a circle.

"What you doing?"

"Fire pit." He looked up at her and grinned, that sinister smile below dark shades doing funny things to her stomach. "I know how you like s'mores."

She guessed he winked from under those dark lenses, but she couldn't be sure.

The sound of an engine firing in the distance had her

looking out at the field. Connor, astride a lawnmower, held up a hand to wave. She waved back.

"Figured if the kids are going to be camping out here," Donovan said, pushing himself up, "they might want to make s'mores and shit."

She didn't hide the amusement in her voice when she repeated, "S'mores and . . . shit?"

"Yeah." His grin widened.

"You smell good." Like outside. A hint of perspiration glistened on his forehead.

Closing in on her, he said, "Me being sweaty turning you on?"

"Everything about you turns me on," she admitted, and heard the catch in her breath.

"What I like to hear." He lowered his head and kissed her lips.

She tasted the salt on his skin, and a hint of coffee on his mouth. Gosh. Why was he so sexy? In a flash, she sympathized with Faith. There was something comforting about the familiar. And even though it'd been years since Sofie had been around Donovan, he was familiar. If she were being honest, she didn't know exactly what she would do if she were in her friend's shoes. After all, here she was with Donny after promising herself she'd never give him another piece of her again.

"I have to run some errands," she said, not wanting to mull over her sordid thoughts. "I came out to see if you could drive me home."

"Not a problem." He gestured with his chin to the fire pit still-in-progress. "We can try this out tonight."

Surprised, she asked, "You want me to come back?"

He ran both hands up her arms, beneath the sleeves of

the T-shirt, his eyes on hers. "Scampi, babe. I want you here every night. Thought that would've been pretty clear to you by now."

It wasn't. Things weren't clear at all. What they were... Well, things were amazing, that's what they were. Her pragmatic, self-aware side wondered how many nights "every night" would end up being. Wondered what happened after he returned to New York...after he sold the house...

She had so many questions but not an ounce of fortitude to ask a single one of them.

"Cute as you look in my shirt, you may want to bring some of your own clothes. Can't guarantee you won't end up in a velour jumpsuit if you rely on what's stashed in the basement."

"Okay, but I may keep the shirt. I like it." It smelled like him.

His eyes grazed over the baggy tee. "Keep it." He put his teeth on his bottom lip and whistled. "Gertie!"

Gertie. He called Dog *Gertie.* Warmth rolled through her chest like a red carpet. For some reason his doing so was significant. A sign of progress, maybe?

"Let me get her inside and we'll get you home," he said, blessedly unaware of her thoughts. Or the hope blooming inside her anew. "Lunch before you go?"

"Um, no. No, thank you."

Gertie bounded around a tree and came to a halt, leaning heavily against Donny's leg. She was panting, drooling, her pale blue eyes squinting in the bright sunlight. What a great dog. Sofie hated the idea of her living anywhere else, of belonging to anyone else. Look at those blue eyes, the look of pure love and devotion she was giving her temporary owner. She was his, through and through.

Sofie tried not to see any glaring similarities between her and the dog. Including the one where they'd both lose Donny in the end.

"The clothes you're bringing over tonight…"

When he didn't finish, she prompted, "Yes?"

White teeth flashed against tanned skin when he smiled. "Those are for Connor's sake. Not mine. When he's not here, I want you naked." He bent and gave her a quick kiss. "Can you do that for me, Scampi?"

"Yeah." She'd do just about anything for him.

Just like the mutt who trailed loyally at his side as he walked to the mansion's back door.

* * *

"No, no, I'm too—" Sofie's protestation ended with a gasp as Donovan plopped her onto the hood of his Jeep. He pushed her skirt over her thighs and heard a soft exhalation, followed by, "—heavy."

"Shut up," he told her, laying his hands on the expanse of thighs gifted to her from the Almighty Himself.

"I don't want to dent the hood."

"Told you a million times, Scampi, you're beautiful." He smashed a kiss against her mouth and she caught his head, thrusting her tongue against his. The slide of their mouths echoed in other parts of his body and he found himself instantly impatient.

"Anyway, you owe me," he teased, snaking his fingers around the legs of her panties and tugging.

She accommodated him by wrapping her ankles around his back and canting her hips. He pulled the material to her ankles. *Pink*, he noticed. He noticed something else, too.

"A thong," he growled.

"It's new." Eyes wide, lips pouting but pursed, she was the picture of innocence. And yet, she'd been wearing the sexiest pair of panties to ever *not* cover her very fine ass.

"Dammit, why didn't you tell me this was under your dress? I should make you put them back on and bend you over this hood instead of set you on top of it."

She grinned. "You're bad."

"You love it."

"I do love it."

When her lips met his, he didn't miss the sensation of his heart clutching. And not because of the kiss—though it was a damn good one—but because she'd said the word *love*.

Love was an emotion he couldn't trust. He understood it—in an abstract way. He got that Evan loved his son, Lyon, that Evan loved his fiancée. He got that Caroline loved to cook. He understood Alessandre loved business and had, at some point, loved each of his four ex-wives.

What Donovan didn't understand were things like if his mother loved him, why had she left him behind? If Gertrude loved Robert, how had she let him abuse Donovan?

Where the Pates were concerned, having their love came with strings, with scars. To be loved was to be burdened. Left behind. *Harmed.*

The pull of Sofie's lips reminded him she was nothing like his family. She loved purely. Loved her friends, loved bacon, loved the color brown. She loved the shower attached to the room he slept in. He knew because she'd talked about it—and what they'd done in it—over and over and over.

And he loved pleasing her. Making her cry out. Loved

the way he turned her on and the way she always brought it up after.

But her love for him needed to stop there. She could love parts of the house, she could love what they were doing together, and she could even love that he was "bad." So long as she didn't love *him*. Love came first, but following closely behind: *problems*.

Plenty of them.

Starting with what she'd expect from him. Because of his childhood, because of his upbringing, because of who he'd become over the past seven years, there were parts of himself he simply wasn't capable of anteing up.

Didn't matter who he blamed. He just couldn't, and that was that.

"Beautiful night," she said as he continued wrestling with the elastic band on her panties. They were tangled in her high heels. Giving up, he tossed her shoes to the ground.

"Michael Kors," she said against his mouth.

He pulled his chin back to look at her. "Who?"

"The shoes."

"Buy you new ones." He kissed her, allowing his hands to wander higher and higher up her thighs. "You feel like silk." He breathed in the scent coating her neck, a blend of something feminine and soft that had the superpower of making his dick throb in sync with his heartbeat. Pushing one hand under her shirt, he cupped a breast and buried his face in her neck. She tasted like she smelled. Sweet. *Incredible*.

A moan echoed in her throat. "You're sure no one is out here?"

Not that he knew of. They'd driven Trixie out beyond

the stables, through the open field where he parked under a massive maple. Thanks to Connor's mowing, the grass was no longer knee-high.

Donovan and Sofie had the field, the trees, and the stars to themselves.

"You worry too much." He slid the dress from her shoulder and pressed a kiss there.

"I do not. I'm not worried about getting dust on the seat of my skirt," she argued.

"That you even thought that proves me right."

He scooted her forward on the hood and stood between her thighs. His erection shoved against his fly.

"Cashing in my *Do Me* rain check, Scampi." This time when he kissed her neck, she tipped her head back to give him room. He took it.

Then his head was being pulled back, her fingers tight in his hair, her expression fierce.

"If I'm going to do you, Donny Pate, you're going to have to let me be on top."

CHAPTER TWENTY-THREE

*S*even minutes in heaven.

Whoever invented that game didn't know what the fuck they were talking about.

Seven minutes in a closet with Sofie's lips on his would have been great, but seven minutes of her riding him, her tits swinging in his face, her breathing escalating, her hands resting against his chest while her hips slammed up and down...

Heaven. Pearly gates included.

Pressure built in his spine until he was sure his vertebrae were exploding one after the other. He came so hard, his upper half lifted off the back of his Jeep. He welded his palms into the cushion of Sofie's ass. Every muscle in his body tightened, then loosened, his head dropping, his eyes closing. He lay there, breathing heavily.

"You swear when you come," she panted above him. He felt her hair tickle his face a moment before her lips covered his.

He pushed the mass of waves away, keeping his eyes closed. He didn't need to see her. He could *feel* her.

"What did I say?" he asked, his voice rough, his throat dry. He had no clue.

"You said, '*Fuuuuuuck.*'" She'd lowered her voice to sound more like him. It was too damn cute.

His eyes opened as his mouth smiled. He smiled a lot around her. It was as refreshing as everything else he did with her.

Moonlight shining bright behind her head made seeing her expression impossible. But he knew Sofie smiled—he could hear the smile in her voice. Could hear light laughter between her shallow breaths. She'd worked hard.

"That was nice," she said.

"No." He palmed her back and pulled her down to him. "*Nice* is not the word for you riding me home, Scampi."

"Riding you home?" A loose laugh came from her lips, her breath washing over his face.

"Uh-huh."

"Well, if not nice, then what would you call it?"

Heaven, he thought automatically.

Instead he said, "Fucking amazing."

"Poetic."

Yeah, well.

After he'd hauled her off the hood of his Jeep, he'd lowered the hatch in the back and thrown her onto an old quilt there for just this purpose. Getting her out here hadn't been hard. He told her he wanted to check the property and see how Connor did. Which was not true. Connor didn't need to be babysat.

The moment she stepped out of the Jeep and tilted her

head to take in the starry sky, he'd made his move. He kissed her and that'd been it. He had to have her.

Damn. She'd been as sexy in her dress as she was out of it. *Almost.*

Using both hands she pushed against his chest. "I should..."

Before she could leave him altogether, his palms closed around her hips.

"Whoa, whoa, whoa," he whispered. "Slowly."

She shifted, letting him loose very, *very* slowly, while he enjoyed the slippery feel of her sliding away. Not as good as when she'd lowered herself onto him, but still.

He made room for her to lay next to him.

"Like it like that," he murmured, holding her close. His arm closed around her shoulders and stroking the smooth skin of her shoulder. Being inside her without barriers was his favorite part of this whole thing with her.

She tipped her chin to take him in, and when he met her eyes she whispered, "Fucking amazing." That cute, crooked smile.

"Didn't peg you for a dirty girl."

She propped her chin on the hand resting on his chest. "I'm a lot of things when I'm with you."

Her comment settled into the air around him. A lot of truth there. A lot for him to think about. A lot for him to own up to. His hand moved lazily on her shoulder. He was a lot of things when he was with her, too. He was relaxed. He was playful. He didn't think about the next thing to do that would take his attention away from bad memories. He just thought of *her.*

Same as seven years ago.

She pressed into him, tits smashing into his chest. He

loved the feel of her skin on his, the way she was touching him now, running her fingers lightly over his chest. The night air was cool, but not too cool. His flesh still burned from having her.

"I wasn't saving it, you know," she said.

His hand stilled.

"My virginity," she said. "I wasn't saving it."

He wondered if she felt his heart kick against her palm.

"Don't get me wrong. I wanted my first time to be special."

His muscles locked. He was guessing her definition of "special" wasn't being accused of being too tight followed by being asked to get dressed immediately after. *God*, he'd been a self-centered asshole.

Finger to his chin, she turned his head so he was looking at her. "None of my high school boyfriends were anywhere near the same town as special."

He could imagine. He was an idiot when he was in high school. Then he dropped out, got his GED, and became a bigger idiot.

"By the time I graduated," she said, "took a few college classes, and went on more than a few not-so-great dates, I still hadn't found what I defined as special."

He never thought of his virginity as special. Then again, he never thought of much of anything as special. Things just . . . were.

"I don't regret it." Her voice went the slightest bit harder. "But I was pissed at you for a while."

She should have been. He deserved any anger she threw his way. Though he was glad she hadn't held on to it. And not just because it would've jeopardized him being here with her now.

"I was hurt for a longer while," she admitted.

And that was the part he hated most. A muscle in his jaw worked as he clamped his teeth together. With the arm wrapped around her shoulders, he gave her a light squeeze. Because he didn't quite know how to apologize for what he'd done, he simply said, "Scampi."

"I was pissed at myself for a while, too. But I never regretted that night. Because I knew what I wanted. At the time, it was you."

He turned his head and felt his mouth compress into a grim line. It was on the tip of his tongue to ask her what she wanted now. What the hell she was doing with him.

Which wasn't like him. He didn't question situations. He lived in the present. Action, reaction. Life was simple.

Shifting his body, he cupped her jaw, brought her mouth to his. He kissed her slowly, deliberately. While their mouths mated, the taste of her, the smell of her, the feel of her naked body brushing his, and the way her fingers slid along the back of his neck, made the pain from his past melt away.

He ended the kiss and heard her sigh, a soft "hmm" sound as her fingertips continued tangling in his hair.

Feeling as if he should acknowledge what she'd said, he muttered, "Shit time for your first."

"What was yours like?" she asked, her fingers tickling his scalp.

"Sixteen. Wild party. She was high, I was hammered." The memory was hazy at best. "Don't even remember her name."

Sofie trailed her hand from his head to his jaw. "Shit time for your first."

God, this woman. She got him.

He kissed her before he reasoned he shouldn't. And

when he did, thoughts raced in his head. He shouldn't be kissing her. The way she made him feel... those feelings were warning signs he continued to ignore. He wished he could make it up to her, that first time in the library, the callused way he'd treated her.

She pushed both hands into his hair and brought his face to hers. As they continued making out, he vowed before he left Evergreen Cove that was exactly what he'd do.

He'd make it up to her.

He'd find a way to give her that first time back.

A good memory to replace the bad.

* * *

Flames crackled and popped in the fire pit. Sofie watched the orange and yellow sparks, enjoying the warmth, enjoying her well-earned exhaustion.

"Beer? I don't have wine."

A cold bottle appeared in front of her.

"I'll drink a beer," she answered, accepting it.

Donovan sat down next to her on one of the huge logs Ant had shaped into rustic benches earlier in the week. The man was magic with a chainsaw. She took a sip of her beer, letting the drink slide down her throat, and looked around the grounds. The outside of the mansion had really come along. The grass was cut, the weeds were cleared, and a few overgrown bushes had been uprooted and burned. She could easily picture a group of kids from Open Arms camped out in the yard or gathered around the fire pit, marshmallows skewered onto the ends of sticks.

"Two days away." He tipped his own bottle and drank. "Happened fast."

Things had happened fast. One moment the dinner loomed three months into the future, the same day she'd stepped out of the back room to find this man standing in her shop. And if someone would have told her she would be sleeping with him, practically living with him, by the time the dinner rolled around, she would have laughed until she seized.

Only a crazy person would jump back into bed with Donovan Pate.

Hmm.

"Connor is showing up for the campout," Donny said. "He offered to help set up the tents, take the kids on a tour, and teach them what plants are poisonous and which aren't."

She smiled. Sounded like something Connor would do. "And you?"

"Me?" Donny lifted a black eyebrow. With his long hair and dark clothes, leather jacket—yes, the same one—and weather-beaten boots, he reminded her of a pirate. "I'm supervising the fire. I hope there are enough volunteers to help keep track of the kids." He frowned as he studied the trees in the distance. "Hate the idea one of them wandering off. Maybe we could put little tracking devices on them or something."

Sofie laughed, causing him to smile over at her.

Another unexpected side effect of being with Donovan— he made her happy. Legitimately happy.

"That'll free you up for the girlie shit you gotta do." He took another drink.

Feigning offense, she said, "*Girlie* shit? What, you don't think I can start a fire? Roast marshmallows? Pitch a tent?"

His throat bobbed when he laughed. "Sweetheart, I *know* you can pitch a tent."

She rolled her eyes, but secretly, or maybe not so secretly, she loved when he teased her.

You love him, period.

The thought came out of nowhere, slapping the smile off her face. Or maybe the thought had come from somewhere she'd been trying to ignore for the last week. She bit her lip and grew silent, staring into the fire for answers. She couldn't afford to love him. She couldn't afford to give him another single part of her. Not after he'd taken the part she hadn't realized was precious until she'd trusted it with him.

"What's your place like in New York?" she asked, desperately needing a change of subject, and to remind herself their time together was dwindling.

He blew out a breath, took another pull of his beer. "It's like ... Not mine."

"Not yours? What are you, like a squatter?"

"Yeah," he answered, his expression serious. "Kinda. Alessandre, you know, the B-and-B guy, has a swanky place in the Hamptons. And by swanky I mean multimillion-dollar new-build perched on the ocean. His kitchen is all glass"—he swept an arm in a wide arc—"and the balcony leads out to a concrete patio. Every damn week he throws cocktail parties for the neighbors. People whose outfits cost more than your car."

He lowered his arm and shook his head. "Last place I pictured myself living, that's for damn sure. Thought I'd be there for a short time. Ended up staying."

"How did you meet him?"

"Caroline."

Wow, she was glad she knew he hadn't had a girlfriend in the time he'd been away or that name may have caused a spike of jealousy.

"My grandmother's former chef," he clarified. "She lived here—at the cottage at the back of the property."

Right. They'd driven by the cottage when he'd shown her the grounds earlier. Shrouded in pines, Sofie hadn't been able to see much of the place.

"Caroline was more than hired help to me." Donny studied the label on the bottle in his hand, but Sofie bet he looked right through it. "She was more my grandmother than Gertrude."

Hearing her name, Gertie lifted her fuzzy head from her place at his feet.

"Sorry to wake you, girl." He ruffled her ears. When he pulled his hand away, Gertie laid her head back on the grass, blew out a heavy sigh, and closed her eyes. "I knew I was leaving the Cove, so I asked Caroline if she had any idea where I could work. New York was as good a choice as anywhere else. I just wanted to get the hell out of here."

She bristled.

He noticed.

"Help if I told you I had decided to leave before the night in the library?"

Twisting her lips, she shook her head.

"Didn't think so." He gave her a sad smile. "Aless didn't need a cook, but he did need a mason. So he put me to work with this guy, Vic, who was in the process of building a wall around the back of Alessandre's property. I helped. Took to it."

"All those visits to the quarry," she pointed out. "Who knew they would lead to a career?"

"Who knew?" His smile was less sad. "I started doing stuff on my own, too. Alessandre introduced me to his ridiculously wealthy friends. They liked my work. Several of them have vacation houses all over the states. I started traveling to them, building whatever they needed me to—fireplaces, mostly. I'd stay for a few weeks, or until the job was done. When I got back to the Hamptons, I'd crash at Alessandre's guesthouse again. It's a small place, nice though, behind his house. Has an attached garage where I can park Trixie. Gives me a place to build, store materials. Practice my next design."

"Sounds like a home to me."

"Other than my clothes and my Jeep, nothing there is mine."

A shiver climbed her spine. She moved closer, propping her chin on his shoulder.

"Sounds lonely." And it did. His life in New York, and elsewhere when he traveled, sounded incredibly, horribly lonely. Seven years of a nomadic lifestyle. Work followed by more work.

"Sometimes." His arm closed around her and he pulled her close, his hand resting on her hip. She melted into him, thinking how nice it was to talk to him, to be here with him. To be held by him.

Once he left, she would be lonely, too. Lonely for him. Hell, she was lonely for him now and he was sitting right next to her.

Which was not good. Not good at all.

"Hate when you feel for me, Scampi."

"I can't help it." And that was the problem. She couldn't help feeling for him. She couldn't help thinking of him.

She couldn't help loving him.

"I don't know about you," he said, his tone lighter, "but I could go for s'mores."

She looked up to see one of his eyes close in a seductive wink. He wanted her, and she wanted him. Even though she knew the physical temporary wasn't enough.

Well, it would have to be. She wasn't anywhere near ready to give him up. And so she returned his wink with a saucy one of her own.

"I'll get the chocolate." She kissed him before standing.

He caught her wrist before she raced inside.

"Dark chocolate or"—he closed his eyes and pursed his lips, sucking a breath between his teeth—"oh yes, oh God... *milk chocolate*."

Teasing her. Again.

She play-shoved him and he chuckled. The sound rattled through her chest like thrown dice. At the patio door, she paused at the entrance to the kitchen, but before she went in, admired his profile lit by the fire behind him.

The way his black hair hung too long and covered part of his face. The way his nose pointed down to full, talented lips. Long lashes swept over eyes with the ability to see right through to her soul.

She etched this moment into her mind, knowing she'd need it when the nights got long and lonely.

And knowing those nights would come sooner than she wanted.

CHAPTER TWENTY-FOUR

"You good?" Donovan nodded at Connor, who was carrying an armload of canvas, poles, and other tent paraphernalia to help the Open Arms kids set up camp.

"Good," he answered.

With a nod, Donovan headed over to Trixie. Ant had cut a sizable pile of wood in preparation for tonight. Donovan needed to load it up and bring it back to the pit.

"Can I go?"

He turned to find one of the older boys next to him. He guessed the kid at twelve, maybe thirteen. Maybe eighteen. It was getting harder and harder to tell how old any of them were. They all looked like babies to him.

The boy's hair was overly long, dark, almost black. He chewed on his bottom lip while waiting for the answer, and turned equally dark eyes up to Donovan.

"Sure, kid."

The boy tried to climb into Trixie twice before he successfully scaled her height, then they were off.

"What's your name?" Donovan asked as the Jeep rumbled and rolled through the bumpy field.

"Ben."

"Ben, I'm Donovan. You an outdoors man?"

He gave a careless shrug, not making eye contact. "I guess."

Okay. Well, he could deal with the strong, silent type. Looking at Ben was a little like looking at a mirror. Donovan hadn't been a chatty or happy kid.

He parked next to the maple, having a fleeting thought about the last time he parked here. He was with Sofie. And just like everything else he did with Sofie, the night was memorable.

"Leave the big pile to me." Donovan pointed around at some of the branches the tree had shed. "But gather some of those sticks and twigs. We'll need them for kindling." Ben picked around the field and Donovan started loading the back of Trix.

Minutes later, his phone rang. He lifted it to his ear. "Yeah?"

"How is my house?"

Alessandre.

"It's, uh, it's good."

The turrets were visible from here, poking just over the trees that obliterated the view of the rest of the house and visitors milling around Aless's future backyard.

"Ready to go," Donovan told him. "The campout's tonight, charity dinner tomorrow." Something about this phone call was making him twitchy. Everything was wrapping up—ending soon. Endings were so damn final, and always smacked with a bittersweet tang.

"Yes, I mailed a sizable donation to Ruby Voss. It's a good charity, one I'll continue to support in the future."

He nodded even though Aless couldn't see him. He could've guessed Aless would send money. An answer of overwhelming support was the only answer he'd expect from the man, given the subject matter.

"She'll appreciate that." Donovan watched Ben stack sticks in the crook of one skinny arm. "I cleared out a majority of the basement, the bedrooms. There were some antique furnishings I thought you might want."

Except for the room full of creepy dolls. Yikes. Those had gone on the last thrift run. He and Connor had stoically packed them into garbage bags and tried not to get freaked out by their sightless glass eyes.

The only thread left hanging was the fireplace in the great room, but that was a few hours' work, an afternoon, tops.

"A few little things to tie up," he told Aless, "then your bed-and-breakfast is ready to go. Not a hundred percent, but close."

"I'm sure everything will be perfect."

It would. Donovan had worked in more than one D'Paolo B-and-B over the years. First doing small repairs to foundation and flooring, patios, and later, after he'd gained some experience, building and repairing fireplaces. He knew what was expected, Alessandre's style, and the way he ran things.

He ended the call with Aless and loaded the remainder of the wood into the back of his Jeep. Ben climbed in—this time on the first try. Donovan smiled to himself. *Resilient.* He'd been resilient, too. Even when he didn't have to be any longer. After a while, it became a habit.

Donovan put Trix into gear and looked over at Ben, making a snap decision. "Ever done a donut?"

Ben smiled. "No."

"Put on your seat belt."

After they tore up a sizable portion of grass in the field, Donovan returned to the backyard at a leisurely speed. Anyone who spotted Ben's messy hair, and the fact there was a few blades of grass stuck to his head, could guess what they'd been doing.

A dozen other kids, a few volunteers, and Ruby herself bustled around. Connor had erected two tents and was working on a third.

Color Donovan impressed.

He climbed out of Trixie, dropped the hatch, and noticed Ruby Voss approaching, her arms casually crossed over her chest, a pleasant smile on her face. He lifted his chin at Ben. "Fix your hair, man."

The kid scrubbed the top and sides of his head before gathering sticks from the Jeep and heading off in the opposite direction.

The older woman nodded in the boy's wake, then turned to Donovan. "Benton came to us two years ago." Ben was out of earshot, focused on his task. "He was one angry twelve-year-old."

So he was fourteen.

"Took a lot to pull him out of silent mode," Ruby said. "Some boys stay angry their entire lives."

Donovan met the woman's flint gray eyes. Something shrewd twinkled in their depths.

"It's nothing short of a miracle when a man pulls himself out of it."

He felt his arms tense.

"I've worked with kids like Ben for a lot of years, Mr. Pate." She cocked her head and he could see the shrewdness didn't stop with her eyes. "I know a formerly angry little boy when I see him."

Pressing his lips together, he turned away from her and said, "Excuse me." But before he brushed past her, she spoke again.

"Ben lived with his uncle before he came to us."

The back of his neck prickled in premonition. He guessed she was about to say something he didn't want to hear. He tipped his chin slightly. She hovered in his peripheral.

Focused somewhere off in the distance, she continued her story.

"The uncle drank, encouraged Ben to drink. Profusely. By the time he got to us, Ben had been drinking for a year. Had a swollen liver to show for it. He went through detox. He's going to AA meetings now."

"AA?" *Jesus.*

"The association allows underage children to attend with an adult if they find solace being at the meetings," she answered. "Ben is mature for his age."

No shit. Donovan looked over at the boy who'd just held on to Trixie's roll bar, hair flying, hooting like a kid with no worries in the world. Unbelievable. Simply unbelievable what assholes adults could be.

"This is the part where I say his uncle was not at fault. That he has a disease. That Ben was an unfortunate side effect of his uncle's disease." Donovan faced her fully. The look in her gray eyes was cold. "I'm not going to say that to you. You know better, don't you, Mr. Pate?"

He did.

"I think it's a fucked-up hand to be dealt," she said bluntly. "Ben deserved better. Any kid trapped in a situation like his deserves better."

Ruby Voss, when she wasn't gushing about his grandmother, was easy to respect.

"I appreciate all you've done. You didn't have to let Sofia use this property. Or your land. I wanted you to know how much this means to these kids. To Open Arms."

He watched as she pulled in a breath, taking in the surrounding acreage. The day couldn't have been nicer: bright sun, blue skies, barely a cloud. Couldn't have mail-ordered better weather.

He dipped his chin in a nod of understanding and turned to finish unloading his Jeep.

"I didn't tell you his story to resurrect your demons," she said before he'd taken a single step. "Just thought you should know that someone sees you. Even if it is a little late, Donovan, I *see* you."

She cupped a hand on his shoulder as she walked by and squeezed. Then she called to a group of girls wandering too close to the trees.

Donovan didn't realize he'd been holding his breath until spots appeared in his vision. He blew out the breath and sucked in another just as Ben approached the Jeep.

"I can help with the big stuff, too," Ben said.

Yeah. Donovan would just bet he could. He pulled two logs out and nodded at Ben to hold out his arms.

"More," Ben instructed. "I can take it."

Kindred spirit, Donovan thought, and piled on another two.

* * *

Donovan had no idea what time it was.

The kids had roasted hot dogs, ate bags of chips, and drank enough Mountain Dew to keep them up half the night. He tipped his head and looked at the moon, guessing half a night was about what was left.

The kids made s'mores, finally crashing from their sugar-and-caffeine-induced highs. Sofie had been inside most of the evening helping organize the ballroom and getting the kitchen ready for tomorrow. Donovan had gone on the nature walk with Connor and the kids, and learned a few things himself. Ben stuck to his side for most of it. Later, Donovan assisted with how-to-roast-a-hot-dog-without-stabbing-or-burning-yourself portion of the evening.

By the time Sofie caught up with him, he was manning a dying fire. But there was enough heat left for her to roast a few marshmallows to golden perfection. He'd watched her eat them, helping her lick gooey marshmallow off her fingers and sharing sticky kisses while he was at it. Shortly after, she'd laid her head in his lap. She'd conked out the second she closed her eyes.

"Mr. Pate?"

Donovan pulled his fingers out of Sofie's hair. Ben stood at the edge of the fire, gesturing to one of the log benches.

"Care if I sit?" he asked, his voice carefully quiet.

"Help yourself."

Ben sat, rubbing his hands together and holding them in front of the fire to warm them. "I don't sleep sometimes."

Yeah. Donovan understood that. His sleep patterns had

been shit when he was a kid. Hard to sleep when the man who raised him might be around the corner waiting to punch him in the face. He angled a glance at Ben. Or give him a drink.

Ben looked from Donovan to Sofie.

"She your girlfriend?"

Donovan ran a hand down her upper arm while he thought. Then up and down again before responding, "Yeah. She is."

For a few more nights.

"She's pretty. She a model?"

Donovan smiled. "I'll tell her you asked." Maybe then she'd believe she was beautiful. "No, she's not a model. She's the one who put this event together."

"That's cool."

It was cool. Sofie was incredible at this planning stuff. She was organized, cared—probably too much—and worked tirelessly. Even while she stayed here with him, she didn't treat those nights like a vacation. He'd noticed her taking phone calls, rushing to the library to get her binder, or scouring the Internet for information.

"The campouts Open Arms did the last few years have been shitty. Not like this." Ben nodded his head in the direction of the tents. "We were in a park last year." He made a disgusted face, his lips curling. "You can't camp out in a park."

Donovan swallowed a smile. He didn't want to insult the kid by laughing. "No. I guess not. I'm not sure camping in someone's backyard is a step up."

Ben smiled and it didn't look strained. Maybe he would be okay. In spite of what he'd been through. Maybe he would grow up and have normal relationships. Donovan stroked his fingers through Sofie's hair. Maybe Ben would have a model girlfriend. A *real* girlfriend, not a woman he would leave behind. Twice.

Donovan tested the softness of her waves between his fingertips. Ben deserved a real girlfriend—hell, maybe he'd have a wife. He had his entire life ahead of him. And thanks to Ruby and Open Arms, had a fighting chance at learning how to accept love when he saw it.

Or felt it.

Too late for Donovan. Long term wasn't something he'd get to have.

Shame.

"You live here?" Ben asked, his eyes on the mansion looming behind them.

For some reason, Donovan answered honestly. "Used to."

"Have any wild parties?" Ben's mouth quirked. So, still a teenager despite the adult drama he'd been through.

"Not here." He'd partied elsewhere.

"Ruby said the old lady who lived here donated a shit-ton of money to Open Arms," Ben said. "That true?"

Unbelievably, but yes.

"My grandmother."

"Nice lady."

"Not really."

Ben nodded like he understood. Probably did.

"Benton," Ruby called, tightening her jacket around her as she stalked toward the fire. "Get in your tent. It's lights out."

Sofie stirred, lifting her head and blinking out of sleep. How she'd been able to sleep soundly on his thigh, her hip on the hard log they shared, was beyond him. She must've been really exhausted.

"We have to be up bright and early tomorrow morning," Ruby told Ben. She threw a smile over her shoulder at Donovan before walking her charge to his tent.

"How long was I out?" Sofie asked, yawning and pushing herself up.

It'd been an eternity since he'd had a warm, sleepy woman in his arms. Come to think of it, had he *ever* had a warm, sleepy woman in his arms before Scampi? He didn't think so.

"Your lap is comfy." She rolled one shoulder. "This log, not so much."

"Let's get you to bed." He liked the sound of that way too much.

Round eyes met his. "Won't it look bad if you and I sleep in the same room?"

"Sweetheart, these kids have seen worse than—" He didn't finish. Because the next words that came to mind were, *a couple sharing a bed.*

She didn't ask him to expound. "Good point." Leaning in, she brushed his face with her lips and whispered, "Put me to bed, Donny."

Damn, but he did think of them as a couple.

Damn.

* * *

Donovan's hips came off the bed, fingers winding into Sofie's hair as he thrust deep into her mouth. She took him, every inch of him, reveling in the way he was losing control under her ministrations.

When she swirled her tongue around the head of his penis and increased suction, he tugged her head gently. Then commanded her not so gently.

"Get your ass up here."

She let him loose and licked her lips. Donovan hauled her up his body. Before she had a chance to straddle him, he rolled her to her back, parted her legs, and slammed inside her.

Her head went back, her mouth dropping open.

"Hard and fast," she said before he could ask.

"That's my girl." Weaving her fingers with his, he pushed one of her hands onto the pillow over her head and pounded into her again. Her feet came up, cupped his ass, and pulled him deeper.

"Donny, *God*."

"I'll take that title." The words burst from between labored breaths as he continued pumping his hips and driving her out of her mind.

Somehow, she managed a laugh. Maybe because she needed one. She wanted to let go of the stress of the charity dinner, of the fact that tomorrow night would be the last night she was here. Because after...

She refused to think about what happened after.

He bent his head and kissed her, increasing his speed, the friction of his chest hair hardening her nipples.

"*Scampi*."

"Harder," she gasped, clawing his back with her nails. Wanting everything he had—wanting to drain him, use him up, before...

Again she killed the thought.

"Roll over," he said on a growl.

Yes.

Yes, please.

He pulled out of her, leaving her empty and she rolled onto her belly. Anticipation was a coiling snake about to strike. Roughened palms gripped her hips, and Donovan hauled her butt into the air. She grasped the pillow in front of her, biting down on her lip. He kissed one of her butt cheeks, then the other before he slicked his tongue along her center.

Sofie moaned.

"Fucking gorgeous," he said, placing a final damp kiss on her ass. Then she felt the slippery slide of the tip of his penis, and that coiling anticipation snapped.

With one long push, he entered her, drawing another low moan from her throat. She hugged the pillow, her teeth biting into her forearms as he began to thrust. Each powerful movement slammed her against his thick, muscular thighs. Each thrust stretched her, hitting somewhere deep, deep in her core. Deeper than she'd felt before, unfurling a reaction she couldn't have stopped if she wanted to.

She didn't want to.

Incoherent words tumbled from her lips, followed by the very real prayer of, *"Oh God, oh God, oh God."*

"Scampi," he grunted, still moving in and out at a mind-blowing pace. "You come when I say."

Not a chance. Her release was building, cresting. *Already.* Incredible.

"Can't," she informed him, gasping, clutching on to the pillow as if it was the only thing keeping her from shattering. "Almost there."

"No, you're not."

"Donny."

"Wait for me." He pulled her hips against his thighs again, sending a drove of tingles through her body.

"Wait," he repeated, his voice breaking.

Biting down on her lip, she endured the next intoxicating slide of his cock with her eyes shut. In an equally broken whisper she managed, "Please, Donny. *Please*."

"Almost, sweetheart." He thrust, his fingers pressing into the flesh at her hips. Bending over her, he reached around with one hand and pinched her nipple at the same time he pushed into her.

"*Now*," he commanded.

She climaxed on a cry. A loud cry he muted by covering her mouth with one hand. She bit down on to his finger as he thrust again and again, spilling into her. The thrusts slowed and he dropped his forehead, his palm leaving her mouth.

She felt his breath fan her back when he spoke. "Loud."

Losing the ability to hold herself up, she collapsed on the bed with a smile that might stay on her face forever. The movement pulled Donovan from inside her.

"Kids outside." He collapsed next to her and kissed her shoulder.

Oops, she'd forgotten about them. She'd forgotten everything, temporarily. Life was only a series of snaps, pops, and zaps jettisoning through her bloodstream. She still buzzed.

"Your fault." She pushed her hair out of her face. "You make me loud." A satisfied smile arched her lips.

A cocky grin overtook his as he continued to catch his breath.

Rolling to her side, she put a palm on his back. "Never done that before."

He mirrored her movement, pulling her flush against him.

"Which part?"

"The...um. The...last part." The from-behind part. *Yowza*.

"More where that came from. My favorite part is your mouth."

He brushed his finger over her lips. She bit him lightly.

"Liked that, did you?" she asked.

"Scampi, I like everything you do to me."

Her heart filled to overflowing at the compliment. She liked everything he did to her. She imagined another reality where they stayed together, where they continued to push boundaries together. Continued one-upping themselves until both of them were panting and pleased every single day.

A fantasy.

Her smile faded. Not a reality at all.

"I'll start the shower." He kissed her on the lips and climbed out of bed. Sofie stuck her hand underneath the pillow under her head and watched Donovan's bare backside move across the shadowed room.

So domestic. *Pretend*, she mentally corrected. Her Cinderella fantasy was winding to an end, her mansion about to turn into a pumpkin, her prince about to return to New York.

"Come on, Scampi"—Donovan stood in the doorway of the bathroom—"my back isn't going to wash itself." He gave her a wink, then ran his fingers through his messy hair. "Neither is my front."

With a roll of her eyes, she clambered out of bed. "I'm coming."

He vanished into the bathroom calling behind him, "Did that already."

She smiled, but her smile felt sad. A black cloud she could no longer ignore loomed in the distance.

Well.

She'd have to forget the cloud for now. As Donovan had said to her before...

"Is what it is," she whispered to the empty bedroom.

CHAPTER TWENTY-FIVE

Sofie fluffed Faith's hair one final time and spritzed her with a quick shot of extra-hold hairspray. She hadn't been in her own apartment for so long, the place felt sort of foreign.

Faith stood from the edge of the bed and turned her head left, then right, studying her reflection in the full-length mirrored closet doors. Sofie had wound Faith's fine, fair blond hair around a large-barreled curling iron and had given her big, fat waves. The length flowed over her golden-tanned shoulders, making her look like a supermodel... well, like *more* of a supermodel.

Faith faced her and grinned. "You are so good at this, Sofie." She propped her hands on her hips and ran a gaze down Sofie's wardrobe to the very high, open-toed black heels on Sofie's feet. "You look amazing in that dress."

Sofie wrinkled her nose. "Really? I was going to change it." Her eyes went to the mirror. She would swear the dress was longer at the store when she tried it on. "The way the skirt flares." She smoothed the back of the dress flat. Courtesy of her round bottom, it flared out again.

"It's gorgeous. If I had a caboose like you, I'd wear short skirts every day."

"You don't think it's too much?" She turned and bent slightly. "I'm not sure Ruby Voss wants to see quite this much of my thighs."

Faith, in her own little black dress, a svelte, sleeveless number that skimmed her sleek figure and ended demurely above her knees, held up a finger. "Do *not* change that dress. Yes, it's shorter than you're used to, but it is in no way inappropriate."

Maybe Sofie was worrying needlessly. After all, she needed something to obsess about in place of obsessing about Donovan. With a last, wary glance at the mirror, she said, "Fine. But if at any point you can see my underwear, flag me down."

"Done."

* * *

Classical music piped through the speakers in the ballroom, the sconces throwing low light on the walls. Evergreen Cove's finest dressed residents milled about, filling the room with the din of casual chatter.

Sofie knotted her hands together as she did another pass of the room. A few of the older kids from Open Arms, dressed in their best clothes for the event, served cupcakes from a table in the back. Others delivered mini desserts from Sugar Hi while a league of waiters in smart black pants, white shirts, and bow ties carried trays of slender champagne flutes.

Dinner was delicious, five courses served to a sit-down crowd. She was still surprised how many items had been donated for the silent auction. One corner of the ballroom was absolutely packed with everything ranging from paintings to photographs to interior decorating packages from Cozy Home. But there were two items in particular that had received the most fanfare.

Gloria Shields had taken the stage early in the evening to introduce Evan and Asher, who were autographing copies of *The Adventures of Mad Cow*. She announced a painting of the illustrated cartoon characters, Mad Cow and Swine Flew. Her tone was a little more strained and a lot less relaxed when she announced the next auction item: a private performance by Asher Knight and the rest of the band from Knight Time. Whatever had happened between Glo and Ash, Sofie guessed it would be a while before those wounds were mended.

If at all.

Proving relationships sucked basically everywhere, Faith, in an attempt to be cordial, was enduring—if not humoring—her ex-fiancé. Michael had shown up to represent Abundance Market, which Faith and Sofie agreed was respectable. Faith wasn't quite ready to forgive and forget the whole "Cookie" incident, but she admitted to Sofie that if he managed not to be a complete jackass while they were in the same room, she would see about forgiving him.

And here she came now, striding over on heels not as tall as Sofie's, but still she towered over her. At five-feet-ten, it didn't take much for Faith to tower. She handed over a pink drink garnished with a cherry and a slice of fresh pineapple.

Faith elevated her own glass. "Who knew something called 'Swine Flew Fizz' would taste as good as this delectable beverage?"

"Where is Michael?" Sofie sipped her own drink.

"I don't know." Faith rolled her eyes.

"Smile, beautiful ladies." Charlie appeared in front of them, camera raised.

Faith and Sofie pressed their cheeks together and grinned.

After the shutter clicked, Sofie said, "You should be about done, right? Have a drink with us."

Faith raised her glass. "They're better than they sound."

"I didn't intend for you to work the entire evening," Sofie told Charlie. "I'm sure you have enough photos to supply Open Arms and me with plenty of advertising and fundraising shots."

Charlie examined the screen on her digital Nikon. "I don't mind. Plus, my fiancé is busy writing his name in children's books." Her smile was proud, and when she locked eyes with Evan, Sofie watched Charlie's smile turn lusty.

Ah, *amore*.

"Maybe I should forget Michael and take a stab at Asher," Faith joked, sipping her Fizz and angling a gaze at the rock star.

"Trust me, sweets," Gloria said in that droll I've-seen-it-all manner she'd perfected, "you do not want a piece of *that*."

Faith choked, startled to find the raven-haired literary agent standing behind her.

"Gloria." With great effort, she cleared her throat. "I hope you know I was kidding. I know Asher is off-limits."

"He's not off-limits to any other female on the planet. Or in his tour bus," Gloria grumbled. "I don't know why you should apologize." She jerked her chin to a group of suits in the corner. Hot men with dashing smiles. "Get you one of those. Millionaires, billionaires, that's the way to go."

"Yes," said Kimber, joining their little group. "Because men with lots of money have zero problems." She winked good-naturedly—the way Kimber approached everything, Sofie had noticed. Gosh, she liked her. Why didn't she live closer?

"Landon just needed a good woman." Gloria elbowed Kimber in the arm.

Evan's oldest brother stood across the room, glass of scotch in hand, his other hand in his pocket. His hair was cut short and neat, a lighter shade of brown than Evan's. The man looked hot in a tux and stylish black glasses. Kimber was equally gorgeous in a chic black dress with a hint of vintage lace along the arms and hemline.

Crickitt August stepped up behind Kimber now, pink drink lifted to her lips. Sofie had met Crickitt earlier. The curly-headed beauty was married to Shane August, Landon's business partner and CEO of August Industries. He was the broad-shouldered drink-of-water standing next to Landon. A head full of wavy, dark hair lay against his head, and Sofie would be lying if she said she hadn't taken an appreciative gander at the way his pants cupped his butt. The man was not hard to look at.

"It's true, Shane is perfect and has never done anything wrong." Crickitt tossed her chin-length curls with one hand and winked at the group. "I'm sure Charlie would agree Evan is similarly fault-free."

"Oh yes," Charlie said, laying the sarcasm on thick. "We most certainly did *not* have an argument this morning about who put the nearly empty cereal box back in the cabinet."

"We went to the mat over where to eat dinner last night," said the very petite, curvy blond bombshell who stepped into their inner circle next.

"Sadie," Crickitt introduced. "These are the girls."

After names were given, Sofie's eyes went straight to Sadie's shoes. "I love those."

"Jimmy Choo. Forty percent off."

Oh yeah, they were going to become fast friends.

"Who won the dinner debate?" Kimber asked.

"Me," Sadie announced proudly. "Because he got his way about bringing the bike here."

Kimber's eyebrows lifted. "You rode from Osborn to Evergreen Cove on his Harley?"

"We did."

Yes, the Downeys—and their cousin, Shane, an honorary Downey—had heard of the charity dinner and swarmed. Like a troupe of well-meaning bees. Evan's sister Angel and her husband, Richie, made the trip up from Tennessee. Sofie talked to the sassy brunette at the start of the evening.

A dark blond head appeared over Sadie's shoulder right then. The man had an open collar, long hair, and scruff on his attractive face.

"Excuse me, mind if I borrow my wife?" He smiled as a pair of sea green eyes swept the group.

"Aiden, meet the ladies." Sadie melted into him, her smile clearly communicating she did not mind being dragged away.

"Ladies," he said, and Sofie would swear all of them—even the happily married ones—heaved a collective sigh.

After he hauled Sadie to the dance floor, Gloria's eyebrows shot up. "Good God. I forgot how potent he was."

Crickitt snorted. "Aiden is a one-woman guy. Trust me."

"That must be something," Gloria commented, her smile falling. "Having a man be yours and only yours." Her gaze tracked to Asher. "*Knowing* he's not going anywhere."

Kimber's arm wrapped around Gloria's elbow.

"Faith," Glo said a second later. "Your cling-on approaches."

Michael strode over, a fake smile plastered on his face.

"Faith," he said, his eyes flitting around the rest of the group but not settling on any one person.

He looked nervous. He ought to be. They knew what he'd done to their friend. He'd just meandered into the lion's den.

Faith's impatient smile said she didn't care how uncomfortable he was.

"Michael. You should join the conversation. We were talking about one-woman men. You know, men who aren't afraid of *commitment.*"

Crickitt and Kimber sipped their drinks. Glo snorted, unable—or unwilling—to hide her amusement. Michael's face blanched. Through his thin pair of wire-framed glasses, he studied Faith through narrowed eyes.

"Can I have a minute?" he asked, clearly frustrated.

"Fine," Faith told him. To Sofie she said, "Catch me up on what I miss, okay?"

"No problem," she promised, hoping her best friend wasn't about to make a huge mistake.

After Faith excused herself, Sofie did as well. She

clipped through the room, needing a break. She had to stop a few times to shake hands and chat with people she hadn't talked to yet. At the door, she met Ben, the fourteen-year-old who shared his testimonial onstage tonight. His story of being an alcoholic at a very young age and how Open Arms had helped him heal. It was incredibly moving. She'd noticed several guests dabbing tears from their eyes.

"Hey, Sofie," Ben said. His eyes went over her shoulder where Ruby stood talking to a group of gentlemen. "I mean, Ms. Martin."

She smiled. "Sofie is fine. You did great tonight. Your story touched a lot of people." Including Crickitt's husband, Shane. He'd written a sizable check this evening to Open Arms after hearing Ben's story. Sofie wondered if there was a story there. If Shane had related to Ben on some level; if Shane's family, like Donny's, had splintered.

"Thanks. Uh, do you think Asher Knight would sign this?" Ben reached into his suit coat and extracted a Knight Time CD.

Sofie palmed it. "I didn't know kids—er, anyone bought CDs any longer."

He shrugged a shoulder, his cheeks darkening in embarrassment.

"You know what?" She waved over his head, catching Asher's attention. "Go over there now. He doesn't look busy. I know he'd love to sign it for you."

Ben pulled his shoulders back and started toward the famous rock star. Sofie took the reprieve and slipped out of the ballroom, desperate for a break from the crowd.

In the hallway she passed a few loitering guests but

didn't pause on her journey to the great room. She pressed the door closed behind her and closed her eyes, resting her head on the panel. Sanctuary. *Finally.*

"Scampi."

She opened her eyes to find Donovan standing in front of the cold fireplace examining the work he'd done. In all her busyness to get ready for the charity dinner, she hadn't seen the final product.

The corner of his mouth kicked up as he plunged his hands into his pockets. In black slacks and a gray dress shirt, sleeves cuffed revealing tattooed forearms, Donovan looked ridiculously sexy. Which would've been fine if the only area that responded was the part between her legs. Yes, her erogenous zones had sat up and taken notice, but they were not the problem. The problem was that her heart sat up and noticed, too. And that was forbidden.

"I needed a break." She strolled over to him, trying to project an air of nonchalance she did not feel.

His eyes moved over her body, making her pull her shoulders back, put a little extra sass in her steps. Him looking at her the way he did now made her feel pretty. No . . . made her feel *beautiful.*

"I needed a break from you in that dress," he said, his voice a sensual husk. "Hard to be professional while sporting a boner."

Sofie tossed her head back and laughed. That shouldn't be sexy. And part of her wished he wasn't—but he was. Everything he said, everything he *did*, was sexy to her. A sure sign she was a goner. Through and through.

He erased the gap between them, pulled his hands from his pockets, and wrapped his arms around her waist. Wide palms covered her butt cheeks over her dress. He squatted down, kissing her deeply and running his hands beneath her flared skirt, up her thighs, and over her panties.

When his lips left hers, a deep growl reverberated from his throat. "*Lace.*"

She raised her arms and looped them around his neck. "Surprise."

He squeezed her ass again. "When is this thing over?"

He was talking about the party. But her thoughts were elsewhere. Because the "thing" between them would be over soon as well. That talk was coming, she guessed.

"Things are winding down," she said. "The auction winners will be announced promptly at ten." She turned her head to take in the clock on the far wall. "I should probably get back in there. I need to draw the winners."

"I'll help." He let go of her rear, his hands smoothing her skirt. He straightened and she turned to make her way to the ballroom. Before she got too far, his fingers laced with hers. "Never showed you," he said, tugging her back to him. "Used your rock."

He stepped away from the fireplace to reveal the jagged heart-shaped stone in the very center of the design. When she'd found it, she thought it was interesting. Not necessarily usable, since the heart was imperfect. But in the design with other imperfect pieces, it was...well, the whole was kind of perfect.

"Wow," she whispered.

"The only piece that could've gone there. I swear to you, there was this exact shaped hole."

A heart-shaped hole. And the only piece able to fill the hole was the piece she'd found. So much symbolism. She said nothing and his comment hung in the air as the clock ticked away behind them.

Running out of time. *They were running out of time* for everything.

"Better get things wrapped up," he said, squeezing her fingers with his. "Sooner we get these people out of my house, the better."

She nodded. The sooner they got these people out of his house, the sooner she would get to be with Donovan alone. And soon after, he would be packing up and leaving the Cove.

Bittersweet emotions clogging her chest, she kept hold of his hand and walked with him out of the great room.

* * *

Donovan and Sofie ran smack into Evan, who was coming from the direction of the ballroom. Asher trailed behind him blowing a trail of vapor from his mouth. Donovan had already given him shit about his new electronic smoking habit, but he knew, a former smoker himself, how hard it was to quit.

"Looking for a drink away from the stiffs," Evan announced.

Donovan looked to Sofie, who gave his fingers a quick squeeze, then let go. After she sauntered toward the ballroom, Donovan said to Evan, "I can help you with that."

His buddy's arched brow said he had thoughts about that silent bit of communication between Donovan and Sofie, but he ignored him.

The three of them walked to the dining room where a handful of people were having cocktails. Faith was in here, too. No sign of her douchebag ex-fiancé, but Connor was nearby. Donovan was glad. He didn't know what Michael was up to, but Faith was better off without him. Hopefully, Connor could run interference if necessary.

Donovan cut through the crowd with a polite smile, ducked behind the bar, and grabbed a bottle of bourbon and a stack of plastic cups.

Five minutes later, Asher, Evan, and Donovan were sitting in the back of Donovan's topless Jeep parked in the field behind the mansion.

Like Donovan, Evan hadn't bothered with the tie tonight, dressed in pants and a button-down shirt. Ash hadn't bothered dressing up at all—in his signature all-black ensemble of jeans and a tee and cowboy boots. Donovan undid another button on his shirt, anticipating the moment he could get out of the stiff slacks and into broken-in jeans.

"Hell of a party in there, man." Asher chucked back a shot and held up his cup.

Evan refilled it. "Yeah, impressed."

Donovan shrugged, finishing his own drink. "Didn't do anything. Just gave Sofie the space she needed." Except the space between the two of them. Where they were concerned, he hadn't given her much space at all. And she hadn't given him *any.* He tried to make that sound bad in his head. Couldn't do it.

"Who woulda thought?" Evan said contemplatively as he gazed in the direction of the mansion. "Us three screwups making something of ourselves."

Asher grunted. "Who says we're there?"

Evan socked him in the arm. "You were on the cover of *Rolling Stone*, asshole."

"You're both famous," Donovan said. "I'm just a layman who builds fireplaces."

"Dumbass." Asher held out an arm. "You own a freaking mansion."

"Yeah, you own a mansion," Evan agreed.

Donovan felt their eyes on his profile, knowing this was their way of trying to draw an answer out of him. The answer they wanted to hear. What they didn't know, or maybe what they did know and were in denial about, was that nothing had changed with the mansion. Donovan was still selling. He was still leaving.

"Mine for now," he said. "But the mansion is going to belong to Alessandre soon."

"You gettin' a new place in the Cove?" This from Evan.

"Nope. Going back."

"So this thing with you and Sofie..." Evan started.

He bit the inside of his cheek. This thing with him and Sofie. What was there to say about that?

"We'll work it out." Not an answer, but the only answer he was willing to give.

"Shit, Donny. You're as big of an idiot as Asher."

"Hey! What the fuck did I do?" Asher grabbed the bottle of bourbon and refilled his cup. Donovan let him fill his cup as well. "Leave him alone, Mr. Almost Married. Not all men are cut out to be dads and husbands."

"Amen," Donovan said, downing his drink in one swallow.

"Idiots." Evan snatched the bottle for himself.

"Maybe," Asher said. "Doesn't stop us from getting what we want. There's something to be said for having your cake, having different cake whenever you want. Having cupcakes in between."

Donovan chuckled at Asher's stupid joke. But that wasn't the case with him at all, was it? Promiscuity was a novelty. A novelty, he knew all too well, that wore thin after a while. A twitching dick was something he could live with. A raging libido was something he could bury—hell, had buried for seven years.

What he couldn't live with was the idea of lashing himself to Sofie and this town. Pretending to be a guy who knew how to be one-half of a relationship when he knew the deep, dark truth.

He wasn't good at relationships. He wasn't good at family.

He wasn't good . . . not for either of them.

* * *

The guests had finally gone, and Sofie was so exhausted, she could collapse.

She'd bid farewell to absolutely *everyone*: Ruby, the kids, and Evan's family, whom she thanked one-by-one for showing up and for their generosity. The Downeys, Shane and Crickitt August included, were an incredibly genuine family.

After the caterers had packed up, and the sound guys wound up their wires and packed up the microphones, two guests were left. Her dedicated employee-slash-bestie, Faith, and practically-live-in landscaper-slash-handyman, Connor.

Michael had left some time ago. That was the extent of the information Faith had shared, come to think of it. No matter. Sofie would get the full story soon enough.

Connor, still dressed in casual pants and a dress shirt, walked side-by-side with Faith into the foyer. They paused at the front door, where Sofie stood, having just seen out an older couple by the name of Townsend.

Faith hugged her. "Great job tonight, babe."

"Yes. Nicely done, Sofe," Connor said, pulling an arm around her neck and kissing her forehead.

"Thank you both for your help."

Connor gave her another squeeze, then let her go.

Faith dug her keys from a small purse as Donovan came around the corner.

Sofie tried to keep her heart from leaping at the sight of him, but it was no use. His jet-black hair had been styled back at the beginning of the night, but now was falling over his forehead in that disheveled way she'd grown used to. Even dressed in the harmless attire of black pants and a button-down shirt, Donovan Pate was a potent mixture of masculinity and danger.

A danger to your heart.

"You out?" Donovan asked.

Connor shook his extended hand. "For now."

For now.

Sofie felt the words stab the center of her chest. She knew Connor planned to do a few minor repairs before the sale. After that, Pate Mansion, the mansion she'd come to genuinely enjoy, would become Evergreen Cove's premiere bed-and-breakfast.

"Thanks for everything, man," Donovan said. "Couldn't have done it without you."

"I know." Connor smiled. "When are you heading back?"

Final. This conversation was so final.

"Hey, Sofie, can you walk me to my car?" Faith. God bless her. She must have known Sofie could use a distraction.

"Sure thing." She followed Faith to the door.

"Be out in a minute," Connor called after them.

Faith bit her lip and nodded curtly.

Well. That was interesting.

The girls stepped onto the covered porch then walked along the cobblestone driveway, looping their arms together to keep from teetering in their heels. Faith's car was parked close by, since she was among the first to arrive, so the walk was short.

In front of her Mercedes, Faith paused. "Are you going to be okay? Are you sure you don't want to leave?"

"Are you going to tell me what happened tonight between you and Michael?" Sofie asked, changing the subject. What she really wanted to know was what was happening between Faith and Connor. She suspected *something* was going on between those two. If not in practice, at least in thought.

"I know better than to believe in second chances."

Sofie met her best friend's navy eyes, chewing on that bit of advice for herself.

"Michael . . ." Faith shook her head as if exasperated. "You know what? I don't want to talk about it."

"Okay, hon. You don't have to." Sofie got that. She really did.

"Thank you." Faith's shoulders fell, the relief evident.

"Drive safe."

Faith's hand stilled on the door handle. "Are you going back inside?"

Sofie nodded.

"Are you staying?" Her eyebrows drifted into a look of concern.

Sofie nodded again. Like she'd be better off if she stopped now? She'd already fallen for Donovan. Already wanted him to stay in the Cove. How could this situation get any worse? But instead of admitting any of it, she simply said, "Straight through."

Faith climbed behind the wheel of her Mercedes and pulled away. Connor came outside next, revved the engine of his gold Mustang, and without a word to Sofie, rumbled down the driveway behind Faith.

Blowing out a breath, Sofie tipped up her chin. The white full moon, the starry sky, the pine trees and maples dotting the yard... she couldn't remember a more perfect night, unless she counted last night. Last night had been pretty perfect, too.

Abruptly, she missed Gertie's presence. The mutt had gone home with Faith yesterday evening. Faith's sister Skylar offered to watch her for a few days. As fun as the mutt was at the campout, a charity dinner was no place for a dog. Sofie prayed Skylar could help find a family who deserved a great pet. If she didn't, Sofie would have to make sure she did. She may not be allowed to have a dog at her apartment, but she refused to send Gertie to a shelter.

"There you are." The low rumble of Donovan's voice wound around her aching heart.

Sofie's eyes sank shut. Much like he'd given up Dog, he was going to give her up in the same way.

And you are going to give him up.

They were both walking away.

Strong arms wrapped around her waist and his fingers linked around her middle. She rested her hand over his. He didn't ask her to stay tonight. But then he'd stopped asking a long time ago.

He settled his cheek against hers.

"Come inside, Scampi. Have a surprise for you."

Before she could stop herself, hope leaped in her chest. Had he changed his mind about selling? Was he staying? Or maybe, he wasn't staying but didn't want to end what they had between them. Her fingers continued to brush his knuckles, but she stayed silent, afraid to give a voice to any of the thoughts in her head.

He kissed her temple and pointed her toward the house, dropping his hand to her butt where he cupped one cheek as they walked inside. As he pushed open the front door and ushered her over the threshold, she tried to lighten the mood.

"My backside was lonely before you came back to town."

She expected him to laugh, but when the front door closed behind her, she turned to find his expression serious. He took her in from head to toe, slowly, *purposefully.* Then he snagged her hand, spun her around, and pressed her body up against the door with his.

The night seven years ago replayed in her mind.

The foyer, barely lit by soft yellow sconces. The light fading into the dark floors, thick drapes, highlighting the raw intension on Donny's face. As if history was repeating, Donny breathed into her ear and bit her earlobe.

She arched her back and rubbed herself against him, feeling his hard length press into her belly.

"Scampi." He tugged her bottom lip with his teeth.

"Donny," she whispered, feeling the significance of this moment. The *weight* of this moment.

He smiled down at her.

She managed a small smile in return. "If this is my surprise, I approve."

"Giving you a do-over, sweetheart."

His hands curved around her ass. He kissed her again.

"A do-over?" she asked when she lost his lips.

"Library." He tipped his head to the room on her right.

Where it had all started. Technically, it started in the parking lot of the Wharf, but they both knew the most significant act had occurred here, at the mansion. Kind of perfect it should end here, too. The charity dinner was over, Gertrude was gone, and Donovan was leaving. But, evidently, not before making good on the vow to give her a do-over on that first night they shared together.

Perfect. *Achingly* perfect.

She twined her fingers into his black hair. "Couch or rug?"

"Good memory." He kissed her softly and repeated his words from that fateful night. "Couch or rug?" He lifted her like he did seven years ago, his hands cupping her backside. Her legs answered by wrapping around his waist.

She continued raveling his hair around her fingertips and staring down into his pale silver blue eyes, wondering if he remembered what came next.

He did.

"Where do you want to make love?" His throat bobbed as he swallowed thickly.

"You didn't mean it then," she couldn't resist pointing out.

"No."

"Now?"

"Yeah, Scampi," he answered. "I mean it now."

She brushed the hair off his forehead as he walked her to the doorway.

"You don't get hard and fast tonight," he told her. "You get slow and sweet. You get what you deserved the first time around. You get me taking my time, making sure you get what you deserve. Tonight"—he kissed her—"you get everything you want."

Not everything, her breaking heart reminded her.

This was Donovan's good-bye. He wasn't going to stay. He was giving back the thing he'd taken from her, only this time, gift-wrapped.

A good-bye present.

She was going to accept. Because she couldn't physically walk away from him while his eyes held hers and his mouth said all the right words. On a very selfish level, she refused to walk away from an evening bathed in the promise of slow and smooth.

Before Donovan left her again, she wanted every bit of him she could get. Every ounce he was willing to leave behind. Because she would treasure it. When the nights got long and lonely, these were the memories she would unpack and curl herself around.

Placing a kiss on the center of his mouth, she whispered, "Couch."

Same as seven years ago, he smiled up at her.

"That's what I wanted to hear."

CHAPTER TWENTY-SIX

Sofie's hair was up, worn in a loose arrangement of curls. Donovan put her on her feet and, resisting reaching for her body, put his hands in her hair instead.

He felt beneath her curls until he found a bobby pin. He pulled the tiny piece of metal free, careful not to take her hair with it. One loose curl spilled out. She turned green, green eyes up to his, and the power of her gaze zapped his chest like a bolt of lightning. He freed another. And another, repeating the process and dropping pins to the hardwood floor in a series of muted clatters.

Once her hair was down, he combed his fingers through the strands, ruffling the curls around her face.

"Gorgeous," he murmured. So gorgeous it hurt.

Her fingers went to his belt. His hand covered hers. Shaking his head, he said, "Not yet. I have more to do."

She obeyed and dropped her hand. He cupped her jaw, tilted her chin, and kissed her. Just a brush of his lips against hers while spearing his hands up through the hair he'd taken his time to undo. The back of her dress scooped down to her waist in a low V, and he ran his hands down her spine, and back up, savoring the shiver flitting through her body as he did.

His hands trembled the slightest bit. Had he ever trembled when he touched a woman? No. Never. And he'd touched the woman gazing up at him too many times to count since he'd returned to Evergreen Cove.

But somehow this was different. All of it was different. This was her do-over. And he was going to do her over *and over*, he thought with a wicked grin.

Leaving her briefly, he lifted a glass of ice he'd brought in earlier and sucked an ice cube into his mouth.

She watched him approach, pulling her bottom lip under her teeth.

Beautiful.

He tipped her chin and kissed her neck, raking the ice along her thundering pulse and down to the hollow of her throat. His fingers went to the zipper low on her back where he drew it open slowly, peeling the dress from her shoulders just as slowly.

By the time he dragged the ice over Sofie's collarbone, she was writhing, head back, her fingers wrenching into his hair.

He bared her breasts, thumbing her skin as he stroked his tongue between them. When the ice melted, he abandoned her body, but only to get another piece.

* * *

Sofie was *dissolving.*

Like the ice on Donovan's tongue currently running

over her pebbled nipple. She sprawled on the red velvet sofa, legs open to accommodate him kneeling before her. Her fingers tightened into his hair as she pulled and pushed and whimpered.

After who knew how many torturous minutes passed, he tracked his tongue between the valley of her breasts and up to her neck where his cold tongue laved her flesh. He pressed a kiss to her shoulder and several along the length of her neck, leisurely working his way up to her ear.

Gone was the Donovan who nipped and bit, who soothed the sting with more kisses. This Donovan was achingly gentle, his touch featherlight.

And fully clothed, more was the pity. Since he'd pushed her dress from her hips and sat her down onto the sofa, she only wore the lace panties she'd chosen with him in mind.

The scalloped edges were high cut, covering her bottom but completely transparent. She'd pulled them on earlier today, guessing she'd be wearing them for about five seconds after he laid eyes on them. But to her continued surprise and delight, he hadn't rushed to strip her bare.

When he promised to give her everything she wanted, he wasn't lying. This was everything she wanted. His attention. This drugging, slow pace.

Against the back of the sofa, she sagged.

"So far so good?" His head came up, his lips brushing hers.

"I think you know the answer to that question." She lifted an eyebrow. "You know you don't have to—"

His finger covered her lips, and she sucked his finger into her mouth, watching his eyes go hot and hungry. Through parted lips, he sucked in a ragged breath.

There. She had him. And soon, she would have him in

her mouth or inside her. She increased the suction, thinking she'd won the battle of impatience, when he lifted her hips with his free hand.

He pulled his finger from her mouth, slipped past the barrier of her lace panties, and slicked between her folds. The breath she dragged in was broken, the emitting sound a full-on moan begging for more.

While his tongue encircled her breast, his fingers danced along her center. Then he slid one finger inside her, followed by another, and let loose her nipple with a suctioning *pop*.

He raised his chin and licked his lips, and damn if her hips didn't lift on their own, driving his fingers deeper.

"Since this is your first time making love to me"— those lips tipped into a naughty smile—"I'm going to make sure you come first." Mouth on hers, he gave her a long wet kiss that had her reaching for his shoulders and pulling him closer. "And come *hard*."

Her panties disappeared, swept down her legs and tossed over his shoulder. His fingers returned and he put his tongue against her clitoris, applied pressure, and lapped her until she was squirming.

He wasn't kidding. She came.

And she came *hard*.

* * *

She was dripping. *For him.* And that undeniable fact had him rock hard.

Despite the very real shake working its way through his bones, he had continued to put his own needs on hold.

Until now.

He'd vowed to give Sofie everything she wanted. Mouth dropped open, her cheeks bright pink, her mahogany curls spread around her over the sofa where he laid her out, he thought probably, they were pretty close.

From between her legs, he tilted his hips, he drove into her wetness, watching her eyes squeeze close, feeling her tightness clamp around him—hold him together.

Yet again.

She was the most beautiful thing he'd ever seen.

It was no secret Donovan was a dog when he was younger. There were a lot of forgettable, hazy nights soaked in a lot of booze. When it came to sex, being as physically close as he could get to another person, there had always been distance. Save for Sofie. She didn't allow distance.

The only distance he'd ever managed with her was the geographical kind. Being over five hundred miles away had been the only way to be away from her.

That night, the dam of emotions had burst, carrying with it a sense of foreboding the moment he slipped inside her sweet, giving body. She had opened for him in every way possible. Tonight was no different. She was relaxed, accessible. This time, it was he who gave and she who took. He allowed himself the privilege to savor every last inch sliding into her warmth.

Her fingers grazed his jaw, her moss green gaze locking on to his.

He couldn't look away. Couldn't hide. Couldn't deny what he saw in her and what he knew she saw reflected in him. As he angled his hips, arranging himself on the sofa too small for them, he stroked her long and slow, taking his time, pulling every drop of passion out of the woman who had once again accepted him into her arms.

She'd accepted him and that was the most beautiful part.

"Donny."

His old nickname riding on a cracked moan undid him most of all. He thought he had left *Donny* behind. Though he didn't want anything to do with the man he used to be, Sofie, in her own way, affirmed who he was. *Who I am.*

Inside and out, she *knew* him. And she didn't deny him. Straight through.

She moved with him now, arching into a rhythm he matched effortlessly. When she breathed his name a second time, another orgasm rocked her frame and milked his from him. Like drawing a loose string from a sweater, he unraveled, coming inside her, and collapsing to his forearms over her supple body.

He gave her all of him. Every drop she'd given to him, he returned. She'd taken his release and in the process cleansed him of the past that had held him prisoner for far too long.

It took a while for him to come down, a long while where he lay, his face buried in her neck, while her fingers stroked up and down his back, over his shoulders. As his breaths slowed, he kissed her chest and untangled his hands from her hair.

When he pulled out, he did so slowly, earning a soft exhalation as she sighed against his lips. He'd planned on getting them both off this damned uncomfortable couch, to move her to the bedroom or any piece of furniture *not* a foot and a half too short for his frame, but once he faced her, he froze.

"Better." She smiled up at him.

He blew out a laugh, but his levity faded as reality set

in. The first time he brought her here, he shouldn't have. He'd known that. But he'd never told her that.

Straight through.

"Seven years ago I was fucked up," he blurted.

Her face softened, but she stayed quiet.

So he continued.

"The night I brought you here . . . my father died earlier that week. Overdose."

Robert Pate had always drunk a ton, but he started hitting the pills hard after Donovan left home at sixteen. With his punching bag gone, he guessed Robert no longer had a place to dump his anger.

"Gertrude was beside herself. My father was her only child."

Sofie slid the hair from his eyes, saying nothing. Comforting him. Unable to keep from it, he lowered his face and kissed her. She flattened her hand against his cheek and held his lips against hers for a beat.

So fucking sweet.

When they parted, he said, "I was done. Done with the whole town, done with this house. I saw where I was headed—knew my life had added up to absolutely nothing. I was going to end up just like him, and I knew it. I was coming here that night to raid the liquor cabinet. Gertrude kept it stocked. I planned on downing a bottle of bourbon or vodka, hell, anything. Then I was going to drive to the quarry and climb a sheet of ice and rock."

Sofie's face melted into an expression of concern. "Dangerous."

"Stupid."

Her palm slid down his face and came to rest on his neck.

"I saw you watching me from across the bar at the Wharf. Then I decided to do something else with my evening. Decided to give myself a little bit of sweet after a week—a lifetime—of bad. I remember thinking... maybe the way out of pain wasn't more pain. Maybe if I buried myself in so much pleasure I couldn't move, I'd be okay." Moving his fingers into her hair, he cradled her head. "You, Scampi. You were the game changer."

"The virgin who ruined your plans."

"You ruined everything." He gave her a small smile. "And you saved me. Saved me from wandering drunk into the snow."

"Then I drove you away."

"I drove myself. I hated myself for taking what I took from you. Just stole what I wanted and didn't give you anything in return."

"But you—"

He stopped her words with a kiss, then pulled away and shook his head. "I didn't deserve an easy out. I didn't deserve you. Knew you were better off without me. I became what I deserved."

Gentle fingers stroked his jaw as honest green eyes flashed over his face. Adjusting them on the couch, he held her close, kissed her long and slow.

When her eyes cleared of their lusty haze, he said, "Ready for some more truth?"

"Hit me."

"Would never hit you."

Her finger trailed along his bottom lip. "You know what I mean."

"Every ounce of love you poured into our first night together... I felt that. I've been hit a lot, I've had bones broken, had needles punctured into my skin to cover the scars. But I swear to you, I've never felt more afraid than the moment I figured out what you were giving me— how you felt about me." He took a deep breath. *Straight through.* "I've never been so unworthy of a gift before or since."

"Not true." Tears flooded her eyes.

"Don't you dare cry for me, sweetheart."

"I think"—her voice broke, and the break echoed in his heart, splitting him in two—"I still love you."

He held her face between his palms.

"Fuck, Scampi."

"I know. It's foolish." She blinked several times, forcing back the tears perched on her lashes. He watched her eyes fill again. "More foolish to admit it." Those swimming eyes found his. "I can't help it."

Gently, he lifted her chin and lowered his mouth to hers, drinking her in, savoring that love on her tongue. It had a flavor: sweetness, pure and simple.

She shifted beneath him, pressing her hips up to his. He was growing hard for her. Already. Before he thought better of it, he angled himself between her legs and slid in to the hilt. He moved inside her, continuing to kiss her— making love to her mouth as well as her body.

"I've never loved anyone," he said against her lips, knowing he was about to make an epic mistake but, like this moment, was incapable of stopping. He pumped into her, watching her mouth fall open, her eyes sink to half-mast.

"Fuck, Sofie," he whispered, his vocal chords tight with emotion. "I love you." The tears she'd been damming spilled over. He brushed them away with the pads of his thumbs and thrust into her again. "I love you so goddamned much."

She smiled through her tears, holding him tightly as he continued pumping into her.

He shouldn't have said it.

After, she would ask questions he couldn't answer. Questions about what would become of them now.

He loved her. He hadn't lied about that. He also hadn't lied about the fact that she was better off without him seven years ago.

But what caved his chest in, even as another orgasm shook his bones, was the fact that she was better off without him now, too.

* * *

Sofie had no idea what time it was.

After the library, Donovan brought her upstairs and laid her in his bed. He made love to her again, showing no signs of running out of steam. And the entire time all she could think of was his admission downstairs. She'd confessed her deepest, darkest feelings for him, and he'd shattered her in the best way.

He loved her. He *loved* her.

They'd left the bed to shower. He soaped her and dried her and kissed her sweetly. Back in bed, he'd tucked her into his chest, enclosed his arms around her, and complained her hair was wet and cold.

She'd laughed, told him to "wait and see what it looks like in the morning," and closed her eyes.

She was on the fringes of sleep when a shrill ring pierced the air.

Donovan stirred next to her, jostling the bed as he moved to answer his cell.

Sofie blinked her eyes open as he murmured "Alessandre" into the phone. Conversational words followed. *Yeah. Not too late. No. Good.*

His next four words jolted her awake.

"The sooner the better."

Rolling onto her back, she pulled the sheets over her naked body. Donovan, sitting on the side of the bed, ran a hand through his hair.

"Yeah," he said. "Ready to get back."

Her stomach tossed. This wasn't happening.

The *sooner* the *better?*

He ended the call and dropped the phone on the nightstand with a clatter. Swinging his legs into bed, he settled against the mattress and let out a long, low breath.

She sat up on one elbow, her damp hair causing gooseflesh to pop up on her bare skin.

"Ready to get back...to New York?" Part of her hoped he'd fervently deny it.

He didn't.

He looked her dead in the eyes in the moonlit room and said, "Ready to get back to work, yeah."

God. Was she hallucinating? Surely this wasn't the same man who was in the library with her earlier. When he said her name—her *real* name—followed by *I love you.*

"So that's it? You're just...leaving?"

"Scampi." A frown bisected his brows.

"Leaving Evergreen Cove." She threw the covers off, unable to quell the anger—the *hurt*—stinging her skin like hundreds of needles.

Leaving her. *Again.*

The pinnacle of vulnerability would be to show how much she hurt. But she couldn't keep from reacting. Couldn't keep the words from coming.

"How can you make plans to go back after...after..."

She couldn't say it.

Eyes on the ceiling, he spoke in an even tone. "Never planned on staying."

"But...you said"—*that you loved me*—"so many things."

Cold blue eyes flicked to her.

"Doesn't mean I'm staying, Scampi."

And there it was. The hairline crack in her heart—the crack Donny Pate had put there—splintered. He'd fractured her tender heart seven years ago; now he obliterated it.

Doesn't mean I'm staying.

But that's exactly what it should mean. In her mind, anyway. Maybe that's where this entire affair had occurred. *In her mind.* Donovan never made her any promises. And she never asked for any. She'd fallen into his arms again, but this time, her eyes were open. He took what he wanted and left her behind seven years ago. She knew him, knew what to expect.

So why are you upset?

Because she started to believe he changed. Believed *she* changed him. Against her better judgment, she'd allowed herself to hope. Worse, she allowed herself to love him. And love couldn't be undone.

Finally, Donovan turned his head and looked at her. "You gonna make me sleep alone tonight?"

She should. She *could.* She could gather the pieces of her heart, what was left of her self-respect, get dressed, and leave. Not trusting her answer, she said nothing.

The palm of his hand brushed her thigh, stroked up her ribs, and closed around her back.

"Don't wanna sleep alone tonight, Scampi."

She found herself folding over him, *folding*, period. Her weakness where he was concerned alive and well. But she didn't have to stay weak.

Faith had pointed out Sofie held the power in this relationship. He may be leaving. But she had the power to let him. She wasn't going to squander their last night together arguing when he would end up leaving anyway.

Untrustworthy emotions swirled in her chest. She sealed them up tight. Oh, she'd feel them later. They'd escape and choke the very air in her lungs. But for now she'd do her best to feel nothing.

She lay next to him, rested her palm on his chest, and her face on his shoulder. One strong, tattooed arm wrapped around her body and pulled her close. Lying there against his chest, listening to his heart beat, listening to his breaths slow, she felt plenty.

Each breath she took scratched her dry throat like shards of glass.

A soft kiss landed on her forehead.

"'Night, Scampi."

Her mind completely blank of all thoughts, she closed her eyes. Finally, with her leg draped over his thigh, and her arm over his stomach, she fell asleep.

$\mathcal{C}$HAPTER TWENTY-SEVEN

$\mathcal{W}$ork.

Getting back to work was what mattered most. Donovan's first job when he returned to the Hamptons was for Mrs. Baron: super wealthy, peroxide-blond-haired forty-something with a body she'd purchased with her millions and rocked publicly without shame.

As if to prove his point, Alyssa strutted out to her patio, long white robe open, tiny black bikini on display, like a model on a catwalk.

"Looking good, Donovan." She offered a glass of iced tea. "Your drink."

"Thanks." He slipped his gloves off and accepted the iced tea. It was boiling-lava hot out here, way into the nineties, and he was sweating buckets. He took the glass and threw back a long swallow, coughing when his throat began to burn. He wiped his mouth on the back of his hand and slid an irritated glance at Alyssa. "What the hell?"

The corner of her red lips quirked. She shrugged.

"I added tequila, a little bit of vodka, some rum. I can't remember exactly how to make a Long Island Iced Tea, but that should suffice."

"A bottle of water next time." He thrust the glass into her hands.

She accepted with an exaggerated pout. "You certainly play hard to get. Maggie told me you did."

Maggie? She must be talking about Margaret Brown, whose fireplace he'd repaired a few months back. Back before he made the apocalyptic mistake of returning to Evergreen Cove.

Alyssa stepped closer, ran a pink fingernail down his T-shirt, and Donovan couldn't dredge up any feelings save for irritation. He took a step away from her.

"Water, Alyssa. I don't screw my clients. If I did"—may as well make himself perfectly clear—"I wouldn't screw the married, desperate ones."

"Are you trying to get fired, Mr. Pate?" One prim brow arched in challenge as she fought to hold her composure.

With a shrug, he gestured to the half-completed fireplace on her patio. "You know someone else who can finish this?"

Alyssa shut her mouth with the snap of her pearly teeth.

She didn't. He'd designed the fireplace custom to fit on her oddly shaped patio and face the sunset. He'd love to see another contractor match the seams. The mortars were mixed sixty/forty dove gray and Russian brown. He'd done a few others in similar fashion—the entire piece echoed his signature style. His commercial style, anyway. This was what people in the Hamptons wanted. Perfection.

Alyssa wanted to impress her snooty friends. She'd commissioned him for this job for that reason. Or so he'd thought. He slid a dismissive glance over her body. Seemed she had another agenda.

"I'll get your water." Closing her robe with one hand, she clipped into the house.

He turned back to the fireplace. Smooth, square bricks stacked ten feet high in front of him. They were pristine. All the same color. The monochrome fireplace on Alyssa's back patio would be a tower of straight, elegant stones when he finished.

Perfect. Regal.

Boring as hell.

Sun beating on his back, he went down to one knee to pick up another piece. As he slapped the brick into place, his mind returned to Sofie. His mind often returned to Sofie. He wondered how much longer he'd have to endure her invading his thoughts, and then he remembered the last time, and figured it'd take about seven years. At least.

Damn, he missed her.

The phone on his belt trilled and for a split second, he thought he'd summoned her. Connor's number lit the screen. Hope pushed against his chest, wanting out. His friend was a connection to Evergreen Cove...a connection to Sofie.

He tapped the screen and brought the phone to his ear. "Yeah."

"Done," Connor informed him. "She's ready for sale."

A chill spread across Donovan's chest. He'd lived in that house, hated that house, and now, the inheritance he never wanted was almost out of his hands for good. Shouldn't he be relieved? But the weight didn't lift from his shoulders. He felt like Atlas with a world made of unyielding stone balanced on his back.

"Good." Maybe he'd believe himself eventually.

Donovan propped the phone against his ear and slapped mortar onto another brick. He didn't want to be here any longer than he had to be.

"Sofie subbed me out for a permanent gig," Connor said.

The brick slipped from Donovan's hand, narrowly missing his boots. Mortar splattered on Alyssa's patio. "Shit."

"Don't hate."

"That's not what I—listen, Connor, I'm busy."

"I guess Sofe gets her flowers from Fern's Floral Shoppe, and Fern is in need of some lavender. Of course, Fern wants the best—mine."

Connor's patented hybrid. Who knew there was money in something like that?

"Guess I should get my plants out of the mansion."

Donovan heard the question in his buddy's voice even though he didn't ask one. Connor wanted to know if there was any chance he'd keep Pate Mansion. If there was a chance he'd return to the Cove.

"Yeah." Donovan scraped up the mortar and slopped it into the bucket. "Sooner the better." Another lie he'd been trying to convince himself was true for way too long. The sooner the better? What the hell did it matter? Nothing would get better no matter how much sooner he sold the mansion.

"Whatever you say," Connor said, his tone flat. He was disappointed and not because he had to move his lavender beds out of the mansion. He was disappointed in Donovan.

"You did fine without me for seven years," Donovan grumbled. "You'll muddle through without me now."

A sharp, humorless laugh scratched through the phone. "How fucking selfish can you be, man?"

Donovan stood and wiped the sweat from his brow with the back of one glove. "You want to say that again?"

"Can if you want me to, but I'm pretty sure you heard me." He could picture Connor, stony glare, arm crossed over his chest. "You think this town is better off without you, that your friends are better off without you. I'm guessing you've convinced yourself Sofie is better off without you."

Sofie.

Nothing weakened him more than hearing her name. Or thinking about her. Or picturing the hurt in her eyes when he'd kissed her good-bye for the last time. Or feeling his chest cave in the way it did when he walked out to Trixie and found the house key on the Jeep's hood. He walked out on Sofie and she'd accepted. Accepted what he gave her, which was essentially nothing.

"I don't want to talk about Scampi."

"I don't care what you want, Donny. Truth is, none of us are better off without you. I don't know if you were looking around while you were here, but we were doing fine and fucking dandy when you *were* here. Now you're gone, and guess what? Dog is homeless, my lavender is about to be displaced, and Sofie...God, Donny. What the hell did you do to her?"

Pain zapped his chest like he'd been electrocuted. Donovan barely got his throat to work, but when he did, he demanded, "What about her?"

"She looks...You know what? Ask her yourself."

Exactly what he wasn't going to do. He couldn't bear

the idea of her hurt. And calling her and hearing it in her voice? It would destroy him.

After a moment of silence, Connor said, "Those Open Arms kids. Having the campout here was good for them. I ran into Ruby the other day. Know what she said?" He didn't wait for a response. "She said she'd love to do the camp at the mansion every year. *Every year*, Donny."

Donovan clenched his jaw.

"Apparently Ben has not stopped talking about you since the night you gathered sticks and built a fire. Sounds like you made an impression on the kid."

"You done?" The guilt train could station any time now.

"Still convinced you're better off alone?"

"I *am* better off alone. I like being alone."

"Keep telling yourself that and you will die alone. Unloved."

Pissed, he ground out, "Deal."

But Connor wasn't done. "You're a runner. I don't think you'd have any friends if not for Evan, Asher, and me flushing you out of hiding every so often."

"Yeah? Then quit doing it." Donovan didn't need anyone. Wasn't that what he'd been trying to convince people for years?

"Gonna tell you what I know."

Great.

"I know plants. I know roots. And I know you don't have 'em. Know how I know?" Again he didn't wait for a response. "Because you can't get roots if you keep taking off and not letting them grow."

"I have roots." They were gnarled and tangled and buried beneath Pate Mansion.

"Yeah, you do. Me. Evan. Asher. Hell, Evan's wife, Charlie, likes you. Faith liked you, too, or did, anyway, before you bailed on her best friend. Bet if you quit being a dumbass, you could have Sofie, too."

Patience thin, Donovan was seething by the time Alyssa stepped outside with water. The glare he shot her must have been glacial. She handed over the plastic bottle and scuttled back inside without so much as a bat of her fake eyelashes.

"You want to talk about running away?" Donovan turned his back on the house and watched the ocean. "Let's talk about Maya. Let's talk about you serving back-to-back-to-back stints in the military because you couldn't face the reality that was your life." If Connor thought he was the only one capable of doling out holier-than-thou, pot-calling-the-kettle-metal insights, he had another thing coming.

"You're right," Connor surprised him by agreeing. "Difference is, I'm back. I'm staying. I'm done running. About time you stopped being a pussy and did the same."

The line went quiet, and the only sounds Donovan heard were his pulse beating in his eardrums and the gulls crying as they swept over the beach below. He wrapped his hand around his phone hard enough to crack the screen.

With anger fueling his work, he stayed at Alyssa's house until the sky grew dark. He skipped dinner, finished the fireplace, and left her house for the last time.

CHAPTER TWENTY-EIGHT

Sofie took the end of the leash from her best friend's hand.

"I'm so sorry," Faith said. "Skylar checked with everyone she knows. I checked with everyone I know. No one can take her, even temporarily."

Gertie was panting, her mouth smiling. Ironically, she looked happy. Her tail wagged back and forth, knocking against the desk.

"Skylar would keep her longer if she could. My mom's new model boyfriend is allergic to dogs." Faith rolled her eyes. "But if you can keep her somewhere for two or three days, he has a photo shoot in New York. I can take her over there."

At the mention of New York, Sofie's heart clutched. She had been trying her hardest not to think of the state, or the man in it, at all.

"Thanks, but I'll figure something out. Don't worry

about it. Maybe she can stay here at the shop..." Not the best plan, but it'd be near impossible to sneak a dog Gertie's size into her cramped apartment. Especially since her neighbor had recently been asked to get rid of her oversized dog by request of the landlord. She could ask her parents... of course, then she would have to explain why she had a dog. And that would mean telling them about Donovan. Maybe she could fudge the details...

"Are you sure you don't need me for anything today?" Faith wrung her hands. "I can work if you need me to."

"It's Sunday. Take the day off. Gertie is not your problem. She's not a problem at all, are you girl?" Sofie bent to nuzzle the top of the dog's head. "You're just a dog without a home."

Without a mansion, she thought sadly. In a weird way, Sofie felt as lost as Gertie. She hadn't been in her apartment much while Donovan was in town, so when he went to New York, staying there felt... strange. "I'll figure something out," she promised the three of them.

Faith started to leave, then turned and pegged Sofie with a look of concern.

Uh-oh.

"I know you don't want to talk about it, but..."

Uh-oh, times two...

"Are you okay?" Faith scrunched her cute nose. "I mean with... Donovan leaving and everything?"

They hadn't talked about Donovan leaving, about how Sofie was dealing with the loss. She was impressed Faith had kept quiet this long. Typically, they talked about everything. But since Michael's awkward departure from the charity dinner, Faith remained stoically silent. And Sofie, not wanting to talk about her own recent heartbreak, didn't bring up Michael for fear the conversation would lead to talking about Donny.

"I'm not okay," Sofie admitted aloud for the first time. Picking up on her mood change, Gertie leaned her weight into Sofie's leg. Absently, she stroked her fur. "Are you... okay?" she asked Faith.

"I don't think so." Faith sighed. "I never told you—"

The bell over the door rang, and Connor McClain strolled in. He dipped his chin at Sofie before his eyes swung to Faith. His mouth flattened. "Hey."

"Hey," Faith returned.

"Hey, Gert." He came to stand next to Sofie and scratched the dog's ears. "Was just gonna talk to you about Fern," he said to Sofie. "Her shop is closed today, but I have her plants. Okay to store them here until tomorrow?"

"No more indoor greenhouse," Faith said. "I forgot about that."

Straightening, Connor faced her. "Yeah. The closing is at the end of the month."

Three days. The mansion would be sold in three days. Sofie would have no reason to go there again. She had already decided as much as her business would flourish from the connection with Pate Mansion, that if Alessandre D'Paolo needed an event planner for his B-and-B, he would simply have to find someone else to do it. She had accepted what she and Donovan had was over, but there was no way she could set foot near the mansion's library without remembering their last night together.

Fuck, Sofie. I love you.

Her stomach dove, and she folded her arms over her middle. The memory was a physical blow. So painful, she'd had a mini-fantasy last night about how they could have a long-distance relationship. He could visit the Cove, and she could fly out to visit him. They could continue plodding along. But plodding wasn't what she wanted, was it? Carrying on a relationship that would never yield any return on her investment... And then when it ended...

No. It was better to cut ties, or so went the tired lecture looping in her head yet again. She had survived the first time. Surely, she would survive the second.

"I have things to do," Faith said suddenly—Sofie guessed so she could get out of the shop and away from Connor. "See you later. Good luck with Gertie." Barely glancing in his direction, she walked out the door.

After the bell clanged against the glass, Sofie raised her eyebrows at the man in her shop. "I guess you don't want to talk about that?"

He shook his head. "Not any more than you would like to talk about Donny."

A beat passed before she said, "You know, I would like to talk about Donny." *Straight through.* Hadn't that been what she'd learned from him this time around? Funny how he couldn't take his own advice. "Does he have anywhere to keep Gertie in New York?"

"Yeah," Connor said sharply. "He has a place to keep a dog. He has space for his three buddies to visit. He'd have room for a girlfriend if he'd pull his head out of his ass."

She smiled weakly.

"Donny isn't the kind of guy who keeps things for himself," he continued. "What he knows is how to hunker down and endure."

"Hunkering down? Felt more like he gave up." And he gave up so much. She was worth holding on to.

"He doesn't trust himself when he's happy."

"Was he?" she asked quietly. "Happy?"

"I've never seen him so light, Sofe. You changed him."

"And he left anyway."

"More like ran."

They fell quiet for a moment.

"He doesn't have a huge network," Connor said. "He's got a few friends who have chipped past the layer of armor he wears all the damn time. Me. Evan and Asher. We know him to his core. We know the guy under that layer. You know that guy, too."

She sighed, weary. Sick of this discussion already.

"When I was in Afghanistan, I served with men like him. Some guys harden because of war; others harden in preparation for it. Easier not to get hurt when you're made of stone."

What a metaphor. She thought of the stone fireplace in the mansion. The rock wall at the quarry.

"Then there were the guys who had families," Connor said. "The guys who had a reason to fight, something to fight for. Those with nothing to lose, those with everything to lose. Both make good soldiers."

Since he'd started talking about war, his face had darkened, shadows prevalent beneath his eyes. She wondered what he'd been through over there. If he ever talked about it with anyone.

"Which one are you?" she asked.

"I'm split, but not fifty-fifty." A sad smile tilted his mouth.

She wound Gertie's leash around her fingers while she thought of how much to say.

"Donny told me he loved me." The sympathy on Connor's face told her he hadn't known. "But if he did, he'd be here."

Connor scrubbed a hand through his short, sandy-colored hair, then shook his head. "He really doesn't make it easy on those of us who love him, does he?"

"No. He really doesn't."

"Makes you want to ding him in his rock-hard head."

"Something like that."

His hand landed on her shoulder.

"You tapped into him, Sofe. Deep. I bet him feeling what he feels for you scared him shitless. He's not in New York because he doesn't love you. He's there because he does and doesn't know what the hell to do about it."

Her eyes sank closed. "That doesn't make me feel any better."

"No, I guess it doesn't. They say war is hell. So is love."

"Don't tell me that. Don't tell me that when I am trying to get over him." She gestured at her surroundings. "When I am in this office trying to focus on work, trying to pick up the pieces. Trying not to hurt every single day." She petted Gertie, who still leaned against her leg.

"See? You get it." Connor bent at the waist, scrubbed the dog's head one final time, and then leveled his eyes with Sofie's. "You're hardening up, too."

He was right. She was.

Conversation over, he moved for the exit. "Mind if I prop the door open?"

"Not at all. Let me put Gertie in the back, and I'll help."

"No, I got it. You and Gert take a walk," he instructed. "Take some time."

At the "w" word, Gertie launched out of her relaxed lean and dragged Sofie, still attached to the other end of the leash, for the door. Connor chuckled, maneuvering out of the way as Gertie dashed outside and Sofie scrambled to keep up.

Take some time, he'd said. Sofie knew he'd meant take some time to think about what he said.

She did—she thought about what he said for the next two days.

* * *

"Lacey, honey, make sure you rinse the soda cans before putting them into the recycling bin," Sylvia instructed.

Lacey rolled her eyes and Kinsley laughed. Sofie may have laughed, but there wasn't a single part of her capable of levity at the moment. Kinsley and Sylvia went out back to admire her mother's herb garden, leaving Sofie and Lacey alone in the kitchen.

Sofie took the now rinsed cans from her sister's hands and dropped them into the bin next to the trashcan.

Lacey dried her hands on a dishtowel. "Thanks."

"Sure." Sofie nodded and walked to the window overlooking the backyard. Gertie dashed after a squirrel, barking. When she successfully treed it, she sat on her haunches and waited for the rodent to come down.

"Why do you have a dog?" Lacey asked, coming to stand next to her.

"She belongs to a client. How goes the wedding plans?" Sofie hoped the question about her sister's upcoming nuptials would bring the dog discussion to a screeching halt.

Her prim sister pushed her smooth, straight brown hair behind her ear. "Jeff was a jerk."

Shocked, Sofie blinked over at Lacey. She was in agreement, of course. Lacey's first fiancé was a completely wrong fit for her, but hearing her admit that? Flooring.

"I never thanked you for being honest." Lacey offered a chagrined smile. "Too proud."

Lacey was that. Type A, perfectionist, and afraid to make a mistake.

Her sister's eyes, a pale shade of green, met hers. "I don't want you to plan my wedding, Sofe."

Well. That nice talk went south quickly.

"I want you to be in it."

"What . . . what about everyone dating the groomsmen . . ."

Lacey nodded at the dog who was now getting a tummy rub from Kinsley. "Is your tall, dark, and sexy *client* available?"

Sofie's mouth dropped open. "How did you . . . ?"

"I read the *Gazette*, Sofie. I recognized that dog the second you walked her in here. And don't think I didn't notice the owner of Pate Mansion and every inch of his fineness." She stroked Sofie's arm. "Whatever happened, I'm sorry. I can see things didn't go the way you wanted."

"You could say that."

Moment over, Lacey stepped outside, turning to face Sofie before she let the screen door shut. "Oh, and I can keep her for you for a few days. Kenneth's house has a great yard."

"Thanks, Lace."

Oddly enough, it didn't feel strange to have the tension lifted between them. Things felt like they'd finally snapped into place—like everyone was where they were supposed to be.

Maybe Donny was where he was supposed to be. Maybe her destiny didn't involve him at all.

With a sigh, she turned from the chattering females outside and tracked down her father, who was in his basement retreat. Golf played in the background, and Sofie plopped down into the recliner across from the couch.

Her dad hit the Mute button.

"There she is," he said, his gentle tone suggesting he'd picked up on her sour mood as well. She really had to get better about hiding her devastation.

"Here I am." She watched the TV without watching it, feeling his eyes on her. Finally, she turned her head.

"Are you going to tell me the real reason behind you bringing a giant dog that is obviously half yours to our house?" he asked.

"Why are you so smart?" She gave him a wan smile.

"You're welcome. You inherited those smarts." He tapped his head.

"Sometimes I'm not so sure."

"Did the fellow who owned Pate Mansion give you the dog?"

She grunted. "Guess that *Gazette* article made the rounds."

"Hid it from your mother," he said. "She'd ask questions. You know how she is."

So Lacey must not have mentioned it, either. Huh.

"He . . . um. He had to go to New York . . . permanently. He left the dog. Here. And I'm . . . uh, watching her."

Her father's eyes crawled up his forehead. No doubt sensing she'd left out a few pertinent details.

"Okay, then. Now are you going to tell me the *whole* truth about this guy, the dog, and the mansion, or do I have to guess?"

"Please don't, Daddy." She gave him a pleading look.

"Sofia." She could tell by his expression he wasn't going to let it go. "I have been watching you go through something for the past couple of weeks. And it hasn't been fun for me to watch. But you know me. I don't get involved unless my girls need me. Do you need me?"

If anything brought forth the tears she'd been damming over the course of those weeks, it was her father's blatant offer. A few spilled down her cheeks.

"I need you, Daddy."

He patted the couch cushion next to him and Sofie stood from the recliner and moved into his waiting arms. He hugged her close, keeping his arm around her. With the TV flashing silently in the background, he silently waited for her to spill.

So she started at the beginning.

"I met him seven years ago. Donny was the one. I mean, I thought he was the one. Turned out he was just the one who got more than he bargained for, then left town." Sofie averted her gaze and asked her lap, "Do you know what I mean by that? Because this would be a lot easier if I didn't have to spell things out."

Her father's hand on her arm moved up and down. "I think I do."

"He inherited the mansion and came back to sell it. When he came back, so did the feelings I had for him. But what I didn't know was he had feelings for me, too."

Those feelings had resurfaced and bubbled over—for both of them. Donny gave her a do-over, and in a way, gave himself one. As promised, he'd made love to her, and she felt certain that was a first for him, too.

"He loves me," she said, the pain of that admission raining down on her like acid. "He said he'd never loved anyone before. He was raised in an abusive home. Gertrude Pate turned her life around at the end, but Donny's father died having never apologized for what he'd done to him."

She could hear the frown in her father's tone. "Abuse."

"Yeah." Sofie's voice broke on the word. "He has these amazing tattoos. He got them to cover the scars. So many scars," she whispered. Then almost to herself she said, "You know my infinity tattoo?"

"The one I see when you wear the bathing suit I think you shouldn't."

"That's the one." She chuckled but it quickly faded. "Donny got an infinity sign to match mine. He said I'm one of his scars, Daddy. But a good one...If that makes sense."

Her father was quiet for a moment before he admitted, "Makes sense."

"I guess I thought after we connected on such a deep level...After we both admitted how much we loved one another..." She shook her head, the loss stinging like a fresh cut. "I thought I could save him."

Her dad was quiet, his eyes on the television screen, but she knew he was thinking. That was his way. She waited, folding her legs underneath her and picking at the hem of her skirt.

"Remember when we went on a family camping trip?" he said, interrupting the silence. "I think you were about eight years old. Cumberland Falls. Beautiful place."

"I remember sleeping in a tent on top of a very sharp rock." She smiled to herself. "I remember loving every minute of it. And I remember Lacey complaining constantly, because her hair was frizzy and there was nowhere for her to plug in her curling iron."

Her father laughed. "And Kinsley was glued to your

mother's side." He elbowed Sofie gently. "But you, you were my partner in crime that trip. Remember the walks we took to get firewood?"

"And the falls. We hiked a mile to get to them."

"Worth the extra effort."

They were. The falls were majestic, and at the time, the most beautiful landmark she'd ever seen.

"And you found the bird," he said.

The bird. She had forgotten. Completely forgotten.

"Oh yeah. The one with the broken leg."

"You were bound and determined to save that little sparrow. It had taken a dive-bomb out of the nest. I knew there was no prayer it would survive."

She remembered now. "I kept him in a Pop-Tart box with some grass. I wrapped the box in a towel."

"You stayed up all night," he said. "Or tried, anyway."

"You took a shift." She smiled up at him.

He smiled back. "It meant so very much to you."

"Even though you knew it was futile."

"Even though."

Sofie dragged in a deep breath, understanding why he'd brought up the bird. Understanding everything. "It was dead by morning. I couldn't save him. No matter how much I wanted to." Tears she'd rather not cry spilled over.

He gave her a squeeze.

"You're saying I can't save Donovan," she said.

"No." Her father took her hand. "Sofie, sweetheart, I'm saying you already have."

Hope flared in her chest. Hope she had no use for. But her father, in a way, had a point. Donovan, who had never been in love, had fallen in love with her. He may have left the dog behind, but not before he gave in and called her

"Gertie." He'd also cared for and slept in the house he proclaimed to hate—pouring his heart into repairing the fireplace. Placing a heart-shaped stone in its center.

Maybe she had saved him. From his anger, his unhappiness. From his haunted past.

Then why didn't he stay?

"But he left."

Her father hummed in the back of his throat. "Is he worth the extra mile?"

She thought of Donovan's cautious smile, the way it felt to be held against him, to be lifted into his arms. She thought of the stories he told her—stories he'd never told anyone. In a way, he'd gone the extra mile with her. Had trusted her more than he'd ever trusted anyone.

I've never loved anyone.

But he loved her. And told her as much as he slid into her body, held her tight, and kissed her lips. Another tear tumbled from her eye.

"Yes," she answered. "He's worth it."

"Even if he doesn't come back to Evergreen Cove? Even if he breaks your heart again?"

"Still worth it." She swiped the tears from her cheeks. Nothing could hurt more than the way she hurt now. Nothing could make things any worse.

"It's okay, you know. It's okay to look like a fool. It's okay to hope against hope. It's okay to put yourself on the line, go the extra mile, even if it is futile. It's okay to see potential where everyone else sees failure."

He pulled her closer. Sofie rested her cheek on his shoulder, her eyes unseeing on the flickering television screen.

"I wouldn't take back one minute of sleep I missed to sit up and watch over your doomed bird," he said.

"Because it meant something to me."

"Arguably, losing that little bird made you who you are today."

"Because I tried."

"Because you *believed*. Not enough believers in this world, you ask me."

He unmuted the Golf Channel and together, she and her dad watched the screen.

She thought of the bird. The waterfall. Gertie.

But mostly, she thought of Donny.

CHAPTER TWENTY-NINE

$\mathscr{D}$onovan learned a long time ago drinking didn't solve problems. Especially his problems. Drinking, women, smoking…none of the vices worked. Which was why he'd adopted the "straight through" approach. Straight through was the only way to erase the pain.

Erasing the pain of losing Sofie wasn't an option, so he'd have to settle for dulling it.

He emptied the liquor into his glass, his vision going blurry. His living room—Aless's living room, technically—was furnished with cheery beach furniture and white wicker. Huge, looming white shelves filled with books Donovan had never read took up an entire wall. The kitchen was eat-in, the bathrooms tidy, the sunroom too bright in the mornings.

Nothing about the cheery rooms, the pastel colors, the modern furniture, was Donovan's. Nothing here was him…except, well, *him*.

"Yay, me," he growled, chucking back the last shot.

Up until tonight, he'd been enduring. Enduring hadn't worked. So now he was drinking. He was relatively sure the drinking wasn't working, either, but luckily he couldn't tell with his vision swimming in and out.

And anyway, who the fuck cared? Who cared what he did to himself? About how blind stinking drunk he got? About his beach-vacation décor? About the fact he sliced his finger open building Bill Yost's brick fire pit yesterday. Not a big deal. Until he'd excused himself to bandage it and thought of Dog's sliced paw. Then he thought of when he sliced his finger open on the great room's fireplace. Then he thought of Sofie trying to patch him up.

That had sent him to the kitchen where he'd dug a half a bottle of rum from under the sink and started in. He didn't have any fight left in him—no more pragmatic arguments cooked up to appease his inner tormenter. And so he decided to wallow until he couldn't feel anything. Or maybe he'd wallow and feel way too much...which was what stage he was in now.

Gertie. He let out a dry laugh. Sofie thought it was sweet to name the mutt after his grandmother. Because Sofie was sweet. Sofie...

God.

Sofie.

His Scampi. The girl who'd seen more in him than anyone else ever bothered. The girl who gave him her virginity, held on to him tight while he slipped into her tightness. The girl who found a way to forgive him. Seven years later, she let him haul her into his arms and make love to her on the washing machine.

He'd wanted to turn her inside out. She turned him inside out instead.

Why? Why the hell did she let him do anything with her after the way he'd treated her the first time? Who in their right mind would let him that close? Would practically move in with him when she knew he was leaving?

That last thought brought about the memories of lying skin to skin with her. Donovan never thought of himself as a cuddler, but whenever Sofie was next to him in bed, he wanted her touching him. He wound his arm around her and pulled her against his side, her breasts smashed up against the infinity tattoo on his ribs. She'd sleep there, her hand over his heart, her leg draped over his while he basked in the quiet between her breaths, not caring if his arm went dead, or if his shoulder cramped. He wanted her close. And she stayed close.

She loves you.

Correction. She *loved* him.

Past tense.

No way did she love him now.

He frowned at the liquor bottle, wishing there was more rum, thinking in Captain Jack Sparrow's boozy accent, *Why is all the rum gone?* and earning himself a drunken laugh that faded and faded fast.

Night blanketed the guesthouse, the lights at Alessandre's lit for safety only. Aless was in Evergreen Cove and was flying back home after the closing tomorrow. Donovan squinted at the clock. One a.m.

Not tomorrow, then. *Today.*

Donovan's mansion—Donovan's *legacy*—would be sold to Alessandre and become a D'Paolo bed-and-breakfast. Pieced and parceled off, the bedrooms would be outfitted with locks and furnished with matching, elegant armoires and beds. Vacationers visiting the Cove would stay in a landmark, sip tea in the great room with the newly rebuilt fireplace, and relax and read in the library.

The library.

He sat up too fast, head swimming from the alcohol, heart beating erratically as those two words echoed off the halls of his head. Dully, his brain chugged, but he managed to make out one clear thought.

No.

The library, the great room, the ballroom, hell, the kitchen. The maple tree at the back of the property, the cobblestone drive. The utility room.

The shower.

God. The shower.

Hell no.

The idea of strangers in the rooms where he and Sofie had made love made him heartsick. Especially the library. Where he told her he loved her.

He still did.

Dammit. He still fucking loved her.

Proving rum the worst ally ever, pain crept in and latched on to his chest, spreading through his lungs and seizing his next breath. Part of him wanted to curl up and hide. Do that wallowing thing he'd set out to do when he uncapped the bottle.

But the twelve-year-old boy inside him, the one who'd straightened his back and threw a punch at his old man, uttered two words. "Straight through."

Donovan reached for his cell phone and dialed Alessandre's number. He had twelve hours to stop the sale. If Aless didn't answer, he'd call Scott Torsett, the prick. Or maybe the realty company. He'd call every number they had. Send a fax. Wait... he didn't have a fax machine.

He frowned at the empty bottle in front of him. Rum certainly hadn't improved his problem-solving skills.

Alessandre's voice answered and Donovan barked into the phone, "Aless! I need to..." His words faded as he realized he was talking to voice mail. He ended the call, tossed the phone on the coffee table, propped his elbows on his knees, and stared it down.

What to do? *What the fuck to do?*

He was too plowed to drive. All he had was his phone. *Connor.*

Connor would know the answer. Connor would stop the sale, or know who to call to stop the sale.

Donovan found Connor's name in his phone, tapped the screen, and lifted the cell to his ear. On the fifth ring, he was ready to give up hope.

Then his best friend answered with a groggy, "What's wrong?"

Donovan smiled. He hadn't smiled in weeks. Of course Connor thought something was wrong. Donny never called his friends. They called him.

"I'm not selling the mansion."

A moment of silence stretched on the line before Connor heaved a sigh. "Shit, man, I just moved my plants out of there."

"I need her, man. I love her." Donovan rested a hand on his pounding forehead.

"I know."

He'd never said it to anyone but Sofie. Never been in love with anyone before Sofie. Saying it now opened him up in a way that felt like letting the sun in after years of blackness.

"What do I do?"

"Don't call her," Connor said. He heard a few muffled sounds like his friend was shifting or sitting up in bed. "You sound deranged."

"I'm drunk." He was. So stinking drunk. The room had started to spin. "I mean it, though. I'm not selling. I love Sofie."

"I know, but you need to tell her that sober."

"I can't get a hold of Aless."

"He was at the mansion earlier. I was there doing some last-minute yard stuff and showed him around. He's probably on his way to New York right about now."

Back to New York? Donny pinched his eyes closed and tried to decode those words with his sluggish, rum-soaked brain.

"Why would he fly back to New York?"

"Dunno. Just said he was headed back. Maybe he changed his mind about buying it."

Maybe. But unlikely.

"Sleep it off, man. He'll be home soon. You can tell him then you're not selling." Connor grumbled good night.

Donovan ended the call. His friend was right. He should sober up and wait him out. But he wasn't going to sleep. He stalked to the kitchen and made a pot of coffee.

He was going to stay awake and wait for Aless to get home.

After two cups, and staring bleary-eyed at an infomercial on TV, Donovan remembered thinking he needed one more cup if he hoped to stay up much longer.

The next thing he knew, he was jolting awake to a clap of thunder shaking the house.

* * *

Donovan spit the mouthwash he'd been swishing between his teeth into the grass. It was pouring, an absolute skin-soaking downpour. The only upside to traipsing to Aless's house across the connected yards was that the rain was washing off some of the booze smell on his skin.

He decided to file that in the plus column. He had a plus column. Go figure.

A stupid grin pulled his cheeks as he saw Alessandre's kitchen light flick on, followed by the bathroom light. Donovan broke into a jog, ran up the stairs along the side of the house, and used the code on the keypad at the back door to let himself in.

He was about to open his mouth and shout for Aless, when the man himself rounded the corner, unbuttoning cuff links, his eyebrows nearly hitting his widow's peak.

"Donovan." He gave him a once-over, then a smile. Alessandre looked like him in a way. Full head of black hair, but the cut shorter, and with hints of gray at the temples, thick eyebrows, similar height. The main differences were Aless's dark brown eyes and an accent muddled from years of travel.

"You can't buy the mansion," Donovan told him.

His smile faded. "No?"

"No." Donovan crossed his arms, shivering slightly in the air-conditioned house.

Aless blinked at him a few times, then crossed his arms over his chest as well. A standoff. In business matters, Aless got what he wanted. One didn't become wealthy and powerful without being good at bargaining. "What would you say if I told you the closing was finished?"

Donovan's heart sank. "What?"

"What would you say if I told you I called Mr. Torsett and we closed a day early?"

Scott Torsett. Who Donovan had foolishly signed over power of attorney for the sale. It had happened without him.

Mind racing, he said, "Sell it back to me."

Aless held up a hand.

Donovan didn't let him speak.

"You can't have the mansion, Aless. I'm going back." Needing his friend, his mentor, to understand, he sucked in a breath and blurted out the truth. "The woman I love is there. And so's my dog," he added, vowing to find Gertie and hoping whoever owned her wasn't too attached. Wondering what he'd have to pay to get her back.

Wondering what he'd have to do to get Sofie back.

Now fighting a hangover from the rum and dehydration from the coffee, Donovan realized he didn't have a plan yet for how to win Sofie. Well. He could come up with something on the flight home.

Home. He waited for the sting of that word. It didn't come.

"You're going back to Evergreen Cove for a woman?" Aless asked.

"Why is not your concern. How much? That's the only question now."

Alessandre raised an eyebrow, unfazed by Donny's anger.

"How much?" Donovan asked on a near shout.

Aless shook his head. "No need to haggle."

"Listen, I want the mansion and you're going to sell it back to me." Donovan wasn't above putting Alessandre in his place. Not for something this important. "I get that you want the house for your next project, but this isn't a project to me. This is my life. You and I have similar pasts. You know as well as I do why we are both single without families." He gave his friend a meaningful glare. "You know."

Donovan learned from Caroline that Aless, too, had an abusive father. It wasn't hard to guess by the man's reverent silence now that Aless knew Donovan's past as well. God bless Caroline's meddling.

"I think of Sofie and you know what I think of next?" Here it went, laying it out for the first time. "A family. Babies, Aless. *Kids*. I never imagined a day I'd want a child of my own."

His only thoughts involving children revolved around how he shouldn't have any lest he further Robert Pate's abominable bloodline. He swallowed thickly. "Never thought I'd have a reason to try."

"I can't sell you the mansion, Donovan."

His chest went hollow. Before he could humiliate himself by begging—which he was not above doing in this case, Aless spoke again.

"I don't own it. And I'm not buying it."

Donovan digested that statement. Alessandre didn't own it. He didn't...buy it? What happened? Not that it mattered. The mansion was Donovan's. Step one. Now to figure out—

"You mentioned a dog?" Aless's eyes went over Donovan's shoulder, and a small smile tipped his mouth.

On cue, a bark sliced through the air. Donovan turned to find a big, wet dog, white-with-brown-patches, pale blue eyes, and tongue lolling, scraping across the wood floors. Gertie bounded over to him, hitting him square in the chest with cold paws.

"Hey, girl." He caught the dog's square head in his hands and squinted at Aless. "Why do you have Gertie?"

"I brought her," a soft voice said.

He turned his head to see a woman step into Aless's living room. A brunette toweling her wet hair, her green eyes rapidly filling with tears.

Gertie's paws left his chest, courtesy of Alessandre. "I'll take her outside and give you two a moment."

But his voice sounded miles away. All Donovan could do was stare at the woman he'd just announced he wanted to have children with.

"Scampi, what are you doing here?"

"Currently?" She blinked a few times. "Crying."

He rushed to her. When she was within grabbing distance, he pulled her into his arms and laid a kiss on her mouth. She melted into him, her lips cold, her tongue warm, wet clothes sticking to his. She tasted incredible, like he remembered, but somehow new.

Because you love her.

So much.

He pulled his lips from hers but didn't loosen his hold on her.

"Sofie, baby."

"Donny." Her hands linked around his neck, her fingers in his hair.

"I love you, Scampi."

"I love you, too." Her eyes refilled, and she bit the inside of her lip as she smiled.

She loved him. *Loved him.* Still.

He hugged her close and buried his face in her neck. "Thank you."

She stroked his hair. He pulled his head up to look at

her but didn't let her go. Now that he had her, he wasn't ever letting her go.

"What are you doing here?"

Eyes shining, she said, "I came for you."

This woman.

"You came for me."

"I showed up at the mansion to convince you not to sell. I found Alessandre there instead."

"You didn't want me to sell the mansion," he repeated, letting that sink in.

"It's ours. I mean, it's technically *yours*, but the rooms…"

"The memories," he finished.

"They aren't all bad for you, are they?" She wound his hair around her fingers again, her green eyes locked on his face.

Kissing her soundly, he slid his hand to her bottom and grabbed a palm full. "You kidding me? I think of books, I get hard. Know how awkward it is to go to a public library?"

She laughed. He'd missed that sound. He'd missed her.

Serious now, he said, "I was gonna come for you."

"I heard."

"Yeah," he said, recalling everything he'd said to Aless while she hovered in the background. "You heard a lot of things."

"Did you mean it?"

Nervous, he swallowed. "Every word."

"You want children?"

"I want you, Scampi. I want you and whatever involves us together. The mansion, kids, Dog."

"Gertie."

"Yeah, sweetheart. Gertie. I want it all." His arms

tightened on her waist. "I have lived without you for too long, Sofie. I convinced myself you were better off without me. You're not. You're better off *with* me. You need me. You need me to rescue you from ladders and keep you from going on bad dates with short lawyers."

She smiled.

"And you need me to make love to you in every room of the mansion."

A feisty glint flickered in her eyes. "There are a lot of rooms in the mansion."

"Thirty-five."

"Thirty-five," she repeated, her voice lilting.

"Nine at my place." He tilted his head in the direction of the guesthouse.

"Nine, hmm." Her smile faded slowly, her expression turning serious. "My answer is yes."

His heart stopped beating for a second before mule-kicking his chest. "Yes to..."

"Sex. At your place."

"Right," he said. Sex. Not exactly bad news, but he wanted to hear yes to more than the sex.

"And yes to the mansion." She pressed a brief kiss on the center of his lips. "Yes to the library." Another kiss. "Yes to the utility room." Another. "Yes to the backyard. Yes to the balcony. Yes to everything, Donny."

He smashed his mouth against hers, pushed his tongue past her lips, and cupped her ass as he brought her up into his arms. Her legs wrapped around his waist, her arms around his neck.

Pointing the direction of the hallway, he said, "There are a few rooms in this house not being used at the moment..."

"Donny."

"Okay. My place." He walked to the back door.

She palmed his face, smiling down at him, her wet hair a tangled mass tickling his cheeks.

"I love you," he said again. He'd have to say it constantly to make up for the years he'd missed out on. All seven of them.

"I want three."

He frowned, not understanding.

"Three children. But I would settle for two if three is too many."

Okay, now his heart stopped beating. Three children. With Sofie's green eyes. With his dark hair. With her sweetness. Her resolve. Her empathy.

He lowered her to her feet, sifted his fingers into her hair and kissed her deeply. *Everything.* She had given him everything. And she'd come here because she loved him. Their lips parted with a soft smooching sound.

"I don't deserve you," he murmured.

"Love is about getting what you don't deserve."

Before he could kiss her again, the back door opened and Aless and Gertie walked in.

"Excuse me," Aless said. "Didn't mean to interrupt."

Donovan pulled his fingers from Sofie's hair and faced the man who fought for him. His friends. They had fought for him. Connor. Sofie. Alessandre. Asher and Evan had been fighting for him since they were all kids. Donovan thought he'd blown his shot at having a family. He was wrong. He had a family. In the Cove, and here, in New York.

Donovan extended a hand.

Aless shook it. "Invite me to the wedding." He scrubbed

Gertie's head. "Come on, pup." He snapped his fingers and trotted down the stairs, the dog close on his heels.

Sofie's mouth was ajar, a waxy pallor on her damp skin, as she muttered, "But...I don't do weddings."

Yeah. *Hell yeah.*

Donovan grinned down at his future wife. "Well, Scampi. You do now."

EPILOGUE

Seven years later

𝒟onovan walked through the front entry of the mansion, pausing to tug the scarf from his neck. He hung his coat on a hook next to Sofie's. Next to hers hung two smaller coats. One dark blue and silver, the other pink.

Gertie, her eyes clouded, her head gray, padded into the room on unsteady hips. It'd been a fairly mild winter, but the cold wasn't helping the old girl's arthritis.

"Hey girl," Donovan said, hanging his coat and squatting to ruffle the dog's ears. Her tail wagged, low and slow, but it wagged.

Three pairs of boots stood drying on a mat by the door. No doubt the kids had bribed Sofie to take them sledding today since yesterday's snow never came. Today made up for it, though, dumping several inches on the Cove. More was expected tonight.

It'd been another late workday. He'd have to make it up to them for taking the extra hours. Upstairs, he saw only dark, no night-lights glowing in the hallway. No plastic gate blocking the stairway. Which meant no one was in bed yet. Maybe they were watching television, or maybe—

"In here, honey," came his wife's voice.

He found Scampi in the library, sitting on the red velvet sofa. Their four-year-old daughter Miranda was curled on her side, asleep, her sock-covered feet sticking out of the blanket and propped on Sofie's lap. Bran was asleep, too, his head on Sofie's stomach.

Sofie put down the book she'd been reading. Donovan walked into the room, tipped her chin, and took a kiss.

"We had a fire," she said, keeping her voice down. "They fell asleep. I didn't have the heart to wake them."

"You shouldn't be carrying them up the stairs, anyway." He lowered his face and kissed her lips again, loving her taste. He bent over Miranda next, pushing the dark hair off her forehead.

Sleepily, she opened huge blue eyes—light blue like his own. "Hi, Daddy."

"Hey, Scallop. Need you to walk upstairs yourself. I have to carry Bran. Can you do that for me, sweetie?"

She nodded and stretched, knowing the extra effort was needed. Donovan lifted Bran into his arms, revealing his wife's baby bump their two-year-old boy had been using as a pillow. Bran didn't stir, not even when his head hit Donovan's shoulder solidly. Hardheaded kid. No doubt where he'd inherited that trait.

Sofie attempted to push herself up, and Donovan looped an arm around her waist to help her. She was only five months, but already very round.

"They're killing me," she grumbled.

"It's my last late night," he promised.

"You bet your sweet cheeks it is. We're gonna need you around here."

"Yeah, Daddy," Miranda said. "Mommy says if the twins are girls you'll be in big trouble." Trouble came out like *twubble*, which made him smile.

One more. He and Sofie had decided to have *one* more child. Then came the news there were two incubating in her belly. Two.

But they could handle it. Together, with their friends and family backing them, he could handle anything. *Straight through*.

"Know what, Scallop? You don't have to worry about me. Your dad is a big, bad, mansion-owning bada—"

"Tough guy," Sofie interrupted, reaching around to discreetly pinch his ass. Careful not to drop Bran, he bent to the side and kissed his wife.

"Tough guy," he repeated to Miranda as he straightened.

Upstairs, Sofie tucked their daughter in, who requested one more story before bed. Donovan put Bran down, who had yet to acknowledge he was being jostled around in his father's arms, then checked the locks in the house, and set up the baby gate.

Once the kids were down, Donovan and Sofie reconvened in the shower under the multiple sprayers, him enjoying the hot, hot water loosening muscles that were aching from the lifting he'd done at work today.

Sofie traced the heart Evan had added to the infinity tattoo on Donovan's ribs.

"Worth it?" she asked.

"I was able to save the original fireplace so it didn't

have to be torn out. You wouldn't believe how particular the historical society is about mortar. But yeah, I think it will be."

He pushed the water off his face and saw a smile curl her lips.

"I mean this life. Leaving New York, living in a huge house that needs constant upkeep. Burying your bad memories in order to stay in Evergreen Cove."

"Worth it, Scampi." He wrapped his arms around her, his thumb coming up to brush the matching heart Evan had tattooed around her infinity sign. "Wouldn't change a thing."

"Me neither."

He palmed her breast.

She kissed him. He savored her, the way he had since he won her back years ago.

"How are you still this sexy?" he murmured against her mouth.

"Hmm. I could ask you the same question."

After another long kiss under the hot water, she pulled away to ask, "So... what are you doing Saturday?"

"I'm planning a quiet evening at home with my wife and kids." He narrowed one eye.

"You only turn forty once." She grinned but couldn't meet his eyes.

"Scampi." His tone was a warning. "We talked about this."

A warning she ignored. "I think you should keep your schedule open."

"No surprise parties."

Her mouth dropped open in feigned offense. "Who said anything about a surprise party? I'm saying be prepared... just in case your friends want to come by and see you. And in case the ballroom is already decorated with black balloons and streamers."

Carefully, so she wouldn't slip, he navigated her until her back was against the tiled shower wall. He pressed against her, as close as he could get around her protruding belly.

"I told you there would be consequences if you plan a party."

"Sounds terrifying." Her eyebrow arched.

Like that, he was hot for her. He'd married the sexiest woman on the planet. No one got him like she did. No one had ever bothered trying.

"I'm not sure you can maneuver around this." She gestured at her belly between them.

"Wanna bet?" His fingers found her nipples. He slid a hand between her legs.

Sofie's mouth dropped open, her head tilting back. He found a familiar sprayer and moved her so she was standing in front of it, and then his fingers went to work.

Then he proved his wife wrong.

He could maneuver just fine.

* * *

Cassidy and Carmen Pate were born at eight forty-two p.m., small, squealing, and bright pink.

Sixteen years later, his twin girls were both driving, both drop-dead gorgeous with long, black hair and their mother's moss green eyes. Against Donovan's will, they also had permission to date.

Miranda's prediction was accurate.

He was in big trouble.

DONOVAN'S SHRIMP "SCAMPI" A LA SOFIE

Inspired by *Rescuing the Bad Boy*

Seven years ago, Donovan Pate was sweating over four sauté pans when he warned his then-coworker Sofie Martin not to sell *one more* Shrimp Scampi special or he'd brand her for life. Sofie took that bet, marched out of the kitchen, and sold *three*. Today, RESCUING THE BAD BOY's broody hero still addresses Sofie as "Scampi," and was nice enough to share his secret recipe for the dare that inspired her name.

Ingredients:

½ lb jumbo shrimp, deveined and peeled, patted dry and laid in one layer on a plate

1½ Tbsp of butter

1–2 cloves garlic, minced

⅓ cup vegetable broth

1 Tbsp freshly squeezed lemon juice

2 tsp lemon zest

1 Tbsp chopped flat-leaf parsley

½ cup orzo pasta

sea salt, freshly ground black pepper, and cayenne to taste

Directions:

1. Fill a medium pot ¾ of the way with water and bring to a boil. Add pasta, cook 9 minutes.
2. Heat a large skillet over medium-high heat. Add 1 Tbsp of butter.
3. Salt and pepper both sides of the shrimp.
4. When butter is bubbling, turn heat down to medium. Invert the plate over the skillet so that all the shrimp hit the pan at the same time. Add garlic. Cook 1 minute. Flip each shrimp, cook 2 more minutes. Set shrimp and garlic aside in a bowl.
5. Add vegetable broth and lemon juice to the hot skillet. Scrape with a wooden spoon to get brown bits off the bottom.
6. Add drained, cooked pasta to the broth mixture in the skillet, then add lemon zest, parsley, and remaining ½ Tbsp of butter. Toss in shrimp. Add more salt, pepper, and a dash of cayenne to taste.
7. Serve immediately, with warm, buttered bread and a cool, crisp salad.

After four years in Afghanistan, Connor McClain moves to Evergreen Cove to keep his mind off the war. And when he meets a certain long-legged beauty, the only thing this bad boy can think about is how to get her into his arms...

Please see the next page for a preview of

A Bad Boy for Christmas.

CHAPTER ONE

Glitter.

Glitter *everywhere*. Lining the seams of the car's seats, sprinkled liberally across the floorboards, and at this point, probably a part of her DNA.

Faith Garrett had spent the day gluing glitter onto the surface of one hundred foam pumpkins in various shapes and sizes. The pink-bedazzled vegetables were for a Breast Cancer Awareness dinner. Meg Dillon, who was in charge of said dinner, had *ooh*ed and *ahh*ed over the dinner's centerpieces, going as far to throw her arms around Faith's neck and sing the praises of Make It an Event, the planning company where Faith worked for her best friend, Sofie Martin.

This was the good news.

The bad news was the shop vac she'd hauled out of the mansion's garage was not working. Tape. Maybe she could use tape. She kicked the Off switch on the machine and ran the back of her hand over her forehead. For October, it sure was warm today. High in the seventies, not a prayer of a breeze blowing through the colored leaves still clinging to the trees lining the mansion's drive.

Yes, her best friend now lived and worked in a mansion. Sofie hadn't expected to be very much entrenched here when she'd planned the charity dinner last year, but neither had she expected the man who'd taken her virginity years ago to sweep her off her feet.

Donovan Pate had come crashing into Sofie's life, and she into his. Faith had a front-row seat and watched it unfold. The year before that, she'd watched her friend Charlie succumb to a similar fate—falling for the last man she never dreamed of falling for: her late best friend's husband. Evan, a widower who'd battled his own demons after losing his wife, had moved to Evergreen Cove with his son Lyon to start over. Charlie and Evan had been inseparable since. She was a mother to an eight-year-old boy, and a very happy wife to a sexy tattoo-artist-slash-illustrator.

Yes, as of late, the Cove had played host to fairy-tale romances. Someone looking in might believe Faith, whose love life came to a screeching halt last year, might want a fairy-tale romance for herself.

That someone would be wrong.

The last thing she needed, the very last thing she *wanted*, was a relationship. Been there, done that, cleaned the toilet with Michael's T-shirt. No, what she wanted more than anything was not a man. What she wanted— what she needed—was to find her independence. Freed of her fiancé and, finally, freed from living with her mother for way too long, Faith was on a path to find her inner strength.

It had to be in there somewhere.

She wasn't going to rely on a man any longer. Donny and Sofie, Evan and Charlie, they may have worked things out, but theirs were extenuating circumstances. Each couple had meaningful history together. There was no man in her past hovering on the edge of her life, waiting to explode back in and rescue her. There was only a handful of unmemorable boyfriends and Michael.

Sad, really.

But, she thought, bucking up, she was moving on. Her life had taken a turn, but not for the worst. For the *better*. She'd see to that.

Leaning back into the car, she snagged her fountain Coke from the cup holder and took a long, delicious, sugar-laden sip. While she stood basking in the noonday sun, she admired Pate Mansion, her home away from home. The quartz blocks twinkled, the gold turrets standing regally against a blue sky with puffy white clouds. Admiring the house that looked more like a castle never got old, not ever. And she'd seen it a lot over the past year-plus. She spent most days here, planning events in the library-turned-office with Sofie, drinking coffee in the gorgeous kitchen, or helping set up the massive ballroom for the occasional fundraiser.

She strode toward the front door taking in the thick, trimmed hedges lining the building, the purple and orange flowering mums interspersed in between. The saplings planted out front stood strong and tall, accepting their new homes in the dirt like they'd been there from the start.

The beauty of the grounds never failed to amaze her.

The door opened, and she turned her head expecting Sofie to appear, cell phone to her ear. Instead, Connor McClain strode out, and Faith's tongue promptly welded to the roof of her mouth. Another thing that never failed to amaze her was the way this man's muscular thighs filled out a pair of well-worn jeans.

Since she was very tall, five-ten to be exact, she guessed Connor around six-one. She couldn't be sure, unless she was within kissing distance of his incredible mouth, but that was something she filed under N for Never happening. Never *ever*, she reminded herself as he grinned at her.

Her heart thrummed.

Broad shoulders molded by a long-sleeved henley, wide frame in perfect proportion, thighs pressing against worn, soft-looking denim. Yeah. There wasn't much about the man she couldn't appreciate. Not to mention the fact he was ex-military, worked tirelessly for his friends, and had a flirty sense of humor that almost threatened to break down the barrier she'd so firmly erected since Michael had raided the Cookie jar . . . so to speak.

Around a penetrating grin, Connor spoke the words, "Afternoon, Cupcake."

Faith was sort of known for her sugar addiction. And last year when all of the crap hit the fan with her ex, it was Connor who'd caught her devouring a bakery box full of Sugar Hi cupcakes. She knew she'd never live that down.

"Good afternoon to you, Beefcake."

His smile didn't budge. Okay, so she wasn't all that creative with the nicknames. But after the third time he'd teased her by calling her "Cupcake" she had to think of a retort.

Those eyes left hers, narrowing and traveling her face.

Self-consciously, she smoothed the hand over her forehead where she felt her hair tickling her face. "What?"

He stepped closer to her, lifted one rugged, workingman's hand, and brushed his fingers along her forehead. Then he held his hand up for her to see. Pink glitter.

She traded the Coke from one hand to the other, frowning down at the glitter still stuck stubbornly to her palms.

"I'll never get this stuff off!" she said.

Brushing his hands on his jeans, his grin widened to a distracting degree. "You? How am I going to explain looking like I had a run-in with a stripper when I go on my date tonight?"

She felt her face blanch as her blood raced from her cheeks to her toes. Not at the stripper reference, even though that was mildly insulting. But the other thing. Connor had a . . . a *date*?

She tried to reel in her emotions but feared it was too little, too late. No doubt he'd seen the abject disappointment briefly flit across her face.

A reaction that made no sense. She should have expected the man to go on a date now and again. Connor was a ridiculously attractive man. This date was likely not the first date he'd had since she re-met him for the second time. Faith knew he had to date. It was just that she preferred not to know who he dated. Or what they did together . . .

Which confused her. He was her friend. She should be rooting for him.

Even though, it took a lot of effort to get the words, "Ohh, a date. Have fun!" past her lying lips.

"Plan on it." His eyes jerked to one side, a strained silence settling between them. "I should get started so I can get out of here on time." He lifted a tool belt full of garden trowels and other implements for digging in the dirt.

"Yeah. I have to get back in there." She showed him her pink-glittered palm. "Try and clean myself up."

His grin returned and she had to remind her knees to stay strong. Her entire body seemed to forget it was a cohesive unit whenever he was around. One by one, parts of her turned to jelly. Kneecaps oozed, her spine melted, and the part between her legs... Well, she wasn't going to think about that part.

"Have a good day," she told him.

"You got it, gorgeous." He stepped past her, not sending another look over his shoulder, not giving her a flirtatious wink, not saying another word. Just a brief interaction before he walked to the far side of the house and vanished around the wall.

Faith reminded herself yet again that what Charlie and Sofie had was fine for them, but not something she wanted personally. One look at sunny, smiling Connor McClain and she'd forgotten.

But she couldn't afford to forget. A relationship with a man from the Cove was not in Faith's future. No man from *anywhere* was in her foreseeable future. Because she had accepted the fact that her mother, Linda Shelby, as harebrained and crazy as she was, was also right.

The Shelby curse was real. Shelby women didn't marry. *Couldn't* marry. No matter how hard they tried.

Faith had attempted an engagement with Michael and failed. A failure that ended up being a blessing. Yes, she thought as she reached the front door.

Things had turned out exactly as they should have.

* * *

Connor sneaked a glance over his shoulder as he walked away.

Legs. Heaven help him, legs up to her neck.

How he encountered a woman who looked like a Victoria's Secret model but was as down-to-earth as they came on a daily basis and hadn't begged her to go to bed with him was an epic accomplishment on his part.

Admittedly, parts of him had wanted parts of her since he laid eyes on her for the first time years ago when they worked at the Wharf together. But then, he'd been an eighteen-year-old busboy, and she the leggy waitress, waify but all woman—even in her early twenties.

When he'd run into her again a little over a year ago, he learned that *want* wasn't just leftover from a horny teenage crush. He still responded to her looks. Then again, who didn't? But he wasn't an idiot. Sleeping with the girl who was his buddy's girl's best friend was the crowning jewel in the crown of Stupid. And, after the shit that went down with Faith's ex, it'd be some time before she was interested in crawling into bed with Connor.

With anyone.

Damn if the thought of her crawling didn't insert an image into his head of her tiny, pert ass in the air, those mile-long legs...

He blinked out of the mirage, blaming her outfit today: a dark blue dress that matched her navy eyes and a pair of shoes that made those long legs even longer. Was she actively trying to kill him?

So, yeah, it hadn't escaped him she was beautiful. And it hadn't stopped him from teasing her as often as possible to get those pink lips to part into a smile. He was a sucker for a cheap laugh, and in spite of what she'd been through, it'd been fairly easy to get her to laugh. Which swelled the head on his shoulders almost as much as the one in his pants.

She hadn't been laughing a moment ago when he mentioned the word *date*, though, had she? He'd be lying if he said he didn't find that more than a little interesting. His "date" was more an appointment—with his sister, Kendra. Ken was having trouble with her car, and he offered to come over and take a look.

One of the many services he provided since he'd moved back to town. Not that he minded. He'd do anything for his two older sisters.

Connor's family was tight. His father owned McClain's Handyman Services, a business that had served the town of Evergreen Cove since before his oldest sister Dixie was born. A few years after, they had Kendra, and five years later, Connor was born the baby of the family.

Roger McClain had been overjoyed. A boy to take over the business. When Connor grew up and showed zero interest in fixing anything, save for himself in front of a science project, Roger began applying pressure. The pressure kept coming, driving Connor right out of the house at age eighteen, where he'd met Donny and the two of them had shared an apartment and made some spectacularly bad decisions.

Last year, after moving back to New York, Donovan had returned, deciding to stay in the Cove after all. They all had Sofie to thank for that. Connor smiled up at the mansion looming in the light, her clean windows shiny, gleaming. He was glad. Donny belonged in this town, and belonged with Sofie.

Connor dug out a pair of shears from his tool belt before dropping it into the grass and starting on the scraggly lavender bush at the side of the house. No matter what he did to save it, the thing tried to die. Part of him wanted to dig it up, toss it in the fire pit, but another, more stubborn part of him thought it might be saved.

A few minutes into his pruning, the patio door opened and out ambled Gertie, a big white and brown mutt Donny had rescued last year. Sofie followed close on Gert's heels. When she reached him, she licked his face without warning—Gertie. Not Sofie.

Sofie gestured to him with her cell phone. "Mrs. Anderson called and asked when you'd be over to set up for the Harvest Fest."

"On the docket for this week." Like he'd told Mrs. Anderson already. *Twice.* Persistent little old lady, he was learning. And tough. He'd attempted to backtalk her once and suffered her wrath. She was not a librarian to be trifled with.

"Sorry, she can be kind of a pain." Sofie wrinkled her cute nose. Donny's brunette girlfriend was a catch and a half. Bright, adorable, and would do anything for anyone. Connor loved her to pieces.

"Kind of?" he asked with a smile.

She laughed.

Sofie had moved into the mansion after Donovan came home for good. She also moved her event planning business here, rather than keeping her storefront on Endless Avenue. Donovan had simply moved his work here. He did custom masonry and fireplace design, indoor and out. He stayed busy.

Connor pushed himself to standing and bent over to

pet Gertie's flank. The dog that had showed up in the backyard skin and bones last spring had put on plenty of weight. Her coat was glossy, her pale blue eyes bright.

"Good girl, aren't you? Yes you are."

Gertie wagged her tail and leaned against his leg, smiling up at him.

"Tell you what," he said to Sofie, "I have a few hours to kill this afternoon, why don't I stop by there and make sure Mrs. Anderson knows I'm on top of things." It was an inconvenience, but not a big one. Like he'd do anything for his sisters, he'd do anything for his friends, too. And that included Sofia Martin.

"Really?" She looked relieved with her hands pressed flat against her collarbone.

"Really." He gathered his tool belt and trowel, then kissed her forehead as he ambled by.

Before he made it to his work truck, she called out, "Faith said you had a date tonight."

Did she, now? He turned and raised an eyebrow, tossing his tools into the front seat. Sofie was fishing and he wasn't giving her anything.

Before he climbed into his truck, he called out, "See you tomorrow."

"Tease!" She threw a hand at him as he reversed out of his parking space.

Yeah, let that get back to Faith. He didn't mind stoking her jealousy. Not at all. Maybe if she thought he was dating someone, she'd openly pursue him. Wouldn't that be something?

In town, he passed Cup of Jo's, Fern's Florist, and the now vacant storefront that used to be Sofie's event planning company.

His company, C. Alan Landscaping, had no home base. Not technically. Right now billing was done on his phone and in his head, and there was a box of receipts overflowing on his kitchen table. Probably he should do something about that.

When he'd first started doing odd jobs for himself and giving fewer hours helping out his father at McClain's, he hadn't needed a fancy accounting system. The busier he became, the more paperwork dogged him. Organization was not his forte.

Sofie was partially responsible for the recent influx of business. She'd referred him for a number of local events. So did Faith. And since she was Sofie's assistant, he talked and worked with her as closely as he did Sofe.

Being around a creature as gorgeous as Faith Garrett tried every ounce of his libido. And because her jackass of a fiancé had cheated on her, she also tried every ounce of Connor's sympathy. He knew what it felt like to be cheated on. The gut-wrenching knowledge that you meant so little to the someone you pledged your life to. He may not have caught Maya in the act, but he'd caught her *after* the fact.

Way after the fact.

At least Faith didn't marry the dickhead. Bullet dodged. That last thought hit him square in the chest. He had dodged a bullet, too. Several of them.

Literally.

He pulled around the back of the library and shut off the engine, resting his head on the steering wheel. Drawing a deep breath, he blew it out while counting down from five. It never erased the horrific visual behind his eyes, but it did enable him in getting on with his day.

When he raised his head, he found Mrs. Anderson shuffling in her orthopedic shoes, her wrinkled mouth pulled taut, determination in her deep-set eyes.

He lifted a hand in greeting and gave her a patient smile.

There was a lot of day to get on with.

Fall in Love with Forever Romance

Fall in Love with Forever Romance

RESCUING THE BAD BOY
by Jessica Lemmon

Donovan Pate is coming back to Evergreen Cove a changed man... well, except for the fact that he still can't seem to keep his eyes—or hands—off the mind-blowingly gorgeous Sofie Martin. Sofie swore she was over bad boy Donovan Pate. But when he rolls back into town as gorgeous as ever and still making her traitorous heart skip a beat, she knows history is seriously in danger of repeating itself.

NO BETTER MAN
by Sara Richardson

In the *New York Times* bestselling tradition of Kristan Higgins and Jill Shalvis comes the first book in Sara Richardson's contemporary romance Heart of the Rockies series set in breathtaking Aspen, Colorado.

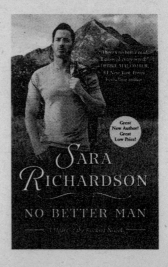

Fall in Love with Forever Romance

**WEDDING BELLS
IN CHRISTMAS
by Debbie Mason**

Former lovers Vivian and
Chance are back in Christmas,
Colorado, for a wedding. To
survive the week and the
town's meddling matchmakers,
they decide to play the part of
an adoring couple—an irre-
sistible charade that may give
them a second chance at the
real thing...

**CHERRY LANE
by Rochelle Alers**

When attorney Devon Gilmore
finds herself with a surprise baby
on the way, she knows she needs
to begin a new life. Devon needs
a place to settle down—a place
like Cavanaugh Island, where the
pace is slow, the weather is fine,
and the men are even finer. But
will David Sullivan, the most eli-
gible bachelor in town, be ready
for an instant family?

Fall in Love with Forever Romance

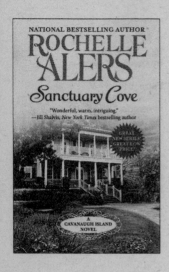

SANCTUARY COVE
by Rochelle Alers

Only $5.00 for a limited t[ime!]
Still reeling from her hus[band's]
untimely death, Deborah [Robin-]
son returns to her grandm[other's]
ancestral home on Cavan[augh]
Island. As friendship with [gor-]
geous Dr. Asa Monroe blo[ssoms]
into romance, Deborah an[d Asa]
discover they may have a [sec-]
ond chance at love.

ANGELS LANDING
by Rochelle Alers

Only $5.00 for a limited time!
When Kara Newell shockingly
inherits a large estate on an island off the South Carolina
coast, the charming town of Angels Landing awaits her...along
with ex-marine Jeffrey Hamil-
ton. As Kara and Jeffrey
confront the town gossips together, they'll learn to forgive
their pasts in order to find a future filled with happiness.